FRIENDS IN LOW PLACES

Eric,

Thanks for the support!!!

Go State Farm buddy!!!

Jim

Friends in Low Places deftly illuminates the intricacies of the male-bonding experience, following five best friends over several annual camping trips that embody everything from side-splitting laugher around the campfire to youth-ful heartbreak to drinking Olympics to crushed lifelong dreams to the ultimate power of forgiveness. There's a lot of love and hope in this novel, an interweaving of lives that shows the importance of vulnerable communing and always offering a hand when the valleys grow deeper. A nostalgic nod to the friendships we hold dear and the kinds of men we've always admired. **Jonathan Starke – author, You've Got Something Coming**

In a normal world it is often easy to forget the impor-tance of the bonds and the friendships we develop in life, especially when we are young and still figuring out what life is all about. Vince Wetzel has masterfully captured the ups and downs and evolutions of those friendships, and how fortunate we are to have them last well into our adult-hood. A treasure. **Rich Ehisen – Creator, the Open Mic and author, In Their Own Words: Twenty Successful Writers on the Craft and Business of Writing**

iii

I couldn't help reflecting on my own camping trips, the rituals of an annual gathering with friends, the laughter around mischief and debauchery, the moments you'll al-ways cherish with your bros, and the times you want to punch those same dudes in the face. Author Vince Wetzel taps into all of these emotions, introducing us to relatable characters that are flawed and funny (my kind of people) and stories that remind us how mistakes can lead to life-long consequences There is healing in nature, there is rec-onciliation around the guys that know you best, and the best rejuvenation is "Friends In Low Places." **Josh Suchon – author, Miracle Men: Hershiser, Gibson, and the Im-probable 1988 Dodgers**

You'll enjoy hanging out with these five high school friends as they carve out an annual weekend together to share their victories and defeats. The author does a vivid job of depicting the messiness of true friendship. A worth-while read. **Pierce Koslowsky, Jr. – author, A Week At Surfside Beach**

The story is rich and absorbing. Throughout, Wetzel touches on the universal themes of human failures, regrets, individual struggles, friendships and family ties. Wetzel's portraits of the lasting male bonding are authentic, and his crisp prose effortlessly navigates the stirring thoughts of his characters. This riveting account will please readers of en-during friendships stories. **The Prairies Book Review**

Friends in Low Places

Vince Wetzel

Contents

To Kristen, who inspires and indulges
my wild ideas

1

Jesse

The plane's wheels touched the ground, the wing flaps went up, and Jesse felt his chest surge forward and his anxiety release.

"Welcome to Sacramento," the flight attendant said.

Jesse switched his phone off airplane mode. He went to the *Danielle* text string.

Jesse: *Landed. Love you.*

He then scrolled down to find Rob's text string.

Jesse: *Landed. Give me about 15 minutes. I'll be outside arrivals.* Three dots appeared after his message turned blue. Rob: *Got it dude. See you in a bit.*

Jesse smiled. For most of the last twenty years, meeting his friends for this trip was a highlight of the summer, sometimes the year. It had always been a time when they regressed to their teenage years of eating and drinking too much, and now it was clear that they had aged too much not to feel the effects.

Jesse didn't need this weekend. He thought he closed this chapter of his life. Yet, here he was, joining his friends one last time to send off one of their own. This time, he was attending out of obligation, and Danielle reminded him that he would not get another chance.

He exited into the terminal, the intimacy of his thoughts now overwhelmed by the stimuli of fellow travelers. Jesse was looking out, gaining his bearings, when he felt a buzz in his hand.

Danielle: *Love you too. Have fun... as much as you can. I'll be thinking of you.*

He smiled. It had taken time, but she could sense what he was thinking even over the distance between Orange County and Sacramento. As he boarded the tram to the main terminal, he thumbed his reply.

Jesse: *Yeah. Part of me just wants to fly back.*

Danielle: *I get that, but you'll be glad you went*

Jesse: *Hope so.*

Danielle: *Give a hug to Tracey*

Jesse: *Will do... will text/call you later.*

Danielle: *OK. I'm here*

For a while, his marriage to Danielle was touch-and-go, the result of her career ambition, being a stay-at-home dad to twin girls, and unexpectedly defying several gender conventions and traditions regarding matrimony and parenting. It took years of therapy and a commitment to each other and the marriage, but he had complete trust in her and her advice.

Another buzz. It was Rob.

Rob: *Close?*

Jesse: *At the Red Rabbit.*

Jesse passed under the public art display that hung over the escalators in the main terminal. With his large canvas duffel slung over his shoulder, he bypassed the baggage claim and went straight through the sliding doors. He looked to his left and found Rob's huge black Ford F-350 pulling up to the curb. Rob's presence in the world was never subtle, and before Jesse had a moment to take in the cool morning air, Rob parked, pulled his six foot four, 320-pound frame out of the cab, and raced around the hood like he used to go after running backs as a linebacker at USC. He was wearing jeans, a local-brewery T-shirt, boots, and a camouflage USC ball cap, which always made Jesse smile. Who needs camouflage in the heart of Los Angeles? Rob embraced Jesse with a bear hug that caused Jesse to inhale.

"Jesse! So friggin' great to see you, dude!"

"Wish it was under better circumstances."

"C'mon, man, it's the trip!" Rob said, slapping Jesse's shoulder and smiling. "Yeah, we have something else to do this time, but c'mon, it's number seventeen and counting."

"Seventeen?"

"Sixteen or seventeen." The number didn't matter to Rob, just the fact that his best friend was here.

"Jim would know," Jesse said.

Rob turned contemplative. His dark beard had more than its share of silver flecks, providing him even more gravitas. "Yeah, he would," Rob said, then his moderated enthusiasm returned. "Let's get your bag in the truck. Everyone's meeting at Jim's, and then we'll be on our way."

Jesse used the truck's running rails to climb in. He was always the smallest of their tight group of five. In high school, they all played football, except Jesse. Rob was the surefire professional-football prospect. Paul was the most popular, David worked the hardest, and Jim was involved in everything. Jesse wasn't an archetype who socialized with this group. He was the small Mexican kid who ran cross country. But their friendship stretched back to elementary school, grew stronger in high school and had endured into adulthood because of this trip. Their shared experiences had stripped away the superficiality of their adolescence and forged a bond stronger than any relationship outside of marriage.

"How's Leslie?" asked Jesse as Rob pulled onto Interstate 5 toward Sacramento. Rob's smile came back bigger than ever.

"She's great. Last week, she shot even par at Lakeridge."

"I saw on Facebook. She looks awesome. Who knew an ex-linebacker would produce a golf prodigy!"

"I wouldn't say *prodigy*," Rob said, trying to hide his pride. "But she's pretty damn good for thirteen."

"Well, you've put a lot of cash into that talent."

"Tell me about it. And my pocketbook's feeling it too. Leslie loves golf. It's all she ever talks about, and if it keeps her attention away from boys, I'll take it."

Leslie had arrived when Rob needed her most. Faced with the realities of professional football, Rob had given in to some of his more self-destructive impulses. Leslie settled him, gave him a purpose, and drove him toward peace of mind.

For the past few years, Rob had been a private investigator in Reno, three hours northeast of Sacramento. The Wild West of northern Nevada better suited his personality, and his dollars stretched further. He could own a house, afford his truck (and the gas), and provide private golf instruction for Leslie.

"Less than four years until I have to deal with boys, and I'm not looking forward to it," Jesse said. He had nine-year-old twin girls, Nicole and Jennifer. "I just hope we can keep them in activities until they're, say, thirty."

"The struggle is real," said Rob. "She's starting to get looks that make me want to go over and pound on those assholes."

"Well, boys only need to see you, and I don't think they'll try anything."

"They don't care, man. Once they're alone, they only think about one thing. I mean, we all know that. What did we talk about in high school if it wasn't sports or girls?"

"Food."

"There's that. But man, the next ten years are going to be tough."

"Credit-card theory," Jesse said. "You pay for boys early when they break stuff and have energy for days. Girls, you pay later...like now...with interest."

Rob smiled. "That's good." Rob switched back to the topic at hand. "If your girls can take up running like you, then they'll be too tired to think about anything else."

Jesse ran cross-country in high school but rarely strapped on the sneakers after graduation. That changed when he and Danielle received a double-wide running stroller at the girls' baby shower. Jesse figured it would be a good way to exercise and give the twins some fresh air. Soon afterward, running became a morning ritual, burning off the anxiety he felt for not working as a casualty of the Great Recession. Even when the girls outgrew the stroller, he continued to run. He enjoyed the discipline that came with being an avid runner, and it helped him keep on top of managing a household, schedules, budgets, and the girls' activities while Danielle was killing herself at her law firm.

Rob slapped the steering wheel. "This is going to be a good trip."

"It's certainly going to be different," said Jesse. He pulled off his hat and ran his fingers through the same full, jet-black hair he had when he was eighteen. "I just feel weird about it."

"Jim wanted this," Rob said.

"We know who wanted this," Jesse corrected and looked out the window.

"That's true, but remember, he's acting on behalf of Jim and Tracey."

"Sometimes, I think he takes being 'Jim's best friend' to the extreme. You knew he was going to find a way to prolong the inevitable. I'm surprised he hasn't moved back up here yet."

"He's trying. I think he was meeting someone this week about a position at a new hotel, which is why he's already here."

David was a hotel executive manager working at a top resort. His career had taken him from Sacramento to San Diego, then

Honolulu, and now Huntington Beach. He had worked hard for it, a poor Filipino kid without the advantage many of his buddies had. While he enjoyed his job, he was ready to move back to Sacramento and explore new opportunities closer to his mom. In the past year, he felt a greater urgency, but he was still waiting for the right opportunity. David was one of Jesse's best friends, but sometimes his love of the dramatic was annoying.

"Regardless of how you feel right now, I think this trip's going to be good for you," Rob said. "For all of us."

"That's what Danielle said. I know I'm being an ass. I just don't want us wallowing in sentiment."

"C'mon, that's what this trip's all about. Always has been. You've got to lean into it and embrace it. You can't *ee*-viate from it."

They both chuckled. Elongating the dee had become an inside joke borne on one of their trips. These repeated jokes were part of what made this trip special for all of them.

"What's the over-under on the number of people who'll stop Paul this weekend and ask about the upcoming football season?" asked Rob.

Paul anchored the sports segment on the evening news for KARC-TV in Sacramento, but he was better known for his time at ESPN and *SportsCenter*. Over the years, they got a jolt of pride and excitement when Paul appeared on a *SportsCenter* commercial or in a clip of a movie playing himself. After some drama back in Bristol, Connecticut, he decided on a change and came back home. To anyone who asked, he was moving back to be closer to his parents, who weren't as mobile and independent as they used to be.

Only eighteen months removed from his national profile, Paul was still recognized anywhere they went, whether it was a restaurant or an airport. While his lack of anonymity was annoying, he took it in stride and predicted scores, gave the odds for a stranger's teams, and smiled through the unintended attention. It became a game for his friends to see how many people would approach him.

"I'd lay the over-under at four and a half for the weekend," said Rob. He turned the corner into Jim's neighborhood, and they saw Paul and David next to Paul's SUV. They turned their heads and smiled. David waved his arms as though Rob hadn't been to this spot hundreds of times before. After Rob parked, David trotted over and embraced Rob. Paul and Jesse opted for the "bro hug."

"You showed up," said David.

"Wouldn't miss it for the world," said Rob.

"Couldn't miss it for the world," Jesse said.

"Well, it's good you're here," said David.

"Have you knocked on the door yet?" Rob asked.

"We couldn't go in without you," said Paul. "We've only been here a few minutes."

Jesse and Rob nodded. In years past, the approach to the house would be loud and immature, but this trip wasn't typical. David took a deep breath, signaling everyone to get ready for the next awkward minutes. This visit wasn't going to be like the countless times they had come by for drinks, parties, and cookouts.

David knocked on the door.

Rob felt his throat tighten. Jesse wanted to be somewhere else and nowhere else at the same time. Paul stood in the back, almost not wanting to be seen.

Tracey opened the door, a smile across her face. They all knew her well enough to realize she was putting on her best front. Underneath her carefully chosen outfit and bouncy blond hair was a woman struggling as much as they were.

"Hey, Tracey," said David and moved in for a big hug. She stood in place in the foyer as each of them came in, embraced her, expressed a small salutation, then stood by the couch.

Tracey exhaled. "I'm so glad you're doing this. I'll go get Jim."

She disappeared down the hall, and the friends just stood there, not knowing what to say. Jesse looked over to the end table and saw Jim and Tracey's official wedding-party photo. Jesse was a bit rounder back then, before his running regimen had sculpted angles out of curves. Paul looked his same photogenic self with perfect hair and teeth, as did David, though he now shaved his head, conceding the fight. Rob had steadily hefted weight onto his huge frame. Tracey somehow looked the same even while Jim's waistline had increased and his face had grown fuller. At least Jim had shaved off that goatee.

"How was your flight?" Paul asked Jesse to break the tension.

"A flight. I hate it when larger people see I'm a small guy sitting on the aisle, take the middle seat, then push their elbows into my space. I used a couple free Southwest drink coupons for a morning beer."

They nodded. They'd been there, judged, or envied others for having those drink coupons. Tracey returned with a small metal box and a well-worn notebook. Each of them took a moment to breathe.

"Who wants to take these?" asked Tracey.

"I'll take the ashes," said Rob. He stared at the small sealed box, amazed that it contained the man he used to tackle, slap around, and call a dear friend.

David received the notebook and handled it like a piece of valuable memorabilia. He smiled with disbelief that it was still intact. Jim's journal had accompanied them on almost all their trips, and it encapsulated all the abuse they had heaped on each other over the years. The cover was stained with white splotches and circles where drinks and food had rested, spilled, and aged. The notebook spiral was bent in every way.

The cover read "Lake Trip Log." They had all seen this cover, but none of them had ever opened it or read a word. They knew Jim's thoughts and recollections on each of their previous trips were recorded in there. They had laughed at him when he brought the fresh notebook on the first trip and said he wanted to start a journal about college. He never wrote about those aspirations but instead focused on that first trip. The journal joined Jim and the friends for every subsequent trip, an unofficial member of the group. The group knew that Jim's remains were really in this notebook, the vessel for which they would remember him and their friendship.

"Are you sure you don't want to join us?" asked David. "You're most welcome."

"I appreciate that, I truly do," said Tracey. "But this is your time to say goodbye. Besides, Willie and I have our half of the ashes to spread."

Willie came out with one of his Harry Potter books under his arm. He made his way to his mom's side and looked at all of them, his resemblance to his dad maturing each day.

"Where?" Jesse asked.

"We're going to the coast," Tracey said. "Half Moon Bay, where Jim proposed to me."

"Of course," said David with a nod, his eyes watering in acknowledgement of these friends gathered in this room. Paul saved David from the indignity of breaking down by shifting focus to Willie.

"Hey, buddy, how are you doing?" Paul said.

"Good," Willie said. He smiled large, and Paul gave him a fist bump to reinforce Willie's inclusion as a junior member of their group. Rob followed, as did Jesse. David recovered and bumped fists with Willie before blowing it up. When they were done, Tracey pulled Willie close with a smile.

"Jim really loved you guys," Tracey said, almost cracking, which caused everyone's throats to tighten. She tried to say something else but stopped.

"He had incriminating evidence against us," said Paul, breaking the tension again. "Especially that guy." Paul pointed to David. "But seriously, a great man, and we're so much better because of him. We thank you for sharing him with us."

"We loved him too," said Jesse, breaking down a bit. He chastised himself for almost losing control like that.

Tracey wiped her eyes and fanned her face. "Let's not relive the memorial. That was too hard the first time. I just wanted to express how much I loved you too."

She gestured with her arms wide for a group hug. The friends gathered around her and Willie as she squeezed David and Jesse. Paul joined the embrace, and Rob enveloped them all with his huge arms. Willie must have felt suffocated and warm at the same time.

"You know this is how we ended our trip every year," said David.

"No, it wasn't," said Paul.

"Burrrrp," belched Rob. "That's how we ended the trip. I hated it when Jim did that."

They sniffed back a giggle.

"Okay, you guys get out of here," Tracey said. She wiped her eyes and cheeks. "You don't want to spend the weekend talking to me. Go relive those silly trips and remember Jim!"

Paul went in for a final hug, followed by Rob, Jesse, and finally David. As Paul, Jesse, and Rob started their way out the door, David bent down to talk to Willie.

"Bye, little man," David said to his seven-year-old godson. "In about fifteen years, you can come along with us. This year, though, it's probably good that you stay with your mom."

As Jesse exited through the front door, he heard Tracey say, "David?"

Jesse continued out of the house and toward Rob's truck, giving David and Tracey some privacy. Jesse understood that David occupied another level of kinship with Jim and his family, almost an honorary uncle. As Jesse approached Rob's truck, Paul was loading his ESPN duffle bag into the back.

"How much ESPN swag do you have?" Jesse asked.

"Less than I used to. When I moved back, I got rid of a lot of the polos and random stuff. But I kept the stuff I'd actually use."

"I have some charities in Reno that would have used anything from the great Paul Buckley. All you'd need to do is sign and send," Rob said. He pulled out the large ice chest with all their food and carried it from Paul's car to the truck.

"Believe me, they weren't that exciting," Paul said. "Beer cozies, ratty T-shirts, golf balls, sweaty hats. How about I sign some photos and good stuff and send them? Besides, how about all your football buddies?"

"Those were tapped long ago," Rob said, who then looked up at the house. "Will he just hurry up?"

On cue, David came out, followed by Willie and Tracey, who stood in the shade of their maple tree. It was already getting warm in the Valley. Paul and Jesse got into the back seats of the cab while David rode shotgun with Rob. Everyone made sure to send a final wave to Tracey as the truck turned the corner and disappeared.

"Okay, let's go! The weekend awaits!" Paul said.

"Well, that wasn't too bad," David said.

"It was easier than the memorial," Rob said.

"Rob, you don't count. You gave the eulogy and barely held it together," said Paul. "For all your Trump crap, you're a true bleeding heart."

"Let's not get into that," said Jesse. "Let's not ruin the trip within the first five minutes."

"That's right," said David. "A moratorium on politics. Plus, isn't anyone else interested to see what's in the Lake Trip Log?"

"Yes, let's do that," said Jesse.

David mock-cleared his throat and began: "1995! It started off as just something to record his hopes and dreams for life after high school, and this is what we got. Well, here you go, he says it right here."

Why am I writing this? Mom said it would be good for me to put down memories in a book so I can look back at this summer when I'm old and remember the good ol' days. I really don't get why, but after this epic weekend, I thought, why not? So here's my recollection of the fun my friends and I had this past weekend.

I guess I'll start from the very beginning, when I first brought up the idea. We were all hanging out at Pete's. I started delivering pizzas there when David was promoted to waiter, and this was our summer gathering spot to fill ourselves with garlic knots, pizza, and sandwiches with our employee discount.

"Those knots were awesome," Rob said, licking his lips.

"Shut up," Paul said. "Let him continue."

2

Jim

1995

G uys, it's the last hurrah before we head our separate ways," I said.

"It's my last weekend before I have to get down to football practice," said Rob. He had an entire combination pizza for himself. The USC coaching staff said he needed to *gain* weight over the summer to be ready for the football season. "I want to party."

"That's the thing; this *will* be a party. Just think: no parents, just us in the mountains making memories," I said.

"But what about the girls?" said Paul. He was heading to Michigan and wasn't sure if the Midwest would compare to California in terms of talent. "What about the girls?"

"I'm sure there will be girls," I said. I didn't realize I would have to do this much of a sell job. "And if not, we'll be fine just drinking and farting and laughing."

"I'm in," said Jesse. "I'm leaving this town, and this may be it."

Jesse was off to Cal State Los Angeles to study accounting. He was also moving away from his mom in Sacramento and staying with his dad in Los Angeles. If the arrangement went well, he may just stay down in Southern California, which was perfectly fine with him. Lately, his mom was getting on his nerves, and he was ready for a change. Jesse said she had become clingy and unwilling to let go.

Jesse was the outcome of a fling resulting in a hasty marriage followed by resentment, varied priorities, and eventual divorce. Jesse's dad was still in his life, but a job transfer to Los Angeles eight years ago changed their dynamic. For a few weeks every summer and for a few days during winter and spring breaks, Jesse would travel to Southern California for a visit. So, when his college choices were either go to a local school or pay for his own room and board somewhere else, his dad offered a room at his apartment and his mom had taken it personally.

"Can you get the time off?" David asked me. "I just got you this job. I don't want to defend your ass against Pete."

"Not a problem," I said. David had worked at Pete's for a year and had to sell Pete to give me a job as a delivery guy. Still, this last trip was a higher priority than a low-paying job. "I know we'll be fine. What do you say, Rob?"

"I don't know," Rob said and focused on the pizza in front of him. It was understandable. He had a football career and coaching overlords that would dominate his life for the next four years. Plus, his dad wasn't exactly a free spirit. As a father coaching his son since the womb, he had a lot invested in Rob. From the breakfast table to the bathroom sink, his dad had an opinion about every move Rob made.

"I'm only going if there are girls," said Paul.

I turned my attention to moving the needle with Paul. If he was in, Rob would cave.

"When I was there last summer with my family, it was perfect," I said. "It's isolated, so there's nowhere else to go, and remote enough so the competition for girls is light, and we'll be on our own...with beer."

"How are we going to get enough beer to make a difference?" said Rob, looking up from his pizza. He could already drink a twelve-pack of Coors Light without much effect. Meanwhile, though the rest of us wouldn't admit it, after four beers we were feeling it.

"My cousin," I said. My cousin Scott was twenty-two and said if I ever needed alcohol to let him know. "I'll call him, and he'll get us whatever we need."

"Okay, I'm in," Rob said, slamming his fist on the table.

"I'm in," Paul said, mimicking Rob and following up with a high five.

Five-for-five. Perfect. A great way to end the summer and our high school careers. Rob reached across the table and grabbed a knot. Jesse poured himself another glass of root beer.

"Do you have a tent?" Jesse asked.

"I have a friend who has a six-person tent," I said. I had already done the research of the campgrounds at this isolated lake located in the Sierras above Fresno. My parents took my younger sister, Katie, and I to the lake last year. At about seven thousand feet above sea level, the air was cool at night and warm during the day with a crisp, fresh breeze. The trees were always green and abundant. The lake water was cold, the kind that would make your manly parts want to curl up and lodge themselves inside your bladder.

There was only one "beach" along the shoreline, and it connected to the boat launch, lodge, cabin rentals, a general store, a restaurant, and a saloon. It still drew crowds when the lake hosted boat races to take advantage of the lake's intense winds. It was a perfect match for a guy's camping trip. With all five of us in, I was ready to start planning.

"Then it's decided," I said with a clap of my hands. "We're looking to leave on Thursday, July 27, and come back on Sunday, July 30."

"Got it," Paul said. "But I may bring my own tent. I'll need the privacy if I get a visitor."

"Oh god," said Jesse, rolling his eyes.

"Hey, it's simple math," said Paul. "Jim and Jesse have girlfriends. Rob will likely get invited to a cabin, and David, well, you couldn't make a move even if she was naked right in front of you."

David seethed, because it was true. He had no moves. Never had. He occupied the "friend zone" with girls. He was a puppy dog and didn't act when there was potential, and before long, they inevitably asked him to set them up with Paul or Rob.

"I may not have a girlfriend soon," said Jesse.

"What?" I said.

"Yeah, Sandra wants to break up, so she's free to explore when she heads off to Pepperdine," said Jesse. Sandra and Jesse had only been dating since he had asked her to prom a few months ago. They were pretty good together, but I guess it wasn't destined to survive.

"Bitch," said Paul.

"Nah, I actually agreed with her," Jesse said. "C'mon, we all know that's where things go with high school relationships. Once you're separated and get a new set of prospects, the high school boyfriend just isn't appealing."

"Still sucks," said Rob.

"But now you and Paul have competition for the ladies on this trip," I said with a smile.

"What's Audrey going to say to you about going to a lake with your buddies looking for girls?" said Jesse. "She can't be happy you'll be with your boys on the prowl."

"Why don't you just break up with her already? She's so controlling," said Paul.

"You guys don't understand her," I said. "She's really cool, and she likes to be close to me when we're together. She wants to be with me."

"She wants to be close so she can give death stares to anyone else who wants to hang out with you," said David. "It's surprising she's let you be friends with us at all."

Audrey and I had been dating for about nine months. My friend Tracey had set us up. They were friends in choir, and Audrey thought I was cute. For a guy who had kissed only one girl, any girl who thought I was cute was worth a look and a date. We went out, and she loved every word I said. She was also attractive. Her brunette hair was cut in the "Rachel" from *Friends*. We spent Thursday nights at each other's houses watching TV and talking about life, dreams, gossip, and silly stuff.

However, my friends thought she was territorial and clingy, and they didn't like that she and I began smoking together. If we were all together as a group, she'd attach herself to me and not let go or we'd go off and share a cigarette. If I was hanging out with them without her, she constantly asked about where I was going and who was going to be there.

"She has nothing to worry about," I said.

"She should," said Paul. "You're like a butterfly about to blossom into a ladies man." He held back a sarcastic laugh.

Rob rolled his eyes. "Jim a butterfly *and* a ladies man? That's an image I want back."

I tried to turn the conversation away from my relationship with Audrey. "So, we're all in for those dates? Make sure you can get the time off. I'll call you about the other details, like costs for the site and food and beer."

Amazingly, everyone's schedules worked out. Rob's dad let him go. Jesse cleared the plans with his mom. Paul had nothing to do anyway, and Pete let both David and I off work at the restaurant. Jesse and Sandra broke it off, and I was left with four bachelors. I was almost a bachelor too when Paul decided to get a rise out of Audrey and shared his hope of using the solo "sex" tent. To Paul's amusement, Audrey shot a look at me, and I was left with the aftermath. I had to reassure her that nothing was going to happen.

Still, it was worth any grief from Audrey. I didn't know if this would be the last time all my friends would be together. Sure, David and I were still in Sacramento. He was enrolled at City College and working while I was heading to Sacramento State.

But who knew what would happen to Rob and Jesse in LA and Paul heading to Michigan?

When July 27 finally came, we all met at David's house. He had a Dodge Caravan that his mom let him borrow. With his tip money, David went to the store and bought all the supplies. Meanwhile, I rendezvoused with my cousin, who bought us enough alcohol to keep us buzzed for the weekend. The cases of beer were itching to be examined when everyone arrived. Unfortunately, David's mom was outside, halfway cleaning up the front yard, partly watching her son and his buddies go on a rite of passage. I think she was looking for beer to be smuggled into the car, which is exactly what we were trying to do. Thankfully, we had Paul, who could charm a nun into the confessional to make out.

As Paul distracted David's mom, I emptied my supply of clothes into some shopping bags and placed the beer and booze in my large duffle bag. David's mom didn't notice the cube shape of my luggage filled with three twelve-packs of Coors Light, another of Corona nor did she see the two other twelve-packs of Miller Genuine Draft in brown bags topped with a bag of Funyuns or the bottle of vodka in the six-person tent bag or even the bottle of Malibu in the portable barbecue. Instead, she was listening to Paul lament his fear of Michigan winters and his hope to join the school-newspaper staff next semester.

We said goodbye to David's mom, who gave each of us a hug. Much to David's annoyance, Paul seemed to take a little longer than everyone else and winked at David while he did it. David got in the driver's seat, and I took my spot as chief navigator in the front. Rob took up the entire back bench while Paul and Jesse had the middle captain's seats.

"Thanks for the distraction," I said. I looked back and gave Paul a high five. "Worked out perfectly."

"No problem. Kathy's a very nice person," Paul said with great emphasis on her first name.

"Kathy?" David said. His hands gripped the wheel a little tighter, and his eyes narrowed at Paul through the rearview mirror. David was protective of his mom, whose cancer had just been declared to be in remission. During her illness, he poured all his strength into her for the fight and we didn't see him much. He was either studying, working, or sitting by her side during chemo appointments. We all tried to help. Paul rallied the football team and organized a food chain to help David's family. He often collected and brought over the meals himself, and the Velascos were forever thankful.

"Yes, she's a very interesting and intriguing woman. Someone a fellow might want to get to know...a little better." Paul enjoyed getting a rise out of David. Even while Kathy Velasco was sick, Paul felt that by discussing her good looks, he was expressing confidence that she would return to health. Paul's playful jabs were meant as a return to normalcy now that she had been cleared and her jet-black hair was formed in a cute pixie cut.

"Dude, that's my mom," said David.

"Settle down," said Paul. "We didn't need to bring my tent over." Paul almost busted up laughing. All of us were on the brink of giggles or full-on laughter.

It wasn't fair that we made fun of David so much. Watching his frustrations boil over was just funny. I mean, I was his best friend, and I knew how far I could take it with him, but I also always tried to dial everyone else back when things got a little too out of hand.

Jesse realized we had teased David enough and got us back on track. "So, Jim, how long will it take for us to get up there?"

"About four hours," I said. "Two and a half to Fresno and then another hour to get up the hill."

"Oh man," said Rob, "I knew we should have bought more snacks."

"Here, have some Funyuns." Paul supplied him with the bag before I pulled out a pack of Marlboros and a lighter and opened the window once we got to a stoplight.

"Dude, not in my car," David said. "Can't you just wait until we get up there?"

"Yeah, man, I don't want my lungs black with smoke when I have to run sprints next week at practice," Rob said. "Just wait until the lake."

"Yeah, c'mon," said Paul. "Keep mijo's car smelling fresh."

I turned back and joined Jesse and Rob with puzzled looks. We all took three years of Spanish and knew that "mijo" was meant as a term of endearment, but David was Filipino, and Paul was the ultimate WASP.

"What?" said David, looking in the mirror. "Mijo?"

"No, I didn't say *mijo*," said Paul. "I said *MIHO*. M-I-H-O...as in 'Mom Is a Hot One!'"

Rob about spit out a mouth full of Funyuns, while Jesse eyes widened at the burn. I just shook my head and held back a giggle. David wrung the steering wheel and whipped his head around.

"I'm going to kill you, Paul," David said and turned back to the highway.

"Settle down, MIHO," Rob said with a laugh. "Just keep driving."

The rest of the drive was typical for five eighteen-year-olds with visions of drinking and great times ahead. Conversations centered around rehashing various hookups we'd had over the years, what girls gave it up to their boyfriends since summer started, who puked during the senior trip to Mexico, and other random gossip we had heard since graduating. We passed the summit and saw our first view of the lake through the trees. The lake was as blue as the sky, which made them both spectacular.

When we approached the small trailer operated by the US Forest Service, I pulled out a scrap of paper where I had written the reservation number a couple weeks prior. Still sites were still first-come, first-serve at the campground itself. I just hoped there was a good spot available.

"MIHO, are you going to check in with Jim?" asked Paul, smiling. We had been calling David "MIHO" the whole trip up. David responded with a nod. He came to just accept it and no longer objected. He figured the shelf life for the name would be a day or at most the length of the trip. "All right then. Jesse, Rob and I'll stay out here,"

David and I walked into the trailer. The interior had the typical signs featuring Smokey the Bear telling us that we can prevent forest fires and another with an owl telling us to give a hoot and don't pollute. At the check-in counter was a fellow camper wearing jeans, a camouflage vest, and a trucker hat. His face had day-old growth, though you could tell he wasn't the rugged type. His boots were right out of the box, and trailing behind him was his daughter, no older than ten with a *Lion King* sweatshirt and matching backpack.

"How is she this week?" he asked the park ranger.

"She's out there, so be sure to keep any coolers up high or in the bear boxes," said the ranger, a short and stumpy forty-something-year-old woman.

Jesse pointed to snapshots of a brown bear tearing through coolers and other food containers on picnic tables. He looked at me and winced.

"Got it," said the man. "Thank you. We'll keep an eye out."

As they turned, the father gave a nod. I nodded back and then approached the ranger, Beth, as indicated by her name tag.

The ranger gave a suspicious look. "Good afternoon. What can I do for you?"

"I made a reservation for a campsite," I said, giving her my information and number. She turned to the large board with at least a hundred clipped yellow tags. She ran her finger down one of the middle rows, pulled one of the tags and came back to the desk."

"Yep, we've got Jim Jenson, staying at a standard tent site for three nights, correct?"

I nodded.

"It's going to be a bit crowded this week with the regatta, but you should be able to find something up at the Rancheria campground. The entrance is back up the hill about a quarter mile.

The lakeside sites are a little boxed in with one another, but you boys will probably see an isolated site that may work better for you."

"We'll take it," I said. I paid for the sites and three bundles of firewood and carried them back to the car.

"We can't be too close to anybody," said David when he described the type of sites available. "With Paul and Rob, we may be a little loud."

"And you never know if the girls will be screamers," said Paul. "It may be X-rated."

Rob rolled his eyes. "Isolated is good. I don't want us to get into trouble. That's the last thing I need."

We found a spot on the backside of the campground. It was the kind of site you would only come across if you couldn't find anything else. For us, it was perfect; isolated with no other sites within fifty yards. After agreeing this was the spot, we unloaded the gear, set up the six-person tent one side and the "sex tent" on the other.

"This will work out perfectly," said Paul, surveying our home for the next three days.

We all grabbed a beer and toasted to each other, this trip, our friendship, and the future.

Because David worked in a restaurant, we assigned him the camp cook. He made it easy on himself with traditional hamburgers and hot dogs. We matched the food with more than our fair share of beer, enthusiastic for our weekend of unsupervised underage drinking that went well into the night.

The next morning, however, we regretted our exuberance. Our bodies were stiff. We shuffled from the tent to the bathroom to the fire ring to the picnic table like grandfathers, regretting each movement and wishing the pain in our heads and stomachs would go away. Even the Pop-Tarts and cereal we brought for breakfast held no appeal.

For much of the morning, we sat in silence and stared at the campfire. But as the day wore on and the alcohol from the night before passed through our systems, our good humor returned, and we were ready or some activity.

"So, is there any place to hike?" Jesse asked. "Seems like a waste to just sit around and drink beer all day."

"What's wrong with that?" said Rob. "Sounds like the perfect time."

"We could do both," I suggested. "There's a trail that leads to this cool waterfall. My parents took my sister and me there last year. We can pack lunch and some beer and hang out on the rocks and take in the scenery."

"So, you mean sit around and drink beer, just at a place we have to hike to?" said Paul.

"Pretty much," I said and smiled.

"Let's do it," said Rob.

We threw some beers and food in a couple backpacks and jumped into Rob's truck. The three miles along a rocky mountain road went painstakingly slow, with numerous switchbacks along harrowing cliffs that didn't help my lingering hangover. When we reached the parking lot at the trailhead, I welcomed the cool, crisp air and my feet on solid ground. The sign indicated we were 1.1 miles away from the falls.

"Oh yeah, we have to hike," said Rob. "Here we go!'

Though the air was cool, the sun was out and intense at seven thousand feet, and before long, our shirts were clinging to our chests. The trail was carved out of one side of the mountain with a stiff incline/decline on both sides. Looking up, the grass was still green, and the yellow and purple wildflowers were in bloom. At one point, I looked back and saw Rob place a beer bottle on the top of a small sapling, causing it to curl over like some drunken summer Charlie Brown Christmas tree. I shook my head. When we reached the falls, we stood before the 130-foot cliff where a stream cascaded off the top, down into a pool, then down the array of granite rocks leading down the mountain. Paul bounded across several large boulders until he found one that was flat enough, long enough, and in the sun to place his towel. We all followed and found our own places.

"Not bad," said Jesse. He looked around and nodded. "Hey, everyone be on good behavior; we've got kids here today."

Indeed, a mother and father were careful to lead their two children, likely under the age of seven, from rock to rock near the waterfall. Their focus was on keeping their kids from slipping, holding their hands and lifting them from one boulder to the next. Their demeanor changed when they saw us. They tensed, their eyes darting back and forth between their children and us. They were more scared of a bunch of teen boys than any wildlife they might encounter.

"Put away your friggin' cancer sticks," David said, looking right at me. I'd just fished out a cigarette. I put it in my mouth and lit up with defiance.

"I'll think about it, Mom," I said through pursed lips wrapped around the cigarette.

David turned away. I could see Paul contemplating a smart rebuke, but instead he just smiled and straightened out his blue towel. "Toss me a beer."

David obliged and sent a Coors Light Paul's way, then one each to the rest of us. We had packed the beers in a plastic bag filled with ice. While the bag had leaked a bit, sending some cold water down David's back during the hike, we all benefited from his sacrifice. In Jesse's backpack we had lunchmeat, rolls, cheese, chips—a teenage picnic.

"Good choice, Jim," said Paul. "Girls will be at the beach tomorrow. Today's perfect for just us guys hanging out, enjoying and contemplating the beauty of life."

"And thanks for getting us off our butts to get here," said Rob. "I needed this before I have to think about football all the time."

"Don't you think about football all the time?" Jesse asked.

"You don't understand how much my dad's prepared every aspect of my life for the next few years and beyond. Me and my career were more important to him than my mom."

Two years before, Rob's mom left the family and divorced his dad. While Rob and his dad had focused on football, she felt left behind. She found someone new who gave her attention, and she took a different course toward happiness. She kept in contact with Rob, but their relationship was strained. Rob felt he and his dad were a solid family unit.

Rob took a last swig of his beer, then motioned to Jesse for another. He also found it was time to change the subject. "Jesse, is your dad ready for you to move in with him?"

"We'll see. I'm not sure if I'm ready either, but I need to get out of Sac, and since my parents weren't flush with cash to save for college, I'll take it."

"Tell me about it," said Rob. "If it wasn't for football, I don't know if I'd be going."

"See what I'm saving by going to Sac City?" said David. "Of course, my mom can't help me at all."

"That sucks," said Rob. "If anyone can do it, you can. You can also get me another beer."

We stayed another couple hours before trekking back down the trail. Rob relieved the Charlie Brown tree of its glass Corona. When we got back to the site, we had an unspoken acknowledgment that it was time to rest and lay low. Rob took a nap. David, Paul, and Jesse played cards while I decided to take a hike down to the lake for some personal time. While I enjoyed hanging out with my buddies, I also found the relative silence of nature energizing and relaxing. Every time I looked at the water, I was humbled by its beauty of green and blue. The deep-blue sky unfiltered by the smog from the valley touched the dark blue of the water, highlighted by the green forest all around. The waves lapped against the boulders and the exposed tree roots of the rocky shoreline.

I hopped from the dirt to the nearest boulder in the water and sat, my knees pulled to my chest, watching across the lake. It was daunting to think about our futures and the different directions they would take us. Three of my friends were going away on new adventures that could take them away from here for the rest of their lives. They would change as they met new people, and I was excited for them but also worried that this could be the last time we'd be this close. And while David was staying local, he was so focused on work, I wondered if he would have the time to hang out with me.

I followed an ant as it walked across the rough surface of the boulder. I wondered how it got across the water and was on this granite island and if it would ever get back. I felt I was trapped too. My parents' finances dictated that Sacramento State was one of my only options. Sac State wasn't a letdown itself. I was a poli-sci major, and the school's proximity to the capitol was an easy choice, but I wasn't leaving. I wondered if my life would change much. I'd wake up in my childhood bedroom, go to class, maybe work, then come home. Where was *my* adventure? I didn't want to leave that spot, but I could only do so much wallowing, and my friends' laughter made it clear that I needed to embrace the adventures up at our campsite. I looked around for my friend, the ant, but didn't see him and leaped to the shoreline and hiked back up the hill to our spot.

We learned our lesson and didn't hit the beer as hard as we had the night before. We woke up Saturday refreshed for a big day on the beach. As I exited the tent, Paul was building a new fire at the firepit with the energy of Paul Bunyan.

"Beach day today!" he said. "Girls."

"Dude, it's seven in the morning."

"Never too early to get psyched up to meet some girls."

"Just don't get your hopes up too high."

"The power of positive thinking."

One by one, each of the guys woke and joined the ring around at the firepit. Paul's anticipation for the day was infectious, and within a few hours we were all ready and packed up for our day at the lakeshore beach. It was still quite early, but this way we could pick out a prime spot with shade and great viewing possibilities.

It turned out that even 10:00 a.m. was a little too late. The parking lot was already full, and the beach was packed with families and crews for the boat races. Most were in their twenties and thirties. Some even had families with young babies running around naked.

Paul looked at me with disappointment. "I thought you said there'd be girls. I mean, even I can't get these twenty-one-year-olds to leave their sailing boyfriends to hang out with us."

"Still early," I said. "I'm sure some girls our age will be coming this afternoon. We'll find some girls for you, Paul."

"We'd better."

Caught between childhood and young adulthood, we tried to navigate between what we knew as a great time when we were kids and the excitement that comes with meeting new people. At various points during that day, we performed backflips and threw each other off the boat launch and tossed the football around with our chests pressed out. After a few beers, I left the group to relieve my full bladder and have a guilt-free smoke. When I returned, I rounded the corner and noticed the guys' attention all focused in the same direction. I followed their gaze to another part of the beach. Ah, the dance had begun. Two girls our age positioned themselves on towels to tease, entice, and observe us. One of the girls redid her tussled, brown ponytail. Another kept looking up from her magazine. They laughed, and the brunette called over to the lake, where a third friend was walking back from the water. I stopped and almost felt Audrey's hand slapping my shoulder all the way from Sacramento. I ignored my absent girlfriend's rebuke and followed this beautiful, tan, blond goddess with a white bikini from the water to her piece of sand next to her friends. The cans of Sprite in front of them were encouraging. When I reached the cooler, Paul came up to me with a big grin and gave me a beer.

"Oh man, it's on."

"What do you mean? Have you talked to them?"

"No, but I'm getting eyes like crazy from the one in the bikini."

"But you haven't talked to them?"

"Nah, man," said Paul. "Got this under control. This is a game."

"It seems things would go a lot quicker if you'd just go over and talk to them."

"Oh, Jim, you've been out of the game too long," Paul said. "Wait, you've never been in the game. This is how it works. You create want. Need. Infatuation. Then you move in. Go in too early, the mystery hasn't had time to build, and they realize they may not necessarily want it. If you wait, the mystery overtakes the actual attraction, and when you can combine both—boom! Magic, and the sex tent gets used."

I shook my head, but I couldn't doubt Paul. There was male bravado, then there was Paul on another level. The crazy thing was that he backed it up. He never was shy and knew the right way to charm everyone. And he didn't have limitations. For every major function in high school, we were introduced to someone new on Paul's arm.

I popped open the beer and looked at Jesse, David, and Rob. After conceding the white bikini to Paul, they were fighting over who would get with the leftovers. Jesse argued that he needed a rebound. Rob was more attracted to the tank-top brunette. Jesse liked the jean-shorts girl. David didn't care. I shook my head as they argued over these girls like they were leftover pizza. I heard Audrey in my ear, raising my conscience about treating women like meat or prizes to be won. She was probably right, but I shook it off. It was too much fun to watch my friends argue.

The game of hormonal cat and mouse continued for much of the afternoon. After about an hour, the unexpected happened...the girls decided to leave. Jesse was the first to notice.

"Hey...*hey!*" he said, nudging Paul. "They're packing up."

"What?"

"What are you going to do now?" I said. I admit, I was happy with this development.

Paul stood, his mind working out the right action to generate the appropriate reaction. We all watched him. Then the girls. Then back to him. He smiled at us before a look of calm and confidence came across his face. He didn't rush to them. Instead, he raised his hand, pointed down, then raised both hands with nine fingers. He repeated the same sequence of gestures.

White bikini gave a smile and a thumbs-up.

Without any words, he had just made a date for us to meet them all back here after dark. Our jaws dropped. Paul turned back to us and took a swig of beer, milking our attention. He raised his eyebrows and smiled. Legend. He was playing chess, and we were learning Chutes and Ladders.

The afternoon and evening were a blend of hopeful predictions of the night ahead and personal grooming to put our best images forward. We even went back into the lake with a bar of soap and bathed and brushed our teeth after dinner. We debated which T-shirts or sweatshirts would look best. We had our doubts, but Paul's mission was focused on the sex tent.

We brought our last eighteen beers to the beach. We thought it would just be the five of us and the girls, but when we arrived, we found ten other teenage mountain delinquents circled around the bonfire. We did the math: five guys, five girls, then the five of us. Four of them—two guys and two girls—looked like they were already coupled. That left White Bikini, Brown Hair, and Pretty Cheeks with the five us, plus three other guys—a sausage fest of eight young men salivating over three pairs of boobs. Even with me acting as wingman, the odds weren't great.

Paul didn't even flinch. Flanked on his left by Rob and Jesse, and the right with David and me trailing behind, the time for subtlety was over. He walked right up to White Bikini, now dressed in jeans, sneakers, and a tied-up flannel over a tank top. As we approached, the three guys, who seemed to be a couple years younger, saw an even ratio just double. They stepped back, if only because of Paul's confidence and Rob's bulk, both equally intimidating.

"Hey, I'm Paul. I'm so glad to finally meet you."

"Finally? You had all afternoon to make your move," White Bikini said.

The three boys chuckled. One had a cowboy hat, a tucked-in T-shirt, and boots. He was next to another boy, whose smile revealed a full set of braces beneath his overgelled hair. The third one had complexion of pizza. They giggled as though they still had a chance.

White Bikini ignored the giggles and said, "We were wondering what you were waiting on. I'm Julie, this is Stacy, and that's Christina."

Both Stacy (Brown Hair) and Christina (Pretty Cheeks) smiled and waved. Stacy's hair was now dry and layered. She was wearing a Clovis West High Swim sweatshirt with shorts and flip-flops. Christina wore a sweater and jeans. Her outfits this afternoon and in the night spoke of a maturity beyond many of the girls her age.

"Well, this is Rob, Jim, Jesse, and MIHO," Paul said. We had grown accustomed to referring to David as MIHO, but this was the first time that David had been introduced as such.

"MIHO?" Said Christina. David blushed and smiled.

"Do you want a beer?" said Rob.

"I guess so," said Julie, and Rob distributed beers to all of us, even the three boys we began to realize had to be fifteen, at the oldest. Ten minutes ago, they must have thought they had hit the jackpot. Now, they realized a free beer was the most action they were going to get.

We all spoke as a group for a while. We found out that Julie and Stacy, like us, had just graduated. Christina was Julie's cousin, a year older and attending Fresno State. Now that we knew she was a college girl, she became even more attractive and intimidating. She was carefree, comfortable with herself, and didn't seem to care about impressing us or her cousin or her friend. There was an ease with the conversation. She reminded me of my friend Tracey. At first glance, she wasn't the prettiest girl in the room, but she seemed to brighten the dark beach as she talked. Julie and Stacy were about to be roommates for their first year at UC Santa Barbara. They were already planning out their dorm room and their unchaperoned lives filled with parties, sororities and the beach. Meanwhile, Christina rolled her eyes—freshmen.

I could see Julie and Paul focused on each other's conversation. Similarly, Jesse and Stacy were pairing off, leaving Christina to talk with Rob, MIHO, and me. As we started to learn more about Christina, the three boys began to stumble around, pumping themselves up with profanity and grimaces.

"Fuck yeah!" Cowboy Hat said to Overgel. We never asked their names.

"C'mon, you can take that tree," Pizza Face said to Cowboy Hat. Cowboy Hat then ran full rush into a pine tree with a three-inch trunk. I wasn't an arborist, but I knew the tree was going to win that fight every time. Sure enough, Cowboy Hat bounced off the tree and fell on his ass, clutching his shoulder.

"That was dumb," said Rob, finishing his beer.

"How many beers did you give them?" I asked.

"Just one. Maybe one more for the three of them to share." Rob shrugged, as if to say, "wasn't me" and walked over to the boys. Having suffered a few injuries making a tackle, he was the most qualified to see what Cowboy Hat had done to himself. Christina, David, and I joined him.

"Dude, you okay?" Rob asked. "Trees don't feel pain. You know that, right?"

"Owww. Yeah," said Cowboy Hat.

"That was awesome," said Pizza. "You're so drunk."

"I doubt that," I said. "Why don't you head back to your campsite or cabin or whatever?"

"We're here with my brother," said Overgel. "He and his buddy are with their girlfriends somewhere." The other couples had drifted off soon after we arrived. They must have thought we would look after these boys while they went and made out in the woods.

"Well, this guy's hurt and needs some ice, and I'm not going to do it," Rob said. "So why don't you either find your brother or your home and go?"

"Yeah, this hurts bad," said Cowboy Hat. "We should probably go."

Christina was impressed with Rob and how he had not only helped the boys but also scurried them away. As we walked back, she started leaning into him and talking in low tones. The pairing was complete. I felt bad for David.

"Guess it's you and me, bud," I said.

"Just as well," said David. "Hanging out with you isn't so bad."

The girls agreed to come back to our campsite, and Stacy followed us back in her white Jeep. While the coupling was understood, we all sat around the campfire continuing the conversation. David and I built up the fire with the twigs and branches we found near the site. We only had two logs left from our bundles, and it seemed we would need the firelight for the evening.

As the fire started again, I noticed Paul and Julie had left. I looked in the direction of the tents and focused on the sex tent. There was no movement, and the bigger tent also seemed unoccupied, which meant they went off into the woods. I began to think about sex in the woods but caught myself being creepy.

"Look what I found," said a gleeful Rob, holding a bottle of Jack Daniels and a bottle of Malibu. "I forgot about these."

Everyone cheered, including the girls. They wanted rum and Coke. The males wanted Jack and Cokes. The found bottles were welcomed as the beer had run out, and none of us were buzzed. If something was going to happen, they would all need some more liquid courage.

The first round went down smoothly, followed quickly by a second. Rob showed off his tolerance while Jesse tried to keep up. We all knew this was a flawed strategy. Jesse never could hold his liquor well and was half the mass of Rob. The four of us continued our stories of prom nights past. David and I started to get a little uncomfortable when Jesse put his arm around Stacy, who then placed her hand on his leg. Christina began to whisper into Rob's ear. That was our cue to leave.

"Let's head to the lake," said David.

We took a flashlight and headed down the hill through the dense trees and undergrowth until we reached the lakeshore and open sky. We heard the water lapping against the shoreline and looked up to see the vast reaches of space and stars.

"Can you believe that some of these stars may not exist anymore?" I said, drawing out a cigarette. "I mean, that's history up there. They're so far away, and the light takes so long to get here, they could have turned into black holes before apes roamed the earth, and we'll never know."

"Crazy shit."

"It's kinda weird that those guys are leaving town and we're not," I said. I lit a cigarette and took a drag. "Do you feel like we're getting left behind?"

"A little," David said. "But we all have to move on from high school."

I blew out the smoke. "I guess so. Will we see each other again after this weekend?"

"I don't know. I think we'll be here, but who knows where life will take them? Their bubble just grew. Ours is kinda the same size right now."

"Yeah." We stood in silence and watched the stars for a while. I felt a little melancholy realizing this could be the last night we would all be together this summer. Who knows, perhaps forever? I took a couple deep breaths.

"Yo! Jim! Where are you lovers?" Jesse sounded as though the Jack hit him good and hard. Usually, he was the quietest of us, but the alcohol dulled his inner voice and self-control. It's funny how alcohol can enable you to yell at the top of your lungs or battle a stationary tree.

"Jesse, calm down," I heard Rob say.

"Shut the fuck up!" Jesse yelled.

As we got back, Paul and Julie had returned. Everything looked normal, except for a wet stain on Paul's crotch. Jesse reached second base as Stacy adjusted her bra. David and I turned away to provide some discretion. Rob gave Christina a big hug with a small peck on her cheek.

"The girls need to head back," said Paul. The three couples separated. Julie, who didn't get into the hard liquor and only had a beer at the beach, got in the driver's seat. She lurched the Jeep forward, and we all waved to them from the side of the road. When their taillights had disappeared behind a curve, the five of us returned to the campfire.

"Dude, I got a handy through my pants," said Paul as he sat on the log close to fire.

"Congratulations," I said and grimaced.

Jesse jerked up with a start. His eyes widened and went from joy to terror. He turned to his right, and a steady stream of puke exited his mouth.

We all groaned. Not more than five minutes since he was kissing Stacy, he was now replacing her taste with bile mixed with beer, Jack Daniels, and Coke.

"Totally worth it," he managed to say when he was done. He fell back onto the dirt just to the side of his puke. We stared at him. He was out.

"Let's get him inside," I said.

Rob, Paul, and I carried him to the sex tent. Nobody wanted him puking on us. We also didn't want him to puke in the tent. Once inside, we put his sleeping bag on top of him and left his head outside the tent, just in case.

"Jesse got fucked up," Paul said.

"Yeah, Christina and I were watching and waiting to see if he'd puke all over Stacy," Rob said. "It was part of the reason why she wanted to leave. The last thing they wanted was for Stacy to return to the cabin covered in puke and try to explain it to her parents."

David and I looked at Rob. "So, you didn't hook up with Christina?"

"No, we didn't. She just wanted to talk. She's got a messed-up life. Her dad just fucked around on her mom, and this was her way of just getting out. I entered the friend zone, unlike my boy Paul here," Rob said. "Paul, how did the handy feel?"

"Fantastic. Great trip, Jim! Well worth it."

"A yearly tradition. No matter what," said Rob. "To the trip!"

"To the trip!" we all answered.

"To the trip, motherfuckers!" yelled Jesse from the tent.

3

MIHO

Thursday at Noon

June 23, 2016

MIHO closed the book. He felt quite strange to read the words from a dead best friend about a trip from more than twenty years ago and reconciling it with his own memories. Some tracked quite well, such as how he got the nickname that still haunted him. At least he'd referred to him as David in the journal.

"I almost forgot the happy ending," Paul said.

"Dude," Jesse said with a wince. MIHO agreed. They were two hours down the road toward Fresno. Throughout the whole entry, MIHO was interrupted several times as the four of them gave their own commentary or recollections. Jim's detail was

43

amazing, but some of the memories didn't jibe with their own. MIHO thought he had cooked a tri-tip sirloin instead of hamburgers and hot dogs.

"I know, the first of many moments I look back and regret," Paul said.

"You were quite a sight," said Rob, who peered into his rearview mirror at Jesse. "Actually, you both were."

"Didn't Jim have a picture of Jesse passed out next to his puke?" asked Paul.

"He did at one point," said MIHO. "It looked like Jesse was dead, but Jim must have lost it."

"Damn, it's good there wasn't social media back then," said Jesse. "I'd hate to have that on the internet."

"Cheers to that and our youth," said Paul, raising an imaginary beer. "That first trip was something else."

"I almost forgot about Audrey," Jesse said.

"Yeah, Audrey," Paul said. "It's the one time I wished he was more like me. He needed to drop her and have a lot more fun. She was a dream crusher."

"He figured it out...eventually," Jesse said.

"I love that we have a record of MIHO becoming MIHO," Paul said.

"I totally forgot what MIHO stood for," Rob said. "The name took on its own meaning."

"I wish that name would just go away," MIHO said. "I've had to live with that for twenty years."

"You'll always be MIHO to us," Jesse said. "I don't even think I can remember calling you David. It's awesome it came out of that trip. Did you guys think we'd keep doing that trip that first year?"

"When Jim first proposed it at the pizza place?" Paul said. "Oh, hell no. I was game because it was a chance to drink with you guys, maybe get laid and have a last hurrah before we headed our separate ways."

"Same here," said Rob. "Things were going to be different once we left home. And, well, they were. But I don't know, the trip was a tether and the best link to reality I had for a while."

"Don't get deep on us now, Rob," said Jesse. "We're not even at Hanky Swanky yet."

Hank's Swank Par 3 Golf Course was a small patch of green near the Fresno airport that Rob discovered when organizing a bachelor party a decade before. They needed a place to meet in Fresno before heading up the hill, and when they were camping, they didn't have the space for golf clubs. It was here at Hank's Swank that a one-club challenge was born. The rules were simple. Players chose only one club to play the course. The holes were no longer than 150 yards and perfect for a normal player's seven iron. Over the years, the clubs varied. Jesse once used a 3-wood. Paul brought a putter, to everyone's amusement.

Over the years, each of them had improved considerably. Paul took lessons and often played at pro-ams and media junkets. As MIHO worked at various resorts, he had access to some of the most exclusive courses and teaching professionals. Rob was a natural athlete and improved his skills by shepherding his daughter through her advancement in the game. Jesse played regularly with his stay-at-home-dads' group. Jim was the only one who wasn't up to their level. He often came in last, but he never cared.

"What's everyone using today?" Paul asked as they fished their clubs from the back of Rob's truck. Rob, who could drive the ball more than three hundred yards, pulled out a nine iron. Conversely, Jesse, who hit the ball short but straight, brought out a six iron. MIHO found his eight iron under his duffle bag toward the front of the truck bed.

"Well, gentlemen, I've got my eight iron," said Paul, pulling out his TaylorMade. Then he pulled out another old, rusty, scratched Wilson. "But I also asked Tracey for Jim's seven. I thought we could all play a couple holes with it, like Jim was here."

"Friggin' A, Paul," said Rob. "Great idea."

"How did you even get it?" asked Jesse. "She welcomed us at the door."

"I asked a week ago and got it. I wanted to take it to the driving range and practice. I still plan to win, with his club or mine."

MIHO chastised himself for not thinking of this. He wanted this trip to be a perfect weekend of reminiscing. He tried to plan the trip like Jim would, doing all the same things, like this round of golf. He should have thought about using Jim's club to add extra resonance, but he was glad Paul had thought of it. It meant MIHO wasn't the only one trying to make this trip special. Over the course of the last few months of planning, he sometimes felt he was the only one truly interested in taking the trip.

The clubhouse at Hank's Swank was nothing more than a single-wide trailer with a counter and coolers of tall boys of

Coors, Bud, Miller, and smaller cans of craft beers. There was also a cooler of Powerade, water, soda, etc. In their more frugal years, they smuggled another twelve-pack onto the course under a fence on the first hole.

MIHO, Jesse, and Paul eyed the variety of beverages behind the glass door and slid it open to pull out tall boys and waters. They didn't smuggle or drink as much anymore. Rob just pulled out a large water and went to the cashier. There was never any pretension with Hank's Swank, and that cascaded to its employees. The man was slumped over on his elbows and more interested in reading a car magazine than a green. When they approached, the man said, "Good afternoon." MIHO watched as his white mustache moved up and down. His bright, well-worn belt buckle matched his plaid, button-down, polyester-blend shirt tucked into his grass-stained jeans.

"The two beers and a round," said Paul.

"That's twenty," said Mr. White Mustache, who was looking at Paul, trying to find the connection to him in his memory. Then it clicked. "Hey, aren't you on ESPN?"

Rob, MIHO, and Jesse shared a quick glance. Rob put his index finger up to tick the first recognition of the trip.

"I was, yes," Paul said and smiled. "I'm now back in Sacramento."

"I thought so. You were the Red Snapper Guy, the "Catch of the Day,'" the cashier said.

During a certain time, it seemed that everyone on *SportsCenter* had a catchphrase. Paul's was "Catch of the Day," where he'd designate a remarkable play by baseball stars like Tori Hunter or

Derek Jeter or wide receiver Randy Moss as the "Red Snapper" or "Wild Alaskan Halibut with a creamy white wine sauce."

"Yeah. I still do those, but mostly I cover regional sports now for one of the stations in Sacramento," said Paul, who went into his often-rehearsed response. "I wanted to get back home and be closer to my parents who aren't getting any younger." While this didn't explain the entire story, it was an easy way to placate interested people. He also knew how to deflect more questions and help make the person's day. "What's your name? I haven't seen you here before."

The man's eyes brightened, and his mustached curled upward. "I'm Bill. I've been here about nine months. They needed someone to keep up the charm of this place and run the ball tractor."

For all of Paul's faults, MIHO always appreciated the way he could relate to anyone he met. He was always polite, gracious, and interested in their stories.

"Right on," said Paul. "Well, we've been coming here for around ten years playing our one-club challenge. Makes sense you haven't seen us before."

"Well, you boys have a good time out there," said Bill. While they were in their late thirties, it always felt good for them to be referred to as boys.

"So, are we going to play the tournament like usual?" MIHO asked as they walked out to the first tee. "How are we handling Jim's strokes?"

"We'll all switch off playing a hole. That gives us eight holes. On the fifth, we'll play a shot each," said Paul, who wrapped his club on the back of his shoulders and began to twist in order to stretch and loosen his back.

"Sounds good," said Rob. "Paul, you tee off for Jim then. This was your idea, and you're probably the one most familiar with his club."

"Sounds good," Paul said. After hitting his own shot ten feet from the pin, he took Jim's seven iron and examined the club. "Did he pick this up at a garage sale?"

"No, a secondhand golf-equipment shop," said MIHO. "Remember? He prided himself on how he paid fifty bucks for these clubs."

"He was ripped off," said Paul. He teed up, waggled, and hit a worm-burner up the fairway. The hole was 130 yards long, and the ball rolled right to the fringe. Jesse followed and overshot the green into the trees behind. Rob almost took a half swing and hit the right side of the green. MIHO's shot hooked left into the rough twenty yards from the pin. Paul finished with a birdie and gave Jim a par. Rob and Jesse also parred, and MIHO birdied. After four holes, Rob and Paul led Jesse and MIHO by a stroke and Jim by another two.

"Man, it's like Jim's still here," said MIHO. "He's still in last place."

Jim's fortunes changed on the fifth hole when Paul mishit Jim's shot, and the ball screamed straight toward the hole, never higher than a foot off the ground. It was aiming to go past the hole and to the sixth hole tee box, but the yellow ball caught an unseen gopher hole in the front of the green, bounced up a couple feet, landed, and rolled to within four feet of the hole.

"Doesn't matter how it got there, but there it is," MIHO said. "Good shot, Paul."

"I think Jim guided that one," said Paul, who laughed and shrugged.

That crazy bounce led to a birdie for Jim and turned around his round. Playing for Jim, they recorded a par on the sixth, another birdie on the seventh, and a par on the eighth. Heading into the final hole, Jim's score was still in contention, tied with Paul and one back of Rob.

"Now it's up to MIHO," Paul said and placed his hand on MIHO's shoulder. "No pressure. Jim's first win in the tournament all depends on you."

With the ninth and final hole, only MIHO was out of contention, and he had lost his touch in the last few holes. If they all could choose someone to bring Jim home, no one, including MIHO, would think he was going to be the guy. Still, it was his turn to play the yellow ball. On his ball, MIHO felt his club turn, and he shanked it off to the right. He slammed his club to the ground and grabbed Jim's ratty Wilson.

"No worries," said Rob. "You're playing for Jim now. He'll guide the way."

"Relax, man," Paul said. "It's okay. I mean, we've set this up for Jim, but in the end, what he'd really want was us to have a great time. And we have, right?"

"Yeah," said MIHO. "I just don't want to let him down."

"It's okay," said Jesse. He smiled. "He's not here, but if he was, he'd just be happy to be in contention. Now, don't shank it like you just did."

MIHO stepped back and observed the ball, the green, and the flag. As he approached, he tried to put Jim in the back of his mind. This was MIHO's shot, his muscle memory, his arms and authentic swing. Jim's club had other ideas. First, the club felt cheap. The grip was worn. Now, it was up to MIHO to deliver.

MIHO waggled in front of the ball and eyed the flag. Good, crisp swing. Put the ball in the air and land to the left of the hole for an easy putt. He took a breath, but instead of blocking Jim from his thoughts, he found Jim filling his heart as he swung, recalling their endless phone calls on the backswing, his smile as he crisply struck the ball, his laugh on the follow-through. The club struck the ball on the sweet spot, and MIHO looked up to track the ball's path through the sky. Jesse, Paul, and Rob also stared.

"Oh my, that sounded good," said Paul.

"Yep, that looks like a great shot," Rob added.

The ball didn't deviate from the path to the flag at all. There was no draw, no hook. It headed straight to the left of the pin, where he wanted to place it. As the ball began its descent, it looked even better, the distance exact. The ball hit around four feet to the left of the hole, and they all cheered. Then it bounced. Now it was three feet. It bounced again to a foot. Then it rolled further right, inches from the cup.

"No way," said Rob.

"Oh my," said MIHO.

The yellow ball kept rolling until it disappeared into the gap between the edge of the cup and the flag stick. A hole in one. An ace!

MIHO jumped up and down and screamed. He was joined by his buddies, and they hugged each other and jumped with their arms in the air. The players on the driving range looked toward them, wondering what had happened.

"I can't believe it," said MIHO. "That's the best shot I've ever hit."

"And coming off that shitty club," said Paul. "What a shot! There was no doubt."

"Wow," said Jesse. "Just wow."

"Fellas, I know we have a no-tanking rule, but I'm done playing," said Rob. "I'd have to make a birdie to tie anyway. My heart isn't even into trying. Jim's meant to take this one."

"Couldn't agree more," said Paul, dropping his club and wiping his hands. "I'm done too. Jesse?"

"I'm good. Jim wins!"

"But MIHO, you still have to buy the beer," said Paul. MIHO grimaced at the idea of fulfilling the tradition that the player who shot a hole in one had to pay the tab for the clubhouse. In a country club, this could be expensive. For Hank's Swank, the damage wouldn't be big. MIHO counted the four of them, plus the five on the driving range, and of course Bill.

"You're getting off easy," Rob said.

"Jim's getting off easy," said MIHO. "It was his shot."

They settled with Bill whose grin expanded when they told him what happened. MIHO bought everyone a beer of their choice—a water for Rob (who was driving) and six additional beers out of the cooler. He offered one to Bill, who promised to open it at home after his shift. MIHO walked to the driving range and offered one to each of the golfers refining their swings. They smiled with gratitude for the beverage and reason for it. Back in the parking lot, the friends toasted Jim and had a beverage in his honor. This trip had started off on a great note and a true tribute to their friend.

As they piled back into Rob's truck, MIHO sensed their enthusiasm now turning to euphoria. When MIHO had organized the trip, he sensed that not everyone was on board. Jesse had even let out a little moan. However, these first few hours had just the right amount of their normal trip with a hint of Jim's memory. Rob drove past the clubhouse and out of the parking lot as they waved farewell to Bill and Hank's Swank. As soon as they were back on the road, Jesse tapped MIHO on the shoulder. "Okay, it's time for the next year in the Lake Trip Log."

MIHO opened the notebook and began flipping through. "All right, so some of these entries are long, like the first year, and others just give a story or just some words we used the whole weekend."

"What do you mean?" said Jesse.

"Well, it looks like in 1996, he gives detailed rules of foil ball and subsequent scores and brackets," MIHO said. "That's it. Oh, and Jesse, you won."

MIHO handed the book to Jesse who flipped through the foil-ball rules. MIHO remembered how foil ball was created because he forgot the decks of cards he was supposed to bring. As a result, they devised a game similar to baseball but also included rules about other players distracting the batter with foil projectiles, and a ball in the bush was an automatic score because, as the rules explained, "Who wouldn't want that?"

"When did Paul threaten to wrestle Jim to the ground?" Rob asked.

"Yes," Jesse said, remembering that story. He flipped the page of the notebook. "That's the following year. It's the only thing he writes about 1997."

Jesse read the story detailing the time they went to the "dance" at the lodge. They mistakenly thought the dance would be like a club, but it was more like a family wedding without the drunk bridesmaids. As the evening progressed, Paul drank more and more, while Jim was sober as the designated driver.

Paul took over the story. "So, apparently, I went up to him and said, 'Jim, you're drunk.' He said he wasn't. I got pissed and told him, 'Tell me you're drunk, or I'll wrestle you to the ground.'" The last bit, Paul slurred. They had all heard this story plenty of times before, and it was funny every time they retold it.

Jesse continued to read: "'So, I could have either told the truth and watched Paul's drunk-assed attempt to wrestle me to the ground...or I could have told Paul I was drunk and exited the situation. The choice was clear. I told him he was right and I was drunk. And Paul said...'" Jesse cued Paul with his finger.

"That's what I thought!" Paul said, putting up a finger and slurring like a drunk.

They laughed again. These trips all centered around creating, telling, embellishing, and retelling these stories.

"How much detail does he go into in 1998?" Rob asked.

"Pretty deep," Jesse said as he flipped through the pages. "Oh, this is right after he broke up with Audrey. Yikes."

"That's right," Paul said. "Didn't he catch her with some other guy at her place?"

"Yeah, he was delivering pizzas nearby and dropped by her apartment," MIHO said. "When he showed up, there was this other dude there."

"Yep," Jesse said. "It says right here: 'I just turned and walked out of that apartment for the last time, got into my car, and peeled out as fast as my Civic could go.' He never looked back."

"That was a relief," Paul said. "What else happened that year?"

"Are you kidding me?" Rob said. "That was also the year with Sean, Becky and the house."

Paul shook his head. "Right. Yeah, another set of poor choices. Well, I can take it. Read away."

Jesse began to read:

This year's trip couldn't have come soon enough. I needed to get away from Sacramento, from my life, from everything. I needed to be with my friends and not care about the world. Most of all, I needed to get away from the life I had with Audrey.

4

Jim

1998

When I picked up MIHO, I was so ready to get out of town. Ever since that day when I knocked on Audrey's door, saw another guy and her look of terror, I was mad at everything that reminded me of her. I felt claustrophobic and confined by Sacramento and the life I thought I knew. I wanted this trip to liberate me from the crap I'd been feeling. I bounded up the steps to MIHO's house. He opened the door and greeted me as excited as I was to get this trip started.

"Are you ready?" I asked him as I gave him a half hug.

"Oh, hell yeah," he said. "I've been working way too hard and need a break before everything gets too crazy again."

This summer MIHO became a valet at the Hyatt Regency in downtown Sacramento for thirty hours a week on top of a full load at Sac State. Last semester, he had an internship, but when that ended, he said he'd take any job at the hotel to keep working and learning as much as he could. So, when he wasn't studying or parking cars, he was finding ways to be useful, sometimes helping out for free.

The only other hobby MIHO had was cooking, and he planned to test out some of his skills this weekend. I had some doubts that he'd be able to pull it off on a camp stove and a portable barbecue, but I figured it would be better than the hot dogs, hamburgers, cold cuts, ramen, cereal, and Pop-Tarts we were used to. We placed the cooler of food and his camping kitchen equipment into the Civic. I just hoped the car could make it up the steep climb into the mountains.

The trip had become more than just an annual hangout with my oldest and closest friends. It was now a thread that kept us all connected. Wherever our lives had taken us over the course of the year, we could count on this trip to bring us back to center.

"Man, I can tell you're ready," MIHO said as we pulled away. "Your smile is so big, it's like you just got laid."

"I don't know about that." I laughed and puffed on a cigarette. "I'm just ready to get away, push reset on my life to start anew without Audrey, and move on. Four years of my life—gone! I'm glad I didn't buy that ring."

Two months ago, I was in the mall and passed a jewelry store. Usually, I just walked on by, not wanting to even give a nod to the thought of long-term commitment. But Audrey had made me stop by the window just to gawk at the diamonds, and on that Saturday afternoon on my way to pick up some shorts, I decided to pop in. I had to learn about what to look for and the price range. It was the first step to making a purchase, and it was significant. Thankfully, I didn't have to take the next step.

"Wow, you escaped that," MIHO said. "I mean, all of us would have seriously raised some shit if you were going to propose."

"I know, you guys didn't like her," I said.

"She wasn't right for you. She was possessive, clingy, and—"

"Dude!" I was getting a little irritated. I knew I was going to get the download of all the pent-up feelings they had toward her, but I was hoping it would be around a campfire with some beer.

"All right, all right. I get it," MIHO said, raising his hands. "You want to hear about my love life?"

"You don't have one."

"Exactly. Maybe I'm just jealous. I'm just too busy to have a girlfriend."

"You're too busy for friends, period," I said. "I'm surprised you're even going on this trip."

"Hey, if I'm going to make it, I'm going to will it to be, baby," MIHO said.

Even though we lived two blocks from each other, and he transferred to Sac State last year, I rarely saw him. While I was either with Audrey, prepping for the next debate competition, or just hanging out with other friends, he was working full time, studying, or sleeping. I admired his dedication and work ethic, but it was hard to understand why he had to work all the time.

"But do you have to work this hard?" I asked. Though I was watching the road, I could feel his eyes staring at me with intensity. This was his life.

"The cards are already stacked against me. I'm Filipino. My mom and I haven't had much money since the cancer. I don't have the advantage you do. I've got to do more than the next guy. That's the only chance I got. So, yeah, you know, I have to work this hard to achieve what I want in life," MIHO said.

"And what's that?"

"I don't know, man, some respect, some money, some authority. But now I've gotta learn everything, be everything, be the best. Otherwise, I'm starting out in a losing position."

This wasn't the first time we had this conversation, but the way he talked about it now was inspiring and a little intense. There was no doubt he had a plan and was going to execute it. We continued down the highway through the small towns, farmland, almond groves, and cattle-grazing lands of the Central Valley. Alone, this drive would be nearly unbearable, but with MIHO the time flew.

"I'm surprised we got Rob to come. I was sure he'd be training and getting ready for the football season," MIHO said.

"Yeah. I had to schedule around his practices. He's only free a couple weekends during the summer."

"Well, next year at this time, we may not see him at all," MIHO said. "I mean, if he's drafted, he may go to an NFL training camp."

Last season, Rob recorded five sacks and forty-five tackles as a junior linebacker at USC. We all watched him on TV from our various spots throughout the country. I found a Sacramento USC bar to sit and watch the Trojans. I had grown up a Cal fan, but when one of your best friends is a starting linebacker at USC, you justify your treachery.

"I know," MIHO said. "The kid who came to my house to play Nintendo may be playing a professional sport in a year."

"Yeah. Jesse says he hardly sees Rob. They try to get together and hang out about once every couple weeks, mostly so Rob can get away from the football craziness."

"How's Jesse?" MIHO said. "He's not coming back to Sac, is he?"

"I don't think so." Some people take to Los Angeles more than others. I never got the appeal of Southern California. But each time Jesse came to Sacramento to visit his mom, the less he saw his hometown as his home. Living with his dad also turned out better than he thought. Jesse had his own room, his own entrance, and his dad treated him more like a roommate. The more he lived there, the less he enjoyed living with his mom, until Southern California became his permanent home. He felt bad for his mom, but he enjoyed going to CSLA and being so close to the beach.

"Well, I'm glad he's coming," MIHO said. "That we're *all* coming. It's great we found a reason to see each other every year."

"Plus, watching Paul is just pure entertainment," I said. "After that first year and that hot girl, he's always chasing the hookup."

Paul moved up in the broadcast-journalism program at the University of Michigan and was scheduled to be the sports director for WOLV-TV, the campus TV station. Not only did he give the daily sports updates on the news broadcast, he sometimes traveled with the teams. Just last year, he covered the football team at the Rose Bowl and followed the team in the NCAA men's basketball tournament. Paul always wanted to be a broadcaster on ESPN, specifically *SportsCenter*. It was appointment viewing to watch Keith Olbermann and Dan Patrick, but he also enjoyed watching the younger guys, like Brett Haber, Craig Kilborn, Stuart Scott, and Rich Eisen. He had met Eisen, a Michigan alum, a few times over the years. In fact, it was a career path he hoped to follow.

MIHO and I met Jesse, Paul, and Rob in Fresno at a small bar in a suburban strip mall that connected the west and east sides of Fresno and was the natural spot for us to connect before heading up the hill. We walked in, and when our eyes adjusted from the midday sun to the darkness of the dive, we found the rest of our crew seated at the far end of the bar, feet on the brass rail, arms folded over the oak. Rob and Jesse, who had driven up from Los Angeles and picked up Paul from the airport, were into their second beer. They were quite a sight with Rob in a well-worn crimson T-shirt with USC Football in gold. Meanwhile, Paul had a dark-blue shirt with a bright-yellow M on it. By contrast, Kramer from *Seinfeld* was emblazoned on Jesse's T-shirt.

"Gentlemen," I said a little loud and prompting a grunt from a fellow patron. "Ready to get this shit started?"

"Fuckin' A!" said Rob. Nobody was going to tell our giant to lower his voice. "I'm ready to not think about blocking protections, defensive schemes, and zone blitzes. And no NFL talk, please."

MIHO and I hung our heads a bit. We wanted to talk about his senior year and a new, exciting chapter in his life, but we also got it. After all, I didn't want to get into it about Audrey. We all had our issues we wanted to set aside to just talk about "guy stuff." So, we just slapped backs and shook hands before sitting next to them and ordering some drinks.

"What's going on, Paul?" said MIHO. "Who's going to be the QB at Michigan next year."

"We've got this guy, Tom Brady," he said. "He's from San Mateo, and we talk California all the time. But anyway, he's likely going to be the starter next year. He's okay talent-wise, just like anyone else. But he does work his ass off. We'll see how that translates. But enough about that, what's up with you guys? How's your mom, MIHO?"

"Oh god." MIHO rolled his eyes. Since that first trip, there were friends at Sac State and other acquaintances who didn't know MIHO as David. MIHO was such a part of our lexicon that he ceased to be David. "I'm not letting you near any ladies I care about. Same with you, Jim, the new free man!"

"So glad you kicked that girl to the curb," Paul said. "She was a real downer."

"He was thinking about rings," MIHO said.

I glanced over at him with a look of betrayal while everyone looked at me in disbelief. I think Paul almost spit out his beer.

"Oh crap," Jesse said. "I didn't know you were in *that* deep."

"I was just looking," I said. I pushed my hands away, trying to downplay it.

Rob stood with his beer and got behind me, his large presence overpowering my space. He placed his large hand on my shoulder like a stone vice and used his other hand to tap my beer with his.

"You're better off without her, man," he said. "I mean, were you even happy?"

"Yeah, of course. When we were hanging out just us, we were awesome. But I guess she thought this other guy, Tony, was better."

"Well, she wasn't *it* for you," Rob said. "She thought she felt love when you were obedient, and you express love by being selfless. It's called co-dependence."

"Boom," said Paul.

"Thank you psych, Spring semester," Rob said. He raised his hands in triumph.

"I hope you got an A," Paul said. "You may have a future beyond football."

"I thought football players didn't attend classes or get 'grades,'" MIHO joked.

"Laugh away, asshole," Rob said, sick of the pervasive impression that jocks got out of tests and homework. "I'm not some dumb jock. Yes, I have access to more study aides, tutoring, and all that, but I still take the courses and the tests."

We finished our beers and lunch and headed up the hill to check into our now-traditional spot, #152. We had a routine of setting up camp. We now had three tents for the six of us, with Rob getting his own because he needed it. When we settled, MIHO began his serious meal preparation. The grilled vegetables, mashed potatoes, and tri-tip far exceeded our expectations.

"Oh my *god*," said Rob. "This is friggin' amazing. I've had tri-tip at our training table, and this is *far* better than anything I've ever tasted."

"It's all about marinades," said MIHO. "If you can get the right flavors soaking into the meat, then it adds to the flavor and cooks with the meat in symbiosis. This one's red-wine vinegar, Worcester sauce, garlic, soy sauce, and liquid smoke."

"Yeah, this is much better than hot dogs and hamburgers," said Paul.

"Well, we do have hot dogs for the beach on Saturday, but with fresh onions, sauerkraut, pickles, and tomatoes, so you can have it New York style or Chicago style," said MIHO.

As the evening turned to night, we pulled on our sweatshirts and built up the fire. We had different lives at our various colleges, but here we could share our communal brotherhood. I had friends in college, but these four other guys felt like they were the ones I'd share my joys, my struggles, and my fears at times like these. Right now, it just happened to be around this fire with beer and frosted cookies, which made the whole thing with Audrey both therapeutic and difficult.

"I think the biggest thing I feel about this whole Audrey thing is shock, and that's wearing off," I said. "And what's weird is I'm not sad or grieving, just a little relieved and excited about what's ahead. Is that weird?"

"Fuck no," Paul said.

I expected him to be the first to speak up. I smiled.

"Man, you're in your prime. You can do so much better than her, right? First off, women love you. You're a nice guy and you do them right. You should hook up this weekend."

I shook my head and giggled. "Dude, I'm not sure if I'm ready for that yet. I'm just happy to be with you guys up here among the stars, beer, and animal-cookie parade."

"What about my cooking?" MIHO asked in mock disappointment.

I threw a frosted animal cookie at him, which hit him in the forehead.

"One good thing about Audrey is that she helped me realize I wanted to teach instead of go into politics," I said.

Well, it was a combination of factors. First, I had interned for the summer in the California State Legislature, and rather than fall in love with the capitol and the constant intrigue and action, I was disillusioned by the backdoor dealing, petty conflicts, and constant plays for power and influence. Meanwhile, Audrey began focusing on education and observing teachers engaging students. While teachers had to deal with students who were frustrating and disrespectful, they also saw the benefits of influencing kids that would go on to do great things. The more I thought about it, the more I liked the idea of switching focus to education. This decision didn't sit well with Paul.

"What? high school? I thought you wanted to run campaigns or run for office or something? Aren't you the student federation president and top master debater at Sac State?"

MIHO laughed and spit out pieces of cookie.

"You're destined to be governor and you're going into teaching?" Paul continued. "Dude, you talk about changing the world."

"And this is how I'm going to do it. I'm going to prepare the next leaders in my classroom."

"See what I mean?" Paul shook his head. "You even make a shit job like teaching seem admirable."

"I like where our boy Jim's head's at," Rob said. "I mean look at his face. Look how excited he is to spend time with teenagers all day. Personally, I don't get the appeal, but not everyone has to have it figured out like you Paul."

Rob threw a bottle cap at Paul, who ducked and threw a half a beer can back.

"Fucker," Rob joked.

"That's right! Don't you forget it," Paul said.

"My brain hurts thinking about all this," I said. "I'm going to bed." I got out of my camp chair and guzzled the rest of my beer, then started toward the tent to get my toothbrush, still overhearing their conversation.

"We broke him," Jesse said.

"Man, if he only knew," Paul said. "He could get laid like that."

"Paul, unlike you, I don't think he's looking for that," MIHO said.

"That's what I mean," Paul said.

As I slipped into my sleeping bag, I could still hear them transition to stories of hanging out with Heisman Winner Charles Woodson, sorority girls, and sex in library study rooms.

I was the first one up the following morning, and that meant starting the campfire. I gathered the necessary kindling under the watchful eyes of squirrels and blue jays, then lit it up with a flip of my Zippo. Once the fire started, Jesse emerged with a great display of bedhead. We gave the requisite nod to signify a good morning, then he sat and watched me add another log to build a good blaze. Soon MIHO and Rob joined us around the ring staring at the flames.

"Where are we hiking today, boys?" I asked. "Should we go to the falls again like the first year or head to the top of the mountain?"

"What if we went to the beach today?" said MIHO. "I just want to relax and not do anything. Friday's lighter, right?"

"Usually, but don't want we want to go on Saturday to meet the ladies?" asked Jesse.

"Nothing to say we can't go both days," said Rob. "But I wouldn't mind just laying low and enjoying the water and drinking some beer."

"Okay, but we're deviating from our tradition," I said, accidentally stretching out the "e" in deviate, which sounded weird.

"*Dee*-viating?" Said Jesse.

Everyone chuckled.

"That sounds *dee*-vious," said MIHO.

"That can be *dee*-structive," said Rob.

Everyone was laughing.

"Oh god, I don't know why I said it that way," I said. "I'm just glad Paul isn't up yet."

"Don't *dee*-ny me this opportunity!" yelled Paul from inside the tent.

Everyone, including me, busted out laughing at Paul's uncanny timing.

"That's *dee*-grading, and I *dee*-mand the opportunity to keep this going all weekend...without *dee*-lay!"

I was grateful there were only a few words that easily came to mind starting with "dee." This led to some needed silence as they racked their brains. As we ate breakfast and packed up for the beach, words would just pop up out of nowhere. "*Dee*-cry!" Followed by a chuckle. When the song on the radio ended and a personality came on air, "*Dee*-jay!" We even got to demilitarized and debase and deduct.

We arrived at the beach around eleven, enough time to find a nice spot with continuous shade. We set our spot, cracked open our first beers, and watched the water and the first Hobie catamarans get out on the water. Watching the lake put me in a trance, and I didn't notice the man in his fifties approach us. His white sunglasses were pointed in Rob's direction, and if that wasn't a giveaway, the crimson sleeveless T-shirt with the gold USC letters was a sure sign. Either he was a fan or a booster—likely the latter, given that he was coming from a full tailgate setup, complete with USC cooler, USC canopy, and chairs emblazoned with USC.

"You're Rob Simpson, right?" asked the man.

"Yeah, how are you doing?" Rob stood up to shake the man's hand.

"Great. I thought it was you. I'm Sean," said the man with a big smile. He rested his hefty arms across his chest and potbelly.

Rob always told us that the athletes were told to respect boosters above all else. For one, you might get a twenty-dollar bill or more. For two, depending on who it was (and you never knew), it could get back to you one way or another. Of course, not everyone was a booster. Some were just USC football fans.

"So, what brings you up here?" said Sean.

"Guys' trip," said Rob. "These are my high school buddies. This is Jim, Jesse, Paul, and MIHO." We all stood and shook Sean's hand.

"Nice to meet you guys," said Sean, who shifted his attention back to Rob. "I thought that was you. We have season tickets, and I've seen you play. I graduated in '76. That's where I met my wife, Colleen, over there." Sean gave a wave to a deep-tanned woman in a white coverall shirt and expensive sunglasses. She waved back. Even though there were a half a dozen people next to and around the canopy, I would have guessed that would be her.

"Hey, I know you guys are doing your own thing, but you're welcome to join us. We're barbecuing up some food and have some extra beers. We're about to set up horseshoes, and my daughter and her friend, they're around your age, should also be here any minute."

When "daughter" was mentioned, Paul's ears perked up like a Doberman.

"Thanks for the offer," said Rob. "We may stop by in a little bit. Just looking to kick back a little, you know?"

"Of course. Of course," said Sean, a little disappointed but trying to play it cool. "No problem. Stop by when you get a chance. You're all welcome."

Sean stepped away, and Paul shot Rob a look. "Dude, free food, free beer, and maybe some girls our age."

"Yeah, but I'm around boosters all the time at school, and it's tiring," said Rob. "You have to almost be someone else. I come up here to get away from all that. This is me. If I go over there, I'll be USC Rob."

Rob looked over and saw their spread, and although MIHO had some dogs of his own planned, we could see many more complementary items, such as macaroni salad, chips, guacamole, and salsa. Our collective salivation was due as much to the food as the prospects of meeting girls.

Rob continued. "I'll tell you what. Let's see what those girls are like. If they're high school, we can't go over there anyway, or if they're ugly, we won't want to. Is that okay for your penis?"

"Yeah," Paul said. His smiled got even bigger. "When these girls show up, we'll *dee*-cide."

Jesse took a long draw of his beer at the wrong moment, and it came out his nose, which made us all laugh harder. As it turned out, Sean's daughter, Kim, was neither in high school nor ugly. Neither was her friend Becky. Kim was a legacy at USC, attending her first year at her parents' alma mater. She was a prototypical USC coed; blond, perky, and tan—but without the sun damage her parents had suffered. Even with a turquoise tank top and sarong, we about drooled. Becky was a tall African American volleyball player who attended Loyola. Once we saw Kim and Becky walk up to Sean and the tailgate, Rob's apprehension of hanging out with boosters was overruled by the rest of our hormones. Plus, we found out the tailgate also included barbecue beef and beans, which was enough additional incentive to go join the party.

Sean's crew consisted of Sean, Colleen, Kim, and Becky, plus Sean and Colleen's friends Larry, Vicky, Bob, and Marilyn. Vicky, Marilyn, and Colleen sat in their beach chairs, drinking Tequizas, involved in their own conversations. While MIHO, Jesse, Rob, and Paul all began angling for ways to make a connection with Kim or Becky, the idea of trying to flirt and pick up women was tiring. I wasn't ready to put myself out there. It didn't matter anyway. Paul zeroed on Kim, and Rob seemed to make a real connection with Becky. Both were college athletes and began speaking a language I couldn't comprehend.

While Sean was introducing all of us, Larry and Bob began setting up a horseshoe pit. I had always thought it was a game for a company or family picnic, but Larry had a legitimate setup, with its own case, measuring tape, and a mallet to pound in the stakes. When it looked as though Jesse, MIHO, and I were going to be on our own, we decided to engage the older men in playing their game.

"You guys play?" Larry asked.

"I've never played before," I said. MIHO and Jesse shrugged their shoulders.

Larry, Bob, and Sean looked at each other. Then Larry rubbed his bald head and pointed to me. "How about you and I team up? We can take on Bob and one of your buddies. Sean and the other one will take on the winner. Sound good?"

Bob shrugged. "Sounds good to me. It'll be nice to have some fresh blood in our game. I'll take this guy." He pointed at Jesse.

"And I'll get this one. What's your name?" Sean asked.

"David," MIHO said.

"His name's MIHO!" Paul said, drawing a giggle from Kim and Becky, who were off to the side, observing. Rob would usually be all over competition, but he stayed away, either because he didn't want to deal with boosters or he was enamored with Becky.

"Okay, my partner's David...or MIHO," Sean said.

The rest of us introduced each other. Sean, Bob, and Larry had known each other for twenty-five years since they all pledged the same fraternity. I saw a lot of ourselves in Sean and his friends. Perhaps in twenty-five years we'd be doing the same thing—bringing our families up to the lake, playing horseshoes, retelling stories of our youth.

They explained the rules and gave us pointers on how to toss the horseshoes to maximize the chances for a ringer. Jesse got the hang of the game, as did I. MIHO was awful. His throws were inconsistent and came off his hand like a flailing duck. If Sean regretted being stuck with MIHO, he didn't let on. Instead, they all seemed to enjoy our company, and it was the first time I had hung out with older men as peers. They asked about our college experiences and career goals and were impressed at how MIHO was working his way up the hotel-career path.

Sean pulled me aside and spoke in a low voice. He looked over at Paul and Kim, who were leaning in for a private chat and giggling.

"So, what's up with this Paul guy?" Sean said. Over the course of the afternoon, Paul and Kim and had become closer and closer. I was sure if Sean wasn't around, his daughter and Paul would be off on their own.

"He's a good guy," I said. "He's a charmer, but beyond that pretty-boy exterior, he'll do anything for his friends."

"That's good," Sean said. "I think my daughter likes him, but you should tell him if he does anything, I'm going after him." He was serious.

"Don't worry," I said, stretching the truth. In fact, I was now worried that Sean's suspicions would come true. "Besides, he's with Rob, and Rob's the best guy. He won't let anything happen."

"All right, but I'm going to keep an eye on them."

Colleen said she wanted another Tequiza, so Sean left to get one out of the cooler.

I looked back over to the four of them. Paul caught us staring and raised an eyebrow like I was creeping him out. I figured it was a good time to go over and give a heads-up to Paul and Rob about Sean. Rob was telling some type of story.

"I was tired and figured it was easier to just nap for fifteen minutes rather than be tired and unfocused," Rob said. "I passed the final and the class."

"I thought football players didn't take finals," said Becky. "Don't you all have tutors who take the finals for you?"

"Not true," Rob said. "At least I don't."

"Well, I'm glad you're not some dumb jock," Becky said. She punched his arm. For the first time, I realized she was almost as tall as Rob. Usually, when girls talked to Rob, they had to tilt their heads so far back that I could feel the strain on their necks.

"I am too," Rob said. "Because then I'd be...*dumb*."

Becky shook her head and rolled her eyes with an easy smile that was flirty but also let him know his ordinary charm wouldn't be enough. Rob took it as a challenge.

Kim looked up as though she remembered something, before her brow furrowed and she made a pouty face. She came over to me and put her arm around me.

"So, I heard you found your lady with another guy. I'm sorry," she said.

I looked at Paul, who shrugged, then I turned back to Kim. It was nice having an attractive girl with her arm around me, though also kind of pathetic. "It's okay. She wasn't the right one. Years wasted."

"Learning experience," Becky said.

"You seem like a good guy. You'll find someone," Kim said. She put her head on my shoulder, then quickly lifted it again with a thought. "Shoot, my friend Lauren was going to come with us, but she had to flake at the last second. She would have been perfect for you."

"That's okay," I said. "I'm with my boys."

"That's right," Rob said, and he gave me a high five. "It's the trip."

Kim let go, and my skin was sad it wasn't touching hers anymore. She walked over to Sean. "Daddy, can Rob, Paul, and the rest of the guys come to the condo for dinner? Paul says they don't have much food at their site."

MIHO shot Paul a look. Just that morning, MIHO had bragged about a slow-cooked pulled pork over rice. Paul shook his head, as if to say, don't screw this up. MIHO glared, and we agreed to come by the condo that evening. After another hour of hanging out, playing horseshoes, flirting, and mooching off Sean, we headed back to the campsite to change clothes, wash up the best we could, and discuss the prospects for the evening.

"Oh, it's on with Kim," said Paul. "That girl's a freak. She gets off on doing stuff behind her parents' backs."

"Dude," I said, recalling my conversation earlier, "Sean's on to you, and if he catches you doing anything with his daughter, man, I know I wouldn't want to be on the other side of that."

"Don't worry, I'll be careful. What do you think about Becky, Rob? You guys seemed to be speaking your own language."

"She's pretty cool," Rob said. "It was nice not talking about football in some type of hero-worship thing. We talked more about what it's like to be an athlete. Seemed like you guys were having a good time with the adults."

"Sean and Larry were having a love fest with MIHO," I said. "I think they wanted MIHO to be their son-in-law."

"Those guys wouldn't want me for their daughters," MIHO said. "They want me to work for them. Larry was trying to get me to think about joining his investment firm. I tried to tell them my interest is in the hotels, not business."

We had planned to wear our nice clothes Saturday night when we headed to the saloon for the first time as legal drinking adults. Instead, we pulled out our clean sweaters and used the single-spigot faucet at the campsite for a cold sponge bath. I mean, it wasn't every night we were invited to a nice cabin for someone else to feed us.

Rob took forever to navigate the switchbacks up to the top of the mountain to Sean's four-bedroom cabin. Before we even got to the front door, Kim was running out of the condo, followed by Becky.

"Ah, you came!" Kim screamed and threw her arms around Paul. Becky smiled at the sight of Rob. We all stood on the front deck, talking about our upcoming fall classes and the recent Southern California heat wave and how Boone's Farms wine had caused each of us to get sick at some point in the last year. Through the window, I could see Sean finishing up the prep in the kitchen.

"Kim, Becky, and all the rest of you college kids, dinner's ready," Sean said. "Grab some food and head to the game room. There's a lot of activities down there."

Kim was disappointed that she had to break away from Paul but excited to show us the game room. We gathered our plates of ribs, beans, salad, and corn, and Kim and Becky led us down a flight of stairs. The game room was huge with a sofa bed, foosball table, dartboard, and an air-hockey table. There was another balcony off the rec room with another great view of the lake. Rob and Becky took up the couch, leaving floor space for the rest of us. We talked about inane things like TV shows: *Friends* vs. *Frasier, ER* vs. *NYPD Blue, Beavis an♦ Butt-Head* vs. *South Park.* Kim wiped off the barbecue sauce from Paul's lip with her fin-ger and put it in her mouth and sucked it. Paul wasn't kidding. We all knew it was just a matter of time before they found a way to break off. Meanwhile, Becky and Rob were engrossed in con-versation like they were old friends, laughing and smiling and oblivious to everyone else.

After we finished the barbecue, MIHO, Jesse, and I knew we needed to leave this awkward situation. I declared my desire to have a smoke, and while Jesse and MIHO never liked my habit, they agreed to join me. We stepped onto the deck, which stood about fifteen feet off the ground, as the cabin was built into the side of the mountain. I pulled out a cigarette, lit it, and took a drag as we leaned against the rail.

"I hate being the odd wheel," MIHO said. "It's just so awk-ward when we have to appease them. I don't know how many times I've seen Paul's tongue down some girl's throat. Or worse."

"Right. One time I was trying to get Paul home and walked into a room where he was messing around with someone and I saw all of him," Jesse said. He then stretched his hands out to about a foot. "All of him."

"Yeah, I've seen it too," I said. "It's hard not to feel inadequate after seeing that snake."

"Really?" MIHO said. "I've never seen it."

"You're better for it," Jesse said.

While I smoked, Jesse and MIHO expressed their excitement for the final years of school. I would still have another year to get my teaching credential before entering the classroom.

"So, you really want to give up politics and teach, huh?" Jesse asked.

"I think so. Unlike the feeling I had when I was working in politics, this feels a little more right. Who knows? Maybe I could also advise the debate team or student government."

"Okay, I can see that," MIHO said. "I've seen you on the debate team helping others, and you do know how student government works."

"If I had to have someone teach my kids, I'd pick you," Jesse said. "And even the stuff with Audrey, you're going to be fine. We're only twenty-one."

"Yeah, the more I think about it, the more I know what happened was for the best," I said. "Still hurts, because I was so blindsided, but I'll get over it."

"Do you think we'll be like Sean, Larry, and Rob when we're older?" Jesse asked. "I mean, come up here with our families and hang out?"

"It'd be cool if we all came back here every year and our kids were doing the same shit we're doing now," MIHO said. "It'd be nice to have a kitchen and a real bed."

"Well, when we're older, we'll be able to afford this type of vacation home," Jesse said, admiring all the amenities in the cabin, from the satellite dish to the sectional couch to the poker table. Through the screen door, we heard Sean descending the stairs toward the game room.

"Kim? Becky? Boys? How are you all doing down here?"

We peaked inside to make sure the coast was clear and saw Becky and Rob disengage from each other and look around for Kim and Paul, who had disappeared. Becky's eyes went wide, and she mouthed "Oh shit!"

Sean appeared in the doorway. I could tell he was trying to give us space but checking in anyway. "Are you guys doing okay?" He asked. "Where's Kim?"

"Umm, she went to the bathroom," said Becky.

"Where's the Paul kid?" asked Sean.

His eyes narrowed and his brow furrowed, then he turned toward the guest bathroom across the hall where we could hear Paul and Kim. Sean reached above the door frame and pulled down the emergency key for bathroom locks. When he opened the door, all I could see was Paul shirtless and his belt undone. I also noticed Kim's bra on the sink.

"What the hell!" he screamed.

Before Sean recovered from shock, Paul ran into the game room. Sean rushed toward Paul with fists of fury. Rob got between them just when Sean swung and caught Rob square on the jaw. Rob stumbled, a little fazed by the punch. Sean continued to come after Paul in a primal rage. I tried to run interference, but I also didn't want to get slugged. Colleen, Bob, Larry, Vicky, and Marilyn stood on the stairs and Bob and Larry went to Sean to try and calm him down. Paul took this time to flee and ran out to the balcony shirtless with his pants unbuckled and his penis out. He looked over the rail, climbed over, and jumped off.

We followed, done with the fight and now resorting to flight. When I got to the balcony, I hesitated at the fifteen-foot drop. Paul was already twenty yards into the wilderness. We should have just left through the front door. Instead, we followed Paul off the balcony. First MIHO, then Jesse. Adrenaline gave me the courage, or the stupidity, toward a leap of faith. Rob was right behind me. I landed, scratching my hands on the ground. From behind, I heard Rob land with a loud thud, followed by a crack and a scream.

"Ahhhhh! My leg. My fucking leg."

I looked back and saw Rob writhing in pain, clutching his right knee. Below the knee, the lower half of his leg veered off at a crazy angle.

"Oh, fuck, fuck, fuck, fuck! Oh god!"

I looked up and saw the balcony occupied by Sean, Bob, Larry, and Becky. All the blood that had filled Sean's face earlier had drained to make it ghostlike as he must have realized the role he may have just played in ending one of his school's top defensive players' year or career. With the scream, MIHO and Jesse returned. From fifty yards away, Paul just turned and stared.

"Where does it hurt?" Jesse asked as he stood over Rob. He and MIHO had returned to attend to Rob.

"Where the fuck do you think?" said Rob. "Does this leg look like it's fine to you?"

While Jesse tended to Rob, I ran back to Paul.

"Doesn't look good?" asked Paul.

"No! His leg's broken, or his knee is toast. Either way, he's fucked. Go back to the site. We'll meet you back there once we know what's going on."

I looked back. Sean, Larry, and Bob had gone through the house, out the front door, and were navigating down the hill. When I returned to Rob's side, Sean, Larry, and Bob were hovering over him and asking questions like the adults we were just learning to be.

"We've got to get him down to Fresno to the hospital," said Sean. He was no longer thinking of what he saw in that bathroom, he just wanted to take care of this young man. He looked us all over. "I bet you guys aren't sober enough to drive."

Our lack of response said it all. Rob was likely the most sober of us.

Sean sighed. "Okay. I'll take him down to the hospital in Fresno. You get your boy down there, pack up your shit, and hopefully by that time, you'll be ready to drive. Larry's going to drive Rob's truck to your campground—Rancheria, right? Do you have his parents' number?"

"Yeah, his dad," I mumbled. I felt sick with the thought we were going to have to call Mr. Simpson.

"Good. Call him and tell him what's going on. He needs to get down here. Rob's going to need surgery. Maybe more than one. But he's going to need his dad here. Can you do that?"

We nodded. We looked at Rob, whose face said it all. The pain of the fall wasn't going to be anything compared to the pain he'd just caused his future career and his father's dreams. We helped Rob up the hill to the road and into the front seat of Sean's truck. Bob got in the back while Larry took Rob's keys to drive his truck to the campsite. Becky, Vicky, and Marilyn had come outside. Neither Colleen nor Kim came out. Becky held Rob's hand and gave him a peck on the cheek. He smiled for the first time. The door closed. Sean started the truck and backed out of the driveway.

"We gotta split," I said to Becky.

"Here, give him my number," said Becky. "Have him call me and tell me he's okay."

"Will do," I said, and we hiked back to our campsite. We didn't say much as we walked the mile back along the road to our site. When we returned, Paul was seated at the picnic table with his head buried in his hands. He looked like he had just slaughtered all the dogs in the world. When he heard us approaching, he sprang up and ran over.

"How is he?" asked Paul.

"Sean took him to the hospital in Fresno, because we were all too drunk to drive," I said. "He basically told us to pack up and that this year's trip is over."

In normal circumstances, I would have bristled at the thought of someone other than my parents giving me a directive like that. But we all knew he was just confirming what was true—we would only spend one night in the forest. We packed with intention and speed. The adrenaline of the past couple hours sobered us up. Before we headed down the hill, we stopped at the pay phone at the lodge.

"Why are we stopping?" asked Paul. He was in my car, while MIHO rode with Jesse in Rob's truck

"You have to call Mr. Simpson and tell him what happened," I said. Paul was waiting for me to let him off the hook, but my eyes conveyed my seriousness. "He's going to have to come down for the surgery."

"Oh crap," said Paul. "What do I say?"

"I don't know. I wouldn't go into great detail about why Rob jumped off a balcony. Might be good to focus on Rob needing him to come to Fresno."

I had never seen Paul look so scared and deflated. On the surface, Paul was cocksure, charming, entertaining, friendly, and arrogant, but he also had kind and thoughtful moments. Still, this was his burden to bear. We didn't know how Rob was going to treat Paul in the future, but this was the first step for Paul taking responsibility. The pay phone stood in a corridor between the saloon and restaurant. When Paul left, we all stood by the cars watching him head up the steps. He pulled out his wallet and a credit card and made the call. He hung his head as he got the connection, then looked up to the sky. He moved his hand through his hair, then turned to focus on some object in another part of the corridor.

"I wouldn't want to be Paul right now," said MIHO.

"Though there were the five minutes with Kim about two hours ago I would have," said Jesse. "Just those five minutes, though."

"Right to the moment when Sean about took Paul's head off," I said.

"And you weren't kidding about Paul's..." MIHO said, his eyes widening. "You know."

"I just hope Rob's okay," said Jesse. "That didn't look good."

"That's not just an ankle sprain, that's a six-months-in-a-cast injury," I said. "No NFL draft for him this year."

Judging by what I saw when I heard the crack, this next year was going to be painful and test Rob unlike he had ever been tested before. He'd spend the next year rehabbing, take an injury redshirt, allowing one more year of college eligibility, then hope for a bounce-back year in 1999 in order to be drafted into the NFL in 2000.

Paul hung up the phone and walked back. His eyes were focused on the ground.

"So?" I asked when he returned.

"He's driving down. He's gotta make some calls to get off work for tomorrow and find someone to take care of the dog, but he'll leave in an hour, which puts him in Fresno in four or five hours. He said to get down to the hospital right away and he'd be there as soon as he could."

"We'd better go," I said. We turned to get back in my car and Rob's truck.

"Yeah," Paul said. "Can you put on the radio? I can't listen to silence, and I don't want to hear it from you either. I know I'm a horrible friend who just ruined one of his best friends' lives. I get it. I'm an asshole."

Part of me wanted to tell him he was just being dramatic. Part of me wanted him to stew in self-loathing. When we got to the hospital, we told Paul to hang back to avoid Sean, Bob, and Larry. When we saw them in the waiting room, Sean gave us an update. Rob had broken his fibula and tweaked his ACL. They were in surgery now. We updated him on Rob's father heading down and that we'd stay until he got there and into the next day. Sean pulled us to the side and stared at Jesse, MIHO, and me.

"I feel absolutely horrible about what happened to Rob. I can't believe what happened. He's a good kid and I'm so sorry for what happened," Sean shook his head and breathed for a moment, trying to gather himself. He pulled out his wallet and a business card and wrote his home phone number on the back. "Please tell Rob and his family if they need anything or help with medical costs, I can help. And please give me any updates."

I nodded. "You're not going to stay?"

Sean shook his head. "No, I don't think it would be good for me to be here when his dad shows up. Right now, he will need to be here for Rob. This other stuff can wait, and I'd rather talk to him when he's had a chance to process everything. Plus, we've got our own stuff to deal with up at the cabin."

He was about to say his goodbye and leave us, but he turned back, his remorse turning a bit into anger. His eyes narrowed at Jesse, MIHO and me.

"Look, I know you boys think finding girls and trying to get in their pants is a big game right now. I know. I've been there. Right now, you all think it's about the conquest and about the stories. But you should know at some point, you're going to be parents and husbands. You'll find that they're not trophies to win by playing silly games. Actions have consequences."

As he pulled away, I was half impressed, half petrified by what he'd said. The man I met in those white sunglasses just eight hours before seemed totally different than the husband and father before me now, imploring us to be more respectful. I suspected his stare would haunt me for years. He turned and left, his head bowed, followed by Larry and Bob.

"Shit," said Jesse, when they turned the corner and left.

"Wow," I agreed. "Too bad Paul wasn't here to hear it."

Eventually, Paul joined us, and we sat and watched the Giants in the waiting room. We didn't speak more than ten words to each other as we waited for Mr. Simpson to arrive.

"Where is he?" Mr. Simpson asked when he entered the waiting room a couple hours later. We followed Mr. Simpson as the nurse led him back to Rob's recovery room. Rob was trying to shake off the drugs and wake up.

"Hey, Rob," said his dad. "I'm here."

"Dad!" Rob said. He had a big smile on his face like his dad made it to the big game. He kept opening his eyes wide, trying to overcome the effects of the painkillers. "You're here."

"Of course, I am, son. What happened?"

"Jumped off a deck and fucked up my leg...oops. Sorry, sir...messed up my leg."

The doctor came in and introduced himself as Dr. Delgado. She explained that she was an orthopedist and the one who performed the surgery.

"You know my son's a football player at USC. NFL talent. That leg's important to his career."

"Yes. Mr. Wilson, who brought Rob here, let me know. I'm the on-call orthopedist for Fresno State, so I understand."

Rob's dad turned to me.

"He's the USC booster we met at the lake," I said. "We were at his cabin when it happened."

"Right," Mr. Simpson said, trying to remember the original conversation with Paul. Dr. Delgado took Mr. Simpson to another part of the recovery room for a private talk.

"Hey guys," said Rob. "Doesn't look like I'm going to get back to the trip." He made a drugged-up pouty face.

"Trip's over, man," said Jesse. "Now that we know you're safe and your dad's here, we should head back home."

"Oh man, why don't you stay? Or go back camping," said Rob.

"It's best we just head back," said Paul.

When Rob looked at Paul, his eyes said it all. They conveyed anger, hurt, disappointment, and betrayal. Rob turned and stared at the wall. He couldn't make eye contact with Paul anymore. It felt completely devastating.

"I'm so sorry," Paul said. "I'm so sorry this happened to you. I didn't know this would happen. I'm so sorry."

Rob continued to focus on the wall. Painful seconds passed, and Paul turned around and retreated to a corner. A few minutes later, Mr. Simpson returned without Dr. Delgado. Rob would stay the night and be released in the morning. Mr. Simpson asked us what had happened. He looked at us in a way that told us that dishonesty wouldn't be tolerated.

We recounted the whole story, including the beach, the dinner, Kim and Becky, Sean's discovery, Rob's efforts to keep Sean from killing Paul, and the decision to race out of the house via the bedroom deck. When we concluded, Mr. Simpson looked at all of us and shook his head. He then stared at us with the same intensity he used on the football field.

"Boys, I'm not proud of you right now. All of you, including Rob, had a role in this, but I'm not going to lecture you. I'm just going to tell you to go home. There's no need for you to be here anymore. Rob and I will head back to Sacramento when he's ready. He needs his rest."

We nodded. The message was sent. Mr. Simpson put a hand to his head and shook it.

"Jesse, I forgot. You're in LA and Rob's truck is here," he said. "Why don't you take the truck back to LA? He'll pick it up when he gets back down there."

"Certainly, sir," Jesse said.

"Oh, guys, don't go," said Rob, his hangdog face begging us to stay.

"No, we gotta go, dude," said Jesse. "We'll talk when you get back though, okay?"

"Oh. Okay," said Rob.

We each gave Rob and his dad a handshake. Paul managed a sincere but soft "I'm sorry" to both of them before we turned and walked out.

"Well, this trip was *dee*-lightful," said Jesse.

5

Paul

Thursday Afternoon

June 23, 2016

As Jesse closed the journal, Paul felt a little ill, and it wasn't the winding highway up to the lake. Eighteen years later, he knew the incident at Sean's house should have been a wake-up call. Instead, it was a reminder of the bad choices he had made over the years. While Jesse read through the journal, Paul kept his eyes looking outside. He didn't dare look at any of his friends, least of all Rob.

Finally, Paul let out a breath and turned to his friends. "I relive that evening all the time, and Jim captured it. Man, it's amazing how that screwed everything up. Why did you guys put up with my shit when I gave you reason after reason not to?"

"You were frustrating as hell," Rob said, keeping his eyes on the winding road up the five-thousand-foot climb through the Sierras. "And I wasn't your friend for a few years. But I should have known not to jump off a balcony like that, and everything else was just bad luck. I've moved on, even if I do still like to give you crap about it."

After that trip, Paul could only follow Rob's football career by talking to Jim and Jesse or by reading the wires at his first job as the weekend sports anchor at a small station in Duluth. As Rob's dream was pulled further and further away, the crack in their relationship became a canyon without any foundation to build a bridge.

After the fateful leap off the balcony, Rob took an injury red-shirt year at USC. This meant he could skip the season without using his final year of college eligibility. When he wasn't standing on the sidelines watching practice or supporting his teammates on gameday, he was working in the weight room and with the physical therapists rehabbing his leg and building back its strength.

When he returned in the Fall of 1999, Rob was in the best shape of his life. He was focused and hungry and ready to excel and prove to the NFL scouts he was going to make it at the next level. Paul watched each of Rob's games at the TV station and cheered every tackle and sack. It looked like the incident at the lake would prove inconsequential and maybe make him mentally tougher.

Then came the game against Notre Dame. Paul watched in the station's control room. Rob was having another good game with three tackles and a sack, but late in the second half a cut block on an inconsequential running play caused a full tear of both the ACL and MCL ligaments in his other knee. Rob went down in a heap. Paul felt ill as he watched his friend carted off the field. He knew he was responsible for this chain of events, even as he watched from a thousand miles away.

Before this second injury, Rob was still projected as a high-round NFL draft pick. After back-to-back surgeries, no team was willing to use a draft pick on him, and he missed another year working his knee back. When he was offered a tryout with the Jacksonville Jaguars the following season, his speed had dropped and his lateral movement had diminished. He still made the team but in a backup and special-teams role and was let go after the season. He decided to take a chance and find exposure in the ill-fated XFL, created by wrestling hustler Vince McMahon in the Spring 2001, playing for the Los Angeles Xtreme. He hoped the extra playing time and TV exposure might help him find a more permanent NFL home. However, he tore his other knee again attempting to make a tackle on the infamous Rod "He Hate Me" Smart of the Las Vegas Outlaws. From the moment he read about the injury, Paul knew Rob's football career was over. Those dreams destroyed by one decision. While they had all moved on long ago, the memory still made him ache.

"Still, seemed that night started off a bad string for you," said Paul. "I changed your life because of my dick."

"It exposed my weakness," said Rob. "I was all football and didn't know life without it. Maybe it was better that I had to find myself without it earlier on."

"How many times have you said that?" said MIHO. "Sounds like you've had to answer that question several times."

"More than you know." Rob chuckled. Regardless of his eventual forgiveness, the story always seemed to create some awkward tension. The consequences of those actions just seemed to reverberate in countless ways that had influenced many of their lives.

"I still can't believe I'm here with you," Paul said. "You should have ditched me."

"Well, you were toxic," MIHO said. "And your penis drove that, but you also had a good side."

"Dude, we love to retell your conquests because they're great stories, but it's all the other stuff that we don't talk about that shows your heart," Jesse said. "Do you remember Moretti freshmen year?"

"Oh, Moretti," Rob said. "What an asshole. Yeah, Paul, you shined in that moment."

Paul smiled. Heading into their freshman year of high school, Jesse had split off their group to join the cross-country team while the rest of them played football. Jesse also hadn't hit puberty and still looked ten years old. He began to eat lunch by himself in order to avoid confrontation. One October lunch period, Jesse crossed the quad to get to his next class. As he passed the steps where the football team hung out, his schoolboy features drew the attention of Jason Moretti, the star quarterback and king bully.

"Hey, shrimp boat," Moretti said to chortles from his buddies.

Jesse kept walking, trying to ignore them. On most days, Moretti would move on to someone else, but this time, he kept after Jesse, referring to him as "pinto bean" and "taquito." It was strange, even the Latino players didn't object to the offensive comments. Perhaps they were afraid to draw Moretti's wrath. Moretti then got up and started walking after Jesse.

Paul, MIHO, Rob, and Jim sat on a wall at the base of the quad with their lunches as they watched Moretti walk after Jesse, who clenched the straps of his backpack and began to walk faster. As Moretti got closer and his abuse continued to escalate, Paul looked around and saw no one standing up for his friend. They didn't hang out that much anymore, but that didn't mean he deserved this abuse.

"This isn't right," Paul said. Before Jim could tell Paul that you didn't challenge the senior star quarterback as a freshman, Paul was already up and chasing after Moretti and Jesse.

"Shut the fuck up," Paul said to Moretti's back.

Rob, Jim, and MIHO followed. Moretti turned to Paul, who didn't back down. In fact, he approached Moretti, with Rob, who had already grown to a giant size, Jim, and MIHO standing behind him.

"I don't think you have any room to talk, freshman," Moretti said.

"Dude, only the weak bully those unable to defend themselves," Paul said, looking at Moretti with disgust.

"Listen, fresh meat, you may be hot stuff on the freshman squad, but you better not get on the wrong side of me and the varsity."

"I'm not on the wrong side of Scott," Paul said, nodding to the senior center Scott Parrish, then to the other senior captains. "Nor Richard, Elliott, Steve, Ronny, or the rest of the guys behind you. They weren't being bullies. Only the small man in front of me."

In that moment, Paul's legend began. He would have gotten beaten to hell if not for separating out Moretti away from his friends. Instead of giving Moretti strength, his teammates gained their own and decided to hold Jason back. Moretti glared at Paul and made the rest of that season hell, but Paul was happy to pay the price.

"Well, that just wasn't right," Paul recalled. "I just did what everyone else was thinking."

"But most people just think and don't act," Jesse said. "Particularly when it could hurt their status. I'll always remember how you stood up for me. And when I didn't like you much, I always went back to that moment. It's hard to turn your back when we know your heart."

"Thanks."

The cab of the truck grew silent as Rob slowly curved up the narrow mountain road. The temperature continued to drop as they climbed out of valley heat into the majestic Sierra Nevadas. They passed over a summit and saw the first slivers of deep blue through the green trees on their left. There was something about the first view of the lake that brought a smile to each of their faces. They were here, including Jim. They passed their old campground and over the bridge, past the marina and the volunteer-fire-department firehouse, where they turned right to reach the cabin.

"And speaking of Sean and Kim's cabin," said Rob. He pointed out the window to the multilevel cabin and familiar balcony. They continued up the hill to their cabin, the same spot for the past three years. Jim had found it on one of those home-sharing sites, and it fit every need. The house had enough beds and rooms for comfort, cooking facilities to satisfy MIHO, and a large deck big enough to eat meals and sip whiskey. The house also overlooked a mountainside of granite, allowing them to build a campfire in the middle without endangering anyone.

"Jim loved this house," MIHO said.

MIHO entered the code for the lockbox to pull out the key to the condo, opened the door, and they walked in. The entryway led to the main living room with a large picture window and sliding glass door. They went straight to the slider and the deck outside and leaned against the railing. They always took a deep breath. Before them was a 180-degree unobstructed view of forest, rock, mountains, and the lake below. It was the closest to heaven they could imagine.

"This is great," said Rob.

"This is amazing," said Paul. "Remember how he always took in this view?"

"Yessir," said Jesse. "Well, let's pick our rooms and get settled."

"Indeed," said Paul.

MIHO took the master bedroom, while Rob picked the second solo room to not subject anyone to his snoring. Paul and Jesse took the third bedroom with two single beds. After they unpacked the groceries, games, and personal effects, they all grabbed a beer and reconvened on the deck. The late-afternoon sun still shone bright, but the patio umbrellas and cool mountain breeze made it comfortable. Paul stepped outside last with a mini humidor. He opened the box.

"I used the connection and got some Cubans," said Paul.

"Same connection as the last time you got us Cubans?" Asked Jesse.

"Kind of," said Paul. "Not as scandalous, though."

"That's good," said Jesse. "I remember that story."

"Right, let's not go into that," said Rob.

"Well, whoever supplied them, I say 'thank you,'" said Jesse as he drew his first full drag after lighting it. Rob, MIHO, and Paul followed. They each sat back and puffed. "I don't smoke these things any other time than on our traditional first sit on the first night. I can't stand them any other time, but here, it's *ee-*lightful."

"This is great," said Paul, and he took a swig of beer. "This is my favorite weekend of the year. Well..." The rest went unsaid, and they raised their bottles of beer and clinked the necks together. They stayed silent for a couple minutes.

"So, MIHO, what's the itinerary for the weekend?" said Rob.

"Well, just all the traditional stuff," said MIHO. "Cards tonight, hanging out tomorrow, campfire tomorrow night. On Saturday, we're going to go to Tom Sawyer's Island and spread the ashes."

They didn't know if that was the name of the island on the lake, but that's what they called it. The island had a footprint of a pretty large playground, along with trees, rocks, and a beach. Each year, Jim suggested they take a boat to the island, but they always dismissed the idea. Who wanted to rent a boat and schlep the gear to the island?

"We're finally going to do it," said Paul. "Man, how many times did Jim want to go out there and we never did?"

"This time, though, he's going to join us," said MIHO, holding the box.

"I bet he figured this was the only way for him to get us out there," Jesse said. "He wasn't above using a dirty trick to manipulate us."

"Do you guys want to read another year of the Lake Trip Log?" asked MIHO.

"No," Jesse said with a sigh. "I need a little break. We have all weekend."

"Right," said Rob. "Let's just enjoy the present for now. Jim would want us to chill out and have a great time. He doesn't want us dwelling on him."

"I think he does," MIHO said. He was a little irritated. "I mean, he wrote this in his will."

"No way," said Jesse. "Jim didn't know he'd die so young. He knew that if he didn't put it somewhere, we wouldn't pull something together. I know I wouldn't be here."

Paul looked at Jesse who had given the same reasoning on the phone the week before. Jesse wasn't one for nostalgia and thought overindulgence in it was neither productive nor healthy.

"C'mon," Jesse said. "If this trip wasn't in the will and we didn't need to spread his ashes on Tom Sawyer's Island, would any of us have organized something this year? We'd keep in touch and see each other regularly, but we wouldn't take a trip together and would eventually drift apart."

"That's true," said Paul. "We'd be those friends who say we're going to go do something, then never get around to it."

Paul looked away from MIHO's death stare. He knew this trip meant something more to MIHO. There was an awkward silence.

Rob, always the peacemaker, changed the subject. "What's for dinner?"

"Just the traditional spaghetti, some homemade meat sauce, salad, and rolls," MIHO said. "It was Jim's favorite."

"I love your sauce," said Rob. "I hope you made a whole pot."

"I'm going to get dinner started," MIHO said.

Rob motioned to Jesse to help and make a peace offering to MIHO. Jesse rolled his eyes.

"Need any help?" Jesse asked MIHO.

"What? This is truly a first. Jesse offering to help me."

"Hey, now that I'm not cooking twenty meals a week, I'm okay returning to the kitchen on my weekend away," Jesse said. "Besides, I have first dibs on your marinara before Rob steals it all."

"I will beat you, Speedy," Rob said.

"Try it Billy Bob," Jesse snapped back and smiled before closing the screen door.

Paul and Rob stayed on the deck, puffing away.

"I just feel for Willie," said Rob, taking another puff. "I mean, he's seven and just about to head into that time when he'll need a father."

Willie and Jim were close. In fact, some people referred to Willie as Jim's mini-me. Not only did they look alike but also had very similar interests—sports, *Star Wars*, even history. They were inseparable at times. As a teacher at the local high school, Jim operated the scoreboard at football and basketball games.

Much of the time, Willie would sit next to him and watch the games.

"He's doing better," said Paul, who had taken Willie to a few Sacramento Kings games, the park, and out for burgers, just to give Tracey a break. "MIHO and I have been trying to spend time with him when we can. I think the most important thing is for him to know that he can both miss his dad and also have fun without him."

"I think it was good for you to move back home," Rob said. "I'm proud of you. You became a positive male role model."

"At some point, I guess we all mature, just at different times."

"That was the best thing to come from that jump off the balcony. It caused me to grow up a lot faster. If I had an easy path to the NFL, I wouldn't be the man I am today. And I kinda think that's a good thing."

"No, you'd be a fourteen-year pro, and you'd own this place. Kidding. I know what you mean. But who's to know if you'd have still dated Becky if you went to the NFL?"

"No, I had time to date Becky because of my injury. I was so bored; I called her because I had the time. I watched her volleyball matches. I went to Loyola countless times to visit her. That wouldn't have happened if I was getting ready for the draft."

Paul remembered hearing how watching Becky play volleyball and getting to know her drove Rob in his rehab. She was supportive of him as he pushed to get back into shape to continue his NFL dream. She was with him for the second knee injury and another round of rehab and when he had to accept the disappointment of not being drafted. Even though she was still at Loyola, she flew out for his first game on the Jaguars roster.

They were living together when his professional-football career finally ended before it had really begun.

"That was the worst part," Rob said. "She was there and all in, even through all the disappointment. But I wasn't. I shut myself off and turned to alcohol more and more to dull the pain. My isolation and resentment began to take a toll on our relationship. We fought more and more, and eventually she decided she couldn't help me if I was unwilling to try."

"And then Leslie came," Paul said. "And you turned it around."

"Not right away. You forget that toward the end, just weeks before she left, I got Becky pregnant, and when she came over to tell me, some other girl who'd spent the night, I don't even remember her name, was wearing one of Becky's shirts. That was it for her. Great move on my part."

"Well, growing up seemed to be a lot more painful for you than a lot of folks," Paul said. "You hit your bottom fast and with a deep thump and crack."

"I don't wish that reality check on anyone. A lot of good came out of it—Leslie, for one—but I wasn't a good person to be around. Even Jesse stopped coming by."

Jesse opened the slider with three waters in hand. He handed one to Rob and Paul, and together they raised them. They all swigged a drink with a smile.

"You all brought me back from that dark time," Rob said. "Thank you."

"Well, I helped put you there," said Paul. "These guys did the bulk of the work, but there's something about a group of guy friends that you can count on them no matter how you've screwed them in the past. I wouldn't be here if it wasn't for all of you. Damn, MIHO's sentimentality is contagious."

"What?" MIHO said as he walked onto the deck.

"MIHO, we need more beers," Paul said. He gave Rob a wink.

"Get it yourself, asshole. Jesse, you were supposed to tell them dinner's ready."

"I can smell it, and I'm sorry that none of you are going to have any," Rob said.

They all stood and walked inside. In the middle of the open kitchen was a spacious island where the night's dinner was spread. Along with a large, overflowing bowl of plain spaghetti was a pot of sauce that smelled like it had been cooked by the matriarch of a mafia crime family instead of a Filipino hotel manager. There was also a wide array of side dishes to complement the spaghetti, including roasted vegetables, garlic bread, and a gorgonzola apple salad. Rob got to the plates first and began piling on the pasta, sauce, veggies, and bread. Jesse followed him while MIHO watched. The cook always dished last.

"Oh, mama," Paul said. He went to a box near the kitchen and pulled out a couple bottles. "I'm so ready for tonight. And for the occasion, I've brought some Napa cabernet to enjoy."

None of them were big wine aficionados, but they did enjoy diversifying their liquid throughout the weekend. At first, the variations from beer had names that started with Jim, Jack, Glen, Tito's, and Captain. Now, they added a lot more water to the mix, plus juice, mineral water, and wine. MIHO knew his wines but never developed a pallet for it. He was fine with whatever anyone brought.

"I love the spaghetti feed," said Rob. "I can't remember how many we'd have before a game, but they were never as good as yours."

"I always ask for the recipe, so I can make it for Danielle and the girls," Jesse said. "But MIHO never shares. Ever!"

"Hey, I have to keep it a secret, man. I can't be giving it out like that. The chef who shared it with me swore me to secrecy. I'd have to kill you, and I don't want to do that."

"Whatever," said Jesse. "Okay, now are we all ready to read the next year?"

"Remember, we took a couple years off," Paul said. "We'd all started our careers. Rob was working through football. I was in Duluth. MIHO finished school and had gotten his first real hotel job in San Diego, and Jim was getting his teaching credentials. So, it was, what, 2001?"

"Yep, 2001," said MIHO, flipping to the page. "One month before 9/11."

6

Jim

2001

I was walking back from the high school cafeteria to my class-room when I saw one of my students wearing a sleeveless USC T-shirt, which transported me back to three years ago and the leap off the balcony.

Lot of things changed after that trip. We watched Rob go from sure-fire NFL star to aimless drunk and Paul start his promising career in TV sports. MIHO, Jesse, and I didn't know how to deal with it. We talked to both of them separately, mostly checking in on Rob to see if he was okay and Paul to see how it was going with the local sports scene. We always stayed away from the topic of that night.

I always felt a pang of remorse, regret, and resentment for that evening. What if I hadn't followed Paul off that balcony and instead pushed up the stairs and out the front door? Would Rob have followed? Or what if we didn't go out for that cigarette, could we have told them not to do anything stupid? Could we have knocked on the door a few moments earlier and got them to put on their clothes? Where would Rob be today? And would we all be together again?

The student in the USC T-shirt reminded me that perhaps we couldn't bring back Rob's NFL career, but maybe we could bring back the trip that brought us closer to each other year after year. I knew that if we didn't change something, our bond would be lost forever. I had to at least try to get us back up to the lake.

By the time I left work and got home, I was resolved to resurrect the trip, and as soon as I arrived home, I dropped my bag and called MIHO in San Diego.

"Hello?" MIHO said. He sounded groggy. I was sure I woke him. He was now a front-desk clerk working overnight shifts at the very posh Manchester Grand Hyatt on the San Diego Bay. For the past two years he'd taken any shift available to move his way up the hotel ladder.

"It's time to go back up to the lake," I said. "I miss that place, and I think we all need to get back together."

"The lake?" I could tell he was processing. "With all of us? You know Rob's a mess, and Paul's in Minnesota, and they aren't speaking. Jesse and I would have to drive up from Southern California."

"That's exactly why we need to get this back together. We need it now more than ever. And Rob *really* needs this one."

MIHO sighed. Rob's life had become a bit of a sad tale. "I've never seen Rob like this before. It's like he's lost all purpose. The cash he saved from his NFL and XFL salaries is running out.

Jesse says he gets up late, sits by the pool at his apartment, and drinks beer, goes out to a club, sometimes brings a girl home, then repeats."

"For some, that would be the dream," I said, but the joke was lost on MIHO.

"For him, it's depressing. He doesn't even go to the gym anymore. He rehabbed his knee enough to be a mere mortal, but it's like he's a zombie. So, yeah, I agree that he needs this, but I'm not sure if we can get him up there."

"Will you be able to go?" I asked.

"Definitely want to. I just hope I can get the weekend off. It's vacation season. And what about Jesse? Can he tear himself away from his new girlfriend? And how about you? Can you two whipped boys have fun?"

Jesse, who joined an internet start-up after college, was in a serious relationship with a receptionist working her way through law school. We joked that his new name had ceased to be Jesse and had become Danielle-and-I.

"Hey, don't compare me to Jesse," I said. "We just started dating, and she's not like the other one."

I ran into Tracey about a month ago. I was sitting at a coffee shop in midtown sipping a double cappuccino to help me slog through student essays. I looked up from a poor essay about post-Civil War Reconstruction and saw her for the first time in six years waving at me from a table across the room. My eyes perked, and my face brightened. I hadn't talked to her since high school graduation. I stopped my Bob Marley's *Legend* CD, pulled off my headphones, and signaled her over.

"Hi Jim," she said. Her smile brightened the room like it always did, regardless of the weather. She was wearing jeans and a T-shirt proclaiming a sorority rush from Fall 1998.

"Tracey!" I said with enthusiasm bordering on creepy. "My goodness, it's been so long. Are you back in town?"

"Oh, yeah, been back about seven months. I work in the Capitol. I didn't mean to bother you. You looked like you were intently reading...papers?"

"Yeah. Did we write this poorly in high school? Believe me, you're a preferable distraction." I motioned her to take a seat at a comfy chair next to mine. "I'm a high school history teacher at Miramonte." I stacked the papers and placed them back in my bag. I could already tell that I'd rather stay up all night finishing these papers if it meant spending time chatting with Tracey.

Over the course of the next three hours, we provided each other with the highlights of the last six years. We discussed MIHO (David to her), Rob, Paul, and Jesse, and she talked about Cal and toiling around the Bay Area for a couple years before deciding to move back to Sacramento and work in the legislature. She was a legislative aide to a state assemblyman from Fremont, California, who focused on maintaining health services for the elderly and people with disabilities. Since she had a degree in rehabilitation, she was a perfect fit to be his expert.

After we'd gotten the updates out of the way, she seemed to take a moment gathering her thoughts before saying, "I'm sure I know the answer, but what happened to Audrey?" Tracey said, her eyes narrowed in sympathy. Of course, she already knew.

"Well, I was committed," I said. "Her...not so much."

"Oh no." She put her hand on mine to express empathy, but it provided a jolt of electricity. "Oh, Jim."

"Why do say that? Did you know something?"

Tracey nodded. "I'd heard through a few people."

"Yeah, I guess I was the last to know. But when I found out, I didn't look back."

Tracey smiled and patted my hand. "Well, I'm glad."

With her I already felt a deeper connection than anything I'd had with Audrey.

My relationship foibles allowed her to disclose hers, including a couple boyfriends she had in college and a bad break up in the Bay Area, which helped propel her back home.

After that chance conversation a few weeks prior, we spent hardly any moments apart. We went to dinner and the movies. We walked in the park and talked and laughed. We weren't even romantic until about a week prior to the trip. It was strange. Our relationship from high school never left, but now it had grown in depth and perspective. It was just so effortless to talk to and care for this person. Still, we decided to take things slow. We'd both been burned, and there were many layers we needed to reveal before it got too serious.

"Paul may be hard to get to come out," said MIHO, bringing me back to the present.

"If he can, he will. He loves this trip, even though he screwed up on the last one."

"Well, that's the thing. Do you think Rob's really ready to hang out with Paul for an entire weekend, given that they haven't spoken in three years? And with the way Rob's been acting lately, do we really want to take a chance on that wildcard?"

MIHO had a point. In Rob's current state and his continued resentment toward Paul, it could get ugly fast. And Paul, while he felt awful for what had happened, hadn't learned from the experience. He was still chasing tail like a jackrabbit.

"I'll talk to Rob and Paul," I said. "If I can get them on board, will you go?"

"Sure, but I'm not convinced even your powers of persuasion can get them both there. But if you can do it, and I can get off work, then I'll come."

"Fantastic," I said and hung up with a mission to resurrect the trip.

My first call was to Rob. He was the key. If I could convince him, I knew the rest would follow. Even Paul would find a way if he knew Rob was okay with it. Jesse would make it work, and MIHO, his worries about getting off work notwithstanding, was going. I called Rob, who picked up and cleared his throat.

"Hey Rob, it's Jim." I tried to be upbeat.

"Oh, hey," said Rob. He seemed to cheer up with my greeting. That was a start. I asked after him. He was just hanging out at home, watching TV. That's what he usually did. Or drank.

"Hey, so I'm thinking of bringing back the trip. What do you think?"

"What trip?"

"The trip to the lake. A little camping, some beers, some hiking. All that stuff. It'll be a good time and a good break for all of us." As soon as I said *break*, I wondered if I'd screwed up before I'd even begun.

"The last trip didn't end so well," said Rob. "I don't know. Is Paul going?"

"I haven't asked him yet. I wanted to talk to you first and see what you thought and if you'd want to go whether or not Paul joined."

Rob was quiet on the other end. I might have heard him take a sip of a beverage.

"I don't know. I mean, Paul...well, there's a lot there, you know?"

I could hear the hurt dripping from his voice. I began to wonder if this was a bad idea. Did I really need to bring Rob all this pain just so I could have a trip with all my friends? I decided this would be good for Rob. Remind him of the guys who really cared about him, not his football career.

"Right," I said. "Still, it might be good to get out of town and make some new memories, so it's not tied to that."

Rob was silent.

"All the reason to create new memories," I said again. "Look, what are you going to do otherwise? Same thing you've been doing. But at least the mountains will be more picturesque."

"I'm just not sure. I haven't talked to Paul since that weekend," Rob said. "I don't know if I can do that whole pick-up-girls thing or even watch Paul and his act."

"You don't have to do anything you don't want to. You can just take walks and clear your head. You can sit and stare at the lake. As far as Paul, we know what he's going to do. But we can keep him from getting crazy or at least getting us in a situation like last time."

"Right. Good luck with that." I could hear him take another sip. Then he sighed. "Okay, I'll go. It might be good to get out of this town and get my head right. But we have to figure something out about Paul."

"Okay, let's do it then!" I said. "MIHO's in. I'm sure Jesse will go. I'll check in with Paul too and share our concerns."

I only pushed the cradle down to hang up the phone before dialing Paul. I remembered he kept strange hours as a sports anchor. He'd go to work at 2:00 p.m., have an extended lunch hour from 7:00-9:00 p.m., then work until midnight. Since he was in the Midwest, he was also two hours ahead. It was 6:00 p.m. I might just catch him during his dinner break.

Paul picked up. "Hello, this is Paul."

"Hey, buddy, it's Jim." I looked at the ceiling. Though I was excited to talk to him and tell him about the trip resurrection, I also had Rob's conditions in mind and wondered how Paul would take it.

"Jim!" Paul screamed into the phone. "How's it going, big dog?"

We spent the next few minutes catching up on the stories he had covered, mostly local stuff since his small market wasn't close to any major sports teams, and talking about my new relationship with Tracey.

"Have you slept with her yet?" he asked. I wasn't surprised.

"No. We've gotten close, but we've both been there, done that too many times to know that we don't want this to be like any of the others."

Paul let out a big laugh. "You remember I dated her, right?"

"Yeah, for like, two seconds. She said you were only interested in getting into her pants."

"She's probably right. And it's a good thing nothing happened. Wouldn't want to have shared the same cave, if you know what I mean."

I did but didn't want to continue this line of conversation. I shook my head. "So, I think I'm going to get the trip to the lake back on the calendar. What do you think? Can you get time off if we do something in August?"

"I could put in some time for vacation, though it's right before the NFL season. I miss that trip. So...is Rob going? Or, is he fine with me going?"

This was the hard part of the conversation. I had to stray into the uncomfortable, but necessary, topics. "Yeah, he's good to go, and he's okay with you going, but, um, he doesn't want a repeat of last time."

Paul laughed. "Of course not. I'm not going to seduce some daughter of a psycho who forces us to jump off a fifteen-foot balcony!"

"Well, a little more than that. He doesn't want chasing girls to be a goal and a focus on the trip this year. He just wants all of us to hang out."

"Oh, gotcha."

I could sense his hesitance and found myself stacking and re-stacking the coins on the kitchen counter, giving my fingers something to do during this uncomfortable exchange.

"I get it. Sure, whatever."

Though disappointed, he shifted back to excitement and talked logistics. I was the only one coming from Sacramento, while MIHO would drive up from San Diego, pick up Jesse and Rob, then head up to Fresno. Paul decided to see if there were any flights into Fresno's small regional airport. If not, he'd come down with me.

A call to Jesse, who only had a moment (he needed to meet Danielle, of course), and the trip was set for us to head up to the lake again. Rob and Paul's possible confrontation could yield irreversible damage and made me a little anxious, but something else told me that it could lead to reconciliation. Mostly, I was hoping we could help Rob reconnect with life and prepare him to be a father.

When the day came for our return to the lake, I packed up my old, reliable Civic and drove down the agricultural heart of California to pick up Paul at the regional airport. It turned out that getting from Iowa to Fresno took the skill of an experienced travel agent. Paul drove from Duluth to Minneapolis, flew to Phoenix, and ran across the airport to make his connection in a small turboprop to Fresno.

"I'm here, and I wouldn't miss it. It's the goddamn trip. I've just missed this for the last three years," said Paul after we loaded his bags and he got into the car. "I'm so ready! Rob's really not doing well?"

"Nope," I said. "It's hard for him. His childhood dream is over. He ruined a relationship with a good woman and has a kid on the way. The life he'd expected for all these years is never going to happen. Now, he has to figure out what he wants in life, who he is, and all that crap."

"I guess he'd blame me for that, eh?"

"Uh...yeah," I said, my sarcasm unfiltered. "So, forgive him if he doesn't want to chase tail with you this time. And to be honest, I don't know how he's going to be. Jesse says he's been drinking a lot, but is that a signal of a problem or is it just a coping mechanism until he can pull himself out of it? Does he need us to help him out? I don't know."

"Right, all right," Paul said, and he looked back out the window as the scenery changed from the oak trees of the foothills to the green pines of the Sierra Nevadas. As we reached higher elevation, we turned off the air conditioning and rolled down the windows to take in that cool, crisp mountain air. It was amazing how the smells and slight coolness reduced the stress and put us in a vacation mood.

We talked about Paul's career and his next move after Minnesota. It was about time for him to start sending out his tapes again to larger markets. He was hoping to get to ESPN in the next few years.

When we checked in, the ranger informed us that we needed to lock up and hide our food. *She* was around. Also, the weather forecast called for a good downpour in the coming days. We had made some of the proper preparations for rain, I had a couple of tarps and some twine, but was unsure if we were ready for a downpour. When we found Space 152 open again, we surveyed the site for waterflow, tree coverage, and slope. We strung the tarp between a few trees over the picnic table, found a spot to put the firewood, and placed our tents on higher ground before pulling out our chairs and tasting our first beer as the clouds were beginning to roll in.

"This was the hardest we've ever worked to prep the campsite," Paul said.

I pulled out my box of cigarettes and tapped it before sliding out a single stick and putting it to my mouth.

"What does Tracey think of you doing that?"

"She's not a fan."

It was true, Tracy didn't like the habit. Audrey was part of the reason I'd started, but I didn't quit when we broke up.

"I'm not a fan either," Paul said. "Those things kill you. You should quit."

"I will. But it's a comfort while I'm drinking and hanging out with you guys."

"Don't put that on me. That's your own bad choice."

We heard the rumbling of a truck coming toward us. It had to be MIHO, Rob, and Jesse. We looked up at the road, and sure enough, Rob's black Chevy rolled into view. MIHO had the window down and leaned out when he saw us.

"Shit, it's going to rain!" he yelled.

"Yep, but look, we're prepared," I said. "Aren't you glad you have friends like us?"

Rob looked at us and at our tarp setup with ambivalence. "Something like that."

Rob parked the pickup on the smaller shoulder of the tiny camp road. I put out my cigarette, and Paul and I chugged our beers and went up to the truck to help them unload the firewood, camp stoves, lanterns, and ice chests. Within a half hour, we were back around the camp ring sitting in those chairs, breathing in the fresh air, and laughing like old times.

"So, Jesse, did you need to get surgery to remove Danielle from your hip to get here?" Paul asked. "Do we need to change the dressing at regular intervals?"

"Oh, come on. I'm not that bad," Jesse said. "I really like this girl."

"Aww, how sweet," I said. "And she's going to be a lawyer. Don't screw her over or you're toast."

"I saw pictures of her too," Paul said. "What's wrong with her?" Paul put Jesse in an endearing headlock and gave him a noogie.

"She's fine," Jesse said, escaping Paul's arm. "I admit, it took a few tries to get her to agree to a date. Her schedule with work and going to law school is crazy. And when we did manage to go out, we skipped the bullshit and got right to the real stuff. It's like the connection was there. I can't explain it."

I did get it. While I wasn't where Jesse was in his relationship, I felt something for Tracey. It was more than just two people hanging out. I felt right at home and would be comfortable wherever we happened to be.

Paul and Rob were engaged in our conversation but not with each other, whether it was our careers, my new relationship with Tracey, or Jesse telling stories. Still, it was progress to just have Rob up here with us and for him to be laughing and joking like his old self. Though we were only a couple hours in, I was hoping this was an indication of things to come. Paul was self-aware and didn't tell jokes or stories about getting laid or hooking up or inappropriate acts with MIHO's mom even when MIHO put him to the test with statements like, "Working for a hotel is hard. The customer's needs are primary, even when you're busy with something else."

In previous years, Paul would have followed up with, "Your mom's always hard at work with me at the hotel too. But I make sure her needs are primary." Instead, Paul just smiled and sipped his beer, like he was sharing a private joke with the beverage.

While MIHO made dinner, Rob decided to join me as I hiked the hundred-yard trek to the edge of the water. There wasn't much of a trail. Rather, it was a path among fallen trees and limbs and undergrowth.

"How was the drive down?" Rob asked. "Lonely?"

"It wasn't too bad," I said. "I had some CDs and time to think about Tracey."

Rob stood on a rock on the shore and looked out. I hadn't seen him since his football career officially ended. He'd gained some weight, close to twenty-five pounds, which, combined with his decrease in muscle mass, was significant.

He turned toward me. "She's good for you. I mean, with Audrey you were limiting yourself because she wanted you to. You're so much happier all around. And you're not making excuses."

"Thanks. It feels a lot different and better too."

This might be the moment to begin the conversation about how he was doing. He'd come down to the lake with me, which had to be an invitation to have a private chat.

"Is there any chance to get back with Becky?" I asked.

"I don't know. I really screwed up, man," Rob said. It was the most sincere and honest I'd ever seen him. "I've been a real asshole, and she needs more than I can give her. What made us great is how we connected around competition. I don't have that spirit anymore, and she probably just thinks I'm a loser."

"But what about the kid?" I felt I was close to prying, but with the incoming clouds and shreds of sunbeams poking through at sunset, it seemed the "mood" was right to push.

"Right. Becky and I talked about it, but she doesn't think I can dry out or be a good partner and parent to the kid. Maybe she's right. I'm not sure if it could survive the stress of parenthood, late-night feedings, diaper changing, baths, etcetera. And that wouldn't be fair to the kid either."

"I guess not. What are you going to do?"

"I don't know. I told the guys on the way up. I don't know what I'm going to do with my life, let alone about raising a child. My life was football. That's gone. Somebody said I could coach. Fuck that. I can't look at a football field right now. I hate it. The pain that the game has given me the last three years makes me angry and helpless and hopeless." Rob looked like he wanted to say something else. He stared out at the water, and his mouth quivered. "And now I've got a helpless baby relying on me. How can I take care of a kid when I can't take care of myself? I just don't know. I don't even know what to do. My football money's almost gone, and I'll have to find a real job."

"You have that degree," I said, trying to be encouraging.

"Criminology? I thought about being a cop. But with my knees? I wouldn't survive academy."

"It's something, at least."

"I'm also angry all the time." Rob looked back at the water. "I used to be able to channel it into football. Now I dull it with alcohol or painkillers. Or I suppress it. Like, I want to kill Paul right now every time I see him holding back a joke. He hasn't fucking changed. He's just trying to hide it."

"He's said he's sorry. He really is. He's felt bad the last three years for the pain he's caused you."

"Easy for him to say. He's living his dream. He's the one who screwed up and his career's on the upswing with everything ahead of him. Look where I am."

I wanted to say something, but no words came. Instead, we focused on the water and the dark clouds rolling in. I just didn't know which would affect the trip more, the upcoming downpour or the inevitable confrontation. I should have tried to force the issue and get everything out in the open. Dealing with it made more sense, but avoidance was easier.

"Wow, there's going to be some rain," Rob said. "We should head back to see if you guys prepped the site right."

It turned out that Paul and I didn't do a great job. For one, the tarp we'd tied to the trees sagged in the middle. Rain would have created a pool of water that would have either broken the twine and dumped gallons of water on us or would have sagged so much we wouldn't be able to see across the table.

While Paul and I didn't get past Webelo's, Jesse, Rob, and MIHO spent a lot of time in scouting. They corrected our poor design by running twine between two trees that ran over the picnic table, then stretched the four corners out so the water ran over the sides of the tarp. About a half hour after we finished the revised weatherproofing, the first sprinkles came down. I had to give our friends credit. As we sat around the table playing liar dice, we stayed dry while the rain hit the tarp and rolled down the sides.

While the rain couldn't dampen our spirits during our first night of renewed tradition, the next morning revealed that nothing is more miserable than camping in the rain. Even with our weatherproofing, we were wet and cold. The only thing we could do was play cards and dice and drink. Around 9:30, we realized that if we were going to sit around the campsite and drink beer over the weekend, we were going to have to head to the store for more alcohol.

"Man, what are we going to do with Paul and Rob?" I asked MIHO as we drove through the campground toward the main highway.

"I don't know. They're either going to kill each other or play an endless game of passive-aggressive tag."

A confrontation was imminent. Rob made a point to slam down the lid of the ice chest as Paul was looking to grab a water. Paul rolled his eyes when Rob had made a comment about USC football. They were on the verge of saying something to each other but held it in.

"And we left Jesse there alone," I said. We giggled. "What happens if they confront each another with only tiny Jesse to hold them back? It could get ugly. I think we should get it out in the open. It just seems we're all held captive by this thing between them."

"Well, it's pretty big," said MIHO. "And Rob's out of football and has a kid on the way."

"Rob didn't have to jump off that deck."

"He was following us."

"But we're idiots! We had nothing other than our health to worry about. He had his career."

"We're all idiots, but that's not the way you want to lead the discussion with Rob," MIHO said. "If so, you're bound to be dick-sanded into the mud."

"Dick-sanded?"

We both laughed at the visual, diffusing our own disagreement.

As we walked up the ramp to the store, we saw a flyer for the lodge cabins for rent. Even though they were rustic and run-down, they started at about $150 a night. MIHO and I walked into the store. The orders were for at least forty-eight more beers and "the biggest bottle of Jack you can find." The store had both, and the money collected from the four other burgeoning alcoholics just covered those costs.

We headed back and found Paul and Jesse playing drinking games with cards, whose only purpose was to get as drunk as possible as quickly as possible. As we got out of the car, I could hear Jesse yell, "Just as long as you don't win! I don't care if I win or lose."

They laughed before noticing us and yelling, "Hey!"

"You raided the store pretty good," said Jesse. "What did you get for Daddy?"

"MIHO...brought his mom," said Paul and laughed, the most comfortable he had been since we arrived.

"Where's Rob?" I asked, opening the ice chest while MIHO unloaded the beer into it.

"He went out for a walk. Said he'd be back at some point," said Jesse.

"Now we can party," Paul said.

"Dude, just stop that shit," I said.

"What?" Paul asked.

"Have some friggin' empathy," MIHO said. "You know what he's been through and your role in it."

"Yeah, I know. I've had to tone down the jokes you've been serving me all weekend," Paul said.

We all looked at him with disbelief. Was he that tone deaf?

"He's going through some tough stuff right now, and he needs our support, not someone working against him," I said. "You've got to be there for him, even if it means admitting your mistakes. In case you didn't know, you do make them."

Paul looked off to the side and bit his cheek. I was expecting him to come back with an excuse or shift blame, but instead his demeanor changed from defiance to resignation.

"Yeah, I guess," Paul said. "I need to do right by Rob. He deserves it."

I looked up as though I'd see Rob strolling down the road. I didn't. Just the steady drizzle coming down around us and a growing pile of beer cans near the tree.

"Geez, we were only gone for forty-five minutes," I said.

"Jesse couldn't get past the river," Paul said. "And he kept challenging me, even though I've been killing him. And I've been drinking just so he doesn't feel too inferior."

I opened my first beer, and we continued to play cards against the backdrop of the constant patter of rain against the tarp. When the rain slowed and reduced to random splats, I was as drunk as everyone else, which made me wonder if the strange sound, like someone banging a wooden stick against a large pot, calling us to dinner, was real. Everyone glanced toward the direction of the sound. That's when we saw a black bear running through the woods just below our campsite, followed a few seconds later by a man in a state of undress—shirt open, pants unbuckled and almost falling down—banging on a big pot. I'd never seen a bear, but I was glad it was running away from us. The man kept running past us on the road, and the banging continued until we couldn't see him anymore.

I looked at MIHO, Paul, and Jesse.

"Oh my god!" Jesse said. "What the…"

"Jesse, the word you're seeking is *fuck*," Paul concluded.

"Oh man," I said. "I guess *she* is around." I'd never seen the famous bear in the fur and was glad I hadn't run into her on a hike.

"How long has Rob been gone?" I asked.

"When did you get back from the store?" Jesse asked.

"About ten," I said.

"It's one thirty now, and he left about fifteen minutes before you got back," said Jesse. "So that's about four hours?"

I walked toward Jesse and Rob's tent. MIHO and Paul also joined us. "Should we go looking for him?"

We knew that Rob was working through some things and that he sometimes took off for personal reflection. We respected that. Still, it was the longest he'd ever stepped away. And with that bear roaming around, there was reason for concern.

"I say give him another half hour," said Paul. "It'll also give us some time to sober up before we try going on a rescue mission. It would make no sense for us to put ourselves in unnecessary danger. Who knows if there are other bears out there?"

"Right! Rob's out there among them," Jesse said.

"He's bigger and hairier than those bears," MIHO said. "Still, we should look for him."

"He went off away from the road and toward the trails," Jesse said and pointed. "We can go in that direction if we need to and do a grid search."

We gathered sticks, stones, and any other rudimentary weapons. MIHO even got his own pot and wooden spoon to bring along. Just as we got to the road and toward Rob's last-known location, he came walking from the opposite direction carrying a Styrofoam cup. His hat and sweatshirt were soaked.

"Hey, fellas," he called. We all turned and looked dumbfounded. "Sun's finally out."

"Oh my god," I said. "Did you see the bear?"

Rob smiled. "Hell yeah, I did! Crazy!"

He took a long drink of coffee. We all looked at him waiting for the story. He had a look of calm I hadn't seen yet on the trip. This was Rob from three years ago. His demeanor fed our imaginations, and we created fantastic stories of him putting down his coffee, getting into a three-point stance, rushing forward, and driving his shoulder into the chest of the bear, bringing the wild beast to the ground for a three-yard loss before picking up his coffee to continue on.

"Yeah, I take it you saw it too," Rob said. "I was just down the road about two hundred yards back. I'm having a nice walk in the drizzle when I see this black bear lumbering toward me. Of course, I ducked to the side of the road behind the biggest tree I could find. It was about twenty yards from me when it turned and went into the forest and up the hill. Man, what a rush to have a bear coming right at you."

"Did you see the half-naked guy with the pot and pan?" Jesse asked.

"Oh, Roy," Rob said. "Yeah, good guy. Right after the bear turned up, he stopped running next to me. He said he was in the outhouse when he heard something rummaging around the trash can at his site. His wife and kids were in the tent. He got off the pot and rushed to the campsite, grabbed a pot and a spoon, and started banging away. The bear noticed the noise and walked away. But Roy didn't want the bear coming back, so he banged it louder and took off after the bear. I guess they must have ran right by you."

"What an idiot." I laughed. "He was lucky."

"Roy said as much. He didn't know what he was thinking, only that he needed to protect his family."

"Wow," Paul said, looking at Rob with admiration.

Rob returned the stare with acknowledgment, quelling any awkward tension.

"Well, one thing we know is that if fatherhood's going to make me a crazy motherfucker who chases bears with a pot and a spoon, then I'll take it," Rob said.

We laughed and started back to the site.

"You were gone a while," said Jesse.

"Thanks, Mom," Rob said. "I just went for a walk and found my way to town."

"I thought you went toward the trails," Jesse said.

"I did. I walked about a half mile down the trail, but then I came back and was about to join you all, but you were whooping it up, and I wasn't ready for that, so I kept walking and thought I'd get to the road. Then I thought I'd go to the ranger station. Then the marina. I stopped and got a coffee and went to the beach and the point. I sat there a while, then got another cup of coffee and walked back. It was good."

A smile of contentment was on his face. That was good enough for me.

"Well, then get a beer. You've gotta catch up."

Rob smiled, pulled out a water from the ice chest, and sat down. He watched as we continued to play various card games. The awkward tension from the previous night was gone. We laughed harder and with more authenticity than any other time the rest of the year. These were the best times and refreshing to my soul. By 9:00 p.m., the small pile of beer cans that Paul and Jesse had started had multiplied, and we were ready to pass out in our tents.

When I emerged from the tent in the morning, the ground was saturated. The trenches we dug around the tents were still diverting water, but another downpour could overwhelm them. The rain had stopped for a bit, allowing me to pull out a chair, sit, and light a cigarette. I listened to the drips of water and the wildlife coming out from their shelters. Sometimes I'd look up and see a squirrel peering its head around a tree to see if we had any food. How nature would rejuvenate itself even after the rain. I wished I was refreshed like the land. Instead, I felt like crap. My insides were turning somersaults. Soon, MIHO also stumbled out of the tent, sat at the picnic table, bent over, and put his head between his knees, looking like he may leave his dinner in the mud. As I stumbled forward, he looked up, his eyes still swollen with sleep, his face like death. But he still smiled.

"Dude." He shook his head. He didn't need to say more. I knew what it meant: *Man, that was a crazy day. Too much drinking. We can't do that again.*

"Dude," I said back. *I know, man. Wow. We either have to watch our drinking or find something else to do.*

"Dude," MIHO said, looking over the campsite. *We're close to getting rained out here. I don't know if we can take much more.*

"Dude?" *What are you saying? Do you wanna leave?*

"That cabin's looking pretty good right now," MIHO managed. "Just an idea."

I admit, it sounded like a good idea. I was soaked and would give anything for a dry cabin and warm blanket. The closest thing to warmth we had was a fire. The ring was soaked, but our wood was dry, and a warm fire before the rain returned justified the effort in building it. I took to chopping some of the wood for kindling, and soon the sound led Paul, Jesse, and Rob to emerge from their tents just as disheveled as MIHO and me. Everyone welcomed a fire to bring warmth and comfort. Even with the moisture in the air, the fire began to blaze in front of us as we all sat mesmerized in our chairs.

"What do you guys think about getting a cabin for tonight?" MIHO asked.

"Let's do it," said Paul, raising his hand like we were taking a vote. "This place is waterlogged, and my body feels like a prune."

"I agree," said Jesse. "How much do you think?"

"Maybe thirty or forty bucks a person," said MIHO. "Hopefully it's not all booked."

"Are you talking about those run-down cabins by the lodge?" asked Rob.

"I think the advertising term is *rustic*," said Paul.

"Yeah, just up the road from the lodge," I said. "We'll need to check on things sooner than later."

Paul mimicked fixing his hair and putting on his TV-personality smile. "We'll get one. I can charm anyone, including MIHO's mom."

MIHO shook his head. I looked over at Rob to gauge his reaction. If it upset him, I couldn't tell. It wasn't like Paul and I had to dress up for prom, but we pulled on some jeans and our jackets and a hat. MIHO grilled up some bacon and made coffee. By the time breakfast was over, the rains were starting, and the fire was beginning to succumb to the moisture.

We drove the Civic to the lodge. As we stepped into the dry reception area, we passed pictures of the lodge from better years—when it was a loggers' paradise to a vacation spot. There were pictures of wood-bottom boats and catamaran races. It was a contrast to the worn carpet, the broken chair in the corner, and some water stains and damage to the ceiling tiles. Paul approached the desk with the confidence of a TV broadcaster used to walking into a room and asking anything he wanted. His smile was warm, and he greeted the woman, who looked to be in her mid-fifties.

"Good morning," he said. "It's pretty wet out there today. What's your name?"

The woman looked us up and down, evaluating whether she'd rent a cabin to us. Paul continued to smile, those perfect white teeth conveying his confidence, warmth, and safety.

"Judith. It's supposed to rain all day. How can I help you?"

Paul leaned on the counter in a casual manner. "Yeah, my buddy and I are camping just over at the Rancheria campground and are probably a few rainy hours away from being washed out. I'm from out of state and would like to stay here just a little longer. Do you happen to have an available cabin for tonight?"

"Let me check," Judith said, opening a binder. "Is it just the two of you?"

"We have another friend back at the site," Paul lied. I guess he figured the smaller the number, the less risk that we'd "tear up" the place. "We'd really appreciate it."

Judith narrowed her gaze on the binder. "Well, we have a cabin with two queen beds for a hundred fifty, or we have one with two queens and two twins for two hundred."

"Let's go with the two hundred-dollar option," Paul said. "We're too big to be bunking up with each other." He laughed.

Judith giggled too. "Okay. Do you have a credit card?"

We'd gathered forty dollars per person in cash.

"I have cash for the room, but you can put my card on file for deposit and incidentals if that works," Paul said.

"That's fine," said Judith, accepting the twenties. Paul also gave her his Visa. "I'll just need you to sign here for the room saying you won't throw parties or be rowdy and disturb the other cabins."

"Right. We'll be field mice, Judith," he said. "No problems from us."

"Okay, then. You can have cabin ten. It's just up this road and to the left. It has two bedrooms, a small kitchen, and a bathroom with a shower."

"Hot water?" Paul asked as he signed some papers and agreements. "My buddies and I could go for a hot shower after being in the rain all weekend."

"Of course!" Judith said with a smile.

"Fantastic," said Paul, who returned the papers. "Looking forward to it."

"Here you go." Judith presented the keys. "Have a great rest of your trip."

"Of course, Judith," Paul said with a wink. "It's been a pleasure."

We left the lodge, victorious. Before we headed back, we decided to hike up the road to the cabin in the light drizzle to check it out for ourselves. The cabin was small with a pitched roof, not bigger than my parents' living room. A small deck with two resin chairs and a plastic patio table acted as the cabin's front porch.

We unlocked the deadbolt and opened the door, walked inside, and saw that it was indeed "rustic." I looked to the left and saw two beds facing each other, backing up to the front and back walls. To the right was a small two-burner stove and oven that looked like something out of a 1950s kitchen with a refrigerator just a few years newer. There was a small sink, a coffee maker, and a Formica dining table with four mismatched metal and wood chairs around it. Paul and I ventured down a hallway that led to another small bedroom with two beds and a door to a small bathroom with a toilet, a sink, and a shower. With our two hundred dollars we were really paying for the location and the scenery, not the accommodations.

"Just remember, it's better than the rain-soaked campground that could flood out at any minute," said Paul.

"Right! It's a mattress, a bathroom, a shower. I'm sure even MIHO will appreciate using this kitchen more than his camp kitchen."

"Agreed," said Paul. "Let's get back and pack up our crap and bring it here. We've got all day and all night to party at the saloon."

With that, we walked down the hill, retrieved the Civic, and went back to the campsite. The boys were happy to have a dry place to stay the night. While it was messier and more difficult to pack up our gear in the rain, we got it done in less time than expected.

"It's not much, but better than where we came from," Jesse said when we arrived and stepped inside.

When we'd settled into our home for the night, we had an important choice to make. We could get some activity in, albeit in the constant drizzle, or we could stay in and continue our binge drinking. We chose a walk in the drizzle and walked the quarter mile to the lake.

For the first time I can remember, there was no wind at the point. As we looked down the length of the lake, we could see the constant gray in the skies with the darker black of the lake water and the dark-green forest between the two. On a typical day, the lake would have deep swells and whitecaps as the wind would push the water. Today, the lake was still.

"It was choppier yesterday," said Rob. "Today's so much more serene."

"Yessir," said Jesse.

"This lake still gets me," said Paul. "Thanks for bringing us out here again." A little sincerity from Paul was as rare as a jewel. Paul kicked some dirt, then looked at Rob. "Look, I know my actions on the last trip were devastating to all of us. It cost you your dream. And I know I've said it, but I want you to know that I'm truly sorry for the role my actions played."

Rob drew a breath. I think he was taken aback, as we all were, by the suddenness and honesty of Paul's admission. I expected him to pull Rob to the side and talk to him, but Paul had jumped on the moment. Rob turned and took a couple steps away. MIHO, Jesse, and I stepped back to give them space and try not to trespass on their moment. Yet, having lived in this cloud over the past three years, we were a part of it. It was like watching the last play of a Super Bowl that would determine the outcome.

"Paul," Rob said, turning back. "The last three years have been hell. And for the longest time I've attributed it to you. 'What if?' has been a question I've asked myself again and again. What if you weren't such a horn dog? What if we hadn't met Sean and his daughter? What if I hadn't met Becky? What if I didn't blow out my other knee? It's all a fucking game, though."

I looked over at Jesse and MIHO, the three of us wondering what was coming. Would Rob pound Paul into the dirt? Would Paul jump off the point into the lake? All we could do was watch and be ready.

"I mean, there's the other side of the 'what if' question. What if we never went on this trip? The memories we've shared wouldn't exist. What if I hadn't met Becky? I wouldn't be having a baby. Right now, that seems scary, but when I hold him or her in my arms, I'm thinking the baby's going to be the biggest blessing in my life. So…I don't know, man. Three years later, I'm still pissed at you, but also I can't blame you for everything without also feeling like you had a hand in bringing me a future blessing."

We were all dumbfounded by Rob's perspective. We thought this clearing of dirt on the point would be the venue for a dick-sanding. Instead, Rob grabbed Paul and brought him in for a big bear hug. This reconciliation was so touching, and we'll forever swear that the rain tasted salty.

"I'm so sorry," Paul said.

"I know. But I'm pissed at all of us for losing the last three years," Rob said, breaking the embrace. "We should have talked and worked things out. Instead we avoided each other."

"I wanted to give you space," Paul said. "I knew you weren't my biggest fan."

"I wasn't. Part of it was being pissed you never called. I thought you were selfish for ruining my dreams and still playing out yours."

"I was selfish. I also didn't know what to do or say. I didn't want to shove my career in your face. I'm sorry."

"Dude, without you, I wouldn't have sniffed USC. You spent countless hours creating those highlight reels that my dad sent to colleges. You called up the newspapers to share my stats and even got a couple features written. Without that publicity, I wouldn't have gotten as far as I did. So, the blame game only goes so far before you get to all that you've done."

MIHO, Jesse, and I approached, and we wrapped our arms around each other's shoulders like we were in a big huddle.

"We have to keep doing this, no matter what," Rob said. "Agree?"

We nodded. The rain came down a little harder. We looked at each other as our jackets were getting soaked.

"It's time to leave the waterworks to God," said MIHO. "Time to *dee*-part and get *dee*-ry."

We returned to the cabin, and MIHO went to the kitchen to start dinner. Somehow, he was able to pull together a fantastic shrimp scampi with toasted garlic bread. He even had some bottles of white wine stored in his provisions. How did we not know that he had those chilling in the bottom of the cooler with the beer?

After dinner and the best shower I'd ever had by myself, we set off toward the saloon. We were supposed to go three years ago before our trip detoured to the emergency room. It was all that we'd expected. The saloon was one large room in a log cabin with a few tables but enough space for a makeshift dance floor if necessary. On the left, a long bar stretched thirty-five feet from one end of the structure to the other. Two bartenders served the lodgers and locals. Along the walls were very antique snow skis, fishing gear, sailing gear, and relic signs. In the rafters hung a saddle. Interesting.

We sat down, and Paul bought the first pitcher. We all joked that we were drinking the same beer we had back at the cabin but paying triple the price. Nobody complained, and we plied the corner jukebox with money to play all the tunes we wanted. And we were dry.

These were great times.

7

Rob

I thought that was the year we first got a girl to go up in the saddle," said Jesse.

The friends finished dinner and sat outside enjoying the remaining Cubans and a special bottle of scotch MIHO had brought. The caramel liquid swirled in their glasses, the single porchlight providing harsh shadows in the night.

"No, that was another year," said Rob. "Remember, it was dead that first year because everybody was smart and went home. It was like we were in a ghost town. It was one of the best years because it was just us, and we weren't trying to hook up."

"I like how you put us all in the collective," said Paul with a smile. "Since it was *me* who was always looking for it."

"You don't have to tell me," said MIHO, who was flipping forward in the book. "It seems the next few entries just tell stories about you and your conquests."

"Shut up," said Paul. He reached over and tried to grab the notebook. MIHO kept the book secure and began to read Jim's accounts of Paul's sexcapades.

Rob smiled at Jim's account of him standing on top of one of the tables to lift a few girls into the rafters and swing their legs into the saddle. The bartenders were so pissed and worried he would break a table or worse. Rob remembered how thin the wall between the men's and women's restroom was when he heard quite clearly one of the girls telling her friend in detail how she had just serviced Paul on an abandoned snowmobile behind the saloon. At the time, Rob was titillated. Now, he just shook his head and sipped his drink.

"I wish he would have skipped that stuff," Paul said. "Do you realize how awkward it is to hear about the bad choices you made when you were younger?"

"What about the next year?" Jesse asked.

"Um...2003 details when Paul was with an eighteen-year-old and a forty-year-old on the same trip," MIHO said.

"Don't remind me," said Paul. "I got a Facebook friend request from the older one a couple months ago."

"Did you respond?" Jesse asked.

Paul looked at Jesse like he was crazy. "Can we just skip to a year where it's not about me hooking up?"

Instead of prolonging Paul's agony, MIHO flipped to 2005. He sighed and then put the book down. Rob pulled it from him and flipped back to 2005.

"Of course," Rob said. He realized why this wasn't MIHO's favorite chapter. Rob thought the trip lived up to its expectations of a double bachelor party. They brought new people. There were great stories they would remember forever, and there was golf, poker, and girls. He knew that MIHO had a different perspective.

"Right, Kyle and Todd," Jesse said. "Yeah, MIHO, your two favorite people."

MIHO wasn't amused. "Yeah, let's do that one tomorrow. Let's play some more cards."

Rob swirled the scotch in his glass. It was as smooth as anticipated. The mark of a good scotch was its enjoyment after a small sip. They didn't need to shoot it or swig it from the bottle. After more than twenty years, Rob felt that they'd learned patience. And yet, one of them wasn't there to enjoy this point in their lives. Rob looked over at MIHO, who was completely lost in thought and staring at his glass of scotch.

"So, speaking of Leslie," Rob said, changing the subject for MIHO's sake.

"We weren't," said Paul with a laugh. "But how does she look for the upcoming season?"

Rob set his glass on the table and leaned forward, his smile beaming while discussing his daughter's achievements. Leslie was neither a volleyball player like her mom nor a football player. Instead, she had taken to golf with legitimate talent. She had the athletic coordination of her mom, the strength and drive of her dad, and the golf intelligence all her own.

When Rob first started to bring her to the golf course when she was eight, he thought it would be a great way to have a few hours of uninterrupted time outside with her. He taught her the basics, then watched as she hit the ball straight and true. After a few lessons, she began to break 100 with regularity hitting from the regular ladies' tees at nine years old.

Rob entered Leslie in a couple youth tournaments, and by ten years old, she was beating thirteen- and fourteen-year-olds. She then started beating Rob too. She would read the course and advise him on shots he should take. She won the high school girls league title as a freshman and hoped to compete on the boys team next year. Regardless of gender, she was one of the top golfers in her age group.

"She has so much talent, it's unbelievable," Rob said. "But I'm not making the mistake my dad did—it's not her whole life. I've still got her taking dance classes, and we'll play *Madden* on PlayStation."

"What the hell?" MIHO said. "How do you all manage schedules, let alone the cost?"

"It's a flipping struggle. Becky and I keep a shared calendar on our phones just to make sure who's picking her up and where she needs to go next. And don't get me started on costs. I can't imagine the twins."

Jesse shook his head. "Thankfully, they're still young enough where they try these things together. But I know there will come a time when they'll both have their own interests, and we'll be screwed. Just think about what you pay for stuff and double it, every time."

Rob shook his head. It was hard enough managing one kid's schedule. He started to think about Tracey and how she'd manage as just one parent.

"It's got to be hard doing this all alone," Jesse said.

"She's not alone. She's got us," MIHO said.

"I've helped Tracey out with Willie and even running him around when she needs it," Paul said. "She needs a little help now and then, and I'm happy to be there for her."

"We're all going to need to be there for Tracey whenever she needs it," Rob said. "It's our obligation to Jim." Rob raised his glass a final time as an honor to Jim, then threw it back and announced he was going to bed. It was 11:00 p.m., which was now late for them. Earlier nights, earlier mornings, and comfortable beds were a must.

Rob was the first to stir the next morning. As an adult, he just liked the time before dawn to be with himself. This morning, he was up with a cup of coffee at 6:00 a.m. Though he enjoyed the comraderie with his friends, the silent time with nature helped recharge him. He would pour a cup of strong coffee into a travel cup, collect a book on philosophy or spirituality to prompt deeper reflection, and walk to an isolated part of the forest. This would set the tone for the whole year. This year, however, he brought a single envelope.

About fifty yards into a trail next to the cabin, he followed a couple sets of deer prints. After his near encounter with a bear a few years ago, a part of him was always a little wary over going on these solitary hikes deep into the wilderness, but he had been a Boy Scout, respected nature, and knew what to do if danger came.

The trail led to a nearby stream, and he stood by the edge. Rob breathed through his nose, taking in the smells of the water, the trees, and the slight hint of deer droppings. From beyond two fallen trees, he spied a grown doe and its fawn quenching their thirst at the edge of the water. They paid no attention to him as though he was just a part of their reality. When they moved on, he turned to see an entanglement of tree roots along the bank that provided a nice perch with which to view the stream without too much discomfort. Rob wiggled his butt on the root and closed his eyes, letting a calm wash over him. He always found this meditation rewarding but could never make the time at home. He focused on his breath and let his anxieties float away.

Once Rob was ready, he pulled out the envelope. Inside was a card that Jim had given him when his dad had passed six years ago. The card itself was a little cheesy with gold-foil lettering and the water-colored birds printed on it, but it felt appropriate at the time. Rob was more interested in the pages inside:

My brother, Rob,

I cannot imagine the grief you're feeling right now. Not only was he your parent, but for your childhood, he was your driving force. He was your father and, for the teen years, your mother too. He was your cheerleader, your coach, your teacher, your big brother, and your men-tor all rolled into one.

I knew him as Mr. Simpson, your dad. As our peewee football coach and one of our high school assistant coaches. He dropped me off at my house after practice in the fall and grilled burgers in the backyard dur-ing the summer when we were hanging out in the pool.

He was also the one person Paul couldn't charm, both to our ad-miration and chagrin. We couldn't get anything past him, even with the smoke and mirrors and misdirection. He always knew where the smuggled alcohol was or when we went to a party when we shouldn't have. He had eyes and ears everywhere, and we loved him for it, even if we cursed him under our breath.

Most of all, he made you, you. You're the standup man you are be-cause of him. Even with the disappointment of the failed pro-football career, you got through it because you were strong. And not just in the physical sense. Your strength lies in the reliance in yourself.

I can already see how you're paying it forward with your daughter. You've had opportunities to make choices that would have been easier. Becky gave you the chance to keep your distance from Leslie. You turned your life around for her. You always put the ones you care about ahead of yourself, and that's the calling of a man of integrity.

As you know, you're one of my best friends, and I'll always be thankful to your dad for making you a person on whom I can forever rely and someone who will always be there for the ones he cares about. You didn't become that on your own, though I'm confident you would always get to that place.

There's no right way to grieve. The most important part is just to let it happen. Don't fight it. Your father will always be there as part of your soul.

I love you, man. You embody the qualities I forever strive, and I thank you for being that shining light for me, and I thank your dad for showing you the light.

With deepest sympathies,
Jim

Rob finished the letter and folded it. He found his cheeks were wet and his eyes swollen as he looked down at the stream and sniffled. He took a deep breath and sighed. The beauty of this setting, reconnecting to the grief over the death of his dad and now one of his best friends, was just too much for him to keep it together. He let go. The wave of suppressed sadness and heartache overwhelmed him, causing him to double over the tree root. Rob hadn't cried like this when his dad died, nor when Jim died. Now, however, the dam had burst, and he was flooded with emotions he never knew he had.

While it felt good and therapeutic, he regained his composure and took a few breaths, inhaling deep and exhaling like a blowfish. He felt lighter and calm. Was it the metaphorical burden that he felt was lifted off his shoulders? He looked at the stream and the endless water winding and folding over the rocks with full appreciation of its beauty. The sounds of the stream were clearer and crisper than before. A smile creeped on his face.

Jim was right about the effect his father had had on Rob. Even though Jack Simpson pushed Rob every day in football and school and prescribed almost every minute of his life, he had also instituted routine and the importance of process and accountability. It was strange. Once he accepted that his football life was finished and it was time to move on, only then did he appreciate these other life lessons. He also hoped that he was improving on those lessons with his daughter. Jim seemed to think so, and Rob agreed.

Rob realized how much he needed this trip for closure. It just seemed appropriate to be here, say goodbye to Jim properly, and be with the guys. He allowed himself one more deep breath to take in the stream, put a hand to his heart, then pointed and looked to the sky. Tears welled up once again, only this time he smiled and stood up, dusting off his butt before beginning the hike back to the cabin.

When Rob approached the house from the back, he saw Jesse leaning over the balcony with a cup of coffee. He looked up and gave a salute to his friend, who raised his cup.

"Good hike?"

"Of course," said Rob. "Good run?"

"The altitude and hills are hard, but yeah," Jesse said. His shirt was still sweaty.

"Anybody else up yet?"

"Not yet. Just got back about five minutes ago."

Rob climbed the cabin steps and headed to the kitchen. He filled his cup with coffee, no cream and sugar, and joined Jesse outside. Rob sat down on one of the chairs and put his feet up on another.

"Where did you go?" asked Jesse.

"Just down the hill to a little stream. Saw a couple deer. I wish I had my rifle."

Rob said it for Jesse's reaction, which turned out to be an exaggerated eye roll. They were a study in contrast. Rob was a giant of a man, while Jesse was compact and tight. Rob was a member of the NRA. Jesse railed against guns in Facebook posts. They often had heated discussions about life and politics, but they knew they were never going to change each other's minds.

Rather, they learned to respect their perspectives and even needled each other without condemnation.

"So, got in some reflection time about Jim?" Jesse asked.

"Yep. I needed to work it through."

"I get that. I guess I'm just not feeling it the way you and MIHO seem to be. This place seems haunting to me without Jim. Don't you feel a little creepy?"

"Not until you just mentioned it. I mean, that hole in one was a little divine, but I think it's just a way to celebrate Jim one last time. And drink beer."

"It just seems MIHO is being a little weird about it. He's trying to make this all about Jim and not about us *and* Jim. I don't know."

"Well, we all need to figure it out in our own way, and I think this is MIHO's process."

MIHO and Paul walked into the kitchen. Rob considered taking a picture of Paul and posting it on social media. Paul's normally perfect full head of hair was strewn in about twenty different directions, and his gray ESPN T-shirt and striped pajama pants belied someone getting up for Saturday morning cartoons. MIHO owned his hipster look with sweatpants, hoodie, and beanie. He might as well have been brewing a craft beer. They grunted at each other, then came outside to join Rob and Jesse on the deck. Paul squinted as he came out into the light.

"Good morning, fellas," Paul said.

"Morning," said Rob, raising his cup.

MIHO just grunted.

"Glad you all could wake up."

"Remember when we'd get up at ten or later? Those were the days," said Paul. "The bladder is smaller, the prostate is older, and it seems we have to go to bed dehydrated just to sleep eight hours."

"Sounds like a personal problem to me," said MIHO. "Nah, I feel ya. I remember when I could drink a gallon of water and sleep ten hours. Sure, my pees were a minute long of strong stream. Now, I have to decide whether the pee at three thirty is worth getting up for or hold it and feel it for the rest of the night."

"What a conversation," said Jesse. "Peeing and prostates."

"Just wait until we're all comparing our prostate exams, colonoscopies, and vasectomies," said Paul.

"I'm already there with the vasectomy," said Jesse. "Jim also had one."

They all looked at Jesse.

"I know Jim had one, but you're snipped?" asked MIHO.

"Oh yeah. After twins, you realize that two is fine, and you don't need to go through that again. It wasn't that bad. Just some swelling and purple balls."

Their faces contorted into a mix of disgust and pain, like it was happening to their own testicles.

"I took Jim's advice and did it on March Madness week and it was soooo worth it," Jesse said. "Four days where I 'had to rest' and watch the tournament...with a bag of peas on my balls. It was the most enjoyable discomfort I've ever had."

Rob shook his head. "Oh man! I don't know if I could ever do that. Changing subjects, because I can't get the image of Jesse's purple balls out of my head, what's the plan today?"

MIHO stood. "Well, I thought a hike might be nice. We can head up the hill toward those rocks up there. I'm sure the view is fantastic."

Rob looked at Jesse. This was the forced spiritual experience Jesse felt MIHO was pushing. Jesse held his mouth together, trying not to voice his frustration. For the good of the group, Rob thought of a more tactful way to decline the idea.

"Are we up for that?" Said Rob. "We haven't touched the horseshoe pit. Just saying."

MIHO looked at him with a little irritation. "Sounds good. Let's rack 'em."

"Dude, that's pool," said Paul with a laugh. "But I like it. After breakfast, let's load up the cooler and head out back to the pit. By the way, MIHO, what are you making for breakfast?"

"Cinnamon-bread French toast with thick-cut bacon and eggs," said MIHO, who took his first steps onto the deck that morning. "But I ain't doing nothing until that kitchen is clean enough to cook in."

"Okay, Mom," Rob said with a groan.

Since Jesse helped, it was up to Rob and Paul to do the dishes. He knew they should have done it last night. That was the responsible thing to do, but after the scotch and the memories, Rob just wanted to go to bed. Now he and Paul were going to pay for it, and they walked into the kitchen and surveyed the damage. There were pots, colanders, wine glasses, whiskey glasses, and spilled sauce on the counter.

Jesse picked up the notebook and flipped it open. "While you wash those dishes, why don't we delve into Jesse and Jim's bachelor party of 2004?"

"Oh, yes, let's go there," Rob said. He had started filling the sink with suds and pulled out the scouring sponge. He took the first pot and submerged it under the bubbles. "I remember that trip had *lots* of stories."

"That's what happens when you bring more dudes along," said Paul. "You find out lots of things about lots of people, eh, MIHO?"

8

Jim

A t first, I thought MIHO and Rob using our annual trip to throw a double bachelor party for Jesse and me seemed like an invasion of our own tight tradition. Then again, I preferred that to a night of strippers and clubs in Vegas or Reno. Our trip was also pretty self-contained with very specific traditions that could help keep us out of trouble.

My only apprehension was inviting new people into our unit. It's not like someone can come in new and integrate into our group dynamic and inside jokes. But Tracey's younger brother Kyle, age twenty-one, would hate me for life if he wasn't invited, and Jesse wanted to invite Todd, a friend from work.

Kyle was five years younger than any of us and about to attend business school while working at Nordstrom's. He and I had similar interests and shared good times at family functions, but he wasn't a "friend" like the rest of the guys. Kyle often put himself in the middle of the conversations or steered the talk toward his latest venture or focus or whatever. With business school just around the corner, he was talking a lot about the GMAT and the importance of getting into a good school. I figured this trip would help me get to know him better.

"If I'm going to make it in your family, I'm going to need to have someone else on my side," I told Tracey when I informed her that I was inviting Kyle. "I'm outnumbered."

"Who says he's going to be on your side?" Tracey said.

"After one of our trips to the lake, he definitely will be."

Todd worked with Jesse at the technology firm and had encouraged him to ask out Danielle, a receptionist working her way through law school. Now Danielle, newly licensed, was a lowly associate at her new firm and billing countless hours, which left Jesse to share happy hour once a week with Todd.

"He's different," Jesse told me when I called him. "He's not like any of us, but I think he'll fit in."

"How so?"

"His interests are different than ours, and that's good for us. He likes to fish and play the guitar, both can be an addition to the normal drinking and … drinking."

"That's not different, just more accomplished than us."

"Well, " Jesse started, but then he stopped and we went back to talking logistics.

By the time the bachelor party arrived in June, we had exchanged countless emails, some so raunchy that they would embarrass my dad. MIHO and Rob had covered every detail, many without my assistance. MIHO handled the camping reservations and food for the weekend while Rob handled the bachelor activities. They both said this would be a year to remember.

In the last year, Rob had moved back to Sacramento to be closer his dad, who had suffered a heart attack and declining health. While he and Becky weren't back together, he somehow convinced her to move to Sacramento with Leslie. Rob had made changes to his life and been a good father to Leslie over the last three years. With the move, the birth of his daughter, and his father's health, Rob knew who he was and his place in the world. As expected, his knees kept him out of the police academy, but as luck would have it, he reached out to Sean for advice on starting a professional career outside football. Sean used his USC network and connections to help him find a job as a junior private investigator for a law firm in Sacramento. It was a simple but rewarding job. Working with more experienced PIs, he learned some of the real-world practical skills to go along with the theories from school.

When our departure date arrived, I kissed a nervous Tracey and bounded down the apartment steps to where Rob was parked. Tracey felt a little insecure, even though she had nothing to worry about. She had seen me go on this trip before without incident. She was more nervous about Paul and his influence over her little brother. Kyle didn't ease her concerns with the big smile on his face. I tried to relieve her anxiety, saying, "At least we're not going to Vegas," but that didn't seem to help.

Kyle and I piled into Rob's truck and were on our way to Fresno. Rob and I engaged in telling and retelling stories of the trips in the past. We wondered what stories we might create this weekend. Kyle was ready for whatever may come. I think he expected to have his own story to rival Paul.

During our email exchanges, Todd suggested it wasn't a bachelor party unless we played golf or had strippers. So, Rob found a small par-three golf course near the Fresno airport to host a one-club tournament. He announced it as the "Tin Cup" tournament, named after the Kevin Costner golf movie and the scene where Costner played a round with just a seven iron.

When we arrived at the course, Todd and Jesse had already picked up MIHO and Paul from the airport and were sitting in the shade. Todd's Toyota Tundra was loaded with lots of gear and a stainless-steel gas Weber. After a set of introductions, we opened the coolers, grabbed a beer for everyone, and toasted the weekend and the two bachelors.

"Gentlemen, this will be one of many toasts," Rob said. "I want to thank you all for joining us to celebrate Jesse and Jim's upcoming nuptials. But before they sign off their bachelorhood, it's our sworn duty to show them a great weekend. So, here's to a fantastic couple days starting off with the first-ever Tin Cup Tourney."

We toasted again. After I threw back the beer, I looked at Jesse. "What's up with the grill?"

"MIHO's idea," Jesse said, glancing at MIHO who was getting his club out of the van.

"The scope of our meals required more equipment than those small tailgate grills we've been bringing," said MIHO. "We needed the big guns, and Jesse agreed to bring his new Weber. And Todd had a truck to haul it up."

When everyone had pulled out their clubs, fished golf balls from their backpacks, and paid for their rounds and tall boys, we gathered around Rob, who explained the rules and groupings. In one group I'd play with MIHO and Kyle while Jesse would play with Rob, Paul, and Todd. He pulled out three tin camping cups from a box.

"As part of the bachelor party, the bachelors each get one of these. For this weekend, this cup entitles them to ask any of the rest of us to fill them with the beverage of their choice—OJ, coffee, beer, jack and cokes or whatever," said Rob, showcasing the engraved cups: *Jim and Jesse's Bachelor Party, 2004.* "I also bought a handheld engraver so we can put our own messages on them. But this third cup goes to the winner of the Tin Cup Tourney with all the privileges of the bachelors." This third cup said, *Tin Cup Tourney Champion, 2004.*

Everyone glanced around. The stakes were indeed big. Not having to get up to get a beverage all weekend was incentive to really try for the top prize. I was very thankful that I didn't have to win the tournament to reap the benefits.

"Oh, it's on!" said Kyle, pulling out his club. "That cup is as good as mine. Get ready to be serving me drinks all weekend, bitches!"

I always enjoyed Kyle's competitive nature, and he backed it up. Unfortunately, his eagerness to win sometimes bordered on excessive trash talk and arrogance. I knew I'd need to have a side conversation for him to dial it back.

I grabbed a broken tee off the ground and set up my ball. I took a few practice swings, feeling seven sets of eyes on me. I took a breath, stepped up to the tee, thought about keeping my eye on the ball, arms straight, a three-quarter swing, looked at my target again, another breath, then swung away hoping for the best. The ball sliced at an absurd right angle, hit a tree, and bounced eighty-five yards toward the hole, about three yards off the green. Everyone let out a big laugh. Jesse even fell to the ground.

"Yikes! We'll have to make sure we're behind you at all times," said Kyle.

"Good thing you already have your own cup," Paul quipped.

"It got there, and it doesn't matter how," I retorted.

Our scores were unimpressive. When we moved to the second hole, MIHO had the lone par while Kyle and I both scored a four. For the next three holes, Kyle indeed stepped up his game, scoring two pars and a bogey to take the lead in our group with MIHO just a stroke behind. After finishing my beer, I pulled out a cigarette and lit it to help calm my nerves. As we turned to the fifth hole, we crossed the second group approaching the fourth green.

"Dude, is Tracy going to let you keep smoking?" Rob yelled at me. He'd just hit his ball onto the green we'd just finished. I was planning to quit after this trip. Tracey thought my smoking was the worst part of me and wanted me to quit. She wasn't going to have the stinky cigarette smoke in her house. So, if I was going to quit, I wanted to make it a point to enjoy this last weekend.

"Just blowing it out, baby!" I yelled back. "What scores you got?"

As expected, Rob led his group and was tied with Kyle overall. Even though I was keeping a scorecard for our group, Kyle had his own, writing down the other group's scores and tabulating the overall standings.

"Hey, MIHO, what did you get on that last hole?" asked Kyle as MIHO was getting ready to tee up his ball.

"I got a four, so I'm just one shot behind," said MIHO.

"No, you're two strokes behind," said Kyle. "You took a double on that hole."

"No, I didn't. I shot the first one right off the green. I chipped to ten feet, then putted to a foot, then put the next one in."

"Then you must have mis-scored the hole before," said Kyle. "You're two shots back."

"No, I'm one stroke behind you," said MIHO, a little irritated. He had to step back from the ball to gather himself.

"It's the right score," I said, annoyed. I showed him my card. "Let MIHO play the hole." I wasn't sure if Kyle had a legitimate misunderstanding or was trying to play a head game with MIHO. It wouldn't be the first time he'd tried to gain an advantage. Whatever games we played during the holiday gathering (whether it was PlayStation, basketball, board games), he was constantly trying to get in my head. If this was his intention, it didn't work this time. MIHO hit a solid shot onto the green, about four feet from the hole.

"Boom! Did you see that shot?" MIHO said to no one in particular.

After an uneventful sixth hole, we saw a lump on the seventh green. Upon further examination, a dead gopher lay on the green, mouth open, eyes plucked out by birds or insects while flies rested on the carcass. The poisoned gopher had made it halfway across before taking its last breath. Our faces contorted as we looked at the gopher.

"Gnarly!" said Kyle.

We kept the gopher in the corner of our eyes as we played out the hole. Kyle then went to the gopher and took my club and picked it up like some oversized chopsticks.

"Dude!" I said. "Don't touch it."

"I'm not. The clubs are."

He balanced the gopher on our clubs and walked over to the hole and dropped it in.

"Oh, dude, that's sick," I said.

We looked back and saw the second group just getting to the tee. They hadn't noticed Kyle placing a surprise at the bottom of the cup. We laughed, giggled, and bit our lips as we headed to the eighth hole. We played our shots while also stealing glances back to the other group on the seventh. The anticipation was almost unbearable. They took so much time to tee up and hit their shots. Finally, we watched Paul walk to the flag stick and start to pull the pin when he yelled at us, "What the fuck! You're all sick fuckers!"

We laughed and pointed. I bent over and grabbed my legs to keep my balance and regain my breath. Paul fished the gopher out of the hole. He looked like he was going to lose his lunch as he flung it into the trees.

With that fun interlude behind us, we returned to the competition. MIHO and Kyle were tied, and this tee shot was going to be crucial. Kyle's shot landed on the green about fifteen feet away while MIHO's shot landed off the green in the rough.

"That could be it," said Kyle. "That could be what gives me the cup."

I looked over at MIHO, who pounded his seven iron into the ground. He didn't care about winning, he just didn't want Kyle to win. MIHO surveyed his shot, measured, and set up. Right before he was to shoot, another ball hit onto the green. MIHO stood erect and turned around, his eyes flush with anger. "What the hell?"

Behind us, Rob was in his follow-through and laughing. "That's for putting that dead gopher into the hole, jackass!"

MIHO's irritation became amusement and flipped off Rob, then set up again. He swung, but his shot was short and didn't roll as much as expected, leaving him ten feet for a possible tying putt. Kyle tapped in for another par, and when MIHO's putt veered right and missed by inches, Kyle put his fist in the air. "Oh yeah!"

Kyle finished with a thirty, MIHO with a thirty-one, and I finished with a thirty-six. We shook hands and stood off to the side to watch the foursome finish their round.

When the second group approached, Kyle paced the edge of the green like a predator awaiting the right moment to pounce. "What's your score?" Kyle asked Rob.

"Don't know," Rob said. He knew but wasn't going to give Kyle any leverage. He was just going to play the hole and see where things lay. That's how he did everything—do the job the best you can, and the rest will follow.

Kyle turned to Todd, who was carrying the card. "What's Rob got?"

Todd looked unsure. He looked at Jesse, who shook his head as he lined up his own shot and didn't want to be bothered.

Still, Kyle asked, "Can I see the card?"

I nudged Kyle. "Dude!" I said and shook my head.

Rob finished with a par. We waited for Jesse, who came in with a bogey. Todd also finished with a bogey, and Paul four-putted the final hole for a double bogey. I hung out with Todd, who was tabulating their scores, while the others started walking back to the clubhouse, except Kyle and Rob.

While Kyle was focused on Todd's score accounting, Rob was hitting stray driving-range balls back to the range with the ease of the Dalai Lama. He'd hit a shot, followed by "Cinderella Story" and other lines from *Caddyshack*.

"Okay, I have Rob with a thirty-one," said Todd. "And—"

"Yes! Fuckers!" Kyle yelled, his arms thrust in the air. "Better get ready to pour drinks into my cup all weekend."

Todd continued. "Rob got a thirty-one, followed by Paul with a thirty-four. I had a thirty-five. Jesse shot thirty-seven."

Kyle came up to me for a high five. I was happy for him, but looking around, I was in the minority. Rob gave Kyle the cup, and he raised it high in triumph, while Jesse and I held ours with a smile, and MIHO took a begrudging picture for posterity. Kyle smiled and laughed and let out one more "whoop" before getting back into Rob's truck.

When we arrived at the lake and our site 152, we all focused our efforts on making the site our home for the next three days. We set up the tents, the firewood pile, and the mobile kitchen. As soon as camp was set, Jesse, Kyle, and I raised our glasses to take advantage of our camping perks. Todd and Rob were happy to oblige and went to the cooler to get our three beers. As we sat at our camping chairs and sipped that first beer, I was struck by how lucky I was to have my bachelor party at one of my favorite spots in the world. I clinked cups with Jesse and Kyle and smiled big. Soon, MIHO yelled that dinner was ready. As usual, the tri-tips, baked potatoes, and grilled veggies caused mouths to water and the campsite to go silent as our attention was focused on the red meat, starch, and vegetables. He even brought a variety of steak and barbecue sauces, garlic butters, and cheeses to help garnish our meal. As if this wasn't already an upgrade and a special occasion, Paul somehow managed to smuggle three bottles of wine on his flight and brought them out for us to complement our meal.

"I thought we'd class it up a little this year," Paul said. He opened the bottles and poured our cups first before serving the rest of the guys. We swirled the wine in our tin camping cups, smelled it, then tasted it with mock sophistication.

"Very full bodied with flavors of earth, berries, and root," Jesse said.

"But it has a little metallic taste to it," I added with a smile.

As the beer flowed, so did the good times. For the most part, Jesse and I stayed in our chairs, our cups never empty. Meanwhile, each of our friends would take the chair between us and spend some quality time. When Paul joined us, he was smiling ear to ear. Jesse and I both noticed and grew weary.

"Dude, please don't tell us you have strippers coming to our site," Jesse said. "We told you we didn't want—"

"No, you asshole," Paul said. "Of course, if you want, they're only a phone—"

"No!" we said at the same time.

"Don't worry," Paul said. "I wanted you both to be the first to know about some big news I got *right* before I left for this trip. My agent called. I made it. I got a job at ESPN."

I yelled out in big surprise, not being discreet at all: "No fucking way!"

"Yes!" Jesse said.

Jesse and I struggled to get out of our chairs, but when we did, we gave Paul high fives and embraced him. He did it. He'd achieved his dream.

"There's some minor contract stuff I need to work out, but I'm going to start off on the 2:00 a.m. *SportsCenter*, 11:00 p.m. out here, along with some field-reporting work. If things go well, I could be asked to do more prime-time reporting or host a show or something."

"That's fricking fantastic, man," I said. "We have to tell everyone."

MIHO, Rob, and Todd were sitting near one of the picnic tables, while Kyle was watering a tree. They looked over, quizzical about what Jesse and I were so excited about.

"Hey, everyone," Jesse said. "My boy Paul here has a big announcement."

"Did he get a girlfriend? That's big news," MIHO said with a laugh.

"Shut up," Paul said. "MIHO, I told your mom that although she wanted to be exclusive, multiple sexual escapades don't make a relationship. No, this isn't about any girlfriends. I'll soon be working for the Worldwide Leader in Sports."

"Duh-duh-duh. Duh-duh-duh," Jesse and MIHO sang the catch jingle at the same time.

Everyone gathered around Paul and shook hands and slapped his back in congratulations. It wasn't every day one of your friends realized their lifelong professional dream in their twenties, particularly one that was on national cable television.

I was proud of Paul. He worked hard. He often came in early and stayed late, trying to find new angles no one else could see and report them. Other local sports anchors would take their leads from the hometown newspaper, but Paul made and cultivated contacts, even when he didn't have a camera person out with him. He had his own sources within the local high schools, colleges, and even the pro squads in the cities that were hours away from his small community. In other words, while he was a goof and a horndog to us, he was a top reporter and effective anchor and deserved the respect and success he received.

"When do you move to Connecticut?" I asked as we all sat back down around the fire.

"I think the contract will start in a little over a month. Don't worry, I had my agent put in the contract the dates of your and Jesse's weddings so everyone knows I'm *not* working those weekends. As soon as we go down the hill and fly back, I'm going to KTRN to say my goodbyes, pack up, and head out. That's what's good about being a bachelor. The most valuable possessions I have are my suits. All the rest of my stuff, including my memorabilia, are at my mom's house."

I smiled, and somehow my cup was full again, as if by magic. At one point, I looked over at Jesse, who also sipped a full beverage. As the night progressed, it got harder and harder to move out of our chairs.

Later in the night, Paul looked over at me. I was staring at the fire. "How are you doing?"

"Word," was all I could say, lifting my beer and nodding.

For the rest of the night, Jesse and I just sat back and listened to all the embarrassing stories about us. There seemed to be too many stories about the fiancé that never was. We retold Jesse's first trip up here when he puked, the story about the bear and, of course, the story of Sean's condo. Jesse missed most of it. He was passed out in his chair, elbows resting on the arms, hands holding up his chin, as if he was sculpted by Rodin. The only thing keeping me vertical was staring at the fire. When in doubt, stare at the fire. The rolling purple and gold light emanating from those logs was a beautiful site. Jesse opened his eyes.

"Hey, guys, I know where the Laker colors come from," he said.

"Oh yeah? Where? They're originally from Minnesota, right?" MIHO said.

"Dude, check out the fucking log. Man. Look. Purple and gold! See?"

The sound of eight men laughing at once is a cacophony of a roar with different pitches, tones, and rhythms. There was the high pitch squeal of MIHO and the low rumble of Rob and the disbelieving "oh" of Paul. We also had the snort of Jesse, the monotone "ha-ha" of Todd and the nasally chuckle of Kyle. I added the symphonic scaling that started with a baritone chuckle and moved up to a falsetto.

The more we drank, the louder we got and I'm sure it was late. So when a man in his 40s appeared at our campsite, I wasn't surprised but I was friggin' startled.

"Excuse me," he said to no one in particular. His long hair was a mess and remnants of toothpaste flecked portions of his beard.

"Jesus Fucking Christ, who the fuck are you?" Todd screamed.

"I have the site down the road and I can hear everything," said the man, looking a little perturbed. "I've got young kids and we all need to get to sleep. Look, I was your age and I don't want to ruin your fun, but just turn it down a bit, ok. Please."

"It's a bachelor party," said Kyle and pointed to Jesse and me. "These two guys are getting married... well not to each other of course. But they're getting married we are not getting strippers. We're just camping." Clearly Kyle was drunk now too.

Paul, the most diplomatic and seemingly the most sober of the bunch, came up to the man and walked him back to the road. Leave it to Paul to save us all from doing anything inappropriate and getting reported to the camp host.

"Shit," said Todd. "The man trying to shut us down."

"Hey guys, just calm it down a bit," Rob said. "He's just trying to keep his kids innocent. We have to respect that."

"We don't have to respect shit," said Todd. "This is camping."

"C'mon," Rob raised his voice enough to get Todd's attention. "We don't want to get the camp hosts over here, so let's just bring it down a notch. We've got plenty of time and fun yet to go." Rob was trying to be the adult. I know I should also say something else too. But trying to get my words out was hard. I had a few.

"I was just want to have some fun, man!" Todd said.

"Well, I'll tell you what's not fun," Rob said. "Going home early. We've had to do that once and I want to keep this going as long as possible for our bachelors."

"Don't fuck this up!" Jesse said. His eyes were closed and he still looked passed out.

That was the inspiration everyone needed to settle things down and go to bed. I was pretty messed up. We got Jesse into his tent with his head out so he wouldn't puke inside. I told everyone I was okay, so I didn't need to sleep with my head outside my shelter. As soon as I fell into the sleeping bag on top of the air mattress, I could feel the tent begin to spin. I tried to do a count of beers I had during the day. I was up to about thirteen when I began to slow the spinning. It had been a while since I'd drunk so much, but I knew if I could just focus for a few minutes and not move, then I could fall asleep before I got sick. It worked, and I slept hard all night long.

When I unzipped my tent, I was, for once, the last one up. The air was warmer than usual, and everyone, including Jesse, was already eating breakfast.

"Look at Mr. Sleepy Head," said Kyle. "We didn't know if we needed to check on you."

I looked over at Jesse. He looked in bad shape. "How are you doing, buddy?"

"Oh, don't go near my tent. Let's just say, I'm glad you guys put my head outside."

"Ouch," I said. I poured myself a cup of coffee and grabbed some sausage to cure the hangover. It was slow going down, but it was the best I was going to get. In a half hour of silence sitting next to Jesse, I felt a lot better. What I needed was a beer, the hair of the dog, to help get me back to normal.

"Beer me up." I smiled as Kyle was close to the cooler.

Everyone laughed, which prompted Kyle to smile back. He opened the cooler and tossed me a Coors Light.

"So, organizers, what's the plan today?" I asked.

"What do you want it to be?" Rob asked Jesse and me.

"I wouldn't mind just going down to the shore and hanging out," I said. "I don't think Jesse and I are in great shape to do anything but hang low."

Jesse nodded. "Agree. Low-key today."

After breakfast, we packed up our coolers, chairs, towels, mini barbecue, hot dogs, buns, chips, other snacks, condiments, plates, cards, football, boombox, sunblock, and a dozen more little things that we "needed" and headed to the shoreline. No surprise, Kyle was the first one to jump off a rock into the frigid water.

"Oh crap, it's cold!" he said when he came up for air. He took some quick, deep breaths.

"Dude, its snow runoff," Paul said with a laugh.

As soon as Kyle moved out of the landing zone, Paul jumped in with a yell, followed by a yelp as he hit the water. The rest of us followed the same path. With the exception of Kyle, we were all in our late twenties, but were transported back to when we were twelve and the joy and thrill of harmless danger provided all we wanted in life before the insecurities of adolescence and hormones dominated our thoughts and self-consciousness.

Eventually, we were all back in our chairs, laughing, and enjoying each other's company. This was what a bachelor weekend should be. We were no longer the responsibility of our parents nor were we in full partnership with our wives. While we still had our own lives, this would be one of the last times Jesse and I would be accountable to just us and not have to worry about the consequences to our spouses, our kids, etc.

Paul got up with a beer and clinked it with his bottle opener. "So, guests of honor, these are your last moments of bachelorhood, and I have a simple question." Paul stared at Jesse and me, almost straight into our souls, like some Jedi mind trick or lie detector. "Why the *fuck* are you getting married?"

Everyone laughed. Jesse and I knew this was coming. As the first married guys, we were going to be the subjects of ridicule. Still, I was confident in my answer, so I went first.

"Look, I love her, plain and simple," I said to groans. "She's someone I trust completely. I feel at home and ready to take on the world. I want to be that support for her as well, and I can see us together when we're eighty watching TV or walking to get coffee or just enjoying life."

Paul rolled his eyes. I didn't know what he expected. Of course, I was going to be classy. I wasn't going to provide any sexual details. Afterward Jesse gave a similar answer, but he threw a little meat to the wolves by adding his preference for screamers. That drew some cheers and bottle clinking. I guess we needed some misogyny at a bachelor party.

"What about the bridesmaids?" Rob said. "Anyone we should know about?"

"Danielle's maid of honor is pretty hot, and I bet she'll look good in a bridesmaid dress," Jesse said.

"I'd bet that dress would look better on the floor, hay-oh!" Rob retorted.

Ah, male bonding and boorishness were alive and well.

"Dude, just as long as I get dibs on Jim's sister, the lovely Dr. Katie in Florida," Paul said. "I've been dreaming of that redhead since she was a freshman."

"Touch her and die," I said, half serious. Paul wouldn't dream of hooking up with my sister...I think. "Plus, MIHO's mom will also be there."

"Well, then it's a lock," Paul said. "MIHO, don't expect her to come to brunch the next morning."

"Fuck you," MIHO said.

It was a great afternoon. Todd had brought his guitar and started playing. Jesse said he was good, but I was impressed by his vast and eclectic catalog. He played, Garth Brooks, Johnny Cash, Van Halen, AC/DC, Guns 'N Roses and even some of his songs. We must have been there for about six hours before we decided to head back to the campsite. MIHO outdid himself again with "drunken chicken," or its cruder name "beer-up-the-butt chicken." It was a great base for another night of drinking and poker. I didn't have high expectations for my chances. I'd lost money to Kyle a couple times and watched MIHO clean up at some poker tournaments in college. Because Todd organized this activity, bringing out a silver case of poker chips, I assumed he was pretty good too.

"Buy in is twenty dollars," said Todd, who organized this part of the bachelor party. "We're playing Texas Hold'em. We'll start with fifty-cent, one-dollar, and three-dollar chips. Seven's a little big for one table, but we'll make it work."

"Love it," said Kyle. "I look forward to taking all your money."

MIHO groaned and rolled his eyes, and Rob and I both chuckled. I think MIHO expressed everyone's reaction, but Kyle didn't see it. I might as well have just thrown my twenty into the pot and left. It would have been less frustrating. It wasn't long before I stepped away and got everyone a beer.

Soon, Rob joined me, and we went to the fire.

Rob said put his hand on my shoulder. "Hey, are you having a good time, Mr. Bachelor?"

"Of course. All my favorite people are here celebrating this time of my life with me. I'm so glad you guys organized it this way. This is much better than going to Vegas or Reno."

"Good. MIHO and I thought about it, but this way we all stay together and keep Paul out of trouble."

Kyle whooped and yelled. "Take that, bitches!" He pulled the chips toward him.

"If you can keep Kyle in check," Rob said. "I think MIHO may break his nose before the trip is finished. And if he doesn't, I might."

"I know. He's a bit...intense. But he can be a pretty nice guy. I've never seen him this bad. Maybe it's a little immaturity mixed with alcohol and the fact that he's not around his family, except me."

Paul and Jesse pushed away from the table, leaving MIHO, Todd, and Kyle. We all worked our way over to the picnic table and positioned ourselves behind the three remaining players. I was behind MIHO, who was playing from behind. He had to make risks and bluffs in order to get back in the game, but that also put him in a dangerous position to lose it all. On MIHO's final hand, he put it all on the table.

It was a small stack compared to Todd and Kyle's, but if he won now, he'd be back in the game. The moment was tense. The spectators tried not to give away anything, and we covered our mouths and shielded our eyes as best we could. MIHO turned his cards over, showing a full house, a hard hand to beat. He let out a smile. Todd flipped his cards over and had the two of hearts and the five of hearts to give him a flush, which didn't beat MIHO's full house. Kyle smiled and flipped his cards over, revealing two tens, four of a kind.

"Yeah, baby!" Kyle yelled with a whoop. "Someone get a fucking beer for the Tin Cup Tourney champion and soon-to-be poker champion."

Kyle raked in his chips, which now gave him a good advantage over Todd. MIHO stepped back from the table. I looked at him and could see his anger.

He walked to me and leaned in for a whisper. "How could the parents who raised sweet Tracey also raise such an ass like Kyle? I'm about to dick-sand him."

Over the past few years, we had grown fond of using *dick-sand* to describe what we'd like to do to someone who pissed us off. Neither of had a specific description of the act. Was it a body slam? A tackle from behind? But looking at MIHO's eyes, he wasn't joking. Todd didn't last much longer, and soon he too pushed all his chips forward. When Kyle called and turned over his hand to reveal a full house, Kyle's grin turned wide, almost evil.

"That's it, baby!" Kyle jumped up, pumped his fists in the air, and let out a loud whoop. "That's for all the haters."

The tension Kyle caused was palpable. Everyone just walked away as he ran around the campsite. When he got to the cooler, he drained the beer in his cup, stood over it, and yelled, "I'm thirsty!"

I exhaled. This wasn't good. Even Rob was irritated. Many times, he'd let things go, but he wasn't keen on cutting the trip short at the hospital or jail. He stood and seemed to expand into a giant. I'd always known him as my friend and not a defensive lineman. But when he stood and beefed himself up, he looked larger than life. All eyes were on him when he joined Kyle at the cooler. Rob stared at Kyle with intensity, opened the cooler, pulled out a beer, and slammed the lid shut. He opened the beer and poured it into Kyle's cup, his eyes focused on Kyle. As Rob finished, he pulled Kyle close to him and said in a low, calm voice, "Look, Kyle, we're going to calm the *fuck* down and be good campers. We're going to still have fun for our boys Jim and Jesse. You're going to calm the fuck down. I'll put you down if I have to. And I'm not fucking around. We're camping, dammit."

There was silence… for an eternity. Then I could hear Paul giggle, followed by Jesse. We all looked over at the two of them standing by the campfire. They were trying to hold in their giggles the best they could. But as we all looked at them, they let out a laughter they couldn't hold back. We were all wondering what they were laughing at.

"Don't be fucking around," Paul said through his laughs. "We're…camping…*goddammit!*" He yelled the last part through laughs that made us all giggle, including Rob.

"I mean, fucking around and camping go hand in hand," said Jesse with a laugh. "Heaven forbid we fuck around and camp at the same time. Otherwise, we *dee*-serve what's coming to us"

Rob tried to look serious, but he bit his lip. Then he broke and joined in the laughter, and the tension dropped. Kyle, who feared Rob, nodded and went to Todd. He gave him a congratulatory handshake, offering that it was the hardest game of poker he'd ever played. Kyle behaved for the rest of night. He even got up to fill his own beer and offered to pick up beers for others. MIHO also calmed down, but he hit the bottle of Jack hard. I guess Kyle's competitiveness had affected him. The alcohol had done a number on me again, and I went back to my tent. As I fell asleep, I could hear Paul describing how he'd hooked up with two sisters on a train from Chicago to St. Louis. I hadn't heard that one before, but soon I fell asleep.

The next morning, I was up at daylight. There is never a quiet way to get out of bed on a camping trip. Between the plastic squawk of an air mattress adjusting to shifting weight, the whine of a zipper opening and closing, a tent and the inevitable grunt of moving a hungover body, I tried to be as quiet as I could. I didn't want to wake up MIHO. I looked over, but he wasn't sleeping in the tent. I guessed he was already up, but when I looked over the campsite, he wasn't around. No matter, an early morning view of the lake was needed to reflect to take stock of the life I'd had and the adventure I was about to begin. I grabbed my cigarettes, a Gatorade, and Pop-Tarts and began the trek down to the lake where I heard some voices.

"Hey, MIHO, you down here?" I asked as I continued on. When I got to the lakeshore, I saw MIHO and Todd on the river's edge. Todd was putting bait on a fishing line. MIHO was sitting on the ground, his pants dirty, and he looked a little flush, like a child who'd been caught playing with matches.

"Are you okay?" I asked

"Yeah, just a little too much to drink last night. I'm not feeling too good."

"Understand that. Thank goodness I didn't hit it as hard yesterday."

I looked out onto the lake and marveled at the trees and sky reflected on the water. I took a puff of my cigarette and had my own reflection on life today versus six years ago. Instead of lamenting a break up, I was admiring my fiancé. Even with her faults, I had come to appreciate her because it's what made me love her more.

"You guys are up early," I said. "Couldn't sleep?"

"I just got up, got my rod, and came to the lake and saw MIHO was already here," he said. "No luck yet, but there's hope."

"Jesse said you liked to fish. He also said you played the guitar, but man you're really good. How long have you been playing?"

"Since high school. I once had dreams of making it big like everyone else."

"I'm sure it's really hard."

"You have no idea. Los Angeles is full of people who are looking for a break. Actors, musicians, even techs. But there's only so much of that pie, you know?"

I nodded. I looked over at MIHO, whose hands were clasped over his head. Man, I guess he did drink too much. Todd cast his line out into the lake again.

"It's funny, when my buddies and I left Arizona to make a go of it, my mom forced me to take practical classes like computer programming. Well, six months into failing, the band broke up, I found out I liked coding and here I am. I still play some coffee houses here and there. It's a good release."

"And you met Jesse and Danielle at your work?"

"Oh yeah. As you know, I got them together, I invited the office to one of my gigs at a coffeehouse and they were the only ones who showed. They sat and flirted the whole time and didn't even hear my gig. But before long, they were dating."

"I've only met her a couple of times. She seems pretty cool, but pretty driven."

"Danielle can be a real ballbuster. She's going to be one hell of an attorney, but when you watch Jesse with her, her demeanor just seems to relax. He adores her. They're going to do well together. I can tell."

I smiled. I was so happy for Jesse. Since we lived so far, I didn't know Danielle that well, but to hear Todd's confidence in their relationship gave me a lot of comfort that we were both going to be okay. After sitting at the shore for a while, Todd conceded he wasn't going to get any bites, and we all returned to the site so MIHO could set up his kitchen for breakfast.

One by one, the rest of the group came out. MIHO made a massive amount of French toast and thick bacon, complete with powdered sugar, butter, and syrup. If I didn't know better, I'd have thought this was a breakfast from a top-flight restaurant.

We had full stomachs as we headed to the beach and set up our pop-up shelters away from all of the families. Jesse and I needed to get the blood flowing. We picked up the football and tossed it back and forth at the far end of the beach.

"Man, this is more than I expected," I said to Jesse. "I was thinking what we always do, just sit and drink, watch Paul work his magic, make fun of MIHO, and call it a weekend. It's only Saturday."

"I know. I feel I should be on my way home. But this is awesome. I think the golf made the difference. Playing a round and having a couple on the course just put us in the right space."

"Sure did," I said.

Before we went back to the group, MIHO said he had to head back to the campsite to prep lunch. Todd agreed to help, and we all gave them crap for leaving so soon.

"We just ate! That lunch had better be good if he's leaving my bachelor party to prep," I said to Rob. He just smiled.

I turned to see what he was seeing. On the other end of the beach was a group of five girls. Paul and Kyle were drooling like wolves in a Tex Winter cartoon. Their reaction was warranted, and I thought our group may fracture before the afternoon was complete. I watched Paul's mind turn through endless internal calculations and scenarios, working out the right way to pick up these women. His eyes caught an idea and grew wide. He came over to Jesse and me and put his arms around us and led us to our pop-up tent.

"Gentlemen, as the guests of honor at this bachelor party, you also have the privilege of being the ultimate wingmen. Boys, you have nothing to lose. If you get rejected, no sweat. You weren't interested anyway. You just need to introduce us."

I looked back at him with mock disdain. Were we just props for Paul's enjoyment?

"Introduce you?" I asked. "I don't know them. How am I supposed to introduce you?"

"Find a way," Paul said. "I trust you." He smiled and slapped my back.

Jesse and I looked at each other. Well, we did have no fear of rejection. In fact, we were courting rejection, which was quite liberating. All we had to do was introduce Paul and Kyle. Jesse shrugged, and I gave a look back of indifference and decided to walk toward these girls with Horndog A and Horndog B behind us.

Whereas we had our E-Z UP tent to provide shade, these girls were content to court skin cancer. They were from UCLA with Bruins logos emblazoned on a bag, a cup or towel. They were at least six years younger than us, maybe even more. Two of them were blonde, one had red hair, while another seemed to be of Asian descent, and another was Latina.

As we approached, three of them ignored us while two others looked up with annoyance. I was sure they'd been approached by several men in just the few minutes since they'd arrived, or they were expecting to as the afternoon went along. Even though we were both going in expecting likely humiliation, I felt like a total jackass for bothering them. However, we were already too far into this farce to turn back. Jesse and I looked at each other to see who'd embarrass himself first.

"Hello, ladies," Jesse said. "How are ya'll doing?"

"Good." One of the blondes looked up from her magazine, irritated.

"Great," Jesse said. "Look, my buddy Jim and I are going to be brutally honest. This is our bachelor party. We're here with those other jokers over there. See?"

They all turned their heads like a bunch of meerkats surveying the Savannah. The joke was purely on us as the guys were all covering their mouths or turning away to hide their hilarity at our expense. Paul was staring at us with his usual smolder. Either he had a poker face he hadn't used last night, or he thought this gambit could actually work.

"Anyway," Jesse went on, "as the attached guys, we had nothing to lose, so they pushed us over here to invite you over for beers."

Three of them returned to books or magazines or their naps. One of the blondes was amused, and the Asian one was interested to see what the blonde was going to do. That look scared me. Did we just poke a hornet's nest?

"Oh really?" said the blonde. "And who are they?" Nodding to Paul and Kyle.

Paul was still staring. Kyle was next to him, his smile wide and toothy.

"Paul's the biggest coward," Jesse said, pointing. "He's the one who sent us over. Kyle's Jim's future brother-in-law."

"Is that right?" the blonde asked. She turned to the Asian-American girl. "Dena, they sent the married guys over here to do the heavy lifting. That's so wrong."

"Right, that's what we think," I said, turning to her. "I mean, we *are* the bachelors!"

"Exactly. Jennifer, we should teach all these boys a lesson," Dena said. She came up to me and looked me up and down with a beer in her hand. "You're cute too. Your future wife is a lucky woman."

"Thanks," I said. "I'm the lucky one."

"Aww, how sweet," Dena said. She had a mischievous look on her face. "Now, I'm going to play with them a little. Don't worry, I'm not going to do anything wild. I'm just going to whisper in your ear to make them go crazy, got it?"

I nodded and gulped. Dena took another sip of her Corona and came up next to me. I could feel her bikini-clad breast against my chest. It took all my self-control not to pop a boner right there. She leaned in, said "Watch this," then bit my ear. The other girls let out a wild "Woooooooooo!"

Jennifer spoke up, loud enough for the whole beach to hear. "Tell your friends, we're not interested! We aren't meat to be conquered. If your buddies think they can charm us with some far-off stares and a gimmick, they must be little boys not worth our time. We're not interested. This is a girl's weekend."

There was a loud "whoop" of agreement before Jennifer concluded. "And they shouldn't be putting you guys out as bait either. Asshole move. You may want to reconsider your friends."

Well, we kind of deserved that, but how dare they tell me who my friends should or shouldn't be. Jesse was about to turn back and defend the guys, but I put a hand on his shoulder and kept him moving forward. Better to take the humiliation and walk back with our tail between our legs than try to start a war on the beach. Besides, I could still feel Dena's lips and teeth on my earlobe, and if I turned back, I might reveal the stiffy in my swim trunks.

When we returned, Paul remained stoic.

"So, it's going to be a challenge," Paul said.

"I don't think they're interested. They called you guys assholes for using us as bait," Jesse said.

"They want to party. They just might not know it yet," Paul said.

Kyle was the only one encouraged by Paul's proclamation. But Paul surprisingly changed course, shook his head and looked at us. "It's Jim and Jesse's weekend. Bros before hoes. Let's give our bachelors a little extra love. Make sure they have drinks in their cups and prime seating for the good food coming."

Jesse and I went from pickup errand boys to kings in a matter of minutes. The guys set up Todd's elite fold-up chairs with footrests and extra-large cup holders for us. They filled our drinks. Jesse and I sat back and enjoyed the moment.

I turned to Jesse. "I hope MIHO and Todd get here soon with the food. I'm starving."

"Same here," Jesse said. "I wonder what kind of meal needs this kind of preparation."

"Whatever, it is, I hope it comes soon. Chips and pretzels and beer can only do so much. I need protein."

Five minutes later, I heard a honk, and there was Todd and MIHO arriving in Todd's truck. Thank goodness. I got out of Todd's comfy chair with a grunt. I was only twenty-seven, but I felt I was getting older by the minute. I'd noticed that endless feasts and beer didn't burn off quite like it had before. Like Rob, my metabolism had slowed. Looking around, only Paul and Kyle didn't have the beginnings of mini beer guts. I suppose, at some point, we would have to change lifestyles, but for the time being, give me a beer and some Funyuns.

When MIHO and Todd brought three large aluminum serving trays onto the beach and placed them on the card table, the rest of the guys cheered and licked their lips.

"What's underneath?" I asked.

Everyone ignored me. Jesse and I were the only ones in the dark. MIHO brought out more aluminum trays, plates, forks, knives, and napkins.

"You guys took forever," I said.

"We thought a special beach lunch would be perfect for your bachelor party," MIHO said, getting ready for the big reveal. He milked the anticipation, then pulled off the aluminum foil. Underneath were ten lobster tails, potatoes, corn cobs, and onions. In another tray was tri-tip, grilled to perfection. "Here's your surf-and-turf lunch on the beach. Lobster and tri-tip."

Jesse and I were dumbfounded, and the rest of the guys cheered and celebrated MIHO and Todd. MIHO also brought over melted butter and a mild cocktail sauce for those who wanted it. In my opinion, it didn't need it. Everything was so delicious. We pumped up the Bob Marley on the boom box.

MIHO looked over and said, "We wanted to do something special. Soon, you'll be settling for meatloaf and casseroles. But today and tonight, we feast!"

This trip had exceeded all expectations. At some point, I wanted to step back and observe from afar. Well, to be honest, I wanted a cigarette. I stepped back about twenty yards from our spot and pulled out my lighter and lit one and took a glorious drag. My timing couldn't have been better. If we were in a Michael Bay movie, a soaring rock score would be blasting as the UCLA girls walked in slow motion toward us with the appropriate amount of sunlight and sweat shine hitting their bodies. Instead, they crossed between me and the guys on their way to the point or the bathroom. While they ignored the guys, Jennifer and Dena looked at me and smiled. Dena even blew me a kiss. After they passed, I looked over to the other guys staring from our pop-up tent. Kyle shook his head, Paul continued to look determined. MIHO and Todd just laughed. When the girls passed by again on their way back to their spot, Jennifer and Dena stopped and talked to me.

"So, what were you all eating over there?" Jennifer said. "It seemed you were having a sausage fest."

"My buddy, who's this awesome cook, made us this lobster boil," I said. "Never had anything like it. It was spectacular."

"Damn," Jennifer said. "Maybe your buddies should have led with that instead of a couple married guys...no offense."

"None taken." I smiled and took a puff of my cigarette.

"Do you have an extra?" Dena asked, nodding to the cigarette.

"Of course."

"Ugh, I hate it when you smoke," Jennifer said. "Come back when you're done."

As Jennifer walked away, Dena rolled her eyes and smiled at me.

I tapped a cigarette out of the pack and handed it to her. She bent down as I flicked on my zippo for her, giving me a look at her perfect cleavage. If my leering was creepy, she didn't remark. I refocused my efforts on lighting her cigarette.

"Thanks," she said as she took her first drag. "I was really craving a smoke since I got here. My boyfriend doesn't like it when I do."

"Tell me about it," I said. It was true. Tracey wanted me to quit before the wedding. Dena asked about the wedding and how I met Tracey. I asked how her friends knew each other. She and her friends were roommates at UCLA, and Jennifer said this was a good place to get away from the city. It was cool, not too many people, and beautiful. They had all agreed not to even look at guys this weekend.

"You don't understand," Dena said. "We get hit on all...the...time. Especially when we're all in a group. And then some of us want to hang out, while others don't, and then it's total drama. So, no guys."

"So why are you smoking with me?" I asked.

"You're getting married, silly," she said with a flirty tone. "You're safe. No drama with you. Plus, I have a boyfriend. Well, kinda."

"What do you mean?"

"We've been together for about six months, but he's kinda like one of your friends over there, the really good-looking one. He thinks he's the center of the universe. It gets tiring."

I smiled, electric with the attention I was receiving. I could just breathe her in. While I was confirmed and dedicated to Tracey, I was intoxicated by Dena's presence. She was tiny and couldn't have weighed more than a hundred pounds. Some may have considered our conversation a little flirtatious, but I wasn't going to do anything, and she wasn't going to try to tempt me.

"Well, I better get back," she said. "Even married guys have their limits, right?"

"Yep," I said.

"Thanks for the cigarette. We're quitting after this weekend, right?"

"Exactly."

"All right, I'll hold you to it," Dena said as she walked back to her group. She looked back at least twice as she did.

"What was *that* about?" Rob asked. Paul was equally intrigued.

"She just wanted a cigarette," I said, trying to dismiss the implication. "And she has a boyfriend. She told me they have a no-guys pact on this trip. They say they get drama whenever they start talking to guys in a group."

Paul's interest waned. "Oh well. Sometimes the Big Paul pheromones aren't the right bait to catch the big fish. No worries. We're here. We're with my boys, and we're all having a good time, right?"

As the afternoon began to wane, I looked over and saw Dena, Jennifer, and their friends start to pack up. A hint of disappointment crossed the guys' faces. I don't think even Paul's Hail Mary hand signals he had used the first year would work this time. Yet, right before they left, Dena came over to our tent. She smiled to everyone, pushed her black hair away from her face, then gave me a sexy, pouty face.

"Would you mind if had another cigarette?"

"Of course, but this is it, you have to quit. *We* have to quit. We're quitting buddies. We can't be that if we keep smoking. We have to be accountable to each other."

She took the cigarette and the light. "Yeah, it's good to have friends with benefits," she said and winked.

Rob, Jon, and Jesse glanced over. I was speechless.

"Are you guys going to the saloon tonight?" Paul asked. One more Hail Mary.

"Yeah, we'll be there," Dena replied. "It's the first time we'll be twenty-one together. I just had my birthday last week."

"Well, happy birthday!" Paul said. "We'll be sure to be there so we can sing happy birthday to you and give one more official toast to the bachelors here."

Dena laughed and smiled at me. Her eyes suggested more. "Sure. Gotta celebrate one of your last nights of freedom, right?"

Dena's friends had finished packing up the car and waved for Dena to finish up.

"Looks like I've gotta go," Dena said. "See you guys tonight, but listen, don't be jerks. Just hang out. No expectations, okay?"

"Sure," Kyle said. "Scout's honor."

She jogged to the car, and I tried to look elsewhere, but it was hard to not follow her with my eyes.

"Oh, damn," Paul said. "It's *on*."

"You heard her. Her friends just want to hang with no expectations."

"Oh, I wasn't talking about them," Paul said. "I was talking about Dena. She's totally into you, brother. She must like your silly goatee. Anyway, be careful, and let me know if you need me to pull her away."

I shook my head. I was feeling uncomfortable about the situation. "Let's just head back. We have an epic game of liar dice awaiting us at the bar."

We packed up and returned to the site for our typical spigot sponge baths and extra application of deodorant to help make ourselves presentable. The leftover lobster boil, which had been placed on ice, made for a perfect cocktail for our dinner.

When we walked in, the saloon was busy. Rob had a full bag of dice and a stack of solo cups. We found two tables in the middle to push together for our epic game. As promised, Dena and her friends arrived. Dena waved to me, and Jennifer gave a wink. Otherwise, they ignored our group. I was both disappointed and relieved that they weren't joining us. Kyle was crestfallen, but Paul ignored them back.

"I thought you wanted to try to pick them up again," I said to Paul between a game.

"This is a guy's weekend! Bros before hos, right? Besides, if they want to hang out, they'll come to us because we're having so much fun."

I was surprised. Restraint wasn't Paul's strongest suit, but maybe he was maturing. It was just as well—three guys closer to their age approached them at the bar. They smiled, somewhat indifferent to this new attention.

"As the pack of females sip sustenance," said Todd with an Australian crocodile-hunter accent, "the male species invade the female pack, sniffing and roaring their approval. This is the first step in the complicated mating ritual. If the first step is successful, the males will present the females with an elixir that makes them more agreeable to the ritual."

I was amused by Todd's audition for the Discovery Channel when I felt a tap on my shoulder. I turned to see Dena, who was as bubbly as ever. Now dressed in jeans and a flannel over a tank top, she was even more stunning. I had to take a quick breath. Jennifer was with her.

"Hey, what's up?" I asked.

"My friends broke our pact," Dena said. "After all that, they want to flirt, and we thought, why not hang with the bachelors? See? Drama."

"Well, their loss," Paul said. "Join us, we're playing some liars dice."

"Sure," Jennifer said, sitting next to Paul. MIHO gave up his seat between Jennifer and me and left to sit next to Todd. Dena sat down next to me, and I looked at MIHO. He was supposed to protect me.

"I don't know how to play," Dena said.

I took a moment to explain the rules. The object of the game is to bluff or call a bluff on the amount of dice on the table and hidden under everyone's cups. The guesses progress as they move around the table until one is forced to call. With each call, a die is discarded, and the last player with dice wins. Dena still didn't understand and sipped her White Russian. Before long, she was down to her final die.

"The trick is to get the call to move beyond you, not to call or get called," I said. "It's the least risky move."

"I like risky, though," she said. She winked and slid her hand underneath my arm and put her head on my shoulder. I didn't want her to do this. But I also enjoyed the attention. Why not?

She was looking great, and between her and the alcohol, it was hard to concentrate.

Soon she was out and watched the rest of us. She cheered when I won a challenge and gave me a pouty face when I lost. The more she sipped, the more she flirted. I looked over at MIHO to help me out, but he was talking to Todd. Jesse gave me a look imploring me to be careful. I wasn't doing anything to encourage this affection. I also wasn't shooing her away. She continued to squeeze my knee or brush my thigh. Another drink and she may get even bolder.

During the third game, I lost early and excused myself to go have a smoke. Todd and MIHO also lost, and we got up from the table together. As we exited the bar, I turned toward the designated smoking area near the bathroom. They turned toward the parking lot and the lake.

"Where are you two going?" I asked.

"To the beach to check out the stars," said MIHO. "It's pretty cool to see the Milky Way up here. Dude, you have to be careful with Dena. She looks like she's about to blow you under the table. Maybe just sit in one of our seats when you get back."

"Good idea. Todd, the stars up here are pretty impressive. No light pollution. Thinner air. It's awe-inspiring."

Todd smiled and gave me a thumbs-up.

I ran my hand through my hair, squeezing my scalp. I puffed a little more on my cigarette wondering what I was going to do to keep my sanity. I looked through a tiny window that showed a clear view of Dena. She was looking at me with a sexy look of desire. If Tracey wasn't awaiting me with a white dress and a future, man, I would have been doing some pleasurable things.

I watched MIHO and Todd walk into the darkness and turned back and saw Dena.

"I knew you'd be out here sneaking a cigarette," she said, taking the cigarette from my hand and putting it in her mouth. After a breath, she said, "What happened to accountability and being friends with benefits?"

I gulped. She smiled and giggled. I motioned that I had to use the restroom and turned and headed that way. Oh my god. What the hell was happening? I entered the small restroom and relieved a few pints of beer, splashed water on my face. I unlocked the bathroom, and Dena was right there. She pushed inside, closed the door, then pulled me down to kiss her.

Her mouth tasted of White Russian, and it was intoxicating. Thoughts flashed through my head. *No one would know. It's my bachelor party. This never happens to me. This is amazing. What if I get caught? What would I tell Tracey? How can I be faithful in the long haul if I let this happen? Oh, wow, she's hot. I love Tracey. I love Tracey.*

"Hey, stop," I said, just as she was putting her hand down my pants. I pulled away. She looked at me with desire, biting her lip. God, she looked hot. "I can't do this."

"Oh, come on, nobody would know. I won't tell anyone. Let's just fool around and then go back. It's your bachelor party. That beautiful penis needs one more tug before it's devoted to one girl. Don't you want me?"

It took every bit of myself, and I mean *every single fucking bit*, not to go for it. I took another breath. I couldn't do this. I knew in my weaker moments for the next fifty years I'd look back and wonder why I didn't take her up on the offer. Instead, I kissed her on the forehead.

"Sorry, Dena, only one woman can have me. I can't do this. I really want to, but I can't." I unlocked the door and opened it for her. When I opened the door, Paul was there.

"What? Hey!" I said, surprised and guilty. "Um, nothing's going on here."

"Damn right, nothing's going on here," Paul said. "It's time Dena returns to her friends and we head back to the campsite."

Paul grabbed my collar and pulled me out of the bathroom, leaving Dena standing in front of the sink. He continued to push me along the side of the saloon. Rob, Jesse, and Kyle were standing just outside and looked as surprised as I did.

"What's going on?" Kyle asked.

"Nothing. Our boy didn't need my help," Paul said. "He made the right choice."

"What?" Rob said. He looked behind me, and I suspected he saw Dena.

"How did you even know?" I asked.

"I told you she wanted you," Paul said. "I thought you'd just flirt and blow her off. But when she went out for a cigarette, her friend Jennifer told me that Dena was planning to get in your pants. I knew if she was successful, your guilt would destroy everything, including your future marriage. As soon as she followed you to the bathroom, I got up and went after you."

"Thanks. I feel like shit," I said, and the wave of guilt overwhelmed me. How did I lead her on? Why didn't I just tell her no at the beach?

"Hey, you're human," Paul said. "You did the right thing."

"Still. How. Could I risk what I have with Tracey for a few minutes?"

Oh my god. What would I tell Tracey? I put my hands on my knees and felt like hyperventilating.

Jesse put his hand on my back. "It's okay, man, you didn't do anything."

"I kissed her," I said.

"No, she kissed you," Paul said.

"I kissed her back."

"But you stopped. You stopped her," Rob said.

The guilt didn't end. *What have I done? How did I almost something so stupid? What would Tracey think if I told her? Should I tell her? What would happen if I did? Oh, fuck. I'm so royally fucked. How can I look at her the next time I see her?*

I just needed to see MIHO and talk it over with him. Because of Audrey, I knew how it felt to be betrayed like this, and he always had a way of showing me the big picture and helping me think through larger things.

"I'm going to head to the beach. MIHO and Todd are checking out the sky," I said.

"We'll come with you," Rob said.

"No. I need some time to walk this off. Thank you. And thanks, Paul."

"I didn't do anything. You stopped it on your own."

As I walked down the dark road toward the beach, I realized I'd made these small poor choices that forced me to make a big unnecessary choice under duress. I could have gone the other way, save for a moment of clarity. At that moment, I looked up to see the vast expanse of the Milky Way unobstructed by light and the earth's atmosphere. In a way, it was comforting. Only in darkness can you see the truth. My ego had led me to believe that I somehow deserved this momentary pleasure, but it would have only led me to a dark oblivion. However, the truth was that Tracey was my light that snuffed out the darkness.

I turned my attention back to the dark road toward the beach and the pier and the best spot for stargazing. Todd and MIHO had made a great choice. It was a perfect night to see the stars. As I walked toward the pier, I heard some sounds like male voices, but it didn't sound like words. I walked toward them. As I got closer, they sounded more like moans.

"Hey, MIHO, Todd, are you guys over there?" I said.

"Oh shit!" MIHO said, and the little light showed one form shifting to two.

"What the hell's going on?" I said.

My mind started racing, and then I realized MIHO's secret.

9

MIHO

Friday Morning

June 24, 2016

Not the best way to come out," MIHO said as he closed the notebook. "I wanted to get each of you alone because it was awkward enough without Kyle around. And Jim was hardly ever by himself to talk about it."

"Well, and you were busy with Todd," Jesse said.

MIHO nodded and dropped into his deck chair next to the horseshoe pit. He laid the notebook on the cooler situated between he and Jesse as they watched Paul and Rob play the first game of horseshoes. He lifted his water to his lips and took a sip. His mouth was parched from verbalizing the pages and reliving a difficult moment in his life.

"Yeah, that was a weird evening," Paul said. "First, that girl sexually assaulted Jim, and I thought that would be the big drama of the night. Then, Jim comes racing back with you and Todd close behind. He was so shocked."

"Looking back, he acted kinda shitty," MIHO said. "Granted, I wanted to come out another way, but I wanted him to be there for me. Instead, he ran away."

"Well, in his defense, he was already upset about what had just happened in the bathroom and whether or not he'd betrayed Tracey," Rob said. "And then he's hit with that bombshell. It could have been a little much for him to process."

"Yeah, he was clueless, and it was a surprise, but it wasn't an excuse for how he acted," MIHO said. "He just left and walked away and refused to talk to me."

The whole episode was a painful third-party treatment of his coming out. The subtext was laced in throughout the entire weekend, culminating on the beach. It was remarkable how his life was just below the surface of Jim's description of the trips.

While in high school, MIHO didn't know about his feelings for other men. He talked about girls for much of his youth and even had a girlfriend for a brief time his senior year. In truth, he was kind of agnostic about women. As he began college and his career, he found that the ideas and fantasies he had expressed about women with his friends, he was having about some of the men he had met. Even then, he didn't act out on his feelings until he moved to San Diego. He first kissed a man after a late night of drinking with friends. Soon afterward, he began accompanying some of his gay friends to Hillcrest in San Diego.

Still, he kept it secret from others at work, his mom, and of course his high school friends, with whom he had his closest relationships. He thought about bringing it up so many times over the years, but he always remembered the homophobic undertones and innuendo they had shared. It made him that much more nervous about coming out to them. What if the people with whom he had shared his life, rejected him?

For years, he danced between feeling shame, guilt, and martyrdom that he somehow deserved this pain. This devolved into an endless string of casual flings of no consequence, which then multiplied his self-loathing. Even when he met someone for whom he had romantic feelings, he thought the sexual relationship kept them from having emotional intimacy. He couldn't understand how Paul kept being a "player" without feeling devalued.

Right before the bachelor party, MIHO's mom visited him in San Diego. By this time, he'd had a couple healthy relationships that gave him the confidence and the assurance that this was who he was. He felt ready to come out and had the self-confidence that he could handle whatever the reaction. He took his mom to a nice restaurant. Even though he had an idea of her reaction, his face was white, and his palms were so sweaty that he clasped the napkin the entire time. When he got around to saying it, he almost hyperventilated. He was close to retreating and transitioning to some other topic when his mom placed her hand on his and smiled. "It's okay, David. I think I know and have known for a while. And I love you and always will."

MIHO smiled. Her reassurance was comforting. "But I have to say it."

She kept her hand on his. "David, I know. It's okay. I'm here."

"I'm gay. I like men," he said. As soon as he said it, MIHO felt a load of pressure lift. He had heard from others that coming out was a freeing experience. He thought it was just a cliché, but there he was. He felt the exhilaration of being himself for the first time in front of his mother. They stayed in that restaurant for three hours. There were tears, but he didn't care who saw them. His mother asked if he had told Jim and his other friends, and then he felt the weight return. He shook his head. Their adolescence and young adulthood had revolved around male bonding and testosterone. He couldn't be sure how they would react. MIHO's mom expressed confidence that he could tell his friends and that they would love him regardless. If they didn't, then they weren't his friends. She also told him that they may be shocked, but they would be there for him.

He preferred to come out to all of them at once in person, but when Rob had suggested making the trip a bachelor party, he realized it could be a little complicated. He just couldn't make the announcement to all of them, plus Kyle and Todd, at once. He figured it would be easier to speak with each of them throughout the weekend. Even that didn't seem to work. There was Paul's own announcement and Jim and Jesse getting drunk the first night, the irritation he felt for Kyle and, of course, Todd.

Todd. There was nothing special about him, but hanging out on the lake shore on Friday, MIHO started to wonder. As he played the guitar, there were moments when MIHO would catch Todd looking at him. They talked a little while he made dinner, and then came poker. He kept looking at Todd and Kyle for tells, but with every glance, MIHO felt a subtle flirtation. He thought at first it was frustration with Kyle, but he was also agitated that he was becoming attracted to someone on the trip. MIHO needed to dull his feelings, so he pulled out the bottle of Jack Daniels and made several stiff Jack and Cokes.

After Jim had gone to bed, MIHO went to use the restroom. On the trail back to the campsite, he passed Todd, who pulled him in close and stole a kiss. The surprise was thrilling. It started soft and increased in intensity. For fifteen minutes, they groped and felt their energy become kinetic, and they may have dropped to the ground in the shadows if not for Rob lumbering down the trail toward them. Instead, they separated, and Todd suggested they get up early and go "fishing" the next morning.

MIHO didn't sleep well. Beyond the spinning, he was caught between feeling he was betraying his friends by sneaking around and excitement for that stolen kiss. Finally, he had his own camping trip story. He resolved he would have a little fun and then pull them aside at the beach. He got up at dawn before Jim and met Todd next to the lake. Todd was fishing and when MIHO approached, Todd put his pole down, moved to him and resumed their kiss. They moved to a rock and sat and groped each other before Jim called after them from up the hill. Todd scurried up and grabbed his pole while MIHO dusted himself off. MIHO felt sick with shame and regret. He was supposed to be coming out to his best friend, not sneaking around behind his back.

Throughout Saturday, MIHO had opportunities to stop things with Todd, but it felt better and easier to be wanted than to reveal his secret and admit his deception. So, he just isolated with Todd, stealing opportunities to be with him, from cooking lunch to swimming. He was so preoccupied with Todd and avoiding his truth that he didn't notice the dangerous flirtation between Jim and Dena.

By the time Jim caught them on the dark beach that night, MIHO was numb. His relief of not having to hide anymore was overwhelmed by the cowardice and remorse for having his friends find out his secret like this. Though it was dark, he could feel Jim's disappointment and judgment. After finding them and asking what was going on, Jim just turned and walked away. MIHO and Todd quickly dressed before they scurried back to the lodge. When they got to the parking lot, Jim gathered the rest of the guys and they headed to the truck. Rob had looked at MIHO with a look of "What the hell?"

"That was an awkward drive back," Rob said. He and Paul were retrieving their horseshoes, clanging them together to knock off the dirt and getting ready for their next throws. "I still remember it. Jim was looking out the window, not saying a word. We all thought he was reconciling what happened with Dena."

"Yeah, I remember saying to MIHO, 'I can guess what happened.'" said Jesse. "I still couldn't believe I knew about Todd but hadn't suspected you were gay until that moment."

"That's how I came out to you," MIHO said. "I said, 'Yep, I'm gay, and I fucked up.' I was trying to find the perfect moment, and then I just had to deal with it."

Paul clanged a ringer to go up 10-7 in the game. "Wait, Jesse, you knew Todd was gay? And you didn't tell us? And you didn't suspect anything that weekend?"

"First off, I didn't think it would be that big of a deal," Jesse said. "I didn't know MIHO was gay. Second, I didn't know Todd would go there. Besides, it wasn't any of our business. And I was too busy keeping an eye on Jim to notice Todd and MIHO."

Rob threw his shoe. "I had my ideas. I remember wondering if I saw something I shouldn't have in the dark, but I was pretty drunk. I also wondered why you were spending more time with Todd than Jim. But I hadn't made the real leap yet."

"Yeah, sorry I couldn't come out to you all. Jesse was my de facto messenger," MIHO said. "I had to go make things right with Jim."

"That was fun," Jesse said with a laugh. He looked at Paul. "You looked like I was trying to explain Einstein's law of relativity to you. You couldn't comprehend it."

"I mean, I've been around gay people before," Paul said. "But this was *MIHO*. I always teased him for never getting laid and just thought it was because he was shy and had no game, not that he wasn't interested. My whole perspective shifted that night."

"You're so enlightened," Rob said. He was now up 14-12. One more point and he'd take the game. "I was just a little mad you hadn't told me. I mean, we would have been ok with it."

"Right, I mean you were still you," Jesse said. "I don't know. I even felt like I knew you better after, like a veil had been lifted and I could see the real you."

"Well, *now* I know that, but at the time, I was so scared of you all rejecting me and it's not something I can un-reveal about myself. And the way I thought Jim reacted confirmed my fears."

"He wasn't rejecting you," Paul said. "He was just mad you didn't tell him."

"All I saw was him storming away, furious and that felt a lot like rejection to me," said MIHO. "When I caught up with him, it was dark, but he confronted me. He said, 'Look, I don't care if you're gay. If that's what you are, I'm good with it.'" MIHO started choking up, and his eyes were watering. "But then his voiced cracked when he said, 'David, we were best friends. I needed you tonight, and you were gone being someone I didn't even know. I had to find out like this? Who are you? Do I even know you?' That really hurt. I felt alone. Jim was only focused on himself, rather than what a friggin' huge deal this was."

Recalling that night became a little too much, and MIHO pulled a beer from the cooler, opened it, and took a long swig. Rob and Paul stopped their throws. MIHO looked to the sky, his voice affected. "It was the one time when I didn't know if Jim would have my back. We both felt betrayed, and it took some time and effort to rebuild that trust. Now, I won't get that time back."

MIHO let out a big sigh. Jim was supposed to be here. MIHO always felt distance meant nothing as long as they had this trip to reconnect. Now, there were no more trips with Jim. Jim's harassing phone calls to commit to the weekend would never ring again. Only these memories would live on. No more new memories.

Jesse tapped MIHO's back. "He trusted you and that was never in doubt. He just had to come to terms with everything. I had to remind him that coming out is a little different than telling everyone you have a new job. He got it."

MIHO smiled. "Yeah, we spent a lot of time on the phone. I came a day early on his wedding weekend, and we got coffee and hashed things out. By the day of the wedding, I remember bending over backward to be the best best man possible. I was working double-time to make sure his wedding was perfect. And, of course, Tracey was my biggest ally and was a bridge back."

Paul and Rob resumed their game. Rob hit a leaner and won. He pumped his fist and grabbed a water. "I'd forgotten that he still smoked on that trip. I guess he'd kept his promise and didn't smoke after the wedding."

MIHO shook his head. "After the thing with Dena, he never smoked again. He told me, every time he had a craving, he'd remember her and how close he was to screwing everything up, and it was enough to put that craving aside."

"So, he never smoked after that night?" Paul asked. "Well, that was one good thing about Dena. Good for him."

"I still can't believe you just shot up and went to save Jim like that," Jesse said. "You got up so fast, I thought you were sick and had to rush outside to puke."

"I knew as soon as she followed him, it was bad news," Paul said. "I mean, if that was me at that time, I would have locked that door, and you know the rest, but it would have been devastating for him to take that path. I had to stop him before he made a huge mistake. But I didn't have to do anything. He made the right choice on his own."

"Paul, you're such an enigma," Rob said. "You'll fuck up your own life but do everything you can to make sure we don't."

"I'm working on it," Paul said.

"We know," MIHO said and offered the chair next to him.

Jesse joined Rob for the next game. MIHO and Paul sat back down on the chairs and watched them play. Since Jim's death ten months ago, MIHO's grief had gone through all the stages. He had felt shock, denial, anger, and bargaining, but he wasn't sure if he was at acceptance yet. He hoped this trip would bring him to that stage. He needed closure that even the memorial service hadn't brought.

When Jim came around to understand why MIHO had kept his sexuality a secret, their friendship grew deeper. Tracey, of course, was a big reason too. MIHO became one of Tracey's good friends. Sometimes, when even Jim went to bed early, MIHO and Tracey would spend the next few hours talking. In the last couple years, he was looking to move back to Sacramento. MIHO's mom had slowed, and MIHO thought it was time to move closer to his mom, Jim, Tracey, and Willie.

All these memories flooded MIHO's mind, and he needed to get up.

"You okay?" Jesse said as he picked up his horseshoes.

"Just need to get something. Anybody need snacks? Are we okay on drinks?"

"Think so," Paul said. He opened the cooler. "Got water, beer, and Gatorade."

MIHO stood and went inside. He half expected Jim to be making a sandwich or getting a beer or coming out of the bathroom. MIHO had only been in this house a total of eleven days, but there were already so many memories here, and they all included Jim. There was the time when Jim was drunk and knocked the bowl of pulled pork onto the floor. He tried to convince MIHO that the top layer of the pork was okay to eat and got on the floor and picked at the meat and put the good pieces back in the bowl. There was another time when they were watching a movie and Jim cradled his chin in his hands and Paul talked to him for twenty minutes without realizing Jim was asleep. There were countless memories of Jim sniffing his first cup of coffee in the morning or leaning over the island to watch MIHO make dinner. He looked at the kitchen. MIHO froze and put his hand on the couch to keep steady until the anxiety passed. He breathed, walked to the counter, grabbed another bag of chips and a jar of salsa he had made for the occasion before heading back to the pit.

"Just in time!" Rob said when MIHO returned. "You're up, and I'm playing for a rule."

MIHO sighed. He was the wrong guy to stop a rule. Over the years, they had decided if one of them won three games in a row, then he got to make a rule applicable to that game for the rest of the weekend. These rules ranged from punishment for losing (such as a drink if you lose) to adding a degree of difficulty to the game (throwing a horseshoe with a non-dominant hand) to adjusting the scoring (four ringers in a row yields an automatic win). Making a rule was a big deal, and now it was MIHO's duty to try and deny Rob's ability to make a rule. Ever since that first time playing with Sean and his friends, MIHO hadn't improved. He could never get a consistent throw. Meanwhile, Rob's hand-eye coordination allowed him to practically throw ringers all day.

"Oh man," MIHO said. "If Jim were here, he'd be the rule stopper. Unfortunately, I don't think I'll be that guy."

"Not with that attitude," Paul said. "C'mon, man. It's up to you! Do it for Jim. Do it for your mom. Do it for Todd, for all I care."

MIHO looked at Paul, who stuck his tongue at him. MIHO flipped him off. He knew Paul wasn't being malicious. Over the last couple years, Paul had grown up and become more selfless, and while he maintained his quick wit, he held in some of his more biting remarks.

MIHO tried to concentrate and think of ways to maintain a consistent throw. Rob threw his first set of shoes and had a leaner and a ringer. He was dialed in. MIHO had to focus. When he reached back, he said the first thing that came to his head that would provide the right tempo for his throw.

"Ogilvie Home Perm," MIHO said. He meant to say it in his internal voice. The shoe flew in the air and rang true around the stake.

"What the *fuck*!" Paul screamed and laughed. Jesse fell out of his chair. Rob covered the ground below him with beer and saliva propelled by his sudden laughter. MIHO laughed too, more because it worked than what he had said.

"Where did that come from?" Rob said, wiping the beer from his chin.

"I needed to find some tempo, and it was the first thing that came to me," MIHO said.

"Whatever works," Rob said. His next shoe flew over the pole. He was too focused on MIHO and not on his own throws.

MIHO threw again and repeated "Ogilvie Home Perm," resulting in another ringer, then a third. After three throws, MIHO was up 9-0. Paul and Jesse looked at MIHO in awe.

"One more and an automatic win!" Paul said. "What's gotten into you?"

"I have no idea," MIHO said as he and Rob picked up and dusted off their shoes.

MIHO lined up his throw and let it go. "Ogilvie Home Perm," he said before another ringer rang true. Jesse and Paul were up on their feet now. MIHO's eyes grew big, and he began hopping around like a bunny. Jesse and Paul jumped up and gave MIHO high fives. Even Rob congratulated him.

"Rule *dee*-nied," Jesse said and gave MIHO another high five.

"I had a great rule too," said Rob. "I was going to have all of us, at the beginning of any game, match, etc. raise our glasses and toast Jim."

"You don't need to win three games for that rule," Paul said. "We can just do it."

Everyone nodded. And just like that, Rob made a rule anyway.

MIHO stayed at the pit, and Paul joined him. For a rare moment, MIHO got to throw the first shoes.

"Okay, Ogilvie," Paul said. "You got lucky once, but not again."

Paul was somewhat right. MIHO couldn't recapture the magic he'd had in that first game with Rob. He was ordinary. He still scored well and was competitive in each game. He even won a couple as they played, laughed, and lost track of time. It wasn't until midafternoon when they were ready to sit on couches and maybe take a nap.

MIHO brought out grapes and strawberries, an addition a couple years ago to at least give a nod toward being healthy. They lounged on the couches, focused on the big screen in front of them. Paul turned on ESPN out of habit, obligation, or hope a game would be on. Instead, he groaned as three talking heads "debating" LeBron James's latest tweet filled the screen.

"Oh man, they gave him a talk show now?" Paul said of the host with the flawless hair. "He was a little twerp who'd just arrived from Biloxi when I was there. He had talent, sure, but man he was horrible to some of the production folks."

"That was you just a few years ago," MIHO said. "Do you miss it?

"Oh, yeah," Paul said. "But I actually like being back in local news. I forgot how much I loved talking to local people. I don't have to cover the sports gods' every move. My obligation is to my community."

"Maybe it's time for another journal entry," MIHO said, picking up the notebook. "It looks like the next big one is the first Lake Trip Olympics."

"Definitely," Rob said. "That was a fun year."

"Wasn't that when we switched to cabins permanently?" Jesse asked.

"Yep, and a real kitchen," MIHO said. "And a TV to watch the Olympics. Ah, Michael Phelps. That body."

MIHO smiled as Paul rolled his eyes. "You know he trained at Michigan, right?"

"Oh god," Rob said. He popped in a grape before his eyes grew big. "I just remembered. This was the year with Tanya."

"Shut it," Paul said and hit Rob with a pillow.

MIHO pulled out a piece of paper folded into the journal. "Jim included the email he sent to us about the Lake Trip Olympics."

"You gotta read that," Jesse said.

MIHO smoothed out the printout and read:

Okay Jackasses,

In honor of the Olympics in Beijing, we're taking the trip to the next level. Not only have we all agreed to switch things up from camp-ing to a cabin, but we're going to have the first ever Lake Trip Olympics (LTO). A series of events throughout the weekend will test your skill, mettle, athleticism, etc. These events will be:

- *One-club golf: Our Fresno golf outing will double as the brief opening ceremonies and event. Remember, you can only bring one club, so make sure it's the right one.*
- *Poker: We all put in our $20 for chips. At the end of the night, the one with all the dough is the gold medalist.*
- *Horseshoes: There will be a round robin to begin the tourna-ment to determine seedings for a bracket.*
- *Bocce: Like horseshoes, this will be a round-robin tournament. Same rules apply.*
- *The Beach Triathlon:* We'll run a course barefoot that leads to the dock where we dive off, swim to the buoy and back to shore, before heading back to the E-Z UP for a round of flip cup.

You'll be competing for your made-up country, so think of some good names, and feel free to think of national colors and a "national anthem" that we can play for any gold medal ceremony. The anthem must be something we can put on an iPod and appropriate for the beach.

We'll award gold, silver, and bronze medals in each event. In addi-tion, three points will be awarded for gold, two for silver, and one for bronze medals. The winning country with the most medal points will receive $40 from the nonwinners (everyone, bring another $10 bill and don't spend it.)

As for the place, we've all agreed to put forth $200 for the cabin and food. MIHO's already working on a menu. We'll meet at the golf course at 1 p.m. Rob and I are meeting MIHO at the Sacramento airport and driving down. Paul has work in LA and will meet Jesse and drive up.

I can't wait to see you guys. Who knew I'd be looking forward to getting sleep on this trip? But I guess that's what happens when you have a six-month-old at home.

Later bitches,
Jim

10

Jim

2008

Why do you have to go this year? We've got so much going on," Tracey said. She was sitting on the edge of our bed while I packed for the trip. We were both exhausted. In the last six months, our son, Willie, was born, we bought a house, and we were remodeling the kitchen.

"I need this break to refresh and come back stronger and revitalized and ready to be a better man," I said.

Tracey rolled her eyes. "Next, you'll say you need to find yourself."

I smiled. "Well, it does help me to reflect on who I am and ways to improve for the coming year. You should have a weekend like this with your friends."

"Oh, thank you for letting me go on my own trip. You forget two aching and huge reasons why I can't go on an adventure and find myself by getting drunk and sleeping in." She pushed up her breasts to accentuate her frustration with breastfeeding.

"Why? I can take care of William for a weekend, and you go out with your friends."

"You stay home, you're a hero. I leave, I'm a horrible mother. Even if I decided to put something together, coordinating schedules would be a nightmare. It's different for men. Plus, you think you could handle a weekend with a six-month-old, but I know I'll get a call in the middle of the night or at a spa with you begging me to come home."

It was clear I wasn't going to win this argument. I had to cut my losses. William was stirring in his room, and Tracey left to tend to him while I finished packing. I'm sure Tracey was pouring on the guilt so I'd stay, but I was resolved to go. For one weekend, I could be accountable to only myself and could reset and appreciate the value of these two people in my life. Was that selfish?

"I'm going to miss you guys," I called out to her. "I don't want to miss anything, but I'll return more energized to be here for you and William. You'll see."

I felt a pang of guilt. I couldn't believe how much I was going to miss them both. Tracey's mother was planning to stay over, which helped. Though I wouldn't tell Tracey this, I suspected she'd get a better rest with her mom there than me. We both needed a little relief.

For the first couple weeks after Willie's birth, we didn't know if we could get through it. As expectant parents, we heard from everyone, "Get some rest. Get ready for no sleep. Oh my, you're in for it," and we laughed it off. But after we brought

William home, we realized the joke was on us. For three days, Tracey didn't sleep. I averaged maybe three hours a night. We didn't know a human being wouldn't care about how much you asked, pleaded, begged, coddled to stop crying. There was one night when I put William in the car seat and drove from Sacramento to San Francisco and back just so Tracey could get some rest.

Eventually, we found a routine. I became the master of the 2:00-7:00 a.m. shift to give Tracey somewhat of a break. This gave her some semblance of a normal sleep routine, while I got to watch Paul on the early morning *SportsCenter*. I smiled every time he'd come on and deliver the highlights, his catchphrases and transitions to expert analysis. A day or so after I had sent the email about this year's trip, Paul called me and dropped surprising news.

"Dude, I have a girlfriend," he said.

I just about spit out my coffee. Paula, whose name didn't go unnoticed, was a producer at ESPN. After a few overtures, she finally agreed to coffee, mostly to see if Paul was the player everyone said he was. Through their shared interest in sports, their relationship expanded, and Paul realized there could be more to a relationship than sex.

"Feels like a match made in heaven," I said. While I doubted if Paul would ever settle down, it was good to see he was trying. I was sure the endless flings would catch up with him at some point. "She knows your history?"

"Yep, and she doesn't care. I'm all in. She even met my parents."

"Whoa, that is serious," I said. "Have any of these girls ever met your parents?"

"No one since Tracey," Paul said. He often liked to tease me about their two-week romance in high school. "It was quite awkward. I was the most nervous I've ever been, even more than being on *SportsCenter* for the first time or doing interviews at the World Series."

"Damn, she must be something," I said.

"She is, but I'm great at the fun, flirty phase of the relationship. I'm not so good at revealing our flaws and then hoping we can make it work, you know?"

"That's the truth. The annoying parts are there, regardless of your feelings. It's just how you react to them. Do you get repulsed? Do they make you pull away? Do you try to change them? Or do you just find ways to accept and enjoy them because they're a part of her?"

"Well, that's deep," Paul said.

"That's a few years of marriage," I said.

"I just hope I don't dominate the trip with Paula talk, like you all do with new girlfriends."

"That's fine. It'll be a welcome distraction, instead of ogling women on the beach."

"Hey now, we're still human." Paul laughed. "But, yes, I pledge not to ditch you all this year."

For the past few years, Jesse and I were growing tired of Paul's endless pursuit of women on the beach. Each year followed the same pattern. Hang out with us Thursday and Friday. Scout the saloon Friday night for prospects. Hit the beach Saturday. By Saturday afternoon, Paul would be flirting, and by Saturday night at the bar, completely ignoring us. With Paula in his life, we hoped this weekend might break the routine.

When Rob arrived the day of our departure, Tracey came out with little William, wrapped in a blanket with his head peering up. Willie had just woken up, his eyes big and looking at Rob. He was always fascinated with my huge friend, so much bigger than the other humans. For his part, Rob was in wonder of Willie. When there are kids in the area, even the closest friends ignore you to say hi to children.

"There's the big guy," Rob said as he looked at William, touching his chubby, soft cheek. "And there's the beautiful mama." Rob kissed Tracey on the cheek. "Thank you for allowing this jackass to go on the trip."

"Yeah, he's leaving me, so you'd better keep him in line," she said with a smile, though there was a lot of truth to her words.

"Of course," Rob said. "He'll be better because of it. Believe me. I always come back loving my girl more than ever."

I looked at Tracey with raised eyebrows as if to say, "Listen to Rob." She ignored me.

"How's Leslie?" Tracey asked.

"She's great," Rob said. "I can't believe she's almost seven. She's growing up so fast, so keep these precious moments. They leave, and you never get them back."

"You mean the lack of sleep, the constant boob ache, the crying. I'm going to miss it?"

"You'll forget that part, but you'll miss and remember those quiet times," Rob said. "Believe me."

I came back and kissed Tracey, then William and gave them both a big hug before climbing into the truck. Rob started the engine, and as he pulled away, I realized I'd never felt such a pain of missing people as I did at that moment as I watched Tracey bring William back into the house and close the garage door.

"Don't worry, you'll see them again in a few days," Rob said, noticing my heart pang. "Besides, you'll be having too much fun to miss them."

"I'd better be. You know that's part of the reason I made up the Lake Trip Olympics so I can stay busy enough with activities to not dwell on Tracey and William. I don't want to be sitting next to the fire missing the heck out of them."

We picked up MIHO from where he was staying at his mom's house before heading to Fresno. MIHO had moved to Hawaii and was working as the Waikiki Marriott convention manager. Now that he was out and dating, he seemed to have blossomed. He'd been dating Charles for four months and talked about him the way I did about Tracey or Jesse about Danielle. However, I still had difficulty wrapping my head around his sexuality. When he first told me about Charles, I realized he was no longer theoretically gay. His relationships were a reality and it took me a little time to achieve another level of acceptance.

Meanwhile, Rob was excited to hear more about new fatherhood stories. After years of spouting stories to blank stares, he could share the blessings of kids with me and Jesse, who was now a father of twin eighteen-month-old girls. Rob was now the sage who could extoll wisdom to us neophytes. As always, the conversations flowed, and we arrived at the golf course thirty minutes ahead of Paul and Jesse.

"Oh, thank goodness you shaved off that goatee, Jim," Paul said as he exited Jesse's truck in the parking lot.

I rubbed my smooth chin. I'd shaved it a little after Willie was born.

"That's about four years too late. Ah, here we are on another trip!" Paul continued.

"Jesse, you're making us all look like out-of-shape slobs," Rob said. Jesse looked as trim as ever, even wearing a fitted T-shirt that accentuated his lean body. I mean, my T-shirts were tight too, but they accentuated my rolls.

"You *are* out-of-shape slobs," Jesse said. "I've made the most of my unemployment."

Jesse had decided to be a stay-at-home dad, but in reality, he was a casualty of the economic downturn. About three months before the twins were born, he was laid off. When Danielle decided to come back from maternity leave, it made sense he'd take care of the girls time until he found a new job. The job never came.

"I'm so glad we're here," I said. My eyes gleamed as we began the opening ceremony. I pulled out my iPod and a plug-in speaker. "I've got some special ideas for the first-ever LTO. Remember I asked you to give send me the name of your made-up country, its colors, and its national anthem?"

Paul laughed. "You've put some thought into this. We now know what you were doing during those late-night feedings."

"So, for Rob, he's playing for Troy, his colors are scarlet and gold, and his national anthem is the USC fight song."

Rob pushed his arms into the air.

"I never would have thought," Paul said, the sarcasm as dry as the desert. "Let me guess, Jesse's country is Raider Nation, his colors are silver and black, and his national anthem is 'The Autumn Wind.'"

Jesse gave Paul the bird.

"You're not going to get mine, Paul," MIHO said. "I'm playing for Aloha, and my anthem is the ukulele-infused 'Somewhere Over the Rainbow' by Israel Z."

"But your colors are the rainbow flag, am I right?" Paul asked, pointing at MIHO, who nodded. "I knew it. And for Jim, he's going to go with something to celebrate fatherhood, and his country name has Willie in it. And his national anthem will be something from Will Smith or Willie Nelson. And, of course, his flag colors will be black and purple, like your Sacramento Kings."

I nodded. My nation was Williamsburg and Will Smith's "Summertime."

"You're all so predictable," Paul said. "All right. Average Joe's is my nation, yellow and red are my colors, and my anthem is 'Playing with the Boys' by Kenny Loggins."

Paul tore off his polo to reveal an Average Joe's T-shirt from the movie *Dodgeball*. I shook my head. If Paul bought into a concept, he went all in. We gave him a hearty clap for his commitment.

"Hey, MIHO, you got enough sunscreen on that dome?" Rob asked. Over the past few years, MIHO was in a battle with baldness. His hairline was now engaged in a two-front war and losing badly. "It gets pretty sunny out there. I'd hate for that balding head to get sunburned on the first day."

"Does Charles know you used to have hair?" I asked. "MIHO, you should just give up the fight. Shave it. Bald is beautiful. I'm sure Charles agrees."

"I don't know," MIHO said. "I mean, it's my hair."

"Believe me, you'd look better shaved," Jesse said. "At least better than right now."

With MIHO now self-conscious, I re-explained the rules and collected ten dollars from everyone to place in the pot for the ultimate winner. Everyone groaned at my formality, but I could tell they could appreciate the effort and making things a little different this year. We were ready to start the first event.

I used my preowned Wilson pro-staff seven iron as it was the safest club in my bag. It didn't matter much. Rob cruised to the gold medal. Paul had a disastrous sixth hole with a triple bogey, which allowed Jesse to leap over him and take silver with Paul taking the bronze. I did birdie the ninth hole, but it was just a tease.

When we returned to Rob's truck, I plugged the iPod into his stereo and lined up Rob in the middle, with Jesse to his right and Paul to his left. I went to the cooler and pulled out a can of Coors Banquet and presented it to Paul. I followed with a Coors Light to Jesse and finally an oil can of Foster's to Rob. I turned up the speakers, then scrolled to the right tune: The USC fight song.

Rob's face showed off his pride in the victory, not only to satisfy his competitiveness but for his beloved alma mater. He raised his hand and waved to the spectating trees and telephone poles that surrounded the parking lot. Everyone cheered after the song ended.

"We should put this on Facebook," Paul said. He pulled out his BlackBerry and began to type in a post.

"Dude, isn't that like Myspace?" Jesse said. "Seems creepy to be sharing shit like that."

Since Jesse and Rob had to drive, against Paul's wishes we placed the winners' beverages back into the cooler filled with the "medals" for the weekend and headed up the hill once again.

I was so excited to have a bed, a shower, and a working toilet. Sure, I felt nostalgic about site 152, but with a new baby, I sure as heck wasn't going to spend my weekend away roughing it with a pit toilet and an air mattress. Now, it wasn't the Ritz. The circular cabin was split into thirds with a large living area and two bedrooms, plus a deck and patio table that overlooked an expansive meadow. I was just happy we all had beds, MIHO had a kitchen, and we had a TV and cable, so we could watch the Olympics, a baseball game, or a movie on DVD.

When we were settled, Rob pulled out his Foster's and handed Paul and Jesse their beers, and we went to the deck to toast the first night. Afterward, MIHO went to the kitchen to start dinner. We were anticipating what he could do with a full kitchen, including a stove and an oven, a refrigerator instead of an ice chest, and a full array of pots and pans. Even though I did the shopping, I bought the food to his specifications. Using a recipe he learned at the Marriott kitchen on Waikiki, he breaded the mahi-mahi, grilled it, drizzled it with aioli, and served it with broccoli and rice pilaf. He also had Rob purchase a bottle of Napa chardonnay to pair with the meal. After seeing MIHO work with a full kitchen, I didn't think we would ever camp again.

After dinner, we commenced the second event of the LTO with a poker game on the deck overlooking the meadow. With the sun setting, we settled around the large patio table and turned on the porch light. Everyone chipped in their twenty bucks and received their chips.

"What's up with your brother-in-law? You know, the one who was a total dick about winning?" Paul asked with a smile. MIHO shook his head.

"Kyle's doing well," I said. "He finished up his MBA and working his ass off at some venture capital firm in San Francisco. This job perfectly fits his personality. He thought we were kind of jerks for not inviting him back."

"If he would have been invited back, I wouldn't have come," MIHO said. "So, good luck with the cooking."

"Speaking of coming, what's up with Todd these days, Jesse?" Paul could barely keep in the giggles.

"Oh my god," MIHO said. "Don't even."

"What?" Paul said, feigning innocence.

"If we are going to go into this, we'd be here all night going over your conquests, starting with grandma last year," MIHO said.

"She wasn't a grandma," Paul said. "Her daughter was just expecting."

"Dude," Jesse shook his head. "So wrong. But in answer to your question, Todd's doing ok. He took another job about a year ago. He's still playing some small gigs. He played at some beer garden near Pasadena about a month ago and we brought the girls. It was a fun night."

"Well, I'm glad the trip is back to just us now," Rob said.

Everyone nodded. It was best just to keep the trip to ourselves. I enjoyed hanging out with Kyle but preferred limiting his companionship to various holiday and family get-together settings, not the annual trip to the lake. Regardless of the circumstances, the trip would be the five of us playing cards, having good food, and enjoying each other's company with a beverage. Speaking of which, Rob poured another three fingers of scotch. I sipped it and let the warmth ease down my throat.

"So, we need to know more about Paula," I said. "Give us the scoop."

"What's to say?" Paul said. "She's great. She's not the hottest girl I've ever been with, but she's the one I've opened up to the most. She gets me, and I can see myself settling down with her, but don't get your hopes up yet, boys, there's a lot of time before that happens."

"Oh man, I thought you were going to make an announcement," Jesse said. "So, she's got you thinking about something more than flings."

"Well, yeah. I mean, she's really good to open up to about stuff." Paul shifted in his seat and took a sip of his drink. I could tell he was getting uncomfortable. He wasn't used to answering questions regarding his feelings and relationships. "Plus, she's takes it up..."

"Dude!" we said in unison. Too much information. We knew he said it to get a rise out of it and to deflect. He was different from us. Whereas we wanted to talk about these women in our lives, he just wanted us to know that there was one he didn't want to leave before the break of dawn.

"The real question is, what do your friends with benefits think about this new girl?" MIHO asked.

On previous trips, Paul had bragged about how he had a network of women in Connecticut and around the country whom he could call for private companionship, and the arrangement was reciprocal. On the road, his network was wide, and it only took an email or a text to have a date for the night.

"Fortunately, a few of those ladies are also in relationships, so they haven't called. Others I've ignored or told I'm unavailable and just don't contact some of them when I'm on the road."

"It's a great start, and we love you for it," Jesse said. "We hope this works out for you. But it does kind of sound like you're keeping a few parachutes out there just in case."

Paul glared at Jesse. The last statement stung a little more than intended. Paul craved validation, not discussion. Just acknowledgment that he had a serious girlfriend was enough.

After two hours, two beers, two more glasses of wine, and three glasses of bourbon, I had to keep refocusing my eyes on my cards. Once again, I went out with a whimper, but I still outlasted Paul and Jesse. As I rose to grab a sweatshirt, I realized the beer, the wine, and the bourbon had made my feet and legs wobbly. I hadn't drunk this much since before William was born. As I passed the bathroom, I was so grateful we had a real toilet that flushed. And a faucet and soap. I was almost wispy as I returned to the living room where MIHO and Rob were locked in a final showdown.

"We have a bathroom!" I announced. "I'm so proud about where we've come."

Perhaps I was more drunk than I thought.

"Someone has new-dad alcohol tolerance," Jesse said, and he and Rob laughed. Jesse came up and swung his arm around me and sat me down on the couch. I was overwhelmed with emotion that I hadn't ever felt for my friends. We'd made it. We'd moved into adulthood intact.

"I'm so glad you're here and I can talk to you about being a dad," I said. "It's so great. But it's so fucking haaarrrd."

"Too easy," Paul said. He was distracted watching ESPN.

Jesse ignored Paul. "Yeah, it can be. But it gets easier, and you figure it out."

"I just hope I can be as good as you and Rob," I said, and my eyes started to tear up. "You guys are such great dads, and I just hope I can be like you."

"Hey, Paul, I think it's time Homer Simpson heads to bed," MIHO said from the table. "I think he's at that level."

"Agreed," Rob said.

I think MIHO and Rob just wanted me out of the room so they could focus on cards.

"Hey, I'm a little drunk, yeah, but I don't need to go to bed," I said. My eyes were getting heavy, and even as I said the words, the idea of sleeping sounded pretty good. I had to protest, though. "We have to do the medal ceremony," I said. "I get a Coors!"

"Not tonight," Jesse said. "We'll do it the first thing in the morning. Don't worry, we won't leave you behind."

"Make sure you don't." With that out of my head, I was very ready for sleep. Jesse led me to my room. I was slow but managed to change into some shorts, brushed my teeth, and slid into bed. It was a real mattress with real sheets. There was a light and a fluffy pillow. No more air mattresses or sleeping bags. *No more dirt* was my last thought before passing out.

The last thing I wanted after my hangover the next morning was to have a cold Coors Banquet, but since I was passed out when MIHO won the poker tournament, they woke me up early in the morning to have the ceremony. It was just their kind of cruelty to pull me out of bed and put a hair of the dog in my hand when all I wanted to do was bury my head under the pillow.

I shuffled my feet into the kitchen and bent over and with a grimace. My body felt eighty years old, my mind at half aperture and my stomach punching me from the inside. I didn't puke, but I wish I had. It would have gotten more of this poison out of me. Such a great role model I was for little William. While he was wagging his arms and batting around toys on his mobile, I was giving my best impression of an alcoholic.

"Father of the year," I said holding up the golden can. I pushed play on MIHO's warrior song. "Somewhere over the Rainbow" played as we all sipped the beer. The first two sips went down hard, but it got easier. Now, I just needed to get down some fatty bacon and a cup of coffee while watching the Olympics and Michael Phelps. We'd all agreed that Phelps deserved the hype, and we'd try to watch what we could live.

"Dude, male swimmers are hot," MIHO said, partly because it was true, and partly to needle our heterosexuality. "Don't you think?"

We all groaned.

MIHO frowned in mock disgust. "Stop with your double standard, you homophobic assholes." He turned to Paul and asked, "Are you checking your Facebook again?"

Paul was flipping through his BlackBerry, seeing what new friends he'd collected over the past few hours. Some of these friends ranged from former colleagues to people from college to high school classmates. He also reconnected with some of the women he'd been with throughout the country as well as other friends from Michigan, Iowa, and Sacramento.

"This is great stuff, man," Paul said. "There are so many people from high school on here. Remember Tanya?"

"Wasn't that Moretti's girlfriend?" Rob said. "I think she graduated when we were sophomores."

"That's her," Paul said. "Guess what? She married Moretti, and they live in Fresno. Well, they're separated, I guess."

"Yikes," I said. "Sucks for them."

"Yeah, I guess Moretti never changed," Paul said. "But she works at the local chamber of commerce or something. She thought about coming up and seeing us."

"No fucking way," Jesse said. "Hell no."

"Why not?" Paul asked. "She just wants to see what we're up to."

"Dude, it's *our* weekend," MIHO said.

"And don't you remember, you have a girlfriend now," I said.

"I'm not going to get with Tanya," Paul said with a wave of his hand. "It's only polite we all reconnect."

"No, I really don't want to," Jesse said. "And I don't want to know what happened to Moretti, so please don't invite her up."

"All right, all right," Paul said. "She's looking pretty good, though. Not bad for three kids, including a teenager."

Paul passed around his BlackBerry, and we all looked at Tanya Moretti. She was thinner than I remembered, her arms fit and toned. Her hair was stylized and looked more sophisticated. Of course, all hair looked better now than the '90s perms.

"That's nuts," Rob said, looking at the photo. "She's pretty hot."

As the morning strung into the afternoon, my hangover subsided, and I slowly kicked a couple waters back. After the initial rounds of round-robin horseshoes, it all turned out as expected. Rob was top seed, followed by me, Paul, and Jesse with MIHO failing again to make the championship round. In the ten years since we started playing horseshoes on this trip, MIHO had never gotten better. His throws were inconsistent, whether at a different pace, release point, or spin. He just couldn't get the hang of it.

As Rob and Jesse began warming up for the championship round, Rob smiled and said, "Let's make this interesting."

"We're not going to bet you," I said. "Then we lose twice."

"No, I'm going to increase my level of difficulty," Rob said with a sly smile. "And if I lose, I won't bitch about it."

"Are you going to throw with your eyes closed?" Paul said.

"Close." Rob went to the cooler and pulled out an empty box of Coors Light and placed it over his head, the slots for the handle acting as eyeholes. He turned to us, his huge frame topped with an absurd-looking helmet that proved he could look intimidating and ridiculous at the same time.

"Oh god," I said. "I think that's as much as a disadvantage to us. I don't think I can concentrate and throw straight with that on your head."

"Just look forward and not to the side," Rob said. "Now throw. Just know that if I beat you with this on my head, you'll never hear the end of it." He smiled, or at least seemed like he did through the box.

When we began the match. Rob pulled the box down like a visor on a medieval knight's helmet. I just focused my gaze on the poles and away from the cardboard knight. Somehow, I managed the win, keeping Rob from increasing his sizable lead. Paul defeated Jesse for the bronze. We had the medal ceremony and cracked open our beers as "Summertime" played on the iPod. After three events:

Rob – 8 points

Jim – 4 points

Paul – 3 points

Jesse – 3 points

MIHO – 3 points

"Man, you boys better start catching up soon," Rob said. "Or else I may not even need to compete tomorrow."

By the time we were finished with horseshoes, MIHO had to start the next dinner. I utilized the downtime to connect with Tracey and William. I missed them, but I was holding up.

"You're having fun?" Tracey asked over the phone.

"Yes. You know these guys. They always put a smile on my face, and if I'm not smiling, they're going to do everything, including physical harm and ridicule, to make me."

"Good for you." I could tell she was happy for me, but wished I was home with her. She just wasn't going to tell me that. It would only lead to guilt, defensiveness, and resentment.

"In a couple days, I'll be back and ready to give you a break," I said. I knew it rang hollow since I knew that implicated that I was doing her "a favor" by helping out. At this point, I knew my biggest job was not to piss her off. She was working on no sleep, and regardless of the help she was getting from her mom, she was still taking care of our kid while I was partying with my buddies. There was also no point in telling her how drunk I was last night. "I miss you guys. Did he do anything new?" He seemed to be learning new things every day.

"He was sitting up on his own and laughing so hard at his mobile today," Tracey said, clearly smiling on the other end. "His laugh was so pure. It was so fun. I recorded it on the camera so you can see it when you get home."

"Can't wait."

"Yes, you can. You're having too much fun."

"I am. But that doesn't mean I don't miss you and William. We need to come up here together sometime."

"Sure. Well, I'll let you get back to your boys. Give them my best. Okay, love you!"

"Love you too," I said and hung up.

When we settled around the table, I gave out the rules for liar dice that would help us determine the gold, silver, and bronze medalists. While we had stake in the games, the value came through in the conversations we had and the comraderie we built.

"I can't believe you all have ladies in your lives right now," Rob said.

"Ummm," MIHO said.

"Sorry, significant others," Rob said. Rob most enjoyed asking about our lives. When we were still teenagers, he'd call this "philosophizing." But now that we were older, we weren't philosophers, we were just men trying to figure out life. As MIHO talked about his boyfriend, I realized he was the most honest and happy that I'd ever seen him. I was just glad someone loved MIHO and that it helped him love himself.

I turned and saw Rob staring at me and smiling, shaking his head. "Dude, your smile hasn't left you all trip. Man, you're tired but full of joy."

"I never knew how great and rewarding fatherhood could be," I said. "I mean, sometimes it sucks and it's hard, but when you get that look, even if it's just gas, I'm happy. Unbelievable. Jesse, I can't imagine what it's like with twins and being a stay-at-home dad."

"I'm not going to lie, it's friggin' hard," Jesse said. "Outside of Danielle, my support system is pretty limited. Parks are filled with moms. My friends and neighbors who are men are working. Meanwhile, Danielle's friends are all talking about their kids and how they love being home, and she feels guilty for being at work. It can be a real mind fuck. But I found a small dad's group, and we go to the park with our kids and talk about what we're all going through. Add in the twins, though, and I feel like I'm the constant winner in terms of tough parenting. But ask me if I care, I don't. I love my girls. They renew me. My soul smiles, even when I'm wiping their asses."

"Oh man." Paul said. He grimaced like he was going to be ill.

"Get used to it," I said. "Dads outnumber you. We're going to start discussing fatherhood and parenting now."

Paul rolled his eyes. "Great," he said and turned back to Jesse. "Don't you feel emasculated by your wife bringing in all the dough? I don't think I could do that."

"I don't think you could either," Jesse said, frowning. "Manliness isn't determined by gender roles. It's about stepping up and owning your responsibilities. Right now, my responsibilities are with Nicole and Jennifer and making sure their needs are met."

Paul threw up his hands. "Hey, man, I'm just saying that you had a career, and now you're home. I'm just asking if you feel regret for leaving your passions and career behind for wiping asses."

"Look, first off. I didn't leave my job. It left me. There was no job. We made this arrangement out of necessity. Sometimes, the best things come out of unfortunate circumstances. Is it weird to be home? Of course. But I have two girls whose reality is me being home, and I'm going to make it the best for them. It's called being an adult."

The implications were left unsaid. We finished our tournament in a subdued tone, and MIHO won. With only two events left, Rob still had a good lead in the LTO, but a win was no longer inevitable. MIHO, Jesse, and I had a good chance to win with a sulking Paul far behind. It was one of the few times during our trips when we all wandered off to bed tense.

When I awoke Saturday, I was proud of my discipline and maturity. Unlike the previous morning, my head didn't pound, my stomach wasn't turning over, and my mind was clear. The impact of drinking more water than alcohol was amazing. I came into the kitchen and heard the drips and pops of the coffee maker pouring the water through the grounds. I looked around and saw the back of Rob through the window sitting on the deck with a paperback resting on his legs. I poured us both a cup of coffee and brought them out to the deck where Rob looked up with a surprised smile.

"What service," he said as he took the cup. "Thanks, my man. Did you sleep okay?"

"You're welcome," I said, sitting in the deck chair next to him and noticing the blue jay expressing his warning to the rest of the forest that I was outside. "I slept great. A fun fact: less alcohol, more water, and you sleep better and don't have a hangover. Something to remember for next time."

Rob laughed. "Imagine that. It's only taken us thirteen years to realize it."

"Right," I said. "With a new kid, it does change your perspective, that's for sure."

"A kid does make things different. But changes for the good."

"So, we kinda left things a little tense last night. Paul seemed a little bitter."

"Yeah, that was strange for him. We were needling him a bit harsher than usual."

"Maybe, but we just don't want him to screw it up with Paula, right?"

"I know, but we should just let things lie. It's his life. He's got to make his own choices."

"You're right."

A squirrel scurried up and around the tree trunk, across a branch, then jumped into the next tree. Rob and I sipped our coffees and watched. Entertainment sometimes doesn't come on a screen.

"Big day today," I said. "Everyone agrees we can't allow you to win bocce."

"Of course not! I win, and I don't even have to partake in the triathlon, which, after liar dice, is my worst event."

The sliding door opened with a whoosh. Paul's sullen demeanor from the night before had vanished, and he was typical Paul. He collapsed into the chair, steadying his cup in his hands. "I'm making it my mission to ensure Rob doesn't win today," Paul said.

"That's lovely," Rob said. "Always the spoiler, never the champion."

"I'll take that role. I'm planning to bring it!"

We laughed. Paul leaned against the railing as Rob and I continued to sit and drink our coffee. I glanced into the living room and saw Jesse, his phone to his ear. His hands kept running through his hair, and he wasn't smiling. I felt I was intruding by staring, so I turned to Rob.

"He and Danielle are going through a rough patch," Rob said. "He doesn't want to make a big deal out of it, but they had a fight about coming here."

I understood. Since I was primary caregiver during the summer, my departure was a life disrupter. I can only imagine the disruption Jesse, the stay-at-home dad, caused his wife. After all, she was the breadwinner, a practicing lawyer with billable hours, and used to fitting the family around her work schedule.

Even if it was now Saturday, this was quite a transition to go from secondary caregiver to primary, even for a weekend.

"Danielle's a very demanding woman," I said. "I don't know how Jesse does it."

"He said it last night. He wouldn't trade it, but he's flying blind most of the time," Rob said. "He said the hardest thing is letting go of the whole gender-expectation thing. He always has to check himself if he thinks Danielle should do this because that's what mothers do, or he has to do that because that's what he's supposed to do."

"But he's getting it done?" I asked.

"Of course. He's Jesse, but all that projection from family and friends has put a stress on them. His dad's always telling him 'that's a woman's job.' Or Danielle's mom lays on the guilt about why she isn't home with the twins. All these outside opinions when it's hard enough to communicate to each other."

The swoosh of the slider returned, and Jesse walked out. The weight of a thousand thoughts and some anxiety that comes with adulthood covered his face. He pulled out a patio chair and sat down, content with letting something else hold him up.

"Trouble?" I said.

"She's got a big deposition coming up, and instead of being at the office, she's got to do all things she does around the house, plus my stuff, plus take care of the twins. She rattled everything off on her task list, and it felt like another shot at me for being away. She loves Jennifer and Nicole, but she has to juggle a little more this week, and she's reminding me how much of an inconvenience that is."

"What are you supposed to do?" MIHO asked. "You deserve a break too."

"I'm just saying it's hard. She's frustrated that while she's got a lot on her plate, I'm here 'doing nothing.'"

"You're not doing nothing," Rob said. "You're competing for second in the Lake Trip Olympics."

"Yeah, that's not an answer I'm giving her," Jesse said. "And besides, I'm only two points behind, and you're not winning."

"Everyone's ganging up on me," Rob said. "What's up with that?"

"Hey, when you're at the top of the mountain, people want to bring you down," MIHO said. "Now, I have to get breakfast ready so we can get out of here and get a prime spot."

Our morning routine went much quicker and smoother than when we camped. We were one of the first groups on the beach and had put up the E-Z UP and our chairs and took our first jump in the lake before the majority of the fellow beachgoers had arrived. We were ready for our next competition in the LTO.

Bocce is typically played on a well-manicured lawn where you read the speed like a golf green and score based on how many of your designated balls you get closest to the white ball or pallino. Our challenge was to take this game of precision and play it on a hilly, rocky, dirt beach that was sloped toward the water and littered with hazards such as rocks, various grasses, rivulets, and bushes.

"Oh, this is going to be interesting," Rob said. "Putting you guys away may be a little harder than I thought."

"Makes it easier for me to play spoiler," Paul said with a mischievous smile.

Paul made good on his promise and eliminated Rob to advance to the final, while Jesse won the other semifinal. Jesse perfected a system of where and how to throw the pallino and beat Paul with surgical precision in the final. Rob beat MIHO for third place and held a one-point lead heading into the final event, the triathlon.

"On your heels, and this could be my best event." Jesse smiled at Rob.

"Not if I play spoiler, baby," Paul countered.

The triathlon was designed to make us look ridiculous, test our endurance, steady hand, and drinking capabilities. It was timed and began with a barefoot run around the beach and down to the pier, followed by a jump into the lake and a swim in cold, open water to a set of buoys and then back to shore. Then one final dash back to the E-Z UP for a round of flip cup.

I was last in the standings and therefore would go first and be the guinea pig for the rest of them. The running course would be the most difficult. The beach area was littered with charred logs from firepits used over the summer, there was gravel near the bathrooms, and the pier had splinters all over. I placed a hand on the corner of the E-Z UP tent, which acted as the starting line. MIHO held the phone with a stopwatch on it. He stood fifteen feet in front of me with his arm out.

"On your mark...get set...*go!*"

MIHO dropped his hand, and I took off. With the first pace, I stepped on a pebble. I winced and kept going. I must have looked ridiculous. I ran up the hill and toward the bathroom and the gravel moat. When I came around the bathroom and started back toward the beach, I welcomed the pine needles that covered the ground. I passed some trees and came to the back side of the lake beach, where the boys waited to cheer me on.

"How's it going back there?" Paul said.

"The bathroom corner is brutal!" I yelled back, but my eyes were trained on the ground. With each step, I was planning my next move, avoiding the pebbles. I was moving my arms like I was jogging, but my steps were awkward and disjointed. I moved to the hot asphalt of the boat-launch area and onto the pier, where a splinter lodged into my toe. When I got to the edge of the pier, I jumped into the water. My body screamed "holy shit!" as the cold water enveloped me. I came up and took a deep breath and began swimming the forty yards to the buoy, but about fifteen yards in, I realized how poor of an idea this was. I was the definition of out of shape. The altitude sapped my lungs. My legs burned. I had to turn over and backstroke the rest of the way. When I touched the buoy, I pivoted toward shore until I could touch bottom, then ran up through the water and to our camp where the flip cup awaited me.

"You're at four minutes," MIHO said. "How are you feeling?"

"Good," I managed. My lungs were burning and trying to take in as much oxygen as possible. I tried to relax for the flip cup. It took a few more tries than I'd hoped, but soon I was pouring the last cup of beer down my throat. The guys were surrounding me and screaming encouragement. I was still breathing hard so I couldn't get it all down. I had to stop four times before I slammed the cup, indicating to MIHO to stop the clock.

"Five minutes, forty-five seconds," MIHO called out as I continued to catch my breath.

"I'm out of shape," I said.

"Drinking shape," Paul said. "I can beat that shit. I'm in plenty of shape."

MIHO was next, and although he was a high school swimmer and now surfing every week with Charles, he still came out of the water and lumbered toward the table. Altitude was still an issue for all of us. He faltered at flip cup, and by the time he finished the beer, he had a time of 5:54.

"I got you by nine seconds," I said.

He came over, put his hands on his knees, and labored in his breathing. "That altitude is no joke."

"Get ready to see me on top of the leader board, boys," Paul said.

Despite being the drunkest one of us, he limbered up, swinging his arms across his body, trying to emulate Michael Phelps. When I dropped my arm, he winked at me and was off. Whether it was the beer that made him numb or just sheer will, he powered through the running course and before long was onto the pier and into the water. Soon, he was running out of the water like David Hasselhoff emerging from the ocean on *Baywatch*. Paul and Rob were the champs at flip cup, and Paul didn't disappoint. He took two tries each on the first two cups. The third cup took four tries, and he chugged the beer with great speed, finishing in 4:30.

"And that," he took a breath, "is how you do it!"

Jesse was up next up and had a clear advantage in this event, and as soon as my hand went down, he began like he would a marathon. His strides didn't include the ginger steps that the rest of us had taken. His form was deliberate, and he disappeared behind the trees and was around the bathroom and on the back side of the beach in the blink of an eye.

"Oh man, he's flying!" Rob said.

Soon he was down the boat ramp, onto the pier, and into the water. He didn't have great swimming form, but he didn't look like he was tiring one bit, and soon he was running out of the water like he'd just started the race. By the time he chugged the beer, he'd obliterated Paul's time at 4:05, and the LTO was as good as his.

"Man, I thought I was going to win this," Paul said, disappointed but amazed at Jesse's time.

"Running and cardio helps," Jesse stated the obvious. "Now the pressure's on Rob."

"Yep, he has to beat 4:05," I said.

"Ass," Rob said. "I'm not going to concede the win, but we all know what the result is going to be."

Even if Rob finished last in the final triathlon, he'd still get second in the overall event. While in college, he was faster than all of us, except Jesse, even with his huge frame. However, thirteen years, knee surgeries, and seventy-five extra pounds had slowed him. Still, Rob wasn't a quitter. He was going to participate even with the result a foregone conclusion.

As my arm went down, Rob jogged through the course the best he could. He didn't try to push anything. He was just deliberate in his jog and in his swim. I was surprised at the efficiency of his movement, and he finished in 5:30, good enough for third place.

"That was amazing," Paul said.

"The running killed me," Rob said. "But hey, I took the bronze and second in the LTO."

"And from the ashes, I emerge as LTO champion!" Jesse said. In winning the last two events, he'd come from a ways back to win.

We passed around the beers, played "Autumn Wind," and sat around for the rest of the afternoon. When we returned to the cabin, we must have contributed to the drought by taking long showers. The hot water rinsed off all the dust, sunscreen, and sweat we'd taken in that day. As I got back to the living room, Paul was out on the balcony, hunched over the railing, his cell phone to his ear. He alternated between standing up and looking at the trees and shaking his head and putting his hands to his eyes.

"Don't go out there," Rob said. "He's on with Paula."

"You have the ears of a bat," I said. "What's going on?"

"From what I gather, he drunk dialed her, woke her up, and wanted to have phone sex. She's got the early shift tomorrow and wasn't appreciative of the call. He pushed her more, and she didn't like it, and now the fight's a bit more significant."

"Ouch!" I plopped on the couch to watch the A's with Rob. We kept the sound at the edge of being able to deny snooping on their conversation while trying to listen in. It took another fifteen minutes for Jesse and MIHO to emerge. MIHO started to make dinner, and Jesse joined us on the couch. When Paul finished, he came in, shook his head, and blew out his cheeks like a blowfish.

"She's pissed. She didn't like that I was drunk and woke her up. She didn't care about the LTO and how I came from behind and played spoiler. I was also trying to share how much I missed her, but I guess she didn't take it that way. It devolved from there."

"Yikes," I said.

"I know," Paul said. "Anyway, she just stopped short from breaking up with me. Maybe this relationship crap isn't for me."

"Dude, I know we've been giving you crap about your commitment, but you don't give up this easy," I said.

"There are going to be bumps in the road," Jesse said. "Take it from me, I've been on a dirt road for a while, but in the end, the road and the journey are worth it."

"I guess," Paul said. "It's just annoying. Who knew I would get laid less in a relationship?"

We all raised our hands.

"Well, I know that, but just seems it'd be different."

I was trying hard not to roll my eyes. "Do you want to be in this relationship? Yesterday, you said you did."

"Not if it's not fun. That phone call was not fun."

"Well, you've got to decide for yourself what you want," MIHO said. "If you want her in your life, you're going to have those hard times, but it's worth it because the good times are the best."

"I guess. I need to take my shower," Paul said and left.

"Well, that's not encouraging," I said.

"He can be so goddamn selfish sometimes," Jesse said. He shook his head. "From what he says, she's a great person, but just because you get in a fight and she's interested in more than just sex with you, you want to end it? So frustrating."

"I want to shake him and wake him to the realities of life," Rob said.

"I had better start up dinner," MIHO said and he provided us with another fantastic dinner of linguini in a white clam sauce. I had a couple glasses of wine and was content to sit and relax and watch movies. Paul had other ideas. He wanted to go to the bar, and his eyes told me he wanted to be on the prowl.

"C'mon, old man," Paul said. "We always go to the bar. Now that we're in a cabin, you get old on us?"

"That's about right," I said. "This is my last night where it's quiet, and I can sleep with no baby and no wife. I can just sit on this couch and not do a damn thing."

"But don't we have closing ceremonies?" MIHO said. He smiled at me, and I gave him a dirty look. Unfortunately, MIHO was right. Closing ceremonies for the LTO were planned for the bar. It's where the prize money would be distributed and the winner would buy a round.

"Ha!" Paul said. "You have to go and stay for a round."

"Okay," I said. "One round, then I'm heading back."

"Me too," Jesse said.

"Whatever," Paul said, and he opened the door and was out as though he was on a mission to have a good time. For him, that meant in the company of women. I looked at MIHO and Rob. Rob seemed ready to go out too. MIHO seemed indifferent.

I just needed a push to get in the mood. Once we filed into Rob's truck and drove down to the saloon, I started to remember all the fun times we'd had there, playing dice, cards, and just listening to music. However, when we climbed the steps to the saloon, I noticed a change. I don't know when the transition happened, but we were now the old guys in the bar. The packed saloon now filled with twenty-somethings. This wasn't our scene anymore.

Jesse and MIHO went to the bar to get the first round while the rest of us found a spot along the wall. I scanned the room. As usual, there were the regulars and the weekend warriors. When MIHO and Jesse returned with the beverages, we gathered for our closing ceremonies.

"Okay," I said. I was the arbiter, the commissioner, the president of the LTO Organizing Committee, which meant I had to express the importance of the events of the weekend, wax poetically about the virtue of competition, and bestow the LTO title to Jesse. "We're gathered here today to bestow a champion. Over three days that tested our athletic prowess, our minds, our pain tolerance, our endurance—"

"And guile," Paul said.

"And *guile*," I repeated, "but in the end, there could only be one LTO champion, and that is Jesse!"

Everyone cheered, and Jesse raised his arms in triumph.

"Everyone, please, let's raise a glass and toast our man Jesse, our champion and the winner of the fifty-dollar pot." I gave him the five ten-dollar bills.

"Well, minus the two pitchers, it's about twenty bucks, but that's okay," Jesse said over the loud music. We all tapped cups and raised them to our lips.

When I looked up, I recognized a woman from my youth.

Paul noticed her too and waved. "Tanya!"

There she was, Tanya Dillon-Moretti, our old high school classmate, entering the saloon. She was dressed in tight jeans and a black top. Gone was her high, brown perm from high school, now straight with blonde highlights. Her youthful curves were replaced by sculpted angles, no doubt created by some CrossFit and/or yoga classes. She looked even better in person.

"You've got to be kidding me," Jesse verbalized what the rest of us were thinking.

Paul was already up and heading over to the door to give her a hug and welcome her to the saloon. They hugged like old friends, though I was sure they hadn't seen each other since Hammer pants were a thing.

I glanced at the rest of my friends. Rob was amused, MIHO was astonished, and Jesse was pissed. Paul led Tanya over to our table. She looked over at Rob, and her eyes grew wide. "Oh my god, Rob Simpson!"

"Hi Tanya," Rob said. "It's been a while."

"Hell yeah, it has. Jason and I followed you at USC and were sorry your football career didn't pan out."

"It happens. That was a long time ago. Now I'm a private investigator for a law firm in Sacramento."

"Really?" She turned her attention to the rest of us. "And here's Jim and David. I remember you guys. And you look very familiar, but you'll have to forgive me for not recalling your name." Tanya squinted at Jesse, trying to remember him in high school. I couldn't blame her for not recognizing him. Back then, he was short, skinny, and preferred to stay in the background. Now, he had grown in confidence and had a rock-solid physique.

"Jesse," he said, extending his hand. "We had the same Spanish class, Mr. Morales."

"Oh my god, yes. You were the smartest kid there. You were so good in that class. I had the hardest time."

Jesse had a different perspective. I remember him telling me about Tanya's veiled racist remarks about how Jesse screwed up the curve because he spoke it at home, then asking if he could bring homemade tamales to the in-class parties they sometimes had before holiday breaks. She was also Moretti's girlfriend, which made him dislike her more.

Paul headed to the bar to order a vodka soda for her.

"It was a hard class," Jesse said. "So, you're not with Jason anymore?"

"No, we're separated. We got married about a year out of high school when I got pregnant. We moved to Fresno so he could be a cop. About three months ago, I kicked him out. He was cheating on me. Asshole."

"Sorry about that," I said. "So, you have a kid?"

"Three. I have a fourteen-year-old son, Tommy, a ten-year-old daughter, Clara, and another daughter, Michelle, who's eight. They are a blessing."

"Yeah, I have a new son, William, he's six months old," I said. "And Jesse has eighteen-month-old twin daughters, and Rob has a seven-year-old daughter too."

"Wow, that's so great, you guys. And how about you, David?"

Before MIHO could answer, Paul returned with Tanya's drink.

"Oh, MIHO's gay," Paul said. "He likes dudes."

"Who? What?" Tanya looked confused.

"Paul's an ass," MIHO said. "Yes, I'm gay and in a relationship and live in Hawaii. MIHO's a nickname these assholes gave me years ago."

"Oh," Tanya said, taking in all the information. "Hawaii? I bet that's a dream."

"It's pretty nice. I can't complain at all. So, what brings you up here tonight?"

"Well, Jason has the kids this weekend, and my friends have a cabin up here that they let me use every once in a while. When Paul said you guys were all up here, I thought I'd come up and have a little reunion." She smiled and slapped Paul's thigh and rubbed it and looked at him starstruck. "I knew you'd be doing something cool but never thought you'd be on TV!"

I tried hard not to roll my eyes. Outside of that comment, Tanya had matured since high school, and it was nice to catch up with her, but I understood that this wasn't a chance meeting at a mountain saloon. Against our wishes, Paul had reached out to her, convinced her to come up to the lake, and was looking to do more than just chat. Not even a "real" relationship was going to keep him from ditching us again. I thought it was time to take Paul outside.

"Hey, Paul, I need to get your extra thing from Rob's truck," I said. I was horrible at being sly, and Paul knew it. Still, he entertained my intention.

We walked to the truck, and as we got away from the saloon, I looked down. "What are you doing? You're trying to hook up, aren't you? Don't screw up what you have back in Bristol over one night at the lake."

"That's the thing. I don't know what I have in Bristol. And Tanya's hot, and I had a crush on her in high school. And it would be kind of a final 'fuck you' to Moretti."

"Dude, who cares about Moretti now? Plus, Tanya's her own person and not his possession. And you're going to ditch us again. You do this every flippin' year. God, I thought with a girlfriend, you'd stay faithful and we'd hang out the whole weekend, but I guess not."

"You guys think I'm going to cheat anyway."

"No. Things come down to little choices. Remember the bachelor party? I made a string of small, bad choices that led to a huge choice, and I barely made it correctly. Right now, the choices are easier. You can just stop, turn around, and go the other way. That's it."

"Well, they're my choices. I'm not married. I'm just dating. I don't have a kid. I can do what I want, and I'm not sure if Paula is forever. So, I'll make my choices. I appreciate you letting me know your thoughts, but it's my life, man."

"You're right."

Paul started to walk back.

"It's your choice but remember that our choices reveal our integrity."

Paul turned and looked back at me, his eyes narrowed. "Are you saying I don't have integrity?"

"I didn't say that."

"Fuck you. You did." Paul got right in my face. "Fuck you and your self-righteous bullshit. You know, you always do this. You try to live this high life, not because you're trying to improve the world but so you can look down on the rest of us. I'm so glad you have your life figured out and you have the perfect wife and the perfect child. But the rest of us are trying to figure it out, and we're doing the best we can. So, save me your condescension and let me be."

I wanted to say something, but I didn't know if I could refute him. During my bachelor party, I'd faced a choice and had made the right one, but I was engaged. He'd only been dating this girl for six months.

"Paul, you're a good guy," I said. "If it doesn't work out with Paula, that's fine. But break it off with her and then go back to messing around. This is about respect for Paula as much as your selfishness."

"You've got to be kidding me," Paul said, shaking his head. "Selfish? I was the one who was there to save your ass before. I don't need your saving here."

Paul walked back inside and went to Tanya. I stood at the base of the steps into the saloon, trying to process the conversation. I wasn't sure anything I said would mean anything. He was going to do what he was going to do. When I returned, Jesse, Rob, and MIHO could tell our talk had not gone well outside. We stayed for about thirty minutes, but every look from Paul was a death stare. He was waiting for me to leave. He only held a smile when he looked at Tanya. The fun times for me were over. It was time to go.

"Should we get back?" I said as I finished my beer. "My last night of sleep!"

"Yeah, I'm getting tired too," Jesse said. Over the course of the night, he softened his opinion of Tanya, but he was also ready to go.

"Oh," Tanya said, disappointed. She didn't want us, well, Paul to leave.

"I think I'll stay out a bit later," Paul said. "Tanya, would you mind driving me back to our cabin if you want to stay out?"

"Sure," Tanya said. "That's fine with me."

Rob looked at the situation, and we all realized we were ditched once again. We finished, settled with the bartender, gave a farewell hug to Tanya, and left. As we walked back to the truck, I recounted the conversation with Paul, and they agreed I was right to remind him what was at stake and that the choices he made were his and we couldn't do anything about it. We drove back, hoping Paul would do the right thing. Ten years ago, we may have rooted for him. Now, we were disappointed.

"Well, you know you can be a self-righteous prick, right?" MIHO said. He put his hand on my shoulder. "It's annoying, but it's a good quality. You're my Jiminy Cricket, a voice that tells me to stop making bad decisions."

"Thanks," I said. "I think."

"Don't worry about Paul," Jesse said. "The one way to get him to do what you want is to tell him not to do it."

We got back and sat on the couch and watched *Wedding Crashers* on DVD with one of the Wilson Brothers and Vince Vaughn. We finished that movie and started *Old School* with Vince Vaughn and the other Wilson brother. The longer the movies went, the more we were convinced that Paul had made the wrong choice. Well, six months was a good length for a relationship for Paul. It was better that it ended sooner than later when damage could really be done. After we finished *Old School*, we headed to bed. Part of me wanted to wait up for him. Part of me knew that he'd come back in the morning. All of me knew he was a grown man who'd made the walk of shame hundreds of times.

When did my impression of Paul's hookups turn from admiration to disappointment? Was it my own maturity? Fatherhood? Just being old? In any case, I wanted him to be back at the cabin, laughing and having a good time with us. We went to bed around one and heard a car pull into the driveway around two. I heard the front door open, some stirring, followed by Paul using the bathroom to brush teeth, use the restroom, then head to bed. When I woke up the next morning, Jesse was already on the deck with his coffee and reading a novel. I poured my own cup and joined him.

"Morning," I said.

Jesse looked up from his book and nodded. "Morning." He closed his book. "So, Paul came back."

"About two," I said. I was done talking about Paul. "I'm ready to get home and see the wife and kid."

"It's about that time," Jesse agreed. "It'll be nice to get back. This weekend was perfect for me to think about some stuff, and I can't wait to get home to talk it through with her."

"Is everything okay?" I asked. I felt that Jesse was a little distracted.

"It's hit and miss. We just have the normal struggles of a home-based spouse and a career-focused spouse."

"Man, sorry. I wish I could help. I'm lucky to have summers off, but it's not like you."

"Well, the time I get to spend with Jennifer and Nicole is something I wouldn't trade, so we just need to work it out."

We sat with our coffee and the crisp mountain air sharing kid stories. MIHO and Rob joined us as we enjoyed our final morning of the trip and the expectation of Paul's story. We all wanted to know what happened.

Eventually, Paul strolled in.

"So?" MIHO asked.

"Nothing happened," Paul said. "Well...I take that back. We went back to her cabin and made out. And we were going to do it, but we didn't have any condoms, so it went pretty cold after that and ended before it started."

"What does that mean for Paula?" Jesse asked.

"What do you mean? I didn't cheat. I just made out. Nothing changes."

"But you would have," I said.

"But I didn't, big difference," Paul said, looking at me with the same face as he had during our argument last night. His stare then lightened, and he took a breath. "Sorry, I'm just a little defensive. I know your hearts are in the right place, and you're just looking out for me. But you don't have to. I'm a grown man, and I make my own choices. And I did make the right choice eventually, thanks to you guys. All I could hear were your annoying voices."

I smiled and patted his shoulder. That was good enough for me. MIHO made breakfast as we packed our stuff and cleaned up. Everyone agreed that the cabin was now a standard. No more camping for us. We were getting too old to "rough it" without showers, a running toilet, a full kitchen, a TV, etc. This was an all right way to spend a weekend.

While we didn't have to pack up tents and sleeping bags, we did have to strip the bedding, empty the trash, and do the dishes so I could get my deposit back. I went through and picked up all the trash in the kitchen and bathrooms. Behind the trash can in one of the bathrooms was a stray box. I was surprised to see it—an empty three-pack of condoms.

11

Paul

Friday Evening

June 24, 2016

O h, Tanya," Paul said. "You know, she used me as much as I used her."

"I was so pissed," Jesse said. "You were such an asshole. I mean, we even told you not to ask her up, and you still did. Man, that was low."

Paul shook his head. It was a well-deserved admonition of his toxic masculinity. His image had become a house of cards that was destined to collapse. Over the years, his friends tried to help him create a stronger foundation, but in the end, all they could do was wait until the eventual fall.

"Tell me about it," he said. "It was a slow downward spiral from there."

Paul slung two fold-out camping chairs over his shoulder and loaded his arms with firewood to take from the house to the campfire. Jim moved them to the house two years after that first cabin, named "the Rock" for the large granite mountainside to which the house opened. The large, barren edifice allowed them to build a campfire in the middle of the mountainside without the fear of catching the drought-stricken forest on fire. In fact, a rock fire ring already existed, and it took two trips from the house to set their evening camp with chairs, a six pack of beer, coffee, and of course a bag of animal crackers.

As Paul walked back and forth to the cabin, he remembered the aftermath. He and Paula had made up and never mentioned Tanya. However, the dam had burst. Just as his friends had predicted, he reactivated his network. Trips out of town became invitations to his hotel room after an assignment. Paul felt bad about lying and betraying Paula, but he was more interested in sleeping away his loneliness.

Two months later, an errant text he meant for a woman in Dallas went to Paula instead. He tried to play it off, but she saw through it. The breakup didn't even wait until he returned home. By the time he had made it back to his apartment, she had removed all trace of herself, including pictures, toothbrushes, clothes, etc. In their place across the living room wall, she had written "ASSHOLE" in permanent marker. He tried to scrub it out but had to repaint the whole room.

In a way, the breakup was a relief. Paul didn't have to lie anymore. He could just be upfront and transparent about his promiscuity. It was understood that his "relationships" came with no strings. In reality, his fun-loving demeanor and short-term companionship masked his profound loneliness and detachment. He often came home to the same cold and empty apartment or to a familiar hotel room. The only voices greeting him were those he could hear through the walls or from the TV he forgot to turn off when he left. There was no one with whom he could relive his day or listen to the highlights of their day. The women were just distractions to fill the time between the end of one shift and the beginning of another.

Paul loved his work. It was what he was meant to do. He enjoyed talking to the athletes and creating reports and having them air. He enjoyed being at the anchor desk and the thrill of live television and operating without a net. It was the time between shifts that he had begun to loathe. At one time, he had loved being on the road and having no family and traveling the world. Now, though, he envied his best friends. They had all found happiness within themselves and found people with whom to share it. Now that he was back in Sacramento, he had found home. It had taken a fall from grace to get there, but he knew who his friends were.

While Rob focused on getting the fire started, Paul looked out at the valley and the colorful sky. It was about twenty minutes past sunset, when the sky begins yellow at the horizon and transitions to a deep purple overhead. As they started the fire, Paul walked toward the edge of the mountainside. He looked up and saw one of the first stars of the night. Paul wasn't a religious man, but he hoped the star was Jim saying a quick hi to him on the rock. He turned and saw his three remaining friends sitting and laughing, highlighted by the flickering orange and yellow light given off by the flecks of the new campfire. They had known each other since before adolescence, each of them with their niche. Rob was the athlete, Jim was the smart one, Jesse the math whiz, MIHO the hardest worker, and Paul was the charmer. Even at a young age, Paul talked his way into good grades and a rendezvous behind the gymnasium. While the rest of them had grown up, sometimes Paul thought he was still that same kid trying to seek validation from others.

Paul found reliving the past through this journal quite painful. Oh, how shallow he had been, and Jim's growing disappointment oozed through the pages. In Jim's writings, Paul was just a caricature, the obligatory asshole in the group. Through therapy, he was realizing that Jim was his hero and had the life Paul had always wanted. The more domesticated and grounded Jim became, the more Paul rejected it and resented him for it. And just when he was beginning to come to these realizations, the one person from whom he wanted the ultimate validation was no longer there.

"Dammit, Jim," Paul repeated the one Star Trek reference they knew and said as a joke. This time, it was said out of anger. Paul's own redemption with Jim was robbed, and he would never have the opportunity to show Jim how good of a man he could be.

Paul picked up a piece of chipped granite and held it in his hand, the course texture rubbing against his palm. It felt the most real thing in his world. Paul looked back up to the darkening sky and chucked the rock sidearm toward that lonely star. The rock disappeared. He picked up another, this one flatter and scraggly, and threw it. He repeated the action again and again, each successive rock thrown harder than the last. Pretty soon, he was grunting. And those grunts turned to sobs.

"Hey," a voice came from behind him.

Paul turned and saw Rob, silhouetted against the fire, a bottle in his right hand. Paul put his hands on his hips. He was breathless.

"Although we're as close to heaven as we can get, I don't think you're going to hit him," Rob said.

Paul smiled and gave a solitary laugh. He wiped his eyes and sniffed, putting his tongue to the side of his cheek, trying to find the courage for words. He dropped the last rock he had just picked up.

"I suppose not," he said, his voice cracking. "I just wasted so much time being this character that I didn't see that all you guys wanted was for me to be real. And it was too late before I figured it out."

"We knew. And it's never too late."

"Yeah, after how many wasted years?" Paul was still angry at Jim and himself.

Rob walked over and wrapped his large arm around Paul's shoulder as they looked toward the dusk.

Rob took a deep breath, understanding that these next important words needed to be expressed. "Paul, you've been through the ringer, and it was of your own doing. But we've always known what was underneath, who you really are. We were frustrated because you were an asshole and couldn't see it. But we always knew."

"I was an asshole. I was a jerk and the worst of us. Yet, you're still here."

"Believe me, it wasn't easy," MIHO said from behind. Rob and Paul turned to see Jesse and MIHO with the fire glowing behind them. "There were times when I wasn't sure why you were still my friend. And yes, we talked about whether to invite you back on the trip. But then we'd remember how you'd have our backs. You may self-destruct but would make sure we didn't."

There were bro hugs all around, bonding once again up here in the mountains, but this time without the linchpin to their friendship. As the dusk turned to night, they went back to the fire. Paul still felt a deep pit of regret and grief, but his friends had given him an infusion of strength. They had grown since the first time they had come up here. Three of them poured themselves a cup of decaf from the thermos as they were on the rock. They stared at the fire, the flames causing them to slip into a trance, thinking of the endless stories of their friendship and Jim. Everyone seemed to relish this time of reflection. Rob needed to do something, so he stood up and put another log on the fire. As he did, embers from the already burning wood drifted into the sky. Dusk had now turned to full night, and even though the light from the campfire kept them from seeing the brilliance of the night sky, they could still make out the millions of stars.

After the fire had a good hot bed of coals, Rob put a beer bottle into the flames. "The game is called 'integrity,'" Rob said. "And the object is to get the fire so hot that the glass melts and you manipulate the glass somewhat without breaking it. It's a challenge for yourself. Can you do it without breaking the bottle? It's harder than you might think."

They all had small sticks to help manipulate the bottles in the fire. Soon the labels burned off, and they watched the flames roll over the glass. About five minutes in, MIHO's bottle exploded.

"Yikes," Jesse said shielding his eyes from any glass.

They all laughed as it looked like the task wasn't going to be as easy as just watching a paper plate catch fire and become an ember.

"Oh, I forgot, you have to make sure the air flow is consistent," said Rob, "or else the air inside will expand and push through the glass, and it will be *ee*-stroyed."

"Well, thanks for letting us know now," MIHO said with sarcasm.

The glass melting gave them all something to focus on and laugh about, although they all thought about Jim. Tomorrow was Saturday, the day they would go to Tom Sawyer Island. They were over the hump on the trip and on the backside of their time together. But tonight, they were playing a silly game with beer bottles and fire and laughing like they were eighteen again.

Jesse's bottle broke. Unlike MIHO's, Jesse's bottle just cracked and fell apart. "That was disappointing," Jesse said. "I didn't even get special effects like MIHO." Jesse sat back and stared at the fire.

Rob was careful to rotate his empty Coors Light bottle, and Paul did the same with Sierra Nevada. Soon, both of their bottles began to warp. Rob and Paul stood with their sticks Their smiles were broad, like a child getting their toys to work for the first time. Rob was gentle as he twisted the stick, which caused the bottle to twist onto itself. Paul just bent his over, making the top and base at ninety-degree angles.

"This is so cool," Paul said. "Who knew you could do this? How did it take this long for us to even try?"

"I went camping with Leslie, her friends, and their dads late last summer," Rob said. "They made the bottles twist and extend. It was clear they'd done it before. I broke two bottles then. This is the first time I've done it right. So cool."

"Who knew?" Paul said. "Now what?"

"The best thing to do is to pull them out with your stick, and if you can, put it to the side of the fire so it can cool," Rob said. "But be careful. You don't want the bottle to explode."

"Right," Paul said being very careful. He used the stick to pull out the bottle and place it next to the rocks. Rob did the same, and somehow, the bottles survived the transfer from the kiln. Rob and Paul gave each other a high five and laughed.

Paul's feeling of elation of completing the task was short-lived, and soon his thoughts returned to the regret he felt for the wasted time he had spent focused on women rather than his friends. The journal captured as much of his carnal pursuits than their shared jokes and experiences.

"I'm going to bed. I'm tired," Paul said. "Tomorrow's a big day."

"C'mon, don't you want to read the next section of the journal?" MIHO asked.

"So, I can see how poorly I behaved? What's the next big section?"

MIHO flipped through a couple pages and found the next section. He winced. This section wouldn't inspire Paul to stay.

In fact, it was another reason to head to bed. "It's the trip to Ann Arbor," MIHO said.

"Oh, hell no," Paul said. "I've relived that year plenty of times and don't have any interest to read how Jim recalls it. I'm going to bed."

MIHO, Rob, and Jesse nodded. Paul started back to the cabin. He took about ten steps, turned, and came back to the fire.

"Look, I love you guys," Paul said. "We all know the path I've taken, and I'd rather not relive it. It's only going to make it more awkward. It's better for me to just turn in and be refreshed tomorrow."

"Understood," Rob said. "We love you too, brother. Good night."

Rob, MIHO, and Jesse all turned in their chairs and looked at Paul. Paul nodded and walked back toward the cabin. Rob, Jesse, and MIHO followed with their eyes before returning their focus to the raging fire. They had a few more logs to burn.

As Paul walked back to the house, he recalled the Ann Arbor trip. It was supposed to be the chance to show his friends his alma mater and his favorite place in the world, the University of Michigan on a college football game day. For 90 percent of the trip, he couldn't have asked for anything more. Unfortunately, that last 10 percent cost him dearly.

Paul walked into the cabin and got ready for bed. He sat on the bed in his dark room and breathed. These moments of mindfulness had become a deep part of his process as he moved back to Sacramento and when Jim died. Paul knew Jim was in heaven, even though he didn't really believe in the afterlife.

Paul just felt Jim was in a better place embedded in the memories and souls of all the people he had touched. He was there with them right now. The journal was painful, but it was also bringing them back together, helping them restore the memories that had brought them closer. This was Jim's afterlife, the impact he had on his friends.

And what about Paul's own impact? He had certainly left a wake of brokenness along the way. In the midst of it all, he justified his behavior by saying that everything was consensual and therefore, ok. But was it? Sure the women were into it, but he didn't care about them more than in the senses of the moment. In the last year, he had realized how dehumanizing this endless string of hookups had been to them and to himself.

Before he climbed in for the night, Paul looked outside and saw the glow of the fire and three silhouettes. One of the silhouettes had a flashlight beaming in front of him. It must be MIHO reading about the best game and worst night of his life.

12

Jim

2011

The buzz against in my pocket was unmistakable. I pulled out the phone and flipped it open.

Paul: *Here's an idea. Instead of a lake trip, Michigan v. Notre Dame for the FIRST-EVER night game at the Big House in September. I'll likely be working it anyway. Go Blue!*

"This is interesting," I said. It was mid-January, and I was in the kitchen with Tracey preparing dinner for our little family.

"What's that?" Tracey said. She was placing green beans on the pan to roast while I was coating the chicken breast with panko breadcrumbs for baking. In February, I began thinking of cabins and places to stay. However, Paul made a preemptive strike, and now I was thinking of whether this could work.

"Instead of the guys' trip to the lake, Paul wants us to go to a Michigan football game."

"Are they playing in California?" Tracey opened the oven and took the pan of chicken I'd just coated and placed it inside. She didn't follow college football and only knew if it was Michigan on the TV by the distinctive helmets.

"No, we'd be going to Ann Arbor. They're playing Notre Dame in September. Paul thinks he'll be assigned to the game and wants us to join him. He thinks it'll be fun for us to go there instead of the lake."

Tracey went to the question I knew she would. "How much is this going to cost?" The trip wouldn't be cheap with a flight, hotel, food, not to mention tickets, which would be exponentially more than a game at Sac State.

"Well, it'll be a little expensive, but it would replace the annual trip."

"If you want to go, you don't need my permission." Tracey grabbed her glass of wine. "Just remember, Willie starts preschool next year, and we'll have those added costs. Don't break our budget for your fun."

Over the past three years, watching Willie grow from a helpless baby to a toddler to the beginnings of a kid had been transformative. Thinking back to the days before him were unimaginable. Things I worried about—sports teams, the front lawn, TV shows—didn't seem to matter anymore. The TV shows I cared about now were the *Backyardigans* and *Dora The Explorer*.

"Are the other guys going?" Tracey asked.

"Paul just sent out the text to everyone. I don't know how the other guys are feeling."

MIHO was still in Hawaii and now the second in command at the Marriott in Honolulu. He had just split from Charles after he let him know he wanted to move back to the mainland. Charles wasn't interested in moving to the mainland or carrying on long distance. I felt bad for MIHO. He enjoyed Charles and Hawaii, but he was homesick and wanted to get back to California to be nearer to his family and his friends. With the prospects of a new job, he may not want to fly twelve-plus hours to Michigan to spend time with us.

Jesse continued to be a great stay-at-home dad, and a weekend away always presented logistical problems. Add in the costs to a one-income household, and he might get vetoed by Danielle, who continued to spend more time at the office than not. It seemed something had to give. Jesse continued to express his frustration over her job and the lack of time she was at home.

Rob was enjoying joint custody of Leslie with Becky, and it seemed all was going okay. I could tell he was still pining for Becky, even if he wouldn't admit it. He often talked more about her and Leslie than he did about himself. Just a couple months ago, he told me shared that Becky was always complaining about her job and looking for a change.

"It could be pretty fun," Tracey said, pulling me back. She leaned against the counter and sipped her wine. I wrapped my arms around her.

"Are you sure you'll be okay with me flying across the country to relive Paul's glory days?" I leaned down and kissed her forehead and smiled.

"I'm okay with you flying across the country to take in a college football game with your friends," Tracey said, giving me a fake look of discontent, "but I'm not sure I'm okay with you reliving Paul's college days. I can't imagine... Never mind, I don't want to imagine it."

Over the past few years, it had become harder and harder to hang out with Paul on the trip. His stories were becoming sadder than vicarious fantasy, and he was less and less interested in hanging out with us than he was meeting someone else. I was getting tired of it and wondered if we needed to give him an ultimatum. Everyone was entitled to getting what they wanted from the trip, but the whole purpose was to hang out together, not find the first opportunity to get laid. Now, we were faced with Paul on a college campus exploding with hormone-crazed coeds, where he was now a semifamous alumnus. Yet, this was less about Paul and more about the opportunity to have a real college football experience with my best friends. I gave Tracey a sympathetic look, brushed the hair from her face, smiled, and kissed her.

"He's inviting us to join him, but I have MIHO, Rob, and Jesse to keep us all on the straight and narrow." I pointed forward. I was focused. No mistakes here. "Even if he does try to get us to do something we don't want to do, the rest of us aren't going to go along. You can trust us. You can trust me."

Tracey smiled. "I trust you. Of course, maybe I'll have to satisfy every sexual desire before you leave so those college girls won't sway you at all."

She pulled me in for a deep, sensuous kiss. We recently decided it was time for us to start trying for another child. With William heading into preschool, the separation of ages was just about right. She lifted her leg around me to pull my growing erection close to her before we heard the quick pattering of small footsteps coming down the hall. Tracey lowered her leg and straightened out her clothes as he turned the corner and entered the kitchen. Her eyes of lust now filled with maternal pride and love.

"Daddy, Daddy, I gotta show you something," Willie said. His smile was wide, and his eyes were big. His floppy brown hair was sticking up in several places. He held a Thomas the Tank engine in his left hand. "C'mon." He held out his hand wanting to lead me to his room.

As I left the kitchen, I smiled back at Tracey. "Maybe later you can show me your superior skills."

I heard her as I rounded the corner, "You can bet on it."

Willie led me to his room where he'd arranged his Thomas the Train engine track in an abstract path that made perfect sense to him but not so much to me. He combined his wooden and plastic tracks to make a virtual city and made Lightning McQueen and Tow Mater a part of the Thomas community.

"Welcome to Willieburg," he said with pride.

"Wow," I said, my eyes filled with joy and surprise. As I watched him explain the intricacies of his town and the relationships between all the toys who inhabited Willieburg, I couldn't believe the love and joy that filled me in that moment. Now, Tracey and I wanted to start that process all over again. We were at the tail end of diapers, and soon we would be changing them again, and then there'd be the late-night feedings. If the next child was anything like Willie, then it would be worth it. I spent the next half hour with him until dinner was ready. After we ate and washed the dishes, I saw several messages from MIHO, Jesse, and Rob, wanting to talk about the direction of the trip. Since I was always principle organizer, they took some direction from me.

"What do you think?" MIHO said as he picked up the phone.

"What do *you* think?" I retorted. "You'll be flying from Honolulu to Detroit."

"I can make it work. I have some vacation time. The question is whether or not Paul will behave himself."

The four of us were relating to Paul less and less, and it broke my heart. He was still stuck in this adolescent bubble, and we were increasingly putting up with him rather than including him. We couldn't force him to grow up.

"Oh, he won't," I said. "We just need to make sure we don't engage in his shenanigans."

MIHO laughed. "Okay, old man. Slow down on your 'shenanigans.' Do you think the other guys will be up for it?"

"We'll find out. They're my next calls."

I followed up with Jesse and Rob. Rob, as expected, wasn't thrilled about watching either Michigan or Notre Dame, and his money was tight. Yet, he could swing it, granted he didn't have any extra added costs. Jesse said yes. He needed a break.

"For all the crap we're sure to endure with Paul being on his home turf with college students," Jesse said, "he's going to give us the best view of the university, and we're going to have a lot of fun."

Paul often ridiculed us for not going to a major athletic powerhouse like Michigan or USC. According to Paul, we'd missed out not living on campus and being able to get away from home like he had. I reminded him all the time that I still had a degree and was doing fine.

"All right, then we're in," I said when I called him back. "One concern we all have is money. Is there anything we can do to minimize costs?"

"Don't worry about the hotel or tickets," Paul said. "I may be able to get both comped by ESPN or the university or both. Just worry about getting flights. Sound good?"

"Sounds great!" I said. While flights still wouldn't be cheap, knowing that game tickets and hotel rooms were taken care of helped ease the concern. "It's just going to be weird not going up to the lake."

"It's time to shake things up a bit," Paul said. "No offense, but we've done the same trip for, what, thirteen years? Nothing wrong with some new experiences."

I couldn't deny that I was excited. It was strange that none of us ever visited Paul when he was in college. It wasn't cheap for poor college students to fly to the Midwest for a simple visit, but none of us ever visited him at college or any of his career stops along the way. He'd been at ESPN for six years, and none of us had ever visited Bristol. Sure, his schedule was nuts and could change at any moment, but as I thought about this trip, I regretted never even considering a visit to our friend.

As the winter stretched into spring and early summer, the trip started to come together. Rob and I were flying from Sacramento. Jesse was catching a flight in Los Angeles, and MIHO had the worst of all of us. His trip would take nearly twelve hours with a layover.

The game ticket prices were in the three-hundred-dollar range. Paul kept assuring me that he had it covered, even if he didn't have the exact tickets just yet. I also asked about the hotel. Even though it was a major university, there weren't many hotel rooms available in Ann Arbor. Many of the hotel rooms were closer to Detroit and the airport. Paul told me not to worry about that either.

"He operates different than you do," Tracey reminded me when I voiced my concerns to her one night in June as we were getting ready for bed. "He's gotten to where he is by making things happen. You do things very methodically. He does things by finding the angles and maneuvering. Two different ways, but both are effective."

"It would be easier if everything was planned with contingencies. What if he doesn't get tickets? What if we don't have a hotel to stay in? What happens then? I don't want to be outside the stadium in a tent with no tickets or having to pay a scalper five hundred bucks for nosebleeds."

"You just have to let go. Have faith. Paul will make it happen."

"I just like to have things in hand."

"Mmm, same here," she said, and she grabbed me and began to move her hand up and down. "Now let's stop talking and see what trouble we can get into."

Just like Tracey had said, Paul came through and confirmed he had two adjoining rooms at a hotel in Ann Arbor and five tickets five rows from the end zone. I exhaled when I saw the text. In addition to the late-night game, Paul confirmed that ESPN's top college football pregame road show, *College Game-Day*, was scheduled to be on campus for the game on Saturday morning. As part of the coverage, Paul would be on campus interviewing key players.

When the Thursday in early September came, I was excited. After we dropped off Willie at preschool, Tracey drove me to the airport. She pulled to the curb, and there was Rob with his duffle bag. His smile got big as he saw us. Tracey put the car in park and popped the back of the RAV4 so I could get my suitcase. Rob gave me a big hug as soon as I got out and before I even got to the trunk of the car to pull out my bag.

"Are you ready?" Rob asked.

"Big House, here we come," I said.

"It's not as good as the Coliseum," Rob dismissed, but he smiled anyway. "Tracey, thanks for letting this guy fly across the country with his crazy friends."

"You guys are going to have fun," Tracey said. "Just don't let Paul get you in trouble."

"Never," Rob said and winked. "We'll be good boys."

Tracey rolled her eyes, then gave Rob a hug and then me. She gave me a long kiss with a big squeeze that left me so happy. "Call me when you get there," she said.

"I will. I love you," I said.

"Love you too," Tracey said, and she slipped into the small SUV, smiled, waved, put the car in drive, and pulled away.

"So, what's the latest with Becky," I asked when we settled into our seats on that first flight.

"She's officially moving to Reno," Rob said. "And taking Leslie."

What began as unhappiness with her job, turned into accepting a job offer and moving to Reno. Rob had told me countless times how she'd lamented quitting and starting over. But when she told him that she was moving, he was stunned, even though she gave him updates from posting to application to interview to background check. Now, it was real.

"I have an appointment with a lawyer next week, and I'm going to take her to court," Rob said.

"Wow, why didn't you do this a few months ago?"

"I always hoped that she wouldn't go through with it and ruin what we have, I thought she'd just come to her senses and stay. That's what you get for optimism."

"That sucks, man."

We sipped more of our loaded coffee. Although Reno was about two hours away, it felt a world removed. As more weekends would be taken visiting his daughter, that would mean less time for us to hang out. But I couldn't imagine the effort Rob would endure driving to Reno a couple times a month, especially during the winter when Donner Pass could be closed due to snow or ice. I listened to Rob discuss the options and his almost desperation of next steps until we exhausted the topic. When the wheels touched down, we turned on our phones at the same time. They buzzed with the same text message: *Welcome to Michigan, bitches! I have MIHO and Jesse, and we're waiting for you. Let me know the baggage claim number.*

"Are you texting him back?" I asked.

"On it," Rob said. He flipped open his phone—he was holding out on getting an iPhone like the rest of us and typed out the gate number where they could meet us.

As we came across the threshold to the carousel area, I saw MIHO and Jesse. Behind and to the side was Paul, who was taking a picture with what must have been a family of four, all donned in Michigan maize and blue. I half expected Paul to blend in with Michigan fan gear until I remembered he was supposed to be working.

Jesse saw us first and motioned to MIHO. MIHO's eyes and mouth went wide as he came up to us for hugs all around.

"Hey guys," he said.

"How can you be awake?" I asked. "Haven't you been on a plane for like twelve hours?"

"Just don't ask me what time it is, and I hope we're not partying tonight. I think I may just crash. We have a big couple days ahead."

"Yeah, maybe a late dinner, then hang at the hotel room?" I suggested. "No worries from here. I don't know what Paul's schedule is, though."

Paul had finished talking to his fans and came over to us with his arms spread. "My boys are here!" He pulled us in close. "Come on in for the real thing. I'm so glad you're here."

"I didn't expect you to be here," I said. "I thought you had to work."

We walked toward the glass exit doors. The doors opened, and in front of us was a long, black limousine with an open trunk and a chauffeur ready to take our bags.

"What the hell?" Rob said. "You got a flipping limo?"

"Only the best for my boys," Paul said. "With a group our size, it's more cost effective than a couple taxis, and it's more stylish, eh?"

"I'm not gonna complain," Jesse said as he provided the chauffeur his bag and climbed in. Rob, MIHO, and I did the same, followed by Paul. The driver got in, and we were off for the half-hour drive to the Marriott in Ann Arbor.

"So, what kind of rooms do we have? The presidential suite?" Rob asked.

"High expectations much?" Paul said. "No suite, but I was able to get adjoining rooms with a rollaway so everyone gets a bed. I hope that's okay."

"Just the fact that we have a hotel room and don't have to crash in some graduate student's spare bedroom is a win," I said.

"Glad it meets your approval," Paul said. He gave me a wink. I'm sure he was sick of me badgering him on the details. "All right, so I'm going to drop you guys off and head back to work. I'm sure you're all tired, so just relax, and we'll get after it tomorrow morning."

"Sounds good. We were just saying we should lay low," MIHO said. "That way we're not chasing rest all weekend."

"I like your thinking," Paul said. "Plus, I won't be much fun. I'll be in very late or early in the morning. I don't want to miss anything with you guys."

Before long, we arrived at the Marriott, and Paul dropped us off at the lobby. He'd already checked in and gave us each a key card. I felt such relief. We arrived and had rooms. I was disappointed that Paul had to go, but we were here together. After settling in, we made it down to the hotel restaurant. I was starving and ready to kick back, have a few, and toast my friends.

"Hey, I wanted Paul to be here with us to announce this, but I can hardly help myself," MIHO said. "I'm moving back to the mainland. I'm now the general manager at the Hyatt Huntington Beach."

"Wow, congratulations," Rob said. "That's fantastic, Mr. Big."

MIHO rolled his eyes. I always knew he was smart, worked hard, and was a good leader, but to move up the ranks as he had was still quite an accomplishment. I couldn't have been prouder.

"Awesome. You'll be closer to us now and not have to fly forever to see us," I said. "But does that mean a full stop with Charles?"

MIHO nodded.

Jesse was happy for MIHO but showed a little mock disappointment. "Man, I missed my chance to get comped accommodations," he said.

"Five years, buddy," MIHO said, raising his hands. "You had your chance. But look at it this way, you can take advantage of a couples retreat just minutes away. I'll hook you up!"

"Thanks, man," Jesse said. He raised his glass. "I also have an announcement. I think I'm ready to reenter the workforce."

This was an even bigger surprise. He was hitting his stride as the primary caregiver. Every time I spoke with him, he glowed about coaching soccer, volunteering at preschool, running and scheduling playdates with their friends.

"I thought you liked being a stay-at-home dad," Rob said.

"Oh, I do. The girls are heading into school, and the law-firm grind is killing Danielle. We never see her. She's only home to sleep, and she hardly does that. She's under constant pressure from the partners, and I can see that it's affecting her physical and mental health. If I can relieve the pressure of her being the sole provider, then I need to do it."

"How does she feel about it?" I asked.

"She's proud, and sometimes that means not telling me she needs help. I think she has this goal of becoming partner stuck in her mind and thinks everything will be fine once she achieves it. I'd rather she just find a smaller practice and be home, even if that means less money. Add in that she thinks I want to be 'the man' and take care of her, and we've had some... 'intense discussions' as our therapist calls it. I didn't know being a man was a bad thing..."

Jesse had gotten himself worked up. He took a sip of his beer to calm himself, and we all did the same, if only to give him a brief pause to collect himself. Jesse placed his glass on the table and stared at the foamy, amber liquid.

Even though Rob was Jesse's best friend, he was unaware of their counseling. "So, you're seeing a therapist?" he asked.

"Yeah. We would have split up years ago if it wasn't for that. If we didn't have a time or place on the schedule to talk through our frustrations and fears and all of it, we wouldn't have found the opportunity to do it at home, and one of us would have given up."

"Wow, that's so interesting," I said. "I know there have been times when I wanted to tell Tracey about something and haven't because Willie came in or we wanted to watch TV or it was time for bed or whatever reason. It's easier to not go there when there's nothing to compel you."

"Exactly," Jesse said.

"Congrats to you, my friend," MIHO said, and we all raised our glasses. "Welcome back to the grind."

"To the drones!" Rob said, and we clinked our glasses. I wished Paul was around for the sharing, but it turned out that he didn't get back to the hotel room until about 1:30 a.m., after we'd gone to bed. It must have been some kind of editing project to keep him out all night.

Over the years, we'd heard every story about the University of Michigan campus, so now that we were finally here, we were excited to get the day started with a tour. After Paul's late night, he had other ideas, and it took Jesse's recently used running shorts draped over Paul's face to get him to move. Paul jolted to everyone's amusement, and before long, we were out the door. Our crew was a group of characters. Paul had on maize and blue, of course. Rob was defiant wearing USC crimson. Jesse and I were nondescript, and MIHO had a bright-turquoise aloha shirt.

"Is this your whole wardrobe now?" I asked MIHO. "What are you going to do when you have to wear suits?"

"I know. That's the one thing I'm going to miss the most."

"Besides being in Hawaii," Jesse said.

"Huntington Beach, Waikiki Beach," MIHO said, weighing both hands. "Ocean, check. Beach, check."

"Meanwhile, USC Rob here stands out," Paul said. "But at least you're not wearing Notre Dame gear."

We weren't a block from the hotel when we came upon a pop-up T-shirt stand with shirts that promoted Michigan or denigrated Notre Dame. Rob spent some extra time with these latter shirts and picked one that declared "Rudy was a Hobbit," poking fun at the fact that Sean Astin had played famed Notre Dame walk-on Rudy Rudiger and a hobbit in the *Lord of the Rings* trilogy. Rob got his XXL and changed shirts right there.

"Happy?" Rob asked Paul.

"Well, I wish you'd warned me about viewing your exposed torso, but yes, that's much more appropriate for our tour."

We walked to all corners of the campus, from landmarks like "the Cube" and "the Diag," to lunch at the famous Zingerman's Deli. Paul showed us all the highlights, including the expansive library, and we saw the crew setting up the *College GameDay* set for the following morning. We made it to the M Den, which is the official University of Michigan gear store, where you can buy anything from T-shirts to pint glasses to authentic jerseys and Jenga. I could have easily dropped a couple hundred dollars, but I held back. Meanwhile, Paul went all out, including buying a special "throwback" jersey for the game.

After about five hours of touring, we were ready to head back to the hotel and get some rest before going out on the town. I had some time to call Tracey and update her on our trip. I went to the courtyard. Since it was early September, it was a nice evening, not too humid and not too hot, just before the Midwest fall took effect.

"So, you're having a good time?" Tracey said. "Glad you took the trip?"

"Definitely. It's good to do something a little different. Plus, there are just so many people. It feels like much more than just a game."

"A little different than Sac State. Even different than Cal."

"Just a little. I bought this Michigan robot action figure for Willie. How is he?"

"He misses you. You want to say hi?"

"Of course." Willie still wasn't sure how to talk on the phone, so after some fiddling and bewilderment, we pieced together a conversation. He was now three weeks into his first year of preschool. He was already adjusting and growing up before me. It was just amazing. He gave me an update about beating Lucero in a race across the playground but losing to Jack. He also talked about some of his latest drawings that he wanted to show me through the phone. He was learning his ABCs and recited them for me. He gave me a full report of his lunch and dinner. Finally, he told me he missed me, which was heartbreaking. I missed them too, but it was time to get ready for our night out. I said goodbye and rejoined our crew back up at the room.

"How's Tracey?" MIHO asked when I entered.

"She's doing well, and William drew me a picture, which made me homesick. I say we go to dinner."

"Yeah, where are we going Paul?" MIHO asked.

"We'll find a place on State Street and then bar hop a little. Sound good?"

We bounded out of the room with excitement and down to the heart of Ann Arbor. The evening was perfect to sit outside as we watched more and more alumni and fans arrive. The food was good, but the time with my friends was better. I wasn't too excited about spending extra cash at various bars, but Paul had been exemplary all day. He hadn't ditched us, and we were willing to follow him. We crawled from one bar to the next. We paced ourselves, chasing water with every drink. Paul toed the line between buzz and drunk. His adrenaline and energy made him the life of the party, but he never drifted into the stage of drunkenness where mere mortals peak and crash in a puddle of vomit.

Being an alumnus and on TV also provided the privilege of bypassing an endless string of velvet ropes throughout the college town. At one point, we entered another club and noticed that we were the oldest people there. We went straight to the back, and I bought a round for us. I didn't look at the credit card receipt. When I returned, I saw two younger men sitting with us. They were dressed in jeans and T-shirts but didn't fit in with the rest of the students. These guys looked too clean-cut. As I approached, Rob introduced me.

"Hey," Rob yelled through the booming music. "This is Troy and Dennis. They're fans of Paul's on ESPN. They just got back from Afghanistan."

I turned to them. "Thank you for your service. I'm sorry, I just bought drinks for these guys. Let me get some for you."

Jesse interjected. "Paul's already on it."

"Thank you," said Troy. He had a square jaw and close-cropped hair. His off-duty attire included a flannel shirt and jeans and some Chuck Taylors. "We can't drink too much tonight anyway."

"Why not?" I asked. "Seems like you're on a college campus, you should have a beverage."

"Nah, we've got some important duty tomorrow, so we can't get too crazy tonight," said Dennis. Whereas Troy was stocky and square, Dennis was lanky and oval.

"Oh yeah? Where do you have maneuvers or are you reporting?" MIHO asked.

Paul returned with a Sam Adams and a Budweiser. Meanwhile, I sipped my vodka tonic.

Troy looked at Dennis, who shrugged. Troy said, "Well, you guys can't tell anyone, but we're Army Rangers, and we're delivering the game ball tomorrow."

"No shit," I said. "That's awesome. But seems like you can deliver a game ball hungover." As soon as I said it, I winced. I must seem like the biggest jackass to be wondering why our military couldn't go to work hungover.

"Well, for us, it's a little more complicated than that," Dennis said. "We're going to be delivering the ball from twenty thousand feet up."

"What?" Jesse said, not sure if he'd heard wrong.

Dennis clarified. "We're parachuting down to the field, and Troy will have the game ball to present to the ref."

We all jumped back in our seats. There was a little bit of disbelief. How was it that of all the bars, we ran into these service men? It was kind of crazy. This never happened at the lake.

"That's awesome!" Paul said. "What a great gig."

"I'm surprised you didn't know," Rob told Paul. "I thought the army would have let you and ESPN know this was happening and a possible opportunity for an interview."

Paul looked perplexed as to why Rob would say this. Troy and Dennis clarified.

"Army policy is that we let the network know for broadcast purposes, but we don't give interviews. We're an army of one, and no one deserves greater coverage than the other. At least not on delivering a game ball for a football game."

"Of course," I said. "That's why you guys are heroes."

Over the next hour, we asked about their missions (classified), the heat in the Middle East (hot as Hades on a heat wave), and why they joined (to get out of rural Arkansas for Troy, to get Osama's ass for Dennis). We added a few other folks to our crew, attracted by Paul's celebrity but staying to hear from Troy and Dennis. In the process, we bought them another beer.

Toward the end of the night, I was talking to Dennis about their "mission" during the game. I had an idea. "Okay, this is what I want you to do when you get on the ground. I want you to take a couple steps, punch the ground, and pull the lawnmower." I gave the motion, punching straight at the ground, then pulling my fist back like I was trying to start an engine.

"We can do that," Dennis said. "I'll do it, and when we do, know I'll remember this fun night with you and Paul and the rest of your buddies. This has been great."

"Awesome," I said, and I told Troy the same thing, just because it was such a great idea in my head that I had to repeat it. We all took a picture, and Paul asked if he could post it on

Facebook. Rob shook his head. Why did everything have to be shared? The Rangers politely declined, again citing the army-of-one principal and that it wouldn't be good to be seen on Facebook drinking the night before a jump, even if it was to deliver a football.

The Rangers left, and we continued to mingle with the college kids. The transition to old man was complete. I no longer looked at these twenty-somethings as peers. I was wondering about their choices and their futures. In sixteen years, would this be Willie? I realized I was too old and out of place for this bar. I suddenly had an urge to head back to the hotel. Jesse, MIHO, and Rob seemed to come to the same conclusion at the same time.

Rob looked over. "Where's Paul?"

I looked around and didn't see his lanky, well-coiffed frame anywhere. "No idea."

Rob and I looked around. We asked Jesse and MIHO, who also hadn't seen him.

"Fuck, he probably left us to get laid," Jesse said. "Fucking Paul."

"Yeah, I have no idea where we are," I said. "How do we get back to the hotel?"

"We can ask someone," MIHO said.

"But we shouldn't have to. Paul should be here. This is his place," I said. I was pissed. All day he'd been good, and then he ditched us for his own pleasure. He didn't even tell any of us or let us know how to get back. I shook my head. Alcohol was challenging me to stay calm and not curse him.

"We can find our way back," Rob said. He pointed to some of the students. "I'm sure one of them recognized Paul and can either tell us where he's at or how we can get back."

No one had seen him leave. Some of them didn't even know he was around. We resolved that Paul was a big boy and would find his way back. We were on the exact opposite end of campus, and by the time we reached our rooms, the adrenaline of the night was gone, replaced by disappointment and anger. Exhaustion won out over everything, and we crashed, knowing we had to wake at nine to make the College *GameDay* show at ten.

Even nursing a solid hangover, I was determined to check out *College GameDay* on campus. As I got up and used the bathroom, I could hear the others stirring. Paul was even in bed. I guess he got home last night at some point. I took a quick shower to wake up and wash off the night before and wondered if Paul would ever grow up. He was in his mid-thirties and needed to start taking responsibility for his life. As I got out of the bathroom, I saw Jesse and MIHO getting ready. Rob was still asleep. Paul was bent over on his bed.

"Dude, thanks for totally leaving us last night," Jesse said to Paul. "We didn't know where we were and how to get back."

"Yet, you're still here," Paul said, gesturing that this was the destination. "I knew you guys would be able to find the place. I had to leave. This psychology student wanted to show me her...thesis back at her apartment. I had to confirm her results. You guys heading to *GameDay*?"

"Yeah," I said, not blessing his actions. "Are you going?"

"Yeah, but I'll meet you there. I want to be incognito," Paul said, pulling out a bright yellow and black mass out of his bag.

"What the…" MIHO said.

"Awesome, right?" Paul said. He stood up and placed the large rubber Wolverine superhero mask on his head "I know I'll be accosted if I go over there as myself, so I'm going to wear this full mask with my Charles Woodson Rose Bowl jersey. It's going to be great."

We laughed. Of course, Paul would pull this out. He was going to be on TV regardless of whether or not he was working.

Rob was still out and snoring. It was amazing how hard he could sleep.

"Do you want us to wait for you?" Jesse asked.

"Nah, I'll meet you over there," Paul said. "Find a good spot to stand, and I'll find you."

"More than likely, we'll find you," I said. "But we'll try to be right in the middle, so look for us."

"I will. I'll be out in about forty-five minutes. I'll see if Rob's up by then."

After yesterday's tour and last night's trek home, we had a better idea of the show's set location. *College GameDay* is ESPN's premier college football pregame show. What makes the show unique is that they travel to a different college campus each week and set up their "studio" with the campus and fans in the background. The TV audience has the pleasure of watching the crazy fans waving homemade signs and flags, trying to get noticed on national television.

A half hour before start time, and the show was already crowded. There were plenty of fans wearing some variations of maize and blue. There were a few good-natured Notre Dame fans there too, though they were outnumbered 50-1. I was still amazed that we were here. We'd forever remember this trip.

As 10:00 a.m. approached, the hosts of *College GameDay* came out. Chris Fowler waved to the fans, acknowledging our enthusiasm. Lee Corso, the old coach, was subdued, which was interesting since he was so animated on the show. When ex-Ohio State quarterback and top analyst Kirk Herbstreit came out, the crowd booed the Buckeye. Those boos, however, turned to momentous cheers as Michigan Heisman Trophy-winner, hero, and legend Desmond Howard came up onto the stage.

As the show began, we watched more of the behind-the-scenes work than we did the actual broadcast. There were so many production people handing scripts to the talent during the commercial breaks and even more staff on headsets. It looked so easy on TV. We noticed Wolverine in a Charles Woodson jersey on the other side of the quad area. We waved our arms and walked over to him. He was dancing and having a good time.

"Hey, man, glad you were able to make it out," I said. "Is it hot in there?"

Wolverine leaned in to hear better. I repeated, "Is it hot in there?"

Wolverine nodded. Then he kept walking and dancing toward the front of the crowd. MIHO, Jesse, and I followed him closer and closer to the stage. He was getting cheers and pats on the back, and the crowd opened up for him, and we just followed. Thank goodness for Wolverine to get us closer to the front, though we felt a little out of place among the hardcore college students. As he danced and gave high fives, Wolverine completely ignored us as if he didn't even know us.

Disappointed with Paul once again, we ventured back out of the student section. We watched as the camera kept capturing the Wolverine standing out in the crowd. Sure, this was his chance for anonymity, but that didn't mean he should ditch us. Just when I was about to shake my head, I felt a hand on my shoulder. I turned and saw another Wolverine in a Charles Woodson jersey.

"Took us forever to find you," said Wolverine in Paul's muffled voice with Rob behind him. MIHO, Jesse, and I looked back to the front of the crowd where Wolverine was still dancing up front. Then we looked back at the Wolverine standing in front of us. This Wolverine in the Charles Woodson jersey had the Rose Bowl logo. The dancing Wolverine, who'd led us to the front of the student section, had a Charles Woodson jersey without the logo. Jesse, MIHO, and I started cracking up. How could there be two Wolverines in Charles Woodson jerseys? We pointed to the front to show Paul. Our Wolverine started to shake with laughter. Rob put a hand to his brow, smiled, and shook his head.

When the show wrapped, Paul removed his headgear to reveal a smiling sweaty face. He placed the mask in a backpack and replaced it with a cap atop his head. We walked through campus again, the energy heightened even from the previous evening. We went down Fraternity Row with endless games of beer pong and cornhole. We stopped by the practice field where the Michigan band was perfecting its halftime routine.

We walked through the endless tailgates until we found ours, led by a man named Carl, who had a twenty-five-foot RV with two TVs set on tables underneath his canopy. He had 100 square feet of Astroturf, which was painted like a football field with a block M in the middle with maize Michigan over a blue field in both end zones.

Carl was a big man in his late sixties with a full head of white hair and a matching mustache. He shuffled from the grill to the serving table, the result of bad knees. His large Weber was grilling beer-soaked brats and buns. On the fixings table, he had various condiments, including dill-pickle spears, grilled or raw onions, tomatoes, sauerkraut, and various kinds of mustard. There was also corn, roasted potato salad, macaroni salad, chicken legs, etc. Alongside the spread, 10 people sat and watched the afternoon games on the TV.

Paul went up to Carl and gave him a big hello. "I want you all to meet Carl," Paul said. We knew of Carl, owner of Carl's Mattress Barn. Throughout college, Paul worked for him, first in the warehouse and then on the showroom floor. "Whenever I get out here, I try to stop by Carl's business and sign some headshots that he gives to customers. Carl was also a lineman for Michigan, class of '67?"

"Yes sir," Carl said. "Nice to meet you boys. I've heard lots of stories about you all, especially you!" Carl pointed at Rob. "Paul said he kept you from having a fine pro career, but before that, he tried to get you to come here. He said you preferred the beach girls to the snow bunnies. I think you made the right choice. It's cold as fuck here."

We all laughed at Carl's unexpected profanity.

"Well, thank you for letting us crash your tailgate this afternoon," Rob said. "Looks like a great game."

"Well, we're going to crush the damn Irish," Carl said. "And, as an SC guy, I'm sure you're in agreement there."

"Damn straight," Rob said.

"So, that's Carl?" I asked Paul as we sat down and started to watch the afternoon games. "I thought he was just an urban legend."

"Oh, Carl's the man," Paul said. "He took a big chance on me, then kept giving me breaks to study and was just so supportive. In turn, I did whatever he asked. I worked my ass off in that warehouse. Later, I worked the showroom and made some great sales. Carl helped teach me how to talk to people and make them feel like they were the most important person in the room."

"Which you sometimes use for evil," Jesse quipped.

"Sometimes, but not always," Paul said. "At Carl's, it was always on the up-and-up. Can't say about after hours, though."

My thoughts returned to the Rangers we met at the bar the night before. "Do you think those guys we met last night are going to jump out of a plane tonight? I think that's pretty cool."

"No way, they were just saying that to get free drinks," Paul said.

"Their story sounded pretty convincing," Jesse said. "They went into great *dee*-tail about how they prepare and how they jump and navigate the crosscurrents to land at the designated point."

"And I heard that there was a planned jump because it was such a big game," MIHO said.

"I still think it was a ruse," Paul said. "They probably heard about it just like you did and used details to be full of shit. I'd be surprised if they did jump out of the plane. Besides, we won't know if it's them or not."

"Yes, we will," I said. "I told them to punch and lawnmower pull the ground when they land to let us know." I followed up with the actual motion.

"We shall see," Paul said. "I'm unconvinced. What do you think, Rob?"

Rob rubbed his chin as if he were contemplating the meaning of life or whether to have another slab of meat. After a moment, he slapped the table. "I say, *bullshit!*"

"That's my guy." Paul laughed and slapped Rob's back.

We all groaned.

"I still think they're going to punch the ground," I said.

"Fifty bucks says they won't," Paul shot back.

"Deal," I said, and we shook on it.

As we had our brats, four twenty-something fans came to each tailgate spot with a large funnel, a long pole, and six hoses coming out of the funnel. Even Sac State had beer bongs, but I never saw one with six hoses, which would be filled with a six-pack or more. It was maize and blue, and therefore we had to partake in the experience. As one of the students raised the pole we kept the tubes up high to keep gravity from pouring the beer. As it kept rising, we placed our thumbs over the tube before placing it in our mouths. For a moment, I realized many mouths had coated this piece of tubing. I could be contracting anything from a cold to the flu to herpes. But that thought was dashed as the beer raced down the tube into my mouth and down my throat. I hadn't done a beer bong in about twelve years, and I still didn't know why it was appealing.

I was thankful it was our last pregame beer and we switched to water. We continued to sample Carl's spread until the calories and fat caught up to us. At game time we helped Carl pack up his valuable stuff and headed to the Big House.

Michigan Stadium doesn't look that big when you first approach. Yet, the stadium has the largest single-game attendance in the country, somewhere over 110,000. As we entered, I'd never seen so many people in one place at one time. The student section all wore yellow, and the rest of the fans were clad in a variation of maize and blue. Paul managed to get us tickets in the end zone, three rows up. I wasn't sure if the tickets had been comped or if he'd purchased them. He wouldn't say. But we were right in front of the Notre Dame cheerleaders and the stupid leprechaun, which upset Rob to no end.

"Please direct your attention overhead for a special delivery," said the stadium announcer.

The jumbotron on both end zones showed a point of view from overhead the stadium. We saw little specks against the dusk sky. The camera jerked and rotated. It was clear it was the paratroopers coming down to deliver the game ball.

"This is it," I said. "We'll see if I was correct or not."

The crowd's excitement grew as people alternated their gaze from the jumbotron to the sky. Soon, the specks took human form, and the parachutes opened, drawing a huge ovation. The Rangers floated down and down. All of us felt we had a little extra invested in this pregame stunt, and it was worth it. The paratroopers guided to each side of the stadium. One was heading toward one end zone, the other toward us. The one on the opposite end of the stadium tripped and fell, but the other landed true. Almost synchronized, they punched the earth, and the entire stadium went crazy, including five friends in the third row behind the end zone.

"Best fifty bucks I ever spent," Paul said with a laugh, conceding the bet and patting me on the chest. "Now let's see if this game tops it."

We hoped the game would live up to the hype. Michigan had one weapon, quarterback Denard Robinson, a dual threat who was more potent running the ball than passing. The previous year he'd torched the Irish with five hundred yards of total offense as a sophomore. Now, the question with a new coach was whether or not he could achieve a repeat performance.

The beginning of the game didn't go so well for the Wolverines. By the end of the third quarter, Michigan was down 24-7. The Notre Dame cheerleaders and the leprechaun continued to taunt us with their glee and antics.

"Doesn't look good," I told Paul. "Three touchdowns in the next sixteen minutes?"

"I don't know," Paul said. "But you gotta believe. College football is full of opportunities and mistakes. After all, these are just talented kids who train more for these moments than we do for anything in our lives."

Within three plays, Michigan scored to make it 24-14, giving the loud 114,000 hope. Paul's optimism in the team was clear, and he could never be objective when it came to the Wolverines. Paul nodded, his eyes focused on the field and his arms folded. Robinson connected with Jeremy Gallon for an-other touchdown to draw the score to 24-21.

"We need another stop now," Paul said. He was rocking back and forth on his feet in a trance, oblivious to our presence.

Somehow, Michigan's defense stopped Notre Dame, and its offense took the field. The tension was palpable. There were two minutes left in the game. I'd gone to some Sacramento State football games. I even made it down to see Rob play in a few big games. But this was the most intense I'd felt at a football game.

Robinson took the ball and ran right, then turned around and threw to his left and found Vincent Smith, who rumbled into the end zone right in front of us. We could have leaped from our seats and tackled him he was so close. The crowd went bananas. Michigan led 28-24 with 1:12 left.

The kickoff went to Notre Dame. It was only a matter of time before the game would be done and the victory assured. Yet now, Paul was nervous. His optimism had turned into dark pessimism. Notre Dame proceeded to move the ball down the field and in forty-two seconds retook the lead 31-28 with only thirty seconds left. What was elation just five minutes ago was despondency and disbelief. How was Michigan going to come back now?

Even Paul's hope waned. "Denard only has so much magic in those dreadlocks. But what a game." His smile showed how much he loved sports and why he was in the right career.

However, the unthinkable happened. On a basic Hail Mary play, Robinson found Jeremy Gallon wide open, and he raced to the seventeen yard line and out of bounds. They had one play to get ready for a field goal, tie the game, and send it into overtime.

Paul looked at me. "They're going for the touchdown."

"How do you know?"

"I just saw Denard's eyes. He gave a tell. I don't know if Notre Dame caught it, but he's throwing it to the right corner of the end zone."

Robinson took the shotgun snap, dropped back, and flung the ball high into the air to the end zone. Roy Roundtree caught his first ball of the game in the end zone, and the Big House went completely mental.

I don't recall consciously jumping up and down, yet I felt myself elevate again and again for minutes. Jesse, MIHO, and even Rob had a look of pure joy. We'd witnessed a game for the ages. I wasn't sure if I'd ever witness a game like that again. I looked over at Paul, who was running up and down the steps high fiving everyone around him.

"Oh my gosh!" I said, my eyes wide with disbelief. "What did we just see?"

"Nothing I've ever witnessed," Rob said. "That was just horrible defense on both sides. My god!"

"No one will remember that," Jesse said. "They'll just see the final ninety seconds."

Paul gave high fives to everyone in our section. The 114,000 people didn't seem to want to leave the Big House, as if leaving would break the spell of what they'd just seen. The White Stripes' "Seven Nation Army" blasted over the loudspeakers. The band was on the field playing versions of "Hail to the Victors."

When Paul returned, he was holding a phone. "Hey, can you guys make it back to the hotel? I just got a text from one of the producers. I might have an assignment tomorrow and need to get to the truck."

"Do you want us to go with you?" I asked. "It would be great to see the truck and the production."

"I'm not sure it would be a great idea. I don't know how long I'm going to be and how crazy it's going to be near the production trailer. Let's just connect back at the hotel in a couple hours. It's going to be wild tonight."

We were disappointed but didn't want to interfere with his job, so we let it go. We watched Paul head back up the stands, continuing his high fives. His phone was to his ear with a smile on his face. It must be some kind of assignment.

We stayed for another ten minutes before finally deciding to leave. I pulled out my phone to text Tracey to see if she watched the game. There were five missed calls and three voicemails, all from Tracey. I grew concerned and stopped to dial my voicemail. I put my hand up to direct the other guys to stop and wait.

"Hey, Jim, ummm, I know you're in the middle of the game and didn't hear the phone, but please call me when you get this," Tracey said with a bit of tension in her voice. "I'm not feeling well at all."

I pressed the button for the next voicemail. MIHO, Rob, and Jesse all looked at me, wondering what was going on. I put my hand up again to be quiet.

"Jim?" Tracey said, this time with a lot more urgency. "I need you to call me, okay? I'm bleeding down there. We've called the ambulance, and they're on their way. My parents are here. I'm scared, Jim. Please call."

My stomach dropped. I felt sick. I pressed play to hear the final voicemail.

"Jim." It was Tracey's dad. "It's Kevin. Tracey's okay. She's at the hospital. But, umm, she had a miscarriage. She's doing fine, but I think she'd like you to call her as soon as you get this. I know you're at the game and haven't heard the calls, but it's important you call back."

Deep sadness overwhelmed me. My face must have aged years in those moments. MIHO, Rob, and Jesse looked at me wondering how it had gone so pale. My legs lost all their strength, and I fell into a stadium seat.

"Jim, what's going on?" Rob asked.

It was hard to get the words out. "Tracey had a miscarriage. She lost the baby. She's at the hospital. This all happened while we were at the game. I missed all the calls."

"Oh crap," MIHO said. "Oh no. She was pregnant?"

"I guess so," I said. Tracey told me she felt a little off on the phone earlier, but I wasn't concerned. In fact, I thought she was trying to lay on a little guilt. In that moment, I'd have given up the last four hours for the opportunity to be with my wife when she needed me the most. I felt tremendous sadness for the loss of this life I didn't know about and guilt for not being there for Tracey. It was a grief and sadness that I'd never felt before. All I wanted to do was talk to Tracey and find a way to get back home as soon as possible.

Everyone wanted to offer their own condolences, but I didn't have time for that now. I had to call Tracey. I couldn't be in that stadium anymore. It was a reminder of my failure as a husband. I stood and ran up all those steps, my breath a little shallow, my legs burning. Just outside the stadium, I raced to the fence as I heard her pick up.

"Jim?" Tracey answered. She was exasperated and tired.

"Yes, it's me," I said. "I'm so sorry I missed your calls. I didn't hear the phone."

"I know, it's okay. But we lost the baby... We..." Tracey broke down in deep sobs that broke my heart. I had to hold it together for her sake. Even though I wasn't around, I needed to be strong for her and support her and comfort her. It was no time for me to break down.

"Are you okay?" I asked. "Where are you?"

"I'm fine. We're just about to leave the hospital. I'm just so very tired. It was so scary. I was just about to turn on the game, even though I wasn't going to watch, when there was a searing pain like a cramp times ten. And I knew what was happening. Thankfully, Mom and Dad were here to play with Willie, and they called the ambulance."

"How's Willie?"

"He was scared. He kept asking, 'What's wrong with Mommy?' But my dad kept him occupied. When I got taken away in the ambulance, my mom came with me. Dad dropped him off with the Davidsons, then came over."

"Oh my god." I felt sick with guilt. "I didn't know. Did you even know?"

"I felt off and different the past couple of days and I was thinking of buying a pregnancy test for when you got back but..." Her voice trailed off. "When can you get home? I want you here."

My flight wasn't until midafternoon on Sunday so I could work off any hangover and get to the airport. But now it was close to midnight, and I wasn't sure if there was a red-eye flight or anything I could catch back to California.

"I'll get a flight as soon as I can. But I'm not confident I can get one tonight. It may be first thing in the morning, and I'll have to pay to change. Is that okay?"

"I want you home."

"I'll do my best to get the next flight back."

"Thanks." She could sense my guilt. "Hey, you couldn't have known this would happen. Was it a good game?" I was amazed. How was she asking about my day?

"Oh my god." I laughed through more tears. "It was amazing, but I'd give it all back to be there with you."

"I know. It's okay. Just get home. They're about to discharge me, so I'm going to go home and get to bed. Text me with what you find on flights, and I can have Dad pick you up."

"Okay. Get some rest. I'll be home as soon as I can. I love you."

"I love you too."

I hung up and exhaled. I turned, and all three of my friends came up and huddled around me. Their touch and condolences were fuzzy, and I couldn't hear them. I felt my heart, though. It was beating with the force of the drum corps of the Michigan marching band.

"I need to get home," I said.

"I'll call Paul. Maybe he can use his connections to get a flight," Jesse said.

"I have better connections than he does," MIHO said. "I'll call my people."

Rob put his arm around me. "We need to tell Paul what happened anyway. Let's head to the truck and see if we can find him."

We started walking toward the bank of satellite trucks on the far end of the stadium.

"No answer from Paul," Jesse said. "I left a voicemail."

We kept walking toward the trucks. MIHO was working his travel magic. Within minutes, he booked a flight back to Sacramento from Detroit through Phoenix. He didn't tell me how much it cost. However, it left at 7:00 a.m.

"I'll just get my stuff and take a cab to the airport tonight," I said. "I can sleep at the airport, if at all."

We reached the production trucks where a security guard stood. Behind him, the crew was rolling cable and packing up to head to the next town. The security guard was holding a clipboard. He'd know how to get a message to the press box and reach Paul.

"We're looking for one of our friends. You know Paul Buckley?" I said. "He works for ESPN. He came here a little bit ago."

The security guard checked his sheet and security sign in. He flipped some pages, then looked up and checked the radio for a Paul Buckley on any of the other check-ins. After about a minute, he turned to us. "Sorry, no Paul Buckley has signed in."

"Really?" Rob said. "He was called to work on something tonight."

"No sir," the security guard said. "No Paul Buckley with ESPN."

A production assistant was walking by when the security guard mentioned Paul. He walked over to us and pushed the microphone of his headset up.

"Did you say Paul Buckley?" The PA said.

"Yeah, is he in there?" I asked.

"No, man, he was suspended last week," the PA said. "The scuttle was some sort of sexual harassment thing, but yeah, he hasn't been around. Is he here?"

"Yeah, he was here with us," Jesse said. "He was here earlier to work as a producer on interviews with the coaches. And then he said he had an assignment they wanted him to do and needed to talk to him tonight."

"Well, unless he was off suspension, he wasn't doing anything for us," the PA said. "Tell him Ted says hi if you see him."

"Will do," Rob mumbled.

"What was that about?" MIHO said as we turned away. We walked aimlessly in a direction that none of us knew. "That guy seemed to have it all wrong."

"Yeah, if he knew, then why didn't Paul tell us?" I said. "But no matter, I can't worry about where Paul is. I just need to get my stuff and go to the airport. Hopefully, we run into him before I leave."

We got our bearings and headed back in the direction of our hotel. Traffic looked horrible with so many folks leaving town. We were all silent for a bit, hit with the dual shocks of Tracey's miscarriage and Paul's disappearance and possible suspension.

As we walked, I felt an anger start in the back of my brain and begin to build. Where the hell was Paul? Had he been lying to us the whole time? Why would he do that? Where was he Thursday? Where was he now? Did he ditch us again?

"We all just saw him take a call and leave," I said. "What's he doing if he wasn't where he said he was?"

"I don't know," Rob said.

When we got back to the hotel, it took me a couple minutes to gather everything and stuff it all into my bag. It was all a silent blur. I zipped up my bag and headed downstairs with everyone. We stepped out of the elevator, and I went to the reception desk to call a cab. As we passed the lobby, I looked over to the hotel restaurant and bar and saw Paul inside with one of the coeds with whom he'd flirted last night.

I took a hard right, so hard that I ran into MIHO. I didn't skip a beat as I continued to walk toward the bar. MIHO, Rob, and Jesse realized where I was heading and followed.

I entered the bar. Paul's back was to the entrance. I tapped him on the shoulder. The girl with whom he was talking looked surprised at the upset look on my face. Paul turned and saw me. "Hey, guys! What a game, right? False alarm with the assignment. I couldn't find you, so I just came here and waited. Do you remember Lisa from last night?"

Lisa was surprised that Paul had said he'd just run into her.

"We went looking for you. We called you," Jesse said. "You weren't at the truck."

"I went to the press box," Paul said. "That's where my bosses are."

"Well, some guy named Ted said you were suspended," MIHO said. "That you didn't have an assignment on Thursday either. What the hell?"

Paul seemed to realize he was caught in a lie and that compounding it with another lie would be a poor move. He resorted to another tactic. "Listen, it's not that big a deal. Big misunderstanding. I didn't want to worry you guys, so I just kept it under wraps. No worries. So, let's have a great time tonight. Why are you all so pissed anyway? Who died?"

At that moment, I understood what rage looked like, and I slugged Paul in the mouth. I didn't even really understand what I'd done until I could feel the bones in my hand connecting with his teeth through his cheek. Paul dropped to the ground.

I didn't wait for the fallout. I just picked up my bags and walked outside.

MIHO followed. "Dude, you just laid out Paul. Now you're out?"

Before I could respond, I felt a hand on my shoulder twirling me around and a fist hitting my ear. I was dazed and had to step back. By the time I realized what had happened and was ready to come back at Paul, both Jesse and MIHO held me back. Rob took care of Paul.

"What the fuck was that about?" Paul glared at me.

"You lied to us," I said. "You're fucking suspended, and you told us you were working."

"I didn't want to ruin the trip. So, I just kept up the charade."

"Where have you been then?" MIHO asked. Although Jesse and MIHO had let me go, and Rob had released Paul, we were all on edge. "Did you ditch us again?"

"You know me, I've had the company of some ladies while I've been here." Paul gleamed a smile, like this would make his actions excusable. "Besides, I knew you'd all be judging me anyway, so I thought I'd relieve you of any wingman responsibilities. And I gotta tell you, when you're a minor celebrity and an alumnus, it's sooo easy."

"That's sad," Jesse said.

"Career goals," Rob said. He rolled his eyes.

Paul, however, didn't see the amusement at his expense. "Don't judge me. I'm having a good time and living my life the way I want to live it. So lay off the judgment, all of you."

"Hey, we aren't judging you," MIHO said.

"The hell you aren't! You've all been judging me since we were in high school. 'There goes Paul and his dick to entertain us. Look at Paul, who's he going to sleep with this year? If it wasn't for Paul, Rob would have an NFL career.'"

Rob started to come at Paul. MIHO and Jesse immediately stepped in front trying to provide some obstacle.

"Hey," I said, beating Rob to stand chest to chest with Paul. "That's enough."

"Jim, stop with your controlling shit," Paul said, and he shoved me.

MIHO moved between us, trying to keep us from tearing into each other. Rob, while back in control, was ready to jump in.

"I'm not sure why you keep us all together. Is it so you can feel good about yourself and what little you've accomplished? Between you and whipping boy Jesse, you guys have wasted your lives."

We were making a scene now. Michigan fans were beginning to arrive back at the hotel and steering clear of our argument. I could see hotel security starting to stir inside the lobby.

"You need to calm down, man," Rob said, moving toward Paul.

"Get away from me." Paul stepped away. "God, all I am is entertainment to you until you don't need it anymore, and then I'm just disposable."

"Where the hell is this coming from?" MIHO said. "Paul, we've been here for you. You're the one with the Peter Pan complex who doesn't want to grow up."

"Fuck you," Paul said. "You know, none of you thanked me for this weekend. I put all you up and gave you tickets, and none of you thanked me. None. This is your first time to Michigan after how many times I've said the invitation's open? You've never been to Bristol. How many times did you visit me when I was at a station in Crapsville, Shitstate, when I was the loneliest I've ever been? Zero. It was always 'Come to the trip. Fly out. C'mon. You've got this.' And never once, 'Hey, I'd love to come visit.' Nope. Great buddies unless I need you. Well, you know what, I don't need to listen to you or get your approval. I don't need you. I don't need freeloading trash in my life. I need to get out of here."

And with that, Paul walked down the street. My heart was beating so hard. Everything was crashing down. Hotel security told us we needed to go or get to our rooms.

"I can't stay here. I need to go to the airport," I said. A cab pulled up, and I got in. The door was still open when I looked up at MIHO, Jesse, and Rob. "I want you to know you guys were true friends tonight, and I know I can always count on you... and fuck Paul."

I closed the door, and the cab drove away. As soon as we left the parking lot, I didn't have the strength to hold everything in. I cried as hard as I ever had. I felt betrayed, hurt, and distrustful, on top of the pain of losing a potential child and the guilt for not being with Tracey. And then there had been what Paul had said. Had we taken him for granted? I didn't think so. And he never mentioned it before. I was so overwhelmed that I cried at different levels of pain for the forty-five minute cab ride.

I arrived at the airport at 12:30 a.m. My flight wasn't until 7:00 a.m. It was so late that security was closed, so I was left to sit in a bank of chairs, looping my bags around my legs to discourage thievery, and settled in for the next few hours. When security opened, I found my gate, boarded my flight, and headed home. I was in a state of haze, shut off from all emotions. All I wanted was to be at home holding my wife.

13

Rob

When MIHO closed the book, Rob just looked at the flames of the fire. Except for the pops and sizzles, there was silence. Rob's face, legs, and chest were getting extra crispy, while his backside was feeling the crisp mountain air. The pile of wood they had brought was gone. Rob, MIHO, and Jesse stood and began to pack up their chairs and coolers.

"That chapter ended ugly," Jesse said.

"There were a lot of things that couldn't be taken back," MIHO said. "Unfortunately. it put a damper on the best game I've ever seen in person."

"That game is forever linked in my mind to the aftermath. I'd take anything over the way that night ended," Rob said. "That look of pure contempt on Jim's face and the vision of Paul walking into the darkness was heartbreaking."

"Remember, he just texted us to say goodbye and he'd pick up his stuff after we left," MIHO said. "I don't even think we texted back."

"I didn't," Jesse said. "I was done."

"He called me about a week later," Rob said. "I looked at my phone and saw 'Paul calling' and refused the call."

"Yeah, he called me too," MIHO said. "I didn't pick up either."

"Neither did I," Jesse said.

"It took me about a month to take his call," Rob said. "I don't know why; I was still pissed at what he'd done. I told him what had happened to Tracey, and he felt really bad. He apologized for what he said, but I could tell he didn't understand it was the lying and the abandonment that was the real issue. I knew he wasn't taking responsibility."

During that call, Paul provided Rob with the whole backstory of his suspension. Originally, Paul was a part of ESPN's game coverage and made all the arrangements in good faith, understanding that he would be partially reimbursed for the hotel reservation. Carl helped secure the costly game tickets, and Paul was very excited for his best friends to come to the place that had such an impact on his life. It was a big deal. It was the first time any of them had come and visited.

Paul explained that he was partially at fault for the sexual-harassment accusations, but it was blown out of proportion. According to Paul, he flirted, and she flirted back. His mistake was to flirt at the same time in which he was supposed to formally mentor her. She took his advances as a quid pro quo. After he realized what he had done, he made things worse by avoiding her and made it hard for her to get good assignments with him.

"Well, then, of course, she reported him," Rob said as they stared at the coals, the evening gear in a pile behind them. "And he admitted to it and showed remorse, so that helped get him a suspension and not a straight termination."

Rob, MIHO, and Jesse were anchored in their spots in front of the fire. They didn't want to leave. The pain caused by that eruption in their friendship had lasting effects on all of them. They all remembered the bitterness they felt flying home that Sunday and the subsequent conversations with each other, trying to reconcile all that had happened that night.

"I can't believe he lied to us the entire weekend," Jesse said. "I mean, he left us multiple times, including right after the game."

"Jim cut Paul off and made it clear to us that he preferred we didn't talk to him either," MIHO said. "I didn't like how Jim could be so vindictive. But we also kept our distance from Paul for a long time."

"And Paul had a point," Rob said. "We never did go to see him. Even though we felt it, we never thanked him for the trip. I feel as though we contributed to the blowup."

"Doesn't excuse him ditching us like that and the other stuff he said," Jesse said.

"No, it doesn't" Rob said. "But you know he gave me this great advice about Becky and Reno that weekend."

On their night out, Paul and Rob were sipping a couple glasses of whiskey at one side of the bar while MIHO, Jesse, and Jim were talking to the paratroopers. Rob filled Paul in on Becky's decision to move to Reno and his plan to sue for sole custody to keep Becky in Sacramento. When Rob finished, Paul shot the rest of his low-shelf bourbon, winced, and stared at Rob.

"Why are you fighting this?" Paul asked.

"Because she's going to take Leslie away from me," Rob answered.

"But what's keeping you in Sacramento? Now that your father's at rest, is there anything in Sac anymore?"

"My job, and it's my town," Rob said. To Rob, the answer was obvious.

"So, you're saying your job and Sacramento are a higher priority than your daughter?"

"No, but she can't just take her away and tell me to deal with it." Rob had put down another drink.

"I get that. I mean, that wasn't right to not discuss it with you. But first off, didn't you kind of do the same thing when you moved back to Sacramento to take care of your dad?"

"That was totally different. My dad needed me. And Becky and I discussed it at length and both decided it was best for Leslie. Becky's just moving."

"But Becky agreed to move with you for Leslie's benefit. Is it too hard for you to do the same? Wouldn't you rather your daughter grow up with both her parents who love her instead of in the middle of this fight between them?" Paul shot his hand up, signaling the bartender for two more whiskeys.

"I guess so," Rob said. "But who's to say I can find a job in Reno? The economy isn't that great."

Paul put a hand on Rob's beefy shoulder. "One thing I know about you is that you'll find something and make it work."

On the flight home from Sacramento, amid the Saturday-night fallout, Rob replayed this conversation over and over in his head. By the time he landed, he decided to investigate what Reno had to offer. He was impressed. There were opportunities, and the lower cost of living might even help him save a little. After some soul searching, he called off his lawyer and let Becky know he was moving with them. Once again, Paul could cut through everyone's bullshit to get to the truth. He just never applied his insights to himself.

Rob broke the trance in front of the fire by taking the large bucket of water and pouring it onto the coals. Even in the dark, a puff of white steam mushroomed in front of them, accompanied by sizzle and a light scream. He turned on the headlamp and picked up his chair and the cooler and began walking back to the house.

"It's time to go bed now, boys," Rob said. "We can't solve any more of the world's problems out here. Plus, I'm cold and tired."

On the walk back, Rob could feel the weight of the last twenty years on his surgically repaired knees. He knew the lifestyle he was living—the red meat, the lack of exercise, the beer—was not good long term. He needed to make some changes. Leslie was worth the effort. He resolved that this trip wasn't just a goodbye to Jim but a transition to a new life of healthier living and exercise. If this last year had taught him anything, death causes such disruption and devastation to friends and families. Rob entered the cabin and had to take a couple extra steps.

"Are you okay?" Jesse said. "Getting old there, Papi?"

"Shut the hell up. I'll break you, you little twerp." Rob smiled.

"We have a big day at the island tomorrow," MIHO said. "Man, this reminiscing is hard."

"Tell me about it," Rob said. "I'm going to bed. Good night."

Rob went to his room, brushed his teeth, and climbed into bed. He pulled out his phone and looked at a picture Becky had sent him earlier in the day with her and Leslie at Lake Tahoe. Becky had typed *Love you, hon. See you when you get back.*

Paul was right, it didn't take long for Rob to find a job in Reno, and he began his new life in Northern Nevada. The transition was easier than expected, and the gesture helped open the door for final reconciliation with Becky. For two years, they made it a tradition to have lunch once a month to make sure they were on the same parenting page. Then lunches became family dinners and movie nights.

One night a little more than a year ago, after Leslie went to bed, Becky invited Rob to stay for an extra glass of wine. As they sat on her couch and recalled their first meeting, Rob saw the same look she gave him that evening in Sean's cabin. He set their glasses of wine on the table and leaned in for a kiss. She also leaned in, and when their lips touched, he felt like he had returned home. As they transitioned from the couch to Becky's room, every move, every caress, every kiss was perfectly in sync.

When they were finished, they looked at one another with the knowledge that this was their new reality. Their exile from each other was over. It didn't take long for Rob and Becky to move in together. The biggest adjustment was for Leslie, who had never lived with them together.

As Rob drifted to sleep, he formed a game plan for his return. He would limit his beer, cut out beef, eat more vegetables, and get a personal trainer to push him back into shape. They spent too long apart working through the disruption of their youth and navigating a path neither of them expected. Now that they had found each other again, he was realizing that he couldn't let this second chance end too short because he didn't take care of himself. He also needed to look good in a tux for when he married Becky, provided she said yes.

When Rob awoke the next morning, he felt the significance of the day ahead. After his trip to the stream, he understood how much their group needed this closure together. So much of themselves were intertwined with one another, a trip to the lake was the only way they were going to move forward as a group without Jim. He woke up with a resoluteness and was looking forward to their "ceremony."

Rob sat on the deck with his coffee, listening to some country music on his phone. He didn't feel like hiking or reading. He'd rather just enjoy the warm sun in the cool, crisp morning air. He heard stirring in the kitchen and figured it was Jesse, the other early riser. Instead, MIHO joined him outside.

"You're up early," Rob said.

"Yeah, too anxious about today." MIHO sat in the chair next to Rob.

"I know. I feel it too." Rob patted MIHO's knee. "This feels like closure."

"I know, right?" MIHO said. "I can't believe that after today, it's really over. I mean, I know I need to move on, and maybe

I'm avoiding it. But since his death, there's always been something to keep him alive, whether it was the memorial service or holidays or this trip. But after today, we'll be done with these remembrances, and I have to accept that he's gone."

Rob pulled out a photo of the five of them on the first trip. The print was grainy, the photo taken on some cheap camera on cheaper film. They were unrecognizable, backlit underneath the shadows of the pine trees with the lake in full light in the background. Rob found it when he moved in with Becky. He handed it to MIHO.

"Oh wow," MIHO said. "We were young. I had hair. You were skinny."

"Oh, thanks," Rob said and shook his head. "Paul looks the same."

"It's my natural charm," Paul said, opening the sliding door and walking onto the patio with Jesse behind him. "What are we looking at?"

Rob showed Jesse and Paul the photo. Jesse smiled as they tried to remember when it was taken.

"So, we're doing this?" Jesse asked. "Going to Tom Sawyer's Island?"

"Yep," MIHO answered. "Spreading his ashes in the lake. It's what he wanted."

They all nodded. MIHO went to the mantle in the living room and removed the box of ashes, where it had sat all weekend. Five years ago, they had discussed the process of making a will. Jim expressed his desires to have his ashes split and for some of them to be spread at the lake by his friends. They all laughed at the idea of a few eighty-year-old men spreading his ashes clad in black socks and sandals.

"I can't believe we're doing this," Jesse said. "I mean, it was just a few years ago when he brought it up."

"I know," Rob said. "I hadn't even made a will, and he'd already planned out his death."

"Jim was a planner," Paul said. "He'd plan and plan some more. I kinda wish Tracey and Willie would have joined us."

"The invitation was there," Rob said. "But I think she knew we needed this for us. She and Willie have their own thing."

"I love those two so much, but this has been a weekend I would've never imagined," MIHO said. "I've enjoyed it just being us."

"I have too, but it's been a little painful." Paul said. "Where did you get in the journal?"

"Michigan-Notre Dame," Rob said.

"Damn, I wished you'd gotten further than that," Paul said, shaking his head, disgusted with himself.

"Hmm, he doesn't write any more until you come back to the trip. There is no writing for three years," MIHO said.

"All the years you guys went without me. Nothing worth noting with me out of the picture."

"Well, it wasn't the same," Rob said. "It was like you were haunting us. We avoided the beach. We went to the saloon early. Jim refused to mention you. We even thought about going somewhere else."

"Oh, thanks," Paul said. "I feel really welcome now."

"Sorry, dude, you pissed us off," MIHO said. "And this place reminded us of it. We even went on a big hike up to the top of the mountain."

"Yeah, even that didn't work out well," Jesse said.

"Oh my god, Jim and I almost died," Rob said. "We were so out of shape."

"I wish I could have been there for that," Paul said. "So, the last entry is last year? Does he gloss over anything?"

MIHO flipped through the pages. "It doesn't pull punches. He re-caps those three years. But in the end, it's good stuff. It'll be okay to read on the island."

"Well, let's get it done then," Rob said. "Let's rent the boat and head out."

"Are we staying the whole day?" Jesse asked. "It would seem a wasted opportunity to head out there and not enjoy it."

"I'm good with that," Rob agreed. "Let's bring bocce and cornhole and a portable grill just like we would at the beach. I don't think there's anything we want to do at the beach, right?" Rob looked at Paul.

"No way," Paul said. "I don't want to step foot on that beach."

Everyone nodded, packed up all the gear, and headed to the marina. The proper rates and deposits were paid and liability waivers signed. They loaded up the boat and headed out. As they approached, they remembered how Jim had always wanted to go out to the island and spend the afternoon. When they were younger, they didn't have the money. Then, Paul would always protest because there weren't women on the island. Then they were just too lazy to go through the effort of renting the boat. It was an unfortunate coincidence that the year that Jim would finally make it to the island would be in a box. Maybe that's why he included this piece in his wishes.

Rob tried to get the boat as close to the beach as possible without risking the boat or its propeller. Once Rob navigated the landing and anchored, they each dropped into the cold lake and brought a load of chairs, bocce, cornhole, barbecue, and the beverage cooler to shore.

"This looks as good a spot as any to set up camp," MIHO said. Facing the eastern shore and the large mountains of trees and granite, they could still spot some of the beach where they used to spend their Saturdays.

Once they had settled into their seats with a beverage, Rob said, "Okay, so when are we doing this?"

"We'll do it, but let's enjoy this with him a little bit here, before we give him away," MIHO said.

"You know he's been dead close to a year, and we've already had the memorial service, and everyone's moved on," Jesse said. "It doesn't matter if we do it now or later."

"Then it doesn't matter if we wait?" MIHO said, looking a little exasperated.

"Why do we have to be extra sentimental about this shit?" Jesse countered.

"This shit?" MIHO said, now on the full defensive. "Look, once we do this, he's really gone. Is it so bad I want to make one more memory with him? He was my best friend."

MIHO turned, waved off Paul, indicating a desire to be alone, and walked toward the other side of the island.

Jesse rolled his eyes with his hands on his hips. "I hate to pull out the stereotype card, but MIHO can be so overdramatic. Jim's freaking our best friend too. It's like Jim's still directing this trip. He did it when he was alive, and now he's doing it in the afterlife."

Rob stepped toward Jesse and watched MIHO disappear through the trees. His voice was low. "Look, we're all processing this differently. I want to get this done too, but I'd rather be there for MIHO, and if that means we wait a couple more hours before we spread the ashes so MIHO has full closure, there's no harm in that, so why not?"

"But, man, MIHO's making this all about him," Jesse said.

"Right, do you really think this is about Jim?" Paul said. "Jim's dead. He doesn't care. This is about us and being there for each other. MIHO needs us and this. So, you know what? We're going to do what it takes to help him. That's it."

Jesse looked at Paul and Rob, put his hands on his hips, and looked in the direction MIHO had walked off. He stared down and kicked the sand and the water. "So, you guys don't care if it's cheesy and sentimental?"

"Of course it is, but we're in this together," Paul said.

"Look, I knew what I needed to do this weekend to move on," Rob said. "Jesse, you probably did too, even if you didn't know it. MIHO needs this and needs our support."

Jesse blew out his cheeks. "All right, I get it. You're right, I'll go get him."

"We'll go with you," Rob said.

They walked to the other side of the island and saw MIHO facing the lake and staring at the various boats crisscrossing the water. As Jesse came to his side, he noticed MIHO's shoulders shaking, accompanied by the sounds of sobbing. Jesse put his arm around him. Rob and Paul moved behind them.

"Hey, David," Jesse said. "Look, I was wrong back there. I'm realizing I'm looking at this trip all wrong, like it was about relieving my own grief. I should have realized this trip was about taking this final step together. It's not about you or me moving on. It's about us and we can't have us with you. I know this has been hard for you. It's okay, we'll do this on your timeline. We're here for you."

MIHO bit his lip and looked off toward the mountains. He was pulling up enough courage to speak. "I'm not ready to say goodbye. I'm not ready for life without him."

"We know," Jesse said. "Whatever you want to do is fine, but let's play some cornhole and have lunch and maybe even finish the journal. Maybe that will help."

"Okay, I just want it to be a perfect memory," MIHO said. "I want us all to look back at this weekend and smile that we did it right."

"We have, but let's make it complete," Rob said. "Together. Let's make this island trip all that Jim wanted it to be."

Jesse patted him on the shoulder and turned. "I, for one, want to *dee*-stroy Paul at horseshoes, for Jim's sake."

"Hey now," Paul said.

MIHO smiled. He took the bottom of his T-shirt and wiped the salty tears from his face. He smiled, nodded, and joined in line behind Jesse as he walked across the island through the trees to their camp. Jesse and MIHO didn't beat Rob and Paul, even with MIHO's Ogilvie Home Perm trick. But it didn't matter as they realized that this is what Jim loved most about the trip—the comraderie, the laughing, and the good-natured trash talking.

When they were done, Paul chimed in. "Can we at least get this last bit of the journal read? If it's okay, I'd like to read. I want to see the last year through Jim's eyes."

Paul took the notebook and looked at both covers and opened the pages. After avoiding the notebook all weekend, he examined the handwriting, the doodles, and the words. It was a living document, and he felt the life oozing from it.

Paul took another deep breath. "Okay, here we go."

I found the Lake Trip Log in my camping gear just a couple months ago. Willie was having a friend over for his birthday sleepover, and I was retrieving the air mattress from my camping bin when I saw the worn cover. Had it been three years since the last entry and the infa-mous trip to Michigan?

Since that weekend, I'd avoided Paul. His texts, calls, even a couple letters went unanswered. As soon as I would see his name pop up, I'd just ignore or delete the text. I accepted that I may never see or hear from him again. If he was unwilling to grow up, then I had better things to do.

Then I got a text, and it felt different.

14

Jim

Paul: *Hey Jim, it's been a while. I know I screwed up things royally, but this time I really nee• to talk to you. It's important. Lots happening.*

I pulled up the message and stared at it for a while. The anger of three years ago returned as if a day hadn't gone by. There are acts and statements that seem unforgiveable. That September night in Ann Arbor proved to be one of them for Paul and me. He lied to us so spectacularly. He was nowhere when I needed him the most, and then he had the audacity to call *me* out. True, my sucker punch didn't help and yes, we may have not appreciated him as much we should have, but I felt we'd been growing further apart for a while. We'd grown up, and he hadn't. He still acted with the toxic masculinity of our twenties. He thought being desired was a sign of success. I knew being loved and needed for support was. He was a jerk, and my life was better without him.

I decided to text Rob, whom I knew had talked to Paul recently.

Me: *Hey I got this text from Paul wante‚ me to call him. WTF?*

Rob: *Would be good to ‚o. He's got some things going on an‚ needs some help.*

Me: *Really? Like what?*

Rob: *Let's just say his issues have come to roost. You should call him.*

Me: *All right, I'll call him tonight. This better not be bullshit.* Rob: *It's not. You'll be glad to reach out.*

I wondered what it could be. What did "issues had come to roost" mean? For the rest of the school day, and into debate practice, I tried to decipher the code. Did it mean he got fired? Did it mean getting some girl pregnant? I finished up with these impassioned teenagers, and when they were gone from debate practice, I pushed call. It took about four rings for Paul to pick up.

"Hey Jim." Paul's voice sounded much more tired and weary than I was used to. "Thanks for calling."

"Well, it sounded important, and Rob said I should call. What's up? Everything okay?"

"Well, I'm coming home to Sacramento."

If was this his news, then it wasn't important. I assumed he visited all the time.

"For a visit? Are your parents okay?"

"No, I'm joining KARC."

I was surprised. Going from a national profile to the third-tier-network station in Sacramento was a definite step down. I still watched him on *SportsCenter*, and it seemed he was still considered a high-profile on-air talent.

"Listen, I'm still not ready to bring you back in my life," I said. "I can't watch your destructive behavior. I—"

"I'm a sex addict."

I was silent. I was stunned. "What?" My mind was trying to grasp what that meant. I realized I had no frame of reference. I knew what a drug addict was and an alcoholic, but what? A sex addict?

"I'm a sex addict," he said again. "I have a problem, and I'm in therapy for it. I've been going for about nine weeks."

"Is that really a thing?" I asked. I still didn't understand. I heard some famous people went into rehab for sex addiction, but that was it. I didn't think it was possible, but I was surprised and interested in what he had to say.

"Yep," Paul said. "I've been told it can be described as a progressive intimacy disorder characterized by compulsive sexual thoughts and acts."

"That sounds clinical. What does that mean?"

"It means I had a mental need to have sex, lots of it and even when I wasn't searching for my next hookup, I was looking at porn. Progressively, that led down a spiral of seeking more thrill and danger until finally..." I could hear Paul draw a large breath into his lungs... "I had sex with my boss's nineteen-year-old daughter in a coat closet at the country club where we were having the Christmas party."

Whoa. Even for Paul, that sounded wild. It sounded like some porn plot, but then I pulled myself out of my own deviance and refocused.

"Oh man," I said. "Were you fired?"

"Pretty much. The official story? I was asked to resign and not say anything. My boss didn't want his daughter to be mentioned anywhere, so we had an agreement to part ways, but my agent negotiated a gag order if I went to therapy. I've been in therapy since."

He sighed. I was silent. I was using the time to process my thoughts. In some ways, it all made sense. The stories we read, the tales he told all led to this moment. If what he said was true, then it explained those nights at the saloon, Ann Arbor, and how he left us whenever there was someone looking to party.

"I'm so sorry, Jim, for all the pain I caused you," he said with the sobriety and seriousness of an address from the Oval Office. "For what I said and everything in Ann Arbor, for lying, everything. Shit, I'm sorry I took you all for granted and hope at some point you can forgive me."

When I began the call, I was packing up my things and getting ready to get home. Now, I was leaning against my desk and staring at the white board scripted with the day's assignments and my bag still open and my computer halfway in. When I walked into my classroom this morning, I didn't suspect I'd be pulling out my personal iPad and googling sex addiction, let alone talking to Paul about it. I wanted to ask so many questions about what and how and why. But the first question that came to me was, "Are you okay?"

"I'm fine." Another deep breath. "I'm okay. Thanks for asking. I appreciate it."

"And you're coming back to Sacramento?"

"I know. After all these years of trying to leave Sacramento behind, I'm coming home, and I'm so relieved." His voice was tired, and I could also sense defeat and disappointment. I realized I'd never heard it in his voice, ever.

"Well, I'm glad for that. I really am," I said. I was surprised by my words. It wasn't forgiveness, but it was genuine. I cared about him, and regardless of his actions over the last few years, I realized I always would. I always wanted the best for him. But now my nagging sense of what happened needed answers.

"How did you get to this place?" I asked.

"Well, it started as we all did, just looking to get laid. But as I've worked through it, there was an underlying issue of depression that I was masking through sexual satisfaction. While you all found connections and relationships, I was continually looking for more ways to get validation that I was attractive and a great lover. The last few years may have made a porn star blush." He stopped, exhaled, and took a moment. "I was always safe, wearing condoms and all that, but I'm still surprised things didn't turn out worse. I mean, I lost most of my real friendships, but it could have been so much worse."

I shook my head in pity and sadness. For so many years, I looked up to him and his career. I struggled to understand what would have happened if I'd gone down the more glamorous path. Now, I heard him, and I was sorry to admit this, but I felt he was pathetic. Just like Rob had said, his actions had indeed come home to roost, and I had to resist the urge to gloat. I put that thought past me and decided to be empathetic and try to understand what this meant for him now.

"So, does KARC know why you left ESPN?"

"Yeah, they do, though they didn't until the interview when I laid out my heart and my therapy and my promise to my hometown station. I also have a no-tolerance clause in my contract that if I even make the slightest questionable joke, they can fire me, no questions," Paul said. "I'll be earning half of what I was at ESPN, but I'll be close to my folks and won't be on the road with the temptations I used to have."

"Wow. When do you get out here?"

"A couple weeks. I know that the last time we saw each other I said some things I immediately regretted. If I'd have known about the pregnancy... Never mind, that doesn't excuse what I said. In any case, I'd like the opportunity to show you I'm worthy of another chance at your friendship."

I hesitated. I wanted to tell him it was okay, but we said too much to let things be forgiven in a moment's notice. "If you need me, I'm here for you. Let me know when you get settled."

"Thanks, man, that means a lot."

We caught up about Tracey and Willie, and when we hung up, I was conflicted. He caused me real pain, but it seemed he'd changed. I wasn't the only one of us hesitant to provide Paul with blanket forgiveness. In some ways, MIHO understood how self-loathing and secrecy fed off each other, and he was the first person to whom Paul had come clean. Rob, who was always looking for the best in people, also was inclined to forgive. Jesse didn't take his call.

On a four-way FaceTime call, MIHO suggested we invite Paul back up to the lake this summer, and Rob agreed. I was still unsure of the prospect of having Paul on the trip. He was a part of some great memories but also painful ones. I also felt he needed to be excluded for what he'd said and done. I wondered if we could relate to Paul anymore. What would his dynamic be now that he didn't have a yearly mission of meeting someone?

"Do we want to go there?" I asked. "Has Paul changed, or are we setting ourselves up for disappointment again? He's lied to us repeatedly. I mean do we really know him? Is he a predator? I don't think I can forgive him just like that."

"He practically ended my dream, and his behavior has been sketchy, but I found a way to let him back into my heart, at your suggestion, if I recall," Rob said.

"Right, and he didn't change," I said.

"This time, it's different," MIHO said. "Look, maybe you can't trust him right now, but trust me. I'll vouch for him. I've been talking to him over the last couple months. He finally gets it. He's very remorseful and has made significant changes."

"Changes he was forced to accept," I said.

"I'll also vouch for him," Rob said. "Trust us, even if you don't trust him."

Rob looked at the camera with determination. They wouldn't be taking "no" lightly. Was Paul was getting off too easy? He'd been an asshole for years. Did we think he was going to change? Jesse broke first. He was still wary of Paul and his sincerity but willing to listen to Rob and MIHO. I looked at my phone and saw all three of my friends imploring me to invite Paul, so I relented.

"All right, I'm willing to give him a chance," I said. "Because of you guys."

We found a date in late June, just after Paul moved back to town. Rob drove down and picked up Paul and I, and we headed down to Fresno. There were some awkward moments, but Paul was still the same person. We talked more about sports and work than his personal life. When we met up at our normal spot at Hank's Swank, he'd opened his arms wide to give Jesse a hug.

"Jesse! This is where we should be," Paul said, his arms outstretched. "Come on. Bring it in."

Jesse didn't embrace him. "You leave yourself open like that, you may get another sucker punch."

"Damn," MIHO said with a laugh. "Tough crowd."

"*Dee*-served," Paul said. "Whatever it takes."

Jesse and I were reserving judgment of how our friendship with Paul would progress after this weekend. We'd agreed to give Paul a chance, and that was more for MIHO and Rob than it was for Paul. During golf, it was the same trash-talking laugh fest it always was but without the constant innuendo Paul always provided. Instead, he focused on my expanding waistline, Rob's bad knees, and MIHO's bald head. In some ways, it was like the last few years never happened. These were the moments that forged our friendship in the first place. We avoided the elephant on the trip until we were sitting out on the patio of the house for our normal whiskey and cigars. We all knew we were going to talk about it and waited until Paul made the first move.

"Hey, so, I think it's time for me to go through my speech of humility, contrition, confession, and all that," Paul said. He took a breath. We could tell he'd somewhat rehearsed what he wanted to say, probably from the moment he knew we were getting together to the moment we were sitting on the deck. "I want to express how much I'm humbled and appreciate this opportunity to try to make amends. You stuck with me the longest, and when I drove you away, I began to realize that my problem was more than I'd thought I could handle."

Paul paced next to the barbecue while Rob leaned against the rail. MIHO, Jesse, and I sat around the patio table.

"Dude, Michigan was three years ago," Jesse said. "If you knew you had a problem then, why did it take you three years and getting caught before you made an effort to get help or do something about it?"

Paul nodded. I assume he expected our skepticism. "That's the thing about addiction and the underlying depression, the more you realize your problems hurt others, the more shame you feel and the more you retreat to that behavior. Having sex was some weird sort of validation and the only way I felt value."

"That sounds horrible," MIHO said. I had a feeling he'd coached Paul, and this was a little scripted. "When did you know it was more than just dangerous behavior?"

"Well, I think when I was using Tinder or looking at porn almost every day, then getting to stuff in public and cheating spouses. And, of course, when I got caught with my boss's daughter in the closet, that was a clear indication I had a bad problem and was on the verge of sinking further into a hole. Getting caught like I did forced me to confront my problem with a therapist."

"So, he's helped?" Jesse asked.

"You chauvinistic bastard," Paul joked. His tone turned serious again. "*She*, the one I had in Bristol, has helped a lot. She helped me realize that my underlying feelings of loneliness fueled my need for intimacy and my narcissism created this game to provide this selfish validation. Basically, I'm pretty fucked up."

"Is it because of your mother?" I asked with a faux-German accent. This time it was me who was trying to crack a joke at the wrong time.

"Nope, she thinks it's my need for sex is connected to my self-worth, and this may stem from deep insecurities and depression. With the move home, I left before we could explore the root cause. I guess I'll figure that out with my new therapist."

"Whoa, that's pretty deep," MIHO said. "We just thought you were horny all the time."

"Well, I thought that too when we were all younger. But while you all found love or at least intimacy, I only felt restrained."

"Now what?" Rob said.

"I've done some bad things, treated people poorly, and I'm lucky I've come away without a disease, an arrest record, or a kid. I just lost lots of relationships and have a career on life support. And while I still think everything was consensual, I find myself questioning everything and it's a painful space. Anyway, I can't promise I'm going to be the best friend ever or even that I have this beat, because I don't. But I'm going to do my utmost to be as good to you as you've been to me. My path to intimacy is to be vulnerable and let people in, and it starts with you."

Rob went over and put his arm around Paul. We all got up and did the same. As soon as we embraced him, Paul broke down. It was like many years ago in the rain, but this felt different, as though he wasn't apologizing for one mistake but for a lifetime of regret. While we huddled there on the deck, like we had in high school before some intramural match, and in the midst sounds of Paul's sniffling and light weeping, Rob's huge arms draped on one side and Jesse's sinewy ones wrapped on the other side, there was a power in this bond that I realized was as close to my bonds with my wife and child as anything I'd ever felt. I'd do anything for these guys.

Afterward, Paul spoke with a depth and transparency I'd never seen before. For the first time, Paul owned his mistakes and discussed his poor choices without trying to justify them or make excuses. I imagined this was a result of therapy, and I was amazed. He had deep remorse for the pain he'd caused others and himself and was working to not be that person anymore. I had to admit, I was deeply moved and impressed. It almost made me ready to forgive and move on.

Paul's vulnerability carried over to a remarkable depth of our conversation that night. Jesse updated us on his wife's burgeoning but manageable law practice of three lawyers and his new job as her bookkeeper, tax guy, and office manager. They found a rhythm that allowed her to focus on the client and the law and for him to deal with everything else. They also had work flexibility. They had dinner together most nights, even if sometimes it meant takeout at the office, and the girls were always picked up and dropped off at school.

I breathed and provided my own news. "Tracey and I have stopped trying for another kid. After four miscarriages in three years, we can't do it anymore. So, we'll have our Willie, and he's such a blessing. We can pour everything we have into him."

"Oh man, I'm sorry," Jesse said. "That must be hard to reconcile. How did you get there?"

"Well, we were at the park a few weeks ago. We were watching Willie, and I just said it. I said, 'Willie's such a good kid. What if we just focused our efforts on making his life the best we can and not worrying about having another baby?'"

"How did Tracey take that?" Rob asked.

"Well, sometimes I'm sensitivity challenged." I shook my head. "I realized that being blunt with my feelings wasn't the way to go. At first, she thought I was calling her a failure, and that wasn't right. Anyway, after a lot of hand holding, listening, talking, crying, all of it, we both wanted to get off the roller coaster and just focus on Willie."

"Wow," Paul said. "So, you got snipped?"

"Yep. Now, we can put that behind us. I mean, it's disappointing that we're now guaranteed to be a family of three instead of four, but we were done with mourning. It's just too hard."

I felt bad for bringing the mood down, but when I looked at Rob, his mouth turned up in a smile.

"Um, I'm also happy to announce that Becky and I have gotten back together," Rob said.

We looked at Rob with true astonishment. While each of us always held out hope it would happen, we were nonetheless stunned.

"Oh wow," Paul said. "It took you this long to tell us?"

"Well, I didn't want to upstage your shit," Rob shot back with a smile. He waved his hand at Paul. "Now that we're done discussing your drama, we can all get on with our lives."

"Touché," Paul conceded.

Rob shared how he and Becky reconnected and reignited the smoldering flame that began in this place. I think we all felt that their reestablished love affair was inevitable, but we were still surprised that it happened. We were all so happy for him.

"I don't have anything to announce," MIHO said. "Other than I *dee*-cided to find a job back in Sacramento to be closer to Mom."

"Dude, we knew that," Paul said. "Doesn't count. Congratulations *dee*-nied."

We laughed, and the good times continued the rest of the night. I think we all went to bed knowing that our friendships were as strong as ever. Paul hadn't regained our full trust, but he was on his way. And while I still harbored some resentment and anger toward him, I knew I'd forgive him eventually.

On Friday, we came across a basketball in the garage and went in search of a hoop. We found one in a condo development down the street and snuck on. The seven thousand-foot elevation only emphasized how out of shape Rob and I were. My body also wouldn't cooperate with my mind, and the moves I could do in my teens were no longer viable. I was defending Paul, who went to his left along the baseline when I felt a strain along my hamstring, followed by pain shooting up my leg. I stood, grunted, and limped off the court to sit on the ground.

"Well, we all knew this would happen," MIHO said. "We're getting old."

"That's what happens when you don't stretch," Jesse said. "You okay, Jim?"

"I'll live," I said. "But no more hoops or other strenuous activity for a while."

For the rest of the day and evening, I resorted to laying on the couch or hopping to the bathroom while we watched mindless action, such as the latest Mad Max movie and *Die Hard*. After the emotion of the previous evening, it was good to focus on movies rather than the issues Paul was working through.

On Saturday morning, my leg was still a little tender but felt good enough to limp around. I didn't have to move much to watch MIHO cook us a large batch of French toast, thick-cut bacon, and scrambled eggs. Rob, Jesse, and I sat on the bar stools surrounding the island watching MIHO work his magic. I sipped my coffee, salivating.

"If you guys don't mind, I really don't want to go to the beach," Paul said.

"Ha, we figured," Rob said. "Don't worry. We haven't been back since the LTO."

"Ah, well, can we go to Tom Sawyer's Island?" I asked. I'd always wanted to rent a boat and head to the secluded island in the middle of the lake. Perhaps this was our chance.

"I wouldn't go that far," Paul laughed. "That's a lot of effort."

"Plus, with your leg, I don't want to carry you," MIHO said.

"I can handle it," I said. "C'mon! New tradition."

"How about next year?" Rob said. "I'm not feeling it. Renting a boat, hauling our stuff over there, hauling it back. Let's just find a spot next to the lake."

I shrugged off my disappointment. After all, we'd still be by the lake, and the company was the main thing. We loaded Rob's truck and found a fire road leading to a secluded shoreline. It wasn't a sandy beach, but it was big enough to play cornhole and had enough shade for us not to need the EZ-UP. Before we sat down for our inaugural beer of the day, we all stood and looked at the scenery before us, the glistening blue water with a backdrop of tree-covered mountains and ski runs beyond that. Through all the years of hanging out together and the ways we'd all changed, this view was still the same.

"Man, why didn't we find this spot earlier in our days?" Paul asked.

"This is awesome," Rob said. "I could go for this all day."

I had no idea how secluded our spot was. Throughout the day, the only other people we saw were in boats enjoying their days on the water, and the only sounds were the laps of small waves against the shore, the music off Rob's phone, the laughter and discussions on politics, sports, and pop culture.

"So, now that we've survived the biggest test to our friendship and this trip, are we going to still be doing this when we're eighty and using walkers to get around?" MIHO asked.

"I could use a walker now," I said. It was true, my hamstring was still smarting, and I sat down with every chance I had. "But why not? We've done it this long."

"What if one of us dies?" Rob asked.

"On the trip? That's pretty morbid," MIHO said.

"No, asshole, what if one of us dies, do we still keep coming?" Rob slapped MIHO on the back of the head.

"We're never going to die, boys," Paul said. "This will be forever."

"All right, let's get this cornhole game going," Rob said. "Jesse, bag up."

I sipped a brew and watched everyone playing corn hole with the backdrop of the lake. I hobbled to the shoreline and put my feet in the cold water. I took a deep breath. This was a great setting to get together, but I wouldn't mind breaking from tradition and going other places if we came back occasionally. But, in my opinion, no other place would match this lake. Paul stood to the right of me. He draped his arm around my shoulder. "Hey, Jim," he said. "I want to thank you again for inviting me back up here. It means a lot, and I'm humbled that you guys brought me back, even though I don't deserve it."

"Not a problem. You're part of the crew. I'm just glad we're back on the same page. Over the past few years, we were moving in different worlds."

"I needed a good kick in the balls to realize it. But throughout all the tribulations of the last seven months, it's led me back, and I'm forever grateful."

"Paul, I wasn't sure if I could say it when we started this trip, but I forgive you. It's been a curse since we were in second grade, but I'll always be there for you. And I'm sorry that I never visited or didn't express my appreciation to you. It seems you needed us and we weren't there and then when you needed us most, I cut you off for three years."

"Don't apologize. It was all my fault. And nothing you could have done would have helped me change until I wanted to change. We're here now. That's what counts and forever into the future."

"Agreed."

We clinked bottles and took a swig and looked out at the lake. For the first time, I think Paul and I got each other. And I knew that now that he was back in town, I'd do my best to be there for him, visit him and help him understand he was not alone in this world.

Breaking from tradition, we didn't head to the saloon that night. Paul had his specific reasons not to go, and the rest of us didn't have any desire to mingle with the crowds. We were done with that scene. Instead, it was another night on the rock and the fire. But this time, there were no tears, regrets, or group hugs. It was just laughing about old times, stories from long ago, stories from our current lives as husbands and fathers and boyfriends and toasts to the future.

15

Jesse

Saturday Afternoon

June 25, 2016

W ell, that's it," Paul said, closing the book. "The journal's
done."

"I can't believe it," Jesse said. "It just ended. Just like his life."

Indeed, after reading all the stories over the weekend, Jesse
was surprised that he wanted more closure. Reliving these memories brought the shock and pain of the last year back into their
lives. He hadn't known what to expect when he started this trip.
He thought it might be an unbearable, soft-light tribute to Jim
and these trips. And it was true that the journal reminded them
of some of their best times. However, Jesse didn't expect some of

the warts and scars laid bare in those pages. It made this weekend more real and important than he thought.

Everyone stood around the rock on the island where MIHO put the metal box. This was the last moment the five friends would be together. Everyone stared at the box, then at MIHO.

"Okay, I'm ready," MIHO said.

"What are we doing?" Paul asked. "I mean, I know we're spreading his ashes, but how?"

"Well," MIHO said, "I thought we can either each take hold of the box and shake it out, or we can each take a turn shaking it. Thoughts?"

"Why don't we take the boat out and spread it out on the lake?" Jesse said.

"We could," Paul said. "But I like the idea of keeping him close to the island he always wanted us to visit but never did. If we ever do come back, this can be the marker where we laid him to rest."

"How about we all go out into the lake and say a quick goodbye, then MIHO shakes the box of ashes into the water?" Rob said.

"Sounds good to me," Jesse said.

Paul nodded, and MIHO also agreed. They left their small camp and went down to the lake's edge, where many rocks and boulders lay on the shore. They waded into the cold water with cautious steps. Each rock had the potential of inflicting pain on their arches or causing them to slip further into the water.

"God, I never get used to the cold water," Paul said. "My balls just shrivel up."

"Thankfully, you don't use them like you used to," Jesse said.

"Okay, before we do this, one final goodbye from everyone," MIHO said.

"Really?" Jesse said. "It's friggin' cold."

"Really! Let's do this right," MIHO said with a little annoyance. He had been thinking about it all weekend, and this was the culmination of the whole planning process. "Why don't you start us off? Just say something about Jim and say goodbye."

"All right," Jesse said. He searched back into what he had been thinking about all weekend. His thoughts raced across the journal, the stories, the memories of him still fresh. Now, he realized what MIHO had meant by saying that he didn't want to say goodbye, that new memories of Jim were over and their group would never be with the five of them again. He didn't know what to say or how to express himself. He just decided to speak and see what happened. "Jim, we were friends since Ms. Garcia's class in the third grade. You always wanted to run and race me, even though I always beat you. It seemed we were always in competition, from running to sports to grades to girls to kids to life. We were the best kind of competitors, never willing to win at the expense of the other but to push each other."

Jesse paused and looked up. This was harder than he'd thought. "I didn't want you to reach the finish line first this time, buddy. I wanted this race to go on forever, you and me. But now it's over for you, and I hope you won the great peace you deserve. Goodbye, my friend."

Tears streamed down Jesse's face. He didn't know he'd had this pent-up sadness and emotion. MIHO was right. These were the last moments with Jim. Now, they would really be four instead of five. He would only live in their memories. Jesse looked over to MIHO and nodded, acknowledging his feelings partly as his own.

Rob looked stunned by Jesse's emotion. To avoid getting caught up, he stared at the water and began to speak. "How many times did Jim drag us here? I think we can all recall the same experiences of a call or a text from Jim in February. He'd say, 'Duuude. It's time to think about the trip. We're just five months away. Have you got the time off?'" Rob mimicked Jim's bulging eyes and the unbridled excitement that he would exhibit when talking about the trip. They all chuckled as Rob kept saying, "'Do you? Do you? Are you coming? Are you coming? C'mon, you gotta come. It's the trip.' We all knew it was the best weekend of the year, but I know I always had to temper his excitement. It was just too infectious. He loved this trip so much. And he'd get you excited, and then, all of a sudden, you have it circled and you're counting the months, the weeks, the days, just so we could be around that enthusiasm. For me, that's what's going to live on from Jim. The joy he got from putting this all together. I want to exhibit that more, and I hope I can. I want to have that enthusiasm and hope his legacy can live on through that."

Everyone nodded. Rob smiled and crossed his arms. They now had MIHO and Paul, and everyone knew that MIHO wanted to go last.

Paul closed his eyes, took a breath, then opened them again. He looked at all his friends in the eyes. "Look, we've read his journal all weekend and got a chance to relive Jim's growing up before our eyes again. He started off as a lovelorn puppy dog just wanting to connect, and he became a man who was always there for a friend, even when they didn't deserve it. He was always a man who had integrity and played by those rules. He was always loyal and wanted us to reach the potential he saw. He always knew we could be better, and that's what he wished for all of us. I knew I wasn't worthy of those expectations, and I got the closest to closing him off, but he truly believed I could be the best person I could, and that gave me belief in myself. I think that's what we all felt when we were around him. We knew there was someone who believed in us more than we did in ourselves. I'll always try to keep that in my head when I struggle."

Jesse put a hand on Paul's shoulder and patted it. All eyes went to MIHO, who was standing with the box in a bag in his hands. His was the last remembrance, and they knew he wanted this the most.

"This is your show," Jesse said. "You've got this."

MIHO stared at the box, believing Jim was watching him too. He looked around at where they were in this lake in the Sierras among these friends. They knew, unlike them, he had planned this moment, if he could only get it out.

"It's so weird how we can be in this place that's been here for centuries and will still be here long after we join Jim. Our time here was very brief in the larger scheme of things, just about fifty full days, or a little less than two months, but here we are, in this water, about to immerse our friend into this final resting place. You guys just talked about the friendships you bore, the relationship you had with him and us. We've all been through a lot together, even through our two months here, but they've had such a lasting impact that has shaped our lives for mostly good. It's hard not to think of Jim as a part of these memories."

MIHO stopped and licked his lips and looked away. The rest of them waited for him to regain his form.

"But...we have to move on, and Jim would want that. As you know, I've been insistent about waiting to say goodbye until this moment. I think it's because he's a part of me, just like he's a part of all of us, and it's hard to say goodbye to a piece of you. He was our glue that held us together, and my biggest fear is now that he's gone, we won't stick. We must commit to this with Jim still in the box, that we won't drift away like some pieces of driftwood. We must promise each other and Jim that we'll continue our connection like he did. We may not get together each year like Jim's persistence insisted, but we need to make the effort. I love Jim. I love you guys. Can we promise to keep together and not drift apart?"

They all nodded.

"Okay, Jim, with your legacy secure, it's time to let you go. It's time to let you be at peace in a place that brought you joy. Let a piece of you always enjoy this slice of heaven where you brought us closer together nearly twenty years ago."

MIHO turned and took two more steps further into the lake. As he placed his foot on one of the algae-covered rocks, his foot slipped and he plunged himself into the water, the box submerging, and Jim's ashing dispersing into the water.

"Shit!" MIHO yelled. He stood up, his body glistening from the water and what seemed like small flecks of ash. Rob, Paul and Jesse looked on in disbelief at first, then began laughing uncontrollably.

"I didn't know you were going to go with the dunking approach," Paul said, trying to keep from falling into the water. "No, seriously, good speech there but that is priceless."

"Shut up," MIHO said. He was embarrassed but had to admit that this was funny. He dipped into the water and to wash off the remaining ashes.

"See ya, Jim." Jesse waved down to the spot where he was dunked. It was over. There did seem to be a new element of closure that Jesse had not anticipated. He had now said goodbye to Jim's physical self. This was good, and he was glad he came.

"What are you thinking?" Rob asked Jesse. They began to turn back toward shore.

"Other than MIHO's dunk is the best I've ever seen? No, I was just thinking about how Danielle was right. This was important. Jim's still with us as long as we want him. Like MIHO said, it's up to us to keep up his legacy, and his best qualities live within us. All we have to do is remember them at the right moments, and he'll always be here."

The walk back to shore wasn't any easier, but they somehow made it. When they got onto the island, Rob pulled out a screwdriver and went to a rock on the edge of the island.

"What are you doing?" Jesse asked.

"I saw this a little bit ago. As much as we believe we're original, other folks have marked this rock in memoriam of people they've lost. I thought we could leave Jim's name as a marker whenever we return."

Rob took a rock and the screwdriver and chiseled Jim's name. When he was finished, they looked at each other and nodded. Jim now had his grave marker.

"Let's see the other parts of the lake," Rob said. They were facing the long end of the lake, and in all the years coming up, they had never gone to the other side. "We have the boat and the time. Let's check it out."

Now that Jim was laid to rest, their obligations were complete. They packed up the gear, placed it in the boat, and pulled up anchor. As Rob pushed the throttle forward and the boat sped across the waves, sometimes with a burst of spray across the bow, they watched the edges of the lake go by, viewing the hundreds of trees that touched the shoreline. As they got to the far side of the lake, Rob killed the power, and they drifted in the middle of the lake, taking in the beauty of the lake, the trees, the clear, deep-blue sky.

"Man, I wish Jim was here," Jesse said. "He would have loved this."

"This is amazing," Paul said. "I'm glad we came."

"Same here," Jesse said. "This puts a great cap on today."

"Truth," MIHO said.

They sat on the boat without a word, just the sounds of water against the hull, motors from other boats, and random cries of joy and jubilation filling the air. After a bit, they turned to one another, and with a simple nod Rob turned the boat back toward the east side of the lake. They felt bad that they had denied Jim his request for an island visit so many times, but they were happy they fulfilled his wishes.

As they unloaded the gear back at the marina, the man who had rented the boat to them greeted them at the dock. "Enjoy your time?" he asked. Like a rental-car agent, he inspected the boat, the gas level, and made sure they didn't leave any trash or belongings.

"Yes, we did," Paul said. "We'd never been to the other side of the lake before."

"Oh yeah? Say, you look familiar. Are you on TV?"

Paul smiled. "I was on ESPN. Now I do sports at a local Sacramento station."

"Isn't that a step down?"

"Not at all. I'm from Sacramento, and it was a great opportunity to come home, be close to family, and maybe settle down a bit. The rat race, you know."

"Yessir. I used to work in Silicon Valley until the mid-2000s. I got sick of it and came up here and started running this marina, renting and repairing boats and snowmobiles. Haven't regretted a second of it. Success is what's inside."

"Very true. Chasing 'success' is pointless," Paul said. They thanked the attendant and piled the gear into Rob's truck.

"Call me nuts, but I think we should go the saloon, have a beer, and toast Jim," Jesse said from the back seat.

"You're crazy," Rob said. "Weren't you the one who just wanted to get out of here?"

"Yeah, I know. But something tells me it would be good to just go to that saloon one last time. We don't have to stay long."

MIHO shrugged. "That seems fine to me. What do you think, Paul?"

"It's early enough that sharing a pitcher would be pretty agnostic. Didn't they add outdoor seating and a fire pit the last time we were there? That could be a good place to chill."

"Then we will," MIHO said. "A proper end to the trip."

Rob pulled into the parking lot, and they saw four open seats around a gas fire pit on the deck. As Rob went inside for a couple pitchers of IPA, Paul, Jesse, and MIHO went to the deck to claim the seats. It was still a bit early for the fire pit to be lit, but the mountain air and relaxed setting was perfect. Rob came back with the pitchers, and they filled their glasses with the deep-amber liquid.

"One last toast for the trip," Rob said. "To a great weekend saying goodbye to our best friend. This was the sendoff he imagined and wished for."

They tipped back the full-bodied bitterness and took in the atmosphere, the trees, the lodge, the vacationers walking about in the early evening. Jesse took another sip. He didn't realize until that moment that the last time he had seen Jim was up here.

"Paul, it's so weird you were the last one to see him alive that night!" Jesse said.

"Yep, don't think I don't relive that last night over and over again."

"Hell, the last year," MIHO said. "I bet we all have our stories."

16

2015

Paul

I should have just let his call go to voicemail. I was busy editing A's highlights when Jim's number popped up on the screen. As a teacher, he had no concept of my shifts at the station. Still, since I was repairing my relationship with him and the rest of my friends, I answered.

"Hey, Jim," I said, picking up.

"Paul, I want to see your place," Jim said.

"Fine, but it's going to look like crap," I said. I'd only moved back into my three-bedroom bungalow in East Sacramento two weeks ago and was still unpacking boxes. "Why don't you just wait until it's all done and you can bring by Tracey and Willie? Afterward, we can take Willie to the park."

"C'mon, it's just me. I'm excited to see how the new-and-improved Paul lives."

"All right. Why don't you come over Saturday? Michigan has the night game against Utah. It's Harbaugh's debut as coach. We can have a couple beers and watch."

"Great. Sounds like a plan."

Now I had to work double-time to make my new house presentable. But who was I kidding? I was just happy Jim and I were on good terms again. During our last trip to the lake almost four weeks ago, I finally understood the totality of what I'd missed when I wandered off to chase some tail. My friends were great guys and knew me better than I did. Even though I basically threw it all away, they were there when I needed them. Their selflessness was a strength I drew from every day.

From the moment I graduated high school, I tried to run from Sacramento as fast and far as I could. I realized that by coming home, I couldn't outrun who I was. I needed roots. I needed personal relationships and to be home. I wasn't sure if it would help with my problems, but I knew I felt less of the pronounced loneliness than I had before. For the first time, I felt comfortable being alone.

Before Jim came over that Labor Day Saturday to watch the Wolverines' season opener, I worked hard to unpack as best I could. I decorated the house with more than just sports memorabilia. "Like an adult should have," as my mother put it.

When I gave Jim the tour, he seemed impressed. He most enjoyed the backyard. It was my favorite part too. It was the selling point since it was where I planned to spend the most time. My yard was more like a courtyard with a brick patio and a fountain.

The previous owners installed a small tiki bar, complete with kitschy wicker and bamboo. I planned to embellish a bit with a kegerator and a TV behind the bar so I could enjoy Sacramento evenings and unwind without going to a bar.

"Oh, we're going to have fun out here," Jim said, surveying the yard. "We put your kegerator here and just sit around all night long."

Jim took a selfie of the two of us in front of the bar and posted it on Instagram. "Hanging with one of my OG best friends. Great times."

"As I said, you and Tracey and Willie are welcome anytime. I'm sure I can set up some fun things out here for him."

"Sounds good. I appreciate that," Jim said.

Michigan fell behind 17-3 and never recovered, ruining Jim Harbaugh's first game as the savior coach of Michigan. We laughed. We ate. We had a couple beers. When the game was over, we cleaned up the stray globs of guacamole, salsa, rice, and beans.

"I'm glad you invited yourself over," I said. "Even though I still have a lot of crap to do here to make it a real home."

"I have good feelings about you here," Jim said. He surveyed the living room, the dark-wood exposed beams and stone-encased fireplace. "I think it's good you returned home. I'm proud of you."

"Be proud when I've been at it longer. But thank you, truly."

"You think you're going to stay here long term?"

"I think so." I hadn't made a conscious decision, but I'd achieved my career goals. Now, I was just doing something I loved, saw the people I loved more often, and could just focus on doing a good job for a good job's sake. "I don't really want to go anywhere anymore. I wouldn't mind just staying here for the rest of my career."

"Dude, that's still a long time," Jim said.

"I know." My face contorted. "But I can't see myself moving anywhere else any time soon."

We both nodded with the knowledge and experience that career ambition isn't always what it's supposed to be. I walked Jim out the front to his car.

"Hey, MIHO's coming out next week to visit his mom. Are you available to hang out?"

I smiled. I had a fleeting retort about MIHO's mom, but I let it pass. "I'll check my schedule, but it's got to be during my dinner break. Do you know where you guys want to eat?"

"We don't have to *dee*-cide on the *dee*-tails right now, but I'll let you know."

"Sounds good," I said and giggled. "*Bee* safe. Talk to you later."

Jim smiled and got into his car. I followed his taillights down the street and around the corner. I went back into the house, closed the tiki bar, and sat down in the living room, watching *SportsCenter*. I felt content. Ever since my sophomore year of high school, my goal was to work at ESPN. I worked hard to reach my goal, but in the end, the peace I craved was here all along. I poured myself a scotch and watched highlights of the first full week of college football when my phone buzzed. It was Tracey.

"Hey, Paul, has Jim left yet?"

"Yeah, he left an hour ago. He's not there?"

"No, that's when he texted, and usually, he's pretty good about coming right home."

"I wouldn't worry. Maybe he got a craving for In-N-Out," I joked.

"Right. I need him to eat better. He's going to have a heart attack."

"Exactly. I'm sure he's fine. You have a pretty good guy there. Better than I would have turned out."

"Oh god, Paul." Tracey laughed. "You were a disaster in the two weeks we dated. But I'm also glad you're here. Jim says you're doing better. That's good. He's proud of you."

"That's kind, and what about you?"

"Well, you know I've heard the stories. And I know all about Michigan, but if Jim's ready to forgive, I'm ready to as well. I'm just happy you're in a better place."

"Thank you. That means a lot. Now, I'll get off just in case Jim wants to ask you if you want a double-double animal style. Let me know if you need anything, okay?"

"Sure thing. Good night."

A couple hours later, my phone buzzed. I assumed it was Jim or Tracey saying Jim had made it home. The text did not:

Tracey: *Jim in a bad wreck. At Sutter Memorial. Please come?*

Me: *Sure. Is Jim OK?*

Tracey: *No. Please come.*

The hospital was a few miles away. I threw on some shoes and grabbed my wallet, keys, and a hat and jumped in my car. I don't remember much about the time between Tracey's call and arriving at the hospital, only that my heart was beating, and I had thoughts ranging from disbelief to shock to misunderstanding. Walking into that waiting room made everything a reality. I texted Tracey I'd arrived.

A few minutes later, Kevin, Jim's dad, found me. His eyes were red and swollen. He looked like all his energy was focused on keeping it together. When he saw me, he opened his arms and took me in. As he pulled me close, he managed to whisper, "He's gone."

The air went out of me. I could hardly breathe. I'd just seen Jim two hours ago, and now he was gone. I held Kevin for a while in that waiting room until he took me back to a private grieving room to see Tracey and the rest of the family. The room was lit warmly in contrast to the sterile fluorescent light filling the rest of the hospital. Tracey's mom sat on a long light-blue couch with white trim next to Tracey, her arm draped over her. Jim's mom was also on the couch, looking up at the ceiling tiles. Tracey's dad was with Willie at the house, still sleeping and oblivious to the tragedy.

"I'm so sorry," I said to Tracey, but even then, my voice broke. I always prided myself on my composure. Being on camera teaches you how to stay focused and not get flustered. However, none of that practice helped in this moment. Tracey came up and hugged and held me, and we both wept. "What happened?"

Tracey couldn't talk, so Kevin spoke up. "All we know is that he lost control of his Jeep and crashed. The CHP are supposed to be here soon. It would be great if you could talk to them."

"Sure, though I'm not sure I'm going to be any help."

"I didn't even get to hug him goodbye," Tracey said. "When he left for your house, he just said he'd see me later. I just yelled 'bye' back, and that was it. That's it!"

Tracey sobbed again and collapsed onto the couch, her mom consoling her. Jim's mom continued to look off to the side, lost in her own thoughts and grief. I couldn't imagine the horrors they were feeling. I'd never experienced this kind of loss before. We stayed in the room for a while, mostly silent among our sniffles and cries when a highway patrol officer knocked on the door and entered. He was dressed in a tan uniform.

"Hello, Mrs. Jensen?" the officer said. "We spoke on the phone. I'm CHP Officer Padilla. I'm so sorry for your loss. Would you mind if I asked you a couple questions?"

Tracey stood and shook his hand. Officer Padilla pulled one of the smaller chairs and sat down. He was tall and lanky with black hair and some gray beginning to sprinkle in. Officer Padilla took out his notepad.

Before he began asking questions, I wanted to know some answers. "So, what happened? Can you tell us how Jim was killed?"

Officer Padilla looked at me with recognition, knowing who I was but still working to connect the dots to Jim. He looked at Tracey to confirm I was supposed to be here. She acknowledged me, and he flipped back a couple pages in his notebook.

"From what we understand from witnesses, your husband was traveling South on Interstate 50. Witnesses say a red pickup may have begun to merge into his lane. He swerved to avoid the truck and lost control of the vehicle. The Jeep flipped onto its roof and slid into the center median, where it impacted on the driver's side. We believe the impact caused some internal injuries. He was unconscious when drivers went to check on him, and then he was brought here."

It was another shock to the system.

"So, was this a hit-and-run?" Kevin asked.

"It's under investigation," Officer Padilla said. "But we don't think so. Witnesses say that Mr. Jensen's Jeep swerved before contact and lost control. There doesn't seem to be any wheel rubs or other evidence to suggest a hit-and-run. It would help if you could tell us where your husband was coming from."

"He was coming from my house. We were watching the football game," I said.

"Was Mr. Jensen drinking?" Officer Padilla said.

"He had a couple beers over the course of the game. They were strong, but he seemed fine when he left. He wasn't a drunk driver."

"Just have to ask the questions," Officer Padilla said, sensing my defensiveness. "It's important to rule out possibilities as it helps us determine what happened."

"Why did you let him go?" Tracey said. I could tell she was trying to reason.

"I wasn't concerned when I walked him out," I said. "He was fine. I thought this would never..." I put my hands to my face and wept. Tracey put her hands to her face and joined me.

"There's nothing you could have done differently," Kevin said. He put a hand on my shoulder.

Officer Padilla asked a few more questions before he offered his condolences again and left. We all sat in that room for what seemed like forever. We just stared at the wall or the floor. At one point, a nurse came for Tracey to fill out some forms, including Jim's death certificate. When Tracey returned, she carried an envelope that held Jim's personal effects, his keys, wallet, watch, change, phone, and receipt. She rummaged through the envelope.

Tracey pulled out Jim's phone and held it and typed in his passcode. When she looked at the screen, she let out another cry. We all went over to comfort her and wonder what caused the sudden outburst. On Jim's phone was the selfie of he and I in front of the tiki bar, the last picture of him ever taken.

"This is it," she said. "He's not coming home again. It's over."

Tracey put her hands to her face and began sobbing again.

"I think we should head home. It's after midnight," Kevin said as he put his arm around Jim's mom. "There's nothing more we can do here. Tracey needs some rest."

"I'll take her home," Tracey's mom said. "Bob's already there with Willie. We'll stay the night and take care of her."

"Sounds good," Kevin said. "Maybe we can all get together sometime tomorrow and figure out what's next."

Tracey nodded. It was clear she was exhausted, and while I wasn't sure if sleep would come tonight for her, she needed a safe space to process. I looked around. I didn't know my role.

"Tracey, is there anything you'd like me to do?" I asked.

"Can you call David and the guys and tell them? David's going to be heartbroken, and I don't think I can do it."

"Sure," I said. I watched as everyone gathered their things. Liz even picked up all the tissues and placed them in the trash can before leaving. I don't think she ever said a word the whole time I was there. I followed them out into the parking lot and gave

Tracey one big hug. When she let go, she didn't look fully present. She was just going where she was told. She stepped into the elevator of the parking garage with her mom. I turned toward my car and just couldn't believe Jim was gone.

MIHO

It started off like a typical Sunday. I woke up, made a cup of coffee, and sat on the balcony of my condo with a partial view of Huntington Beach and checked my phone and read the latest news, Instagram posts, and twitter feed.

The phone buzzed; it was Paul calling. Wow, it was early, but I saw on Instagram that Jim had spent the evening watching football at Paul's. I'd need to stop by and check out his house when I came up next week.

I answered the call. "Hey, buddy, I saw your cool tiki bar last night. Looks like you and Jim had a good time."

There was silence. Had Paul butt dialed me?

"Paul, you there?" I thought I heard crying. "Paul?"

"Yeah, I'm here," Paul said, though his voice was shaky.

"Are you okay? Is something wrong?"

"Ummm, Jim," Paul said. He almost broke but held it together. "He was in a car wreck heading home from my house, and he's dead."

"Dude, that's not funny. Don't fuck around, Paul."

I half expected Paul to either break out laughing or apologize. I didn't expect him to continue his silence for what seemed like forever.

"I was at the hospital with Tracey and her mom and Jim's parents. He's really gone."

I stood up and walked inside. I couldn't focus. However, I couldn't stand either, let alone walk, and I stumbled inside and collapsed on the couch. I couldn't wrap my brain around it. I stared at my coffee table, focusing on the grain of the wood.

"David? You there?"

"I'm here," I said. I couldn't believe it. I know he said he was at the hospital, but Jim had called me yesterday, and he was fine. "You've made a mistake. He's fine."

"No, he's gone, David. He's dead."

Maybe it was the emphatic tone in his voice or him calling me 'David,' but it clicked, and the wave of grief and terror and sadness erupted inside me like a nuclear reactor.

"Oh my god," I said. "Oh my god. Oh shit. Oh my god. No. No. No. No."

"I know, it's unbelievable," Paul said.

I remember Paul telling me about the wreck and something about a red truck and a wall and his time at the hospital with Tracey and the parents and everything else. It was all such a jumble as I tried to process the information. I cried several times as he talked, and Paul would tell me he was sorry and say it's okay and tried to comfort me.

"I need to call Tracey," I said.

"Well, she told me to call you," Paul said. "I'm not sure if she's ready to talk on the phone. Maybe text her. I know she was going to try to get some rest last night, then tell Willie, and then everyone was going to figure out what's next."

"Oh my god, Willie," I said. I realized at that moment I knew exactly what Willie was going through. My own father had died when I was just about the same age. Though my dad had died of a brain aneurism, we both were linked by the sudden deaths of our fathers. I knew I had to take the next flight I could find. "Well, I'm getting a flight and heading up. I was going to be up there anyway to see Mom. I'll just take a couple more days off."

"Are you sure? You don't need—"

"Yes, I do," I said. I was emphatic. I needed to be there for Tracey, for Willie, for Jim, for myself. "I'll get a rental car and stay with Mom. Thanks, though. And thanks for being with them last night. I'm sure Tracey appreciated it."

"I think she did," Paul said. "I feel awful that I'm the one who saw him last. If he hadn't come over, well..."

I admit I had that same feeling, but I also knew Paul wasn't to blame. "It's not your fault. Just...horrible."

I felt a wave of pain rush through me. How could things just happen like this? How does fate rob you of your best friend, of a father, a husband, a teacher? How do things "just happen?" I put my hands to my face again, feeling my palms moisten. He was gone, and there was nothing I could do about it. Paul and I promised to text throughout the day, and he even said we could maybe have a FaceTime chat with Jesse and Rob, whom he was calling next. I said that was a good idea.

I hung up and made my flight arrangements and called my mom. She was just as surprised as I was. Jim was like a second son to her. But, like all moms do, she turned her attention to me. She heard the pain and loss in my voice.

"David, how are you?" she asked. "Are you going to be okay?"

"I don't know, Mom. I feel numb, like I still can't believe he's dead. And that terrifies me because I already feel so sad. I can't imagine how it's going to feel when the grief hits me."

"I know what you mean," she said. "That's what happened when your dad died. So, what's your plan?"

I told her I was leaving for the airport and was going to rent a car and go directly to Jim and Tracey's house. After I got off the phone with Paul, I texted Tracey my plan and asked if I could stop by. She said of course. To Tracey and Jim, I was like their brother. I asked if she needed me to pick up food. She wasn't hungry, but pizza would be easy.

By the time I arrived at their house, it was nearly 4:00 pm. I had barely put the pizza down when Tracey came to me and hugged me with the warmth of a mother bear. I embraced her and didn't realize how much I needed her touch. We held each other for a long time, before Kevin directed me to the couch.

"I just can't believe it," I said. "I just keep thinking he's going to come in from the garage any moment and wonder what's going on."

"I know," Tracey said. "And unfortunately, Willie believes his dad is away and coming home soon."

I looked around. "Where is Willie?"

"My parents took him to lunch and the park. I knew I needed some time to process this so I can help Willie when he needs it. Don't worry, I know it's going to take a very long time to understand what I'm feeling, but I—"

"You don't have to explain it to me," I said. I took her hand. "It's okay. Don't guilt yourself here. You're going to need to take care of yourself first if you're going to be able to take care of Willie."

"Thanks," she said before she buried her face in her hands. When she recovered, she took my hand and led me outside to the back patio where we walked around the yard, the sunshine peeking through the leaves. We held hands, a needed touch of endearment and comfort.

"It was weird. Last night, I saw his body under a sheet," Tracey said.

"Don't tell me you had to identify the body," I said.

"No, thank god," she said. "Kevin thankfully took care of it. But they let me go in and say goodbye. It was weird, I didn't feel it was Jim. I could already feel that he had left and now was a part of me. It was like his presence had changed from being physical to a feeling that I wanted to embrace and hold."

I pulled her around and embraced her again. We just rocked back and forth underneath the shade of the tree. We didn't cry together this time. I led her in some breathing—inhaled deep through the nose, exhaled through the mouth. She looked up at me.

"Damn, this is hard," Tracey said, her voice trapped in her chest. All she could do was whisper. "When I woke up yesterday, he was next to me, and that's the last time I'll ever roll over and see him. I don't think I can get through this without him."

I kissed her forehead. Jim's death had rocked me, but I couldn't imagine how it was for Tracey. She would need those around her to be strong so she could be strong herself. I smiled at her and looked into her eyes.

"You're going to do it," I said. "Jim would tell you to keep at it and that he has every confidence in you. You must be there for Willie, to be both parents. Me, Paul, your parents, and Jim's parents will have to pick up the slack, and we'll do that the best we can. Jim will be around. He'll be around in all of us."

"Thanks, David." Tracey buried her head under my chin.

We went back inside and reminisced about Jim, cried, laughed. Willie and Tracey's parents came back, and I hugged Willie and took him to his room so he could share with me all of his new toys. I needed some mindless pretend time with a child. I caught a few Jim-isms, and I hoped they'd stay, even though Jim wouldn't be around anymore. In time, I'd share my own experiences of losing my dad at such a young age and try to relate to him. I stayed until after the parents went to bed, and Tracey read Willie a bedtime story. I was reading one of Jim's *Sports Illustrate*✦ magazines when Tracey returned and plopped down next to me on the couch.

"How did Willie go down?" I asked.

"I can tell he's exhausted and thank goodness he still doesn't know what's happening. I know it's going to get harder once reality sets in."

"Well, you know you've got help," I said.

"Yes, I do, thank you," she said and squeezed my hand. "As I lay there waiting for Willie to go to sleep, I started thinking about the memorial service. Isn't that nuts? This feels so unreal. Well, anyway, I wondered if you'd want to deliver the eulogy."

"Oh no, I'd be a wreck," I said. "Don't let this queen on the mic with sadness in my heart. Ask Rob."

"Not Paul?"

"Nothing against Paul, but he'll always be the guy from ESPN and a mini celebrity. Rob has always been there. He's seen Jim through everything."

"That feels right. If it's not going to be you, I want it to be Rob."

"I agree," I said. "Okay, I have to go to Mom's. I'll be back tomorrow, and as I said, anything you need, put me to work."

"Will do. Good night. And thanks for coming up so soon."

"Not a problem at all. I love you. I love Jim. We're family."

Rob

Wow, I'm honored, Tracey, but are you sure you want me to give the eulogy?" I asked. "You don't want Paul or MIHO?"

Becky and I were sitting with Tracey on her patio a week after Jim's death.

"I'll admit, I asked David, but he wasn't confident he could deliver it, and I want you to do it," Tracey said. "You've been there for him, and you've been such a steady influence on him all these years. Plus, what you said at your dad's funeral was so touching. I know you can do it."

I sipped my beer as the memory flooded back from five years ago. Unlike Jim, my father's death was expected, almost somewhat welcome, as his body shut down and relieved him of his pain. His heart attack had made him human, but then his kidney failure and finally his liver and brain cancer brought this strong and proud man down. In my youth, he was such a formidable and powerful person, but before he died, he was using a walker and attached to an air tank. He needed help to bathe and go to the bathroom, and he was a withered shadow of himself.

So, when I gave my dad's eulogy, it was with relief. Of course, I still wished he was alive, but I came at it from an entirely different perspective. I knew death was knocking. I had a chance to talk to him about his life. I could draw on the memories of him raising me into the man I was now.

With Jim, I was still in shock a week later. Normally, he and I would be at this patio table watching football, while Leslie would play video games with Willie.

I was floored when Paul called me that Sunday morning. I thought I'd heard wrong. I thought he was hurt but not gone. Paul had to tell me three times that Jim was dead. I can't imagine how tough that was, giving bad news three times in succession.

I needed some time alone, so after I broke the news to Becky, I drove up the back side of Lake Tahoe, periodically banging on the steering wheel so hard, I thought I might break it. When I reached Incline Village and got out of my truck, I wanted to barrel into a tree or find a bear and wrestle it to the ground or break something to give me the desired outlet for my anger. I walked along the edge of the lake, sometimes skipping rocks, mostly muttering to myself. Finally, I sat on the edge of the water for hours, trying to reconcile my feelings and anger with reality. At some point, probably when the sun had set behind the mountains and the air cooled, I realized it was time to go. This lake had the soothing effect I'd needed, and when I returned, I was fine and ready to be there for Tracey and Willie, and of course MIHO, Paul, and Jesse.

"Well, if you want me to, then I will, and I hope I can speak with enough eloquence to celebrate and honor his life." I got up and hugged Tracey. She almost disappeared in my embrace. "When is it?"

"Two weeks," Tracey said. "It's going to be at the Methodist church where we were married."

"Oh, the one with the orange carpet," I said and smiled. It was a beautiful church with huge pipe organs and tall, majestic ceilings, stained-glassed windows lining the sides, and the most hideous orange carpet in Sacramento. "I'll be there, and I'll be ready."

"Thanks, Rob. Now, it would be great to take my mind from everything right now and say congratulations! I can't believe after all these years, you guys are getting back together!"

Becky smiled. It was a relief to shift away from Jim, if only for a moment. I let her tell the story to Tracey. This was the first time Becky had ever been to the house and she was finally entering the inner circle after so many years on the periphery. While our news was initially pushed aside as we dealt with this tragedy. I admired Tracey so much in that moment. Here she was, a week after her life had been upended, so focused and listening to a woman she'd only met a few times.

"I'm just so happy for you both," Tracey said. "Jim told me when you all got back from the last trip. He always said he thought you were the last two to realize you were in love and that you could be together. I'm just very glad he got to hear about it."

"I am too," Becky said. She put her hand on Tracey's. "That first time we met, all those years ago, I knew it, but I didn't realize it would take so long for it to be right."

"That's how I was with Jim," Tracey said. "I think he and I had an idea that we clicked, but then I had to go and screw it up by setting him up with Audrey. What a disaster that was. Of course, if I would have acted on my feelings back then, who knows if we would have had the years we did."

The three of us talked for another couple hours, before we had to drive back up to Reno. As I drove, my mind kept thinking about what I'd say in a couple weeks. It felt morbid to think about giving his eulogy since he was still alive in my mind. He was younger than me. It just proved how precious and fragile life is. It wasn't disease or war or some perilous act. He died driving home from a friend's house.

"Are you doing okay?" Becky said. We were driving over Donner Pass and about ready to pass Truckee before heading down the grade toward Reno. "You're pretty quiet over there."

"Just a little nervous about the responsibility of the eulogy."

"You'll be great. You knew him like a brother."

"But I still can't believe it's real, that he's dead."

"You have a couple weeks. You'll be fine." She reached over and gave me a reassuring rub on my shoulder and the back of my neck. For so many years I'd missed her tenderness.

I had my doubts, but I took time over the next two weeks to flesh out some ideas whenever I had a free moment. My thoughts were on Jim, Tracey, and Willie, and by the time we all drove back to Sacramento for the service, I'd written a eulogy I hoped was worthy of one of my best friends. The process was more therapeutic than I thought and helped me work through my grief in ways I hadn't expected. Writing one for Jim was different than writing it for my dad.

The mid-September day was perfect for late summer. The weather was pleasant, there was a breeze, and I knew that the church would be packed wishing to pay their respects to Jim Jensen. Becky, Leslie, and I arrived at the church an hour early and was taken to the church library. We weren't the first ones there. Tracey was there with Willie, Jim's parents, and his sister, Katie, who flew out from Florida. Tracey's parents were also there, along with MIHO. Leslie went to see what Willie was playing on his iPad, while David and Tracey sat in front of a stained-glass window featuring Jesus talking to children. Kevin paced around as though he couldn't wait for the service to start. Liz knitted as she did when she was nervous.

I hugged everyone, and we all sat around waiting for the service to start. After a while, Becky took Leslie to the sanctuary to take a seat. I decided to stay with the family and MIHO, their honorary member. MIHO took in a deep breath and exhaled. It was so loud that everyone looked at him, even Willie from his electronic entertainment. MIHO looked around with an expression of guilt like he'd just passed gas at church, which made me laugh.

"Jim wouldn't have let that pass, MIHO," I said. "He'd have said something like, 'Did you just fart?'"

That seemed to break the tension for the room. Everyone started laughing.

Willie let out a big belly laugh and repeated, "Did you just fart?"

The grandparents giggled. Tracey rolled her eyes, and MIHO's cheeks grew red.

"Hi," the pastor said when he entered the library. "Is everyone about ready? There are a lot of people here to remember Jim."

Everyone looked at Tracey. She nodded, and the pastor led us to the front-side entrance to the sanctuary. The pastor went in first, followed by Tracey's parents, Kevin and Liz, with Katie and David escorting Willie and Tracey. I brought up the rear. All of us had the center-front pews. Paul, Jesse, Danielle, Nicole, and Jennifer were in the second row, along with Becky and Leslie and a space for me. I nodded to Kyle, who was in the second row with his pregnant wife. As I sat down, I looked up at the sanctuary amazed. The church was packed. Not only was the bottom section filled with people, many of whom I recognized, but the balcony was also packed with Jim's students, former students, friends, colleagues, bosses. I was wowed by the amount of people who'd showed to pay their respects.

When we were seated, the pastor welcomed everyone and gave introductory comments about Jim and his impact on our lives and the memories we'd all cherish for years to come. After the pastor's words, a slideshow of Jim played on the screens set to the music of U2's "One." Pictures of Jim as a baby, in high school, and to present day came across the screen. It took every bit of myself not to break down.

After Bono concluded, the pastor directed Jesse to read John 14:1-4.

"Let not your hearts be troubled. Believe in God; believe also in me. In my Father's house are many rooms. If it were not so, would I have told you that I go to prepare a place for you? And if

I go and prepare a place for you, I will come again and will take you to myself, that where I am you may be also. And you know the way to where I am going."

When it was my time, I looked at Becky who nodded at me. I passed Tracey and leaned in and gave her a kiss on the cheek and shook Willie's hand. As I walked to the lectern, I remembered the directions Tracey gave to me:

- Be succinct and leave them wanting more
- Keep it PG
- No talking about his actual death
- Make it worth it

I buttoned my suitcoat and adjusted the mic and my stance to maximize my delivery.

"Jim used to beat me up."

Laughter.

"My good friend Paul asked me to say that to loosen everyone up because, while this is a solemn occasion, Jim would be the first one to try to add some levity. Hey, Paul, it worked!"

More laughter.

"Well, Jim and I did get in a fight when we were young. We were in sixth grade and playing football in PE class. We'd been talking trash to each other all game, and on a kickoff, we ran toward each other. When I got to him, he reached down, grabbed my foot, and flipped me over his shoulder. At the time, I was a little smaller, so it was a tad easier. As soon as school was over, we met behind the lockers, and as boys often do, we had a great shoving match before our friends 'conveniently' broke us up.

"The next day, we were on the same team. So instead of pushing each other, we combined forces and talked trash and flipped two other guys over. This time, however, no one pulled us apart. I tell you; it was a great sixth-grade fight, and it was the first time that we both had each other's backs, and it's been like that ever since.

"Here we see the countless students and teachers and community members whom he touched with his grace and integrity. We see his friends and family who saw him as a person who'd provide any bit of help whenever it was asked or needed. Over the course of the last fifteen years, Jim influenced thousands of students. He taught history beyond the facts. He discussed the lessons learned from history and how they could help us better ourselves, our community, and our society. When he talked about his debate team, he didn't tell me about the accolades they won, though there were many, but what his team was learning about points of view, about conflict resolution, about empathy and integrity. His success was tied to the people his students were going to be, not the results of the moment.

"Anyone who knew Jim also knew his love and devotion to Tracey. Theirs was a marriage and a love affair to which all of us aspire. Over the years, I had the opportunity to interact with them, and they were the ultimate complements to one another. Jim was a stickler for detail and planning while Tracey likes to take things as they come. Tracey enjoys going on trips and living life. Jim made sure they'd saved accordingly to pay for these excursions. Their relationship had a solid base that could withstand many things, but even when they found some cracks in that foundation, they did what lasting married couples did, they worked together and mended those cracks and became stronger. I've been fortunate to find someone I love, and Jim taught me that the key to that search is to be the type of man someone would want to build that foundation with.

"Jim was also a dad to Willie. When I first saw Jim with Willie, I found Jim's true purpose, to be a dad for this boy. Jim was always selfless, and he believed the most important lessons he would ever teach would be to his son about life. I know, Willie, that your dad didn't get a chance to finish teaching you all his insights and principles, but between all the people who love you and your dad, we'll do our best to instill those Jim-isms we respected so much.

"Many of you know that Jim organized an annual trip for his closest high school friends. We've been doing this for much of the last twenty years. I reflected on those trips recently and how they marked the times in our lives. From tragedy to triumph, from deep personal revelations to tear-inducing laughter, the memories of him that resonate most with me are from those trips. Paul, Jesse, David, and myself all became who we are through those trips, and you can guess who organized them and kept us coming year after year.

"It's no hyperbole that Jim was the best guy. Many of you agree, or you wouldn't be here. But I think he wouldn't want us to remember him for being a great guy. He'd want us to think about what made him a great guy and how we could include those best qualities in our own lives. He'd hope that if he could leave anything, it would be to encourage us to be better people to the world, the society, the community, and to each other. So, I'd ask you to preserve Jim's memory and think about the principles by which you live and make sure your actions and choices align with those principles. I know that if all of us did this in his honor, he'd be proud of his legacy. Rest in Peace, Jim."

Jesse

Rob only showed cracks a few times during his eulogy. I was proud of him. I gave him a discreet high five as he left the lectern before he sat down next to Becky and Leslie. We listened to the pastor provide his words of loss and hope and aim at helping us understand what this all meant. My mind wandered to the moment when Paul called that Sunday morning. I was outside our condo, my earbuds in, stretching, about ready to play an audio book and start my running app.

Of course, I was shocked when Paul told me, but then for some reason I just took off running. I didn't even go inside to tell Danielle. I just texted her from outside to say my run today would be a bit longer. Instead of playing an audio book, I just ran. It was a beautiful morning. When I began, there was still a marine layer hugging the coast. I ran by UC Irvine and pushed through some hills along the coast before reaching Newport Beach and the pier. Overlooking the ocean, I stopped and walked back and forth wondering how and why this could have happened. Neither the wind nor the surf had any answers. They just kept blowing and crashing, unfazed by the devastating news. It was like life went on, even without Jim. It didn't matter that he was one of my best friends. The seagulls still flew around looking for food. Even the surfers just kept looking for the next wave. I envied all of them. The pain never existed, and they could just keep living. As I ran back my eyes watered, swelled, and became red, but I kept running because I didn't know what else to do.

When I got back, I was ready to talk to Danielle and act like the wind and surf. One thing about being a stay-at-home dad to twin girls is you learn that you must be in the present or you're going to get overwhelmed. I took that approach with Jim's loss. Understand what it was but move forward. I still dedicated at least one run a week to Jim and thought about the times we spent together, the times we talked on the phone about wives and kids and what movies were playing. Our time had passed, but Jim would still be with me for the rest of my years.

After the service and reception, Tracey invited us back to her house for an informal wake. She ordered all of us to wear comfortable clothes and that we were going to watch college football and barbecue just like Jim liked to do on Saturdays. I had no complaints, and the girls were happy that they could play video games with Willie and Leslie. Danielle held my hand and gave me a comforting touch any time she could. Since our decision to start her own practice and our continued couples therapy, we began to understand one another and embrace the good and tough in our relationship. She knew what I needed, and right now it was just her presence.

We were the last to arrive at Tracey's house. When she called it casual, she meant it. Tracey was wearing Jim's favorite Chris Webber Kings jersey, and Willie was wearing an old Michigan T-shirt Jim had bought during that trip to Ann Arbor. Sure enough, the Texas A&M and LSU game was on the TV Jim had installed on the wall. Rob was putting some tri-tip and chicken on the grill when Willie asked the girls to the game room to play video games. I think Willie was happy to have other kids help him take his mind off the gravity of the day.

"That was a nice service," Kevin said. "Rob, you did well with your eulogy. I think you captured it. I remember that little fight you two had in sixth grade. When I picked him up and heard he got in a fight, I think he was prouder to have found you as a friend than scared of what punishment lay ahead." Kevin laughed.

As we talked, we also looked at the muted football game. It was good to have something to focus on. I knew if I met eyes with anyone for a prolonged moment, I'd break.

"So, what happened on these trips?" Liz asked. "What kept you guys coming back year after year?"

"Jim," Rob said. "Quite honestly, he was the guy who kept it all together. If it wasn't him, we probably wouldn't have organized anything."

MIHO looked up at the patio cover and took a breath, like he was trying to keep control of his emotions. "Rob, what you said was true. Those trips mark milestones in our lives. I can't think of my life without the lake, without Jim, and without those memories. I'm going to miss him so much. It's hard to think of him not being around anymore."

MIHO put his hands to his face, which gave us all permission to break down. It was as though the damn had burst, and we all wanted to just contribute to the flow. Paul stood and picked up the box of tissues and went around to everyone offering them up. We all took one and dabbed our eyes. It was another of a series of cries we'd have that afternoon and evening over barbecue, football, and beer.

Just like the beach, things returned to normal over the next few months. Rob, MIHO, Paul, and I exchanged texts and sometimes scheduled a FaceTime call to catch up. MIHO kept wanting to bring up Jim, which sometimes became exhausting. In January, MIHO got us all on a call together to make an announcement.

"So, remember Jim made a will? Well, he wanted some of his ashes spread at the lake."

"What?" I asked before laughing. "Even in death, he's badgering us to go to the lake?"

"Right," Rob said. "So, are you saying we're going to do the trip again this year without Jim?"

"I think so," MIHO said. "It would be our last goodbye to Jim."

"I already said my goodbyes. I'm good," I said.

"Well, that might be fun," Rob said. "It will certainly be different."

"I think we should consider it," Paul said. "As Rob said, he'd want us to keep our connections. What better way to keep that legacy than by continuing the trip?"

"So, are we going to do it?" MIHO asked. "It's in the will."

"I'm game," Rob said.

Everyone looked at me. I breathed out and sighed.

"Fine. MIHO, make the arrangements, and let's do this."

17

Last Call

June 25, 2016

The four friends sat in silence on the patio of the saloon, their eyes focused on the flames. They sipped their beverages. Through their memories, it felt like they had lived a lifetime in only one weekend. Perspectives of their own lives and how they related to one another gained greater clarity as they read Jim's in-the-moment recollections.

MIHO shook himself out of the trance, dove into his backpack, and pulled out an envelope. It felt like a lifetime ago when Tracey had given it to him right before they left the house.

"Oh! I almost forgot. We have one more thing to read," MIHO said.

"What's that?" Jesse said. "I thought Paul read his final entry."

"He did," MIHO said. "This is from Tracey."

"You haven't read it?" Rob said.

MIHO showed them the unbroken seal of the envelope. "No, she gave it to me like this and made me promise to read it at the end of the trip. She says it's a letter to all of us."

They all looked at each other with surprise, apprehension, and anticipation. There was no telling what Tracey had written.

"Okay, let's read it then," Jesse said.

They watched MIHO tear open the envelope and pull out two pages of handwritten script.

Dear David, Rob, Jesse, and Paul,

I'm so glad you all took this final trip with Jim up to the Lake. This trip meant so much to him. Around February, his eyes would brighten when he would begin talking to you all, getting possible dates and then securing the house. Each month, he'd mention the trip more and more until the last few weeks would become almost unbearable.

We've all been struggling this past year. It's been agonizing to go through all the "firsts" without him—the first Christmas, Willie's first birthday, the first anniversary, even the first Kings game and Super Bowl. Each day, it gets better, but his void will never be filled.

I stumbled onto his "Lake Trip Log" a couple months ago. I read it from beginning to end and learned what really happened on these trips. I remember him telling me all these stories, though the version he told me about the bachelor party and Dena was a bit more sanitized.

I laughed at some of those silly inside jokes. I cried as I relived our miscarriage through his eyes, and I found out about all of you in new ways as you dealt with the various crises you weathered and shared with one another. And Paul, I'm glad you got your s#!% together. I understand why he anticipated these trips and was so refreshed after-ward.

Reading the Lake Trip Log was like Jim returned for one more visit. I cherished it so much and wanted to make sure you had the op-portunity to feel that too. I asked David to organize this trip so you could read the journal and relive those great times you all had to-gether. I hope it brought you closure or helped you support one an-other.

Jim had an impact on our lives, and I'm so glad he had this trip with you. Because of you, he was a better man. He loved better, lived better, was a better father. I hope you all realize how much Willie and I are grateful for your friendship.

With love,
Tracey

"Oh wow," Paul said, wiping his eyes.

They had all been trying to keep it together as MIHO read the letter.

"It's been a tough year for everyone," MIHO said. "But I'm so glad you guys have been around to share our grief over our friend. I love you guys."

MIHO looked at Tracey's letter and then placed it into the fire. He raised his glass again, and they all took their final swigs of beer and watched the flames catch the underside of the envelope and the paper, soon turning it to black wisps of ash, some of which floated into the air.

"So, MIHO, are you going to be okay?" Paul said, slapping MIHO's knee. "Did this trip help you move on?"

"It did. I know you guys thought I was being an overdramatic stereotypical gay dude."

"Nah, you were just being a dude who needed closure to deal with the loss of his best friend," Rob said. "Though, those pink shorts of yours..."

"They're salmon," MIHO said. Rob shrugged his shoulders. MIHO kicked at his ankle.

"I want to say something," Jesse said. "I didn't want to come up here."

"Really? I never would have guessed," Paul mocked.

"Okay, maybe I wasn't subtle, but I wanted to move forward, and I didn't see how looking back would help us move on," Jesse said. "All I know is that I realized this wasn't so much about Jim but about all of us and how we continue on, the four of us. I thought this would be the end of an era, but it's the beginning of a new chapter."

"The middle-age years," Paul said.

"I mean, it's an opportunity," Jesse said. "I wouldn't say we've been stagnant in our friendships, but we've got plenty of adventures left beyond this lake."

Each of them considered this new proposition.

"How about this," Rob said. "What if every year we rotate organizing responsibilities? So next year, Jesse picks the place and secures accommodations. After that it's Paul's turn, then it's MIHO's, then mine, and then we can come back here every five years."

"Sounds good to me," MIHO said. "One part of his legacy secured. Now, what about Tracey and Willie? It's our duty to look after them."

"Definitely," Paul said. "I kinda feel as though everything that happened to me was to put me in position to be there for when they need me. Whenever MIHO gets up here, between the two of us, we'll help fill the void when she needs us."

They raised their empty glasses in agreement.

"Okay, one more thing then, since it's a new chapter," MIHO said. "It's been over twenty years since I've been given the name MIHO. Can we retire that name and just call me David or something else?"

"C'mon, you're MIHO," Paul said. "When we say MIHO, everyone knows it's you."

"I don't even know you as David anymore," Rob said. "You're always MIHO."

"Man, you just don't know how I get grief from other people when someone here's my name as MIHO. It's just weird."

"What else would we call you? David?" Jesse said. "That's so boring."

"Just something else," MIHO said. "Anything but MIHO."

They contemplated MIHO's proposition. He did deserve some respect for all that he had done for Jim, in this life and beyond, and for them. Still, it was a nickname from their teens, and you couldn't just abandon that.

"Dominique?" Paul said. "After NBA great and master dunker Dominique Wilkins?" They all laughed at the image of him in the water with flecks of ashes on his body.

"That's better than Slips," Rob said.

They roared.

"Or Submerge," Jesse said.

Even more laughter. MIHO even laughed at the notion that his name would stay MIHO for the rest of his life with these friends of his. He would never admit it, but he actually liked the name. It had moved beyond the anagram and was their unique term of affection for him.

They all looked back at the gas flames coming off the fire pit. Garth Brooks came on the stereo from inside the saloon. They smiled and listened to the words before joining in the chorus. They were friends who spent time in low places, but it was their bond that helped bring them back.

When the song was over, they got up from their spots. Their evening at the saloon was over by 7:00 p.m. From the outside deck, they peeked into the bar and went in to pay their final tab. Paul waved off his friends as he pulled out his credit card and slapped it on the bar. Jesse and MIHO left to go outside. As Paul signed his name, he noticed a cute young blonde and her friends at the end of the bar. She was the type of girl he would flirt with at a moment's notice.

He smiled. The scene was reminiscent of a bygone era in his life. Next to her, a twenty-something-year-old guy was talking to her. She giggled as they flirted. Paul turned to see the guy's friends playing darts and giving him a hard time for leaving them to make his move. The guy tried to play it cool.

Paul looked back to Rob to see if he noticed. Rob rolled his eyes. They shared a smile of acknowledgement. Been there, done that. Paul put his credit card back into his wallet, pulled out three twenty-dollar bills, and placed them on the bar.

"Apply this to their bar bill at the end of the night," Paul said, pointing to the five friends. "Looks like good memories and friendships are being made."

The bartender smiled and nodded, understanding.

Paul turned back to Rob, who put his hand on Paul's shoulder, and they walked out together.

Acknowledgements

An undertaking such as writing and self-publishing a novel cannot happen without the love and support of a network of family and friends. My deepest thanks to my wife Kristen, who not only provided some initial reads, but also provided critical feedback on character development and motivation. Without my children, this novel would only be half complete. The maturity of fatherhood to two great kids helped me gain perspective and inspiration. Thank you to Rich Ehisen, a writer to whom I turned when I had a 549-page first draft with no idea of what to do next. His guidance through the business of writing helped me set realistic expectations and a road map to get here. Appreciation to Scott Haner, David Fabionar and Mike McDoniels, all camping buddies, who read early drafts and let me know that it was readable. Thanks to Emily Olivarri, another early reader, who provided great feedback. Finally, many of the stories of Jim, MIHO, Rob, Paul and Jesse are inspired by the friends that have made the annual trip to the mountains. Along with the aforementioned readers, Nick Herndon, Scott Zanutto, Ryan Plescia, Joel Harworth, Dave Jans, Danny Price, Cotton Dean, Johnny Ward, Jim Krueger, Pete Holland, Chris Buti, Jarret Smith, Shane Haldeman and many more provided the laughter, the discussion, the endless games of horseshoes, cornhole and cards that have helped shape my life. I am forever grateful for our friendship.